BIRTH OF AN ARMY

Cassius drew the Sun Sword along the length of the shell, splitting it open. A huge, strange-looking lizard slipped out in a slime-covered ball, panting and stinking of sulfur. Its body shape was more or less humanoid, with a lanky neck, two long arms, and a pair of sturdy legs, but the semblance ended there. It had a scaly head with smoky, emotionless eyes, a beaklike snout, and a grinning reptilian mouth that looked as though it could swallow a dwarf whole. It was covered head to toe in small, brightly colored scales, and its body had a sinuous, vaguely cylindrical look that seemed more serpentine than manlike.

Cassius squatted down to look into its black eyes. "So you're an enkav . . ."

THE OATH OF STONEKEEP

The Oath of Stonekeep is a brand-new, original novel that bridges the thousands of years between Stonekeep I and Stonekeep II, the bestselling PC games from Interplay.

The Oath of Stonekeep

Troy Denning

An Original Novel Based on the
Bestselling Computer Game from Interplay

BERKLEY BOULEVARD BOOKS, NEW YORK

THE OATH OF STONEKEEP

A Berkley Boulevard Book / published by arrangement with
Interplay Productions

PRINTING HISTORY
Berkley Boulevard edition / October 1999

Book design by Tiffany Kukec.
Cover design by Jill Boltin.
Cover illustration by Justin Sweet.

For information address: The Berkley Publishing Group,
a division of Penguin Putnam Inc.,
375 Hudson Street, New York, New York 10014.

The Penguin Putnam Inc. World Wide Web site address is
http://www.penguinputnam.com

ISBN: 0-425-17065-9

BERKLEY BOULEVARD
Berkley Boulevard Books are published by The Berkley Publishing Group,
a division of Penguin Putnam Inc.,
375 Hudson Street, New York, New York 10014.

PRINTED IN THE UNITED STATES OF AMERICA

10 9 8 7 6 5 4 3 2 1

For the Cooks,
our friends in the land of "Bake and Shake"

ACKNOWLEDGMENTS

Many people contributed to the writing of this book. I would like to thank them all, and make special notice of the aid provided by the following people: Andria Hayday, for her invaluable suggestions—and of course for her many patient hours of review and rework on the first draft; David "Zeb" Cook (designer of Stonekeep II) for involving me in such an interesting project, for our many long discussions, for the information he shared . . . this list goes on and on, but most especially for being so much fun to work with; Marti Cadenasso, for getting the ball rolling and sending me everything I needed to know about Stonekeep the Game (except how to sneak past those pesky trolls on Level Eight); Justin Sweet, for his artistic dedication and attention to detail; the Interplay Technical Support staff for helping the "twitch-impaired" navigate Khull-khuum's labyrinth; Chris Taylor and the entire Team Stonekeep for making the place so much fun to be lost in (and to add on to in my own humble way); all the people at Interplay Productions for their willingness to help—no matter how weird the request; Barry Neville, for his enthusiasm and early story suggestions; and my editor, Robert Pulciani, for his many contributions and insightful comments, without which Cassius might have remained a very lonely fellow indeed.

Prologue

There were dark things down in the valley, a string of murky silhouettes stealing from tree to tree, gliding south across shadow-striped snow, a host of throgs and shargas and hell-forged creatures sweeping out of the frozen wilderness to murder and ravage and take what men were too weak to defend.

Wahooka was observing the invaders from the wind-blasted watchtower of an abandoned border fort, high on a rocky peak that overlooked the surrounding forest. Though the tower could be seen as far away as Brookbury Basin, he did not worry about being noticed. He was just tall enough to peer over the windowsill, so that little more than his round pate and sunken eyes showed above the ledge. And even if some sharp-eyed creature of darkness did happen to see him, the thing could hardly mistake Wahooka the Trickster for a sentry. With his upright tusks, long pointed ears, and blue-green skin, Wahooka was much too handsome to be a mere man.

He looked down into the empty compound that enclosed the tower. At one time the fort had been home to a hundred mounted men—a small force, perhaps, but large enough to delay invaders until help arrived. Now the barracks stood vacant and roofless, the stables sheltered nothing but wild boars, and the water well had been choked by centuries of windblown dust. Only the outer walls and the watchtower itself, both constructed of interlocking granite blocks, remained in good repair. When the citadel had been built, at least, Stonekeep had understood the value of readiness. Now the High Lords understood nothing—not their own history, not the danger trapped beneath their city, and certainly not the gratitude they owed Wahooka for imprisoning it there.

For three hundred years they had left the Trickster to skulk about the fringes of the kingdom serving anyone with the wealth to pay him, forced to change identities as often as men changed clothes. The ingrates! Who but Wahooka could have saved Stonekeep all those centuries ago, when mad Khull-khuum had plunged the entire city into the depths of an inescapable abyss? Who else could have molded a hapless boy into a god-vanquishing warrior, or taught him to rule after he resurrected the land? No one but Wahooka! Stonekeep had the Trickster—and the Trickster alone—to thank for its legendary King Drake, for its far-flung colonies and its gleaming towers and its long centuries of peace. And how did they repay him?

Wahooka spat in disgust at the answer, then spun away from the window and crossed the tower. Sculpted into the wall above the stairwell was the visage of a doe-eyed goddess with flowing cascades of wavy hair and a sheaf of wheat hanging to each side of her head. He stopped at the stairwell and craned his neck to look up into her vacant eyes.

"How now, Thera?" he asked. "Your flock is about to be sheared, and you sleep as soundly as your dogs."

The stony icon came alive, lowering its gray gaze to look down upon Wahooka. "I am watching, Wahooka." Thera's voice was as soft as a dove's song. "I am always watching."

"Then you have seen the invaders?"

Thera's gaze flicked toward the valley. "A few throgs

and shargas. I doubt they will topple Stonekeep, Little One.''

The Trickster flattened his ears at the disparaging nickname. ''Perhaps not. The High Lords might stop preening long enough to rush an army north. They might even quit squabbling with each other and beat the invaders back . . . but what about next time?''

Thera narrowed her eyes. ''What next time?''

''The next time there are more than just a few throgs and shargas, dear child,'' said Wahooka. He scuffed his foot along the floor, raising a dust cloud that billowed up as high as his waist. ''Your way hasn't worked, Thera. Your peace has made Stonekeep as complacent as your prosperity has made it fat, and now there are dark things out in the wilderness, watching and waiting. When they see what has become of Stonekeep, they'll come running . . . how they will come running!''

Thera stared down into the dusty cloud swirling around Wahooka's waist. The Trickster smirked and said nothing. There was no need. The art of persuasion lay in what was left unsaid, and Thera was both the brightest of the Young Gods and the friendliest to humans. She would see for herself what needed to be done—and then beg him to do it.

When Thera's gaze returned to Wahooka's face, her expression had changed from one of suspicion to one of concern. ''I am aware of Stonekeep's peril. The kingdom is like an old black oak—strong outside, but soft of heart.''

''Soft? The heartwood rotted away centuries ago! There is nothing left except grubs and humus.'' Wahooka looked away coyly, then shrugged. ''But why should that matter to me?''

Thera frowned. ''Indeed, why should it?''

''Certainly not because of the honor I am shown.'' Wahooka glanced around the room, making a point to linger upon each of the divine effigies that decorated the other walls. None of them depicted his round, beady-eyed face. ''Where are the idols to Wahooka, the golden shrines studded with gem and jewel?''

Dark furrows appeared in Thera's granite brow. ''There

is more to being worshiped than offerings and idols, Little One. Worship must be earned.''

``But I have already earned Stonekeep's worship! The citizens should honor me as their savior!'' Wahooka spun southward, as though looking into the heart of the distant capital. ``Instead, they call me King of the Goblins, hint that faerie swill runs in my veins! They buy my blessing with sparkling bits of glass, drop scraps of tin in water, then beg me to hide their petty frauds. In the Ballads of Drake, they even vex my tongue with the words of a moron!''

``You should not hold the Ballads against them,'' said Thera. ``It has been five hundred years since Drake lifted the city. Human memory cannot be trusted over such a span.''

``Trusted!'' Wahooka exploded. ``Their 'memory' is nothing but lies and self-serving fables! They claim I only 'helped' Drake imprison Khull-khuum!''

``Surely, you do not suggest that the Shadowking's defeat was your doing?''

``When Khull-khuum plunged Stonekeep into the abyss, who spirited little Drake to safety?'' Wahooka jabbed a long-taloned finger into his own chest. ``I did.''

``That is hardly—''

``And when Drake returned as a young man, who saw to it that he was well armed?''

``You helped him find a firedagger and a few oil bombs!'' Thera objected. ``I was the one who prepared him to face Khull-khuum.''

Wahooka inclined his head in mock deference. ``Far be it from me to argue with the Great Mother! You *were* the one who ripped his soul from his body and hurled it into the abyss, so that he had no choice except to fight Khull-khuum for it!'' The Trickster paused, then looked up and spoke in a gentler tone. ``I wonder how many others you sent down before him?''

The idol's eyes flashed at the insinuation. ``How many does not—''

``And who led him into the Palace of Shadows?'' Wahooka demanded, not interested in the answer to his own question. "I did! Had I not been there, you and all the rest of the Young Gods would still be locked in Khull-khuum's orbs!" He jabbed a long green fingernail to his chest. "If not for me, do you think Drake could have set you free? Do you really believe a hapless boy could have defeated the Shadowking?"

"I believe you are exaggerating your own importance." Thera fixed Wahooka with a thoughtful stare. "But, as you say, why does this matter to you? If Stonekeep is so ungrateful, what do you care if throgs and shargas overrun the whole kingdom?"

"Who says I do?" Wahooka looked away. "But I did watch over Stonekeep for many years, and I'm curious about what you're going to do."

Thera held her answer until Wahooka finally looked back to her idol, then said, "I will do what is best for Stonekeep—nothing."

"Nothing?" Wahooka did not understand. "What do you mean, nothing?"

"Exactly that," Thera answered. "I will not interfere. The invasion will be good for Stonekeep. It will shock the High Lords to their senses, and they will be better prepared next time."

Wahooka's mouth fell open, displaying his four lower tusks. "Don't you understand what I'm telling you? If the High Lords don't dispatch these raiders quickly, more will follow—"

"Which is why we must do nothing," Thera said. "Despite what you say, Little One, I know you still care for Stonekeep—but we cannot make the realm strong by shielding it from its enemies. If Stonekeep is to survive as a true kingdom, it must learn to fight its own battles . . . domestic and foreign. I think you learned that the last time you interfered."

Thera gave Wahooka a smile she must have intended to be patient, but which the Trickster found condescending. He felt the anger rushing to his face and did not try to conceal it.

"I was not the one who interfered," he growled. "You turned Stonekeep against me so you could take my place."

"I did no such thing!"

"No?" Wahooka flung open his cloak and displayed its glimmering lining. There were emeralds and rubies, diamonds and sapphires, topaz and opals—gems of every size and shape, all set in gold and polished to a gleaming luster. "I have proof!"

The idol rolled its eyes. "What do a few baubles prove?"

"These were given to me by Drake, Drakeson, and Calvar!" Wahooka pointed to a ruby as large as his thumb, then to a sapphire and a diamond each the size of his little finger. "The Kings of Stonekeep worshiped me for three generations . . . for three generations, until you debauched young Terris!"

Thera's eyes narrowed in fury. "Debauched! How dare you!" A fierce gust of wind howled from the idol's mouth. "Recant!"

"Then you deny it?"

"A mother does not debauch her children! Recant!"

Another gust howled across the stairwell, nearly sweeping Wahooka off his feet. He braced himself and glared at the idol. The wind only continued to grow stronger, and finally a pair of tiny blue lights began to flicker in Thera's stone eyes.

Wahooka looked away. "Very well, I recant." He waved a dismissing hand. "All that is between you and House Drake anyway, and it is not what I asked. Prince Terris named you the official goddess of Stonekeep, did he not?"

"After he banished you from the realm." Thera paused to calm herself, then added, "And you brought that upon yourself—or have you forgotten renouncing Terris in favor of Ulger the Cruel?"

Wahooka's beady eyes darted toward the far wall. "I can hardly be blamed for that. Ulger was the lawful regent."

"Only until the rightful heir came of age," Thera reminded him. "Had you pledged allegiance to Terris, there would have been no war. Is it any wonder he banished you?"

Wahooka thrust out his chin. "What I did, I did with Stonekeep's best interests at heart."

"Provided those interests kept you in gems and power." Thera studied him a long time, then added, "And now I am beginning to see why you find these marauders so interesting."

Wahooka began to inch toward the head of the stairs. "My concern is for Stonekeep . . ."

"If that it is so, you will not interfere. You will stay here, and you will not use this invasion to ingratiate yourself with Stonekeep or its High Lords."

"The High Lords?" Wahooka snorted. "I wouldn't dream of ingratiating myself with those fools."

"Wahooka!" The flickering lights reappeared in Thera's eyes and grew larger, becoming a pair of brilliant sapphire irises. "Wahooka, I forbid you to interfere."

"Forbid me? You Young Gods really have grown too full of yourselves." Wahooka stopped at the head of the stairs. Still glaring up at the idol, he opened his cloak and reached into one of its magical pockets. "You sit up there in your heavenly palaces and never set foot on earth, and you think you can forbid me?"

"I am warning you—"

"No, Thera . . . I am warning you!"

Still fumbling inside his cloak, Wahooka gathered himself up, as though preparing to leap over to the narrow ledge beneath the carven idol. Thera's eyes flashed brilliant blue, and two beams of hissing magic streamed down from her stony irises.

The Trickster did not jump. Instead, he tore open his cloak and withdrew a small buckler of gleaming silver, then cowered behind it like a frightened child. When the bolts struck the shield, they shot back into the idol's eyes and shattered the stone into a thousand pieces, hurling rubble out the windows and filling the watchtower with a deafening clap.

Hoping he would not be too late to sound the alarm,

Wahooka rushed down the stairwell and started south. From the shattered remnants of the idol above came a chorus of tiny voices, almost too garbled to identify as those of the goddess.

"Wahooka, wait!"

Of course he did not obey.

The stag lay half-buried in the snow, calmly eyeing its pursuers from beneath the twisted boughs of a bristlecone pine. The beast had shaggy hair the color of cream and silver antlers with thirteen tines, and every so often it would snort derisively, then exhale a plume of white breath into the cold morning air. Its ivory eyes never strayed from the men and their horses, but Cassius had the feeling it had long ago noticed the white-cloaked stalker he had sent around to take it from behind. They had been after the creature for four days now, and not once had it let anyone close enough to hurl a lance.

Abruptly, the stag lifted its chin and looked into the valley, peering down a steep slope over the spirelike crowns of an ice-crusted pine forest. Nearly a thousand paces below, dozens of dark silhouettes were skulking south at a brisk pace, fluttering in and out of view as they passed through the trees. All of the figures appeared rather gaunt, with long torsos, gangling arms, and small blocky heads. Over their shoulders, some carried slender sticks that might have been lances or polearms, while others wore long shadows at their hips that could only be sword scabbards.

Cassius pinched his eyes shut, thinking that he was finally starting to see things after three nights in the saddle. Certainly, a waking dream was easier to believe than the ridiculous possibility that someone was raiding his father's lands—Kural was, after all, a province of Stonekeep!

When Cassius looked again, the silhouettes remained. Without taking his eyes off the dark figures, he said quietly, "My friends, I fear I'm seeing things."

"I fear you aren't," said Gareth, Cassius's most trusted companion. The son of the most celebrated knight in Kural, Gareth spent nearly as much time at Castle Kural as at his own family's manor, and the two had grown up like brothers—save that their childhood fights had been far fewer and rarely as bloody. "Let's be careful, Cassius. This fellow might be dangerous."

"Fellow?"

Cassius glanced at his companions and saw that they were not looking into the valley below. He followed Gareth's gaze back to the tree, then gasped. In the stag's place crouched an ugly little man, dusting the snow off his knees. He had a pair of dead branches stuck into his leather headband and a cape of cream-colored fur wrapped around his shoulders. His face was leathery and round, with a huge arrow-shaped nose, skin the color of porridge, and long deformed ears that stuck out from his head like those of a sheep. He could not have stood higher than the breastbone of most men, and the four tusks jutting up behind his lower lip gave him a vaguely swinelike appearance.

Cassius rubbed his eyes.

The man tore the branches from of his headband and strode across the mountainside, moving as swiftly as the stag he had been a moment before. Cassius's white-cloaked stalker scurried along behind the fellow, struggling to catch up in the deep snow.

Cassius posted his deer lance on its stirrup rest, ready to defend himself if the need arose. "Who are you?" he demanded. "What are you doing on these lands?"

"And a fine morning to you, too!" retorted the little man. "What I am doing here is my own concern—I was here long before you or your kind.'' He came to within a pace of Cassius and stopped, looking the young lord up and down. ''As for who I am, I imagine your father speaks of me quite often.''

Cassius cocked a doubtful eyebrow, for his father had never mentioned anyone matching the fellow's description.

''Lord Alban calls me Pendaran,'' the little man prompted. ''Pendaran Tremayne. I was of great service to him some years back.''

Cassius thought for a moment, then shrugged. ''I don't recall hearing the name.''

The little man scowled, his leathery face becoming a mass of wrinkles. ''Typical,'' Pendaran grumbled. ''You are Cassius of Kural, are you not? The only son of Lord Alban?'' He pointed to the ruby signet on Cassius's little finger. ''Or did you steal that?''

''Of course not!''

The stalker finally arrived and quietly took up a position behind the intruder, just outside of striking range. The slim, white-clad girl carried no weapon except her hunting bow, and Cassius fervently hoped that matters with Pendaran Tremayne did not come to blows. The orphaned daughter of a bear hunter, Brenna the Swift was not the type to forgo a fight.

Pendaran ignored the girl, save to rotate one sheeplike ear in her direction. ''Good. If you're not a thief, then you're the one I'm seeking.'' He grinned suddenly, fully exposing the snaggled tusks behind his lower lip. ''Now stop wasting my time, young lord, and pay me.''

''Pay you?'' This startled reply came from Gareth. ''For what, little man?''

''For leading you here, of course.'' Pendaran's eyes darted toward the valley, where the shadows were still gliding through the snowy woods. ''To warn you of Kural's danger.''

''You could have just told us,'' Cassius complained, reaching inside his cloak. ''But I suppose we can afford a *terris* or two.''

"Coins?" Pendaran spat into the snow. "No worthless scraps of tin for me! I want jewels."

Cassius pulled his hand out of his cloak. "Don't be ridiculous. Even if I had any jewels—"

"You do." Pendaran pointed at Cassius's ring.

"My signet? You must be joking!"

"Surely an entire province of Stonekeep is worth a single gem—especially when that province is your home."

"A few raiders are hardly going to sack all of Kural," Cassius said, eyeing the marauders below. The valley they were descending was a deep, snowy gash that opened into the Dark Wood Canyon, which in turn led straight down to the fertile lands of the Brookbury Basin. "It's been a hard winter. They're probably just hoping to loot the Swafham granary and escape back into the wilderness."

"I beg to differ," Pendaran said. "Throgs and shargas have no taste for cereals."

"Throgs? Shargas?" scoffed Gareth. "Not bloody likely, old man. Kural hasn't seen the likes of them in two hundred years!"

Cassius was not so quick to disregard the warning. While it was true that the Council of Eight had long ago purged its lands of all green-skinned beasts, it was equally true that as Stonekeep's northernmost province, Kural would be the first to notice if the creatures returned. Besides, Pendaran Tremayne was clearly a sorcerer, and sorcerers were not to be dismissed lightly.

"Well, throgs, shargas, or whatever they are, we'd better put a stop to them." Cassius motioned Brenna toward the back of the hunting party, where her horse was being held by a fellow hunter. "Brenna, when we draw near the marauders, you'll leave us and ride home to sound the alarm."

The young woman frowned. "But if there's going to be a fight—"

"There *is* going to be a fight," said Cassius. "That's why you must alert Lord Alban and Castle Kural."

Brenna's green eyes darkened to stormy emerald. "But I'm the best arrow here! You're only sending me because I'm a woman."

"Because you're a girl," the young lord corrected. Brenna had come to live at Castle Kural five years earlier, after a winter disease claimed both of her parents, and she had instantly become something of a shadow to Cassius. "And because you're our fastest rider. When you turn sixteen, you know I'll be proud to fight beside you."

"As will I," said Gareth. "I've crossed tips with more than a few swordladies who can hold their own in any fight I care to have."

Brenna ignored Gareth's flattery and continued to glare at Cassius. "But I'm almost sixteen now." She pointed at the youth holding her horse, then added, "Maris is barely that himself—and I'm not that much younger than you, Cassius."

"Which means you should know better than to argue with me." Cassius spoke sharply, but without anger. "We are no longer hunting, Brenna. You will do as I command."

The girl's face fell. "Yes, milord."

"Good. We don't know how many raiders might have slipped into Brookbury Basin already. If there's trouble, no one among us will be more able to find a way through."

Brenna rolled her eyes at the obvious flattery, but dutifully swung into her saddle.

Cassius nodded his approval, then used his lance to trace the curve of the valley around the mountain's near shoulder. "The rest of us will ride down into the Dark Wood Canyon and cut the invaders off at the south end."

"Cut them off?" Pendaran gasped. He ran his gaze over the hunting party. "With what? Nine warriors?"

"They're only throgs—and I didn't count more than three dozen of 'em," countered Gareth. "Besides, we have you."

Pendaran's eyes grew large. "Oh no!" he said, shaking his head. "I did not come to fight. I am here only to warn you."

"Which you have done," said Cassius, turning his horse toward the shoulder of the mountain. "But *we* must fight. If we let those beasts into Brookbury Basin, there's no telling how many peasants they'll kill before Lord Alban arrives."

Pendaran grabbed Cassius's reins. "Wait! You haven't—"

"I have made my decision." Cassius jerked his reins free and urged his horse forward—then remembered the payment Pendaran had demanded. Thinking better of angering a sorcerer, he pulled the ruby signet off his finger. "But here is your payment!"

He tossed the ring over his shoulder and raced off at a gallop, leading the way across the side of the mountain. When they reached the shoulder ridge and started down toward the Dark Wood Canyon, Brookbury Basin came into view. It was a large, oval plain directly to the south, ringed on all sides by snow-mantled hillsides and the darker furrows of small canyons. The white-blanketed fields were veined with silver streams and speckled with the stone barns of peasanthold farms. In the center of the basin stood the daub-and-wattle houses of Swafham, clustered together around the village's dome-roofed granary, and at the far end gaped the Giant's Gullet, a narrow gorge leading south to the rest of Kural. To reach Castle Kural, Brenna would have to ride down the canyon and through the Wilshire Bottoms, a journey that would take much of the morning—even at a gallop.

As Cassius and his companions made their way down to the mouth of the Dark Wood Canyon, they spied nearly twenty marauders slinking into Brookbury Basin. Though clearly not men, neither were they the throgs and shargas of epic paintings. With faces that seemed more skeleton than flesh and knobby-jointed limbs as thin as axe handles, the throgs looked like ghoulish mockeries of the lanky monsters portrayed in the galleries of Castle Kural. About the only thing that remained the same were the steel bucklers slung across their impossibly gaunt backs.

And the shargas, lesser cousins to the throgs, were even smaller than the ones in the paintings, standing no higher than a man's belt. Their green hides had turned scaly and brown, and their fingers ended in curving talons so long they could barely grasp the shafts of their barb-bladed halberds.

Brenna left the group and descended the back side of the mountain, circling away from the invaders so she would not be delayed by fighting. Cassius divided the rest of his band, sending three men to ride down the marauders that had already entered Brookbury Basin. He and five others thundered down to block the mouth of the Dark Wood Canyon itself, where the gorge narrowed to a flat-bottomed bottleneck choked with tangles of bog spruce and scrub willow. As they entered the snarled thickets, he lost sight of the intruders and saw nothing but gray trunks and snow-draped branches—until a surprised throg suddenly spun around, betraying its presence in the shadows beneath a black pine.

Cassius could not tell whether the creature's flesh had withered into shriveled black leather or simply rotted away, for the thing's face looked like a scorched skull, with an ugly set of holes where it should have had a nose and eyes as sunken as wells. It squawked in surprise and grabbed for its sword, but the young lord was on the thing in two hoofbeats, planting his deer lance in its skinny chest and galloping past.

Cassius came to a dark, icy creek and glimpsed the head of a halberd on the near side. He splashed around behind a log tangle, buying enough time to draw his sword. The weapon was a long, light-bladed tuck designed more for riding down deer than battling foot soldiers, but it proved adequate for knocking aside the startled sharga's halberd as the little beast spun around to defend itself. The creature dropped its weapon and bared a mouthful of needle-sharp fangs, then hurled itself at the foreleg of Cassius's horse. The nimble mount, well accustomed to dodging charging boars and slashing bears, simply danced aside, allowing the young lord to behead their attacker in a single smooth stroke.

A barrage of whacks and thuds echoed through the trees as Cassius's companions dispatched their prey. From every direction came the squeal of wounded shargas and the half-hissed groans of dying throgs, and the air began to reek of fetid blood and spilled entrails. The young lord crossed the creek, then turned to search for more marauders. He found his four companions doing the same, their horses prancing nervously through tangles of fallen branches and bleeding foes. If any raiders had survived the charge, they were too frightened to show their heads.

A dozen paces up the canyon, astonished intruders began to gather in groups of two and three. The throgs glared at Cassius and his companions from the depths of their cavernous eye sockets, while the shargas' beady eyes darted to and fro, searching for a way to sneak past the unexpected obstruction. As more of their fellows arrived, the throgs began to take the bucklers off their backs and form a rough battle line. Cassius eyed their increasing numbers with dismay.

"We'll hold them off with arrows," he called, exchanging his sword for his hunting bow. "Pick your targets carefully, and stay mounted in case we need to make a quick getaway."

In one swift motion, the young noble nocked an arrow and planted it through a throg's throat. Four more bowstrings throbbed beside him. Four more throgs went down. The survivors hurled themselves to the ground, disappearing behind logs and into snarled thickets, and that was the end of their battle line.

Cassius nocked another arrow and looked up the canyon. When a careless sharga wandered into view, he let the shaft fly. The little creature fell screaming, still searching for the enemy that had killed it. Another hunter fired, and a throg began to howl and claw at the shank now sprouting from its abdomen. The marauders began to yell up the canyon in a strange, chortling language that no man had ever spoken. The advance slowed to a crawl, and it was several seconds before another of Cassius's companions found a target.

With the marauders stalled, the young lord guided his horse a few steps up the canyon wall so he could see the companions he had sent out into Brookbury Basin. The three hunters had left a line of ten marauders dying in the snow behind them, but their charge had exhausted itself at the edge of a peasant's field, where a stone wall had given their prey a chance to recover. Now they were surrounded by a dozen throgs and shargas, all hacking at the trio's already bloodied horses with square-tipped swords or hook-bladed halberds. Cassius's friends responded valiantly with flashing steel and flailing boots, trying to slash and kick their way out of the mob.

It was not to be. Even as Cassius watched, a horse screamed and reared, the shaft of a long halberd dangling from its chest. The sharga on the other end of the polearm pushed forward, forcing the agonized animal to come down across the neck of another rider's mount. The two beasts stumbled and went down.

Cassius screamed and loosed an arrow at the mob, but the distance was too great for his short hunting bow. As the shaft landed harmlessly in the snow, the third rider wheeled his mount around, bleeding and staggering. For a moment the invaders fell back beneath a flurry of slashing hooves and biting steel—then a barbed halberd shot out of the crowd and took the horseman through the ribs. His head rolled back, and he dropped his sword and slipped from the saddle. The riderless mount lashed out with a hoof and smashed the skull of the sharga that had killed its master, then fell itself to a tempest of black blades.

Cassius's heart sank. He began to feel sick and guilty, and it was no consolation that Sir Vinn—Gareth's celebrated father—had said many times that a single well-mounted warrior was worth ten on foot. Three of his friends were dead, and he had given the order that killed them. His hands began to tremble, and he found himself wishing that he had sent Gareth along to lead the riders in the basin—and wondering if he had been right to attempt a holding action at all.

The mob stopped hacking at the three hunters and started back toward the canyon mouth, threatening to sandwich the rest of the party between two assaults. Cassius guided his horse down the slope, intending to call his companions and flee.

Instead, he found Pendaran Tremayne standing on a log, holding up the ruby signet. "Cassius of Kural, I swear you will never marry well! Do you know how long it took to find this in all that snow?"

"At the moment, sorcerer, I couldn't care less." Cassius started to order the retreat, then realized that Pendaran's arrival provided the advantage he needed to prevent his friends' deaths from being in vain. He raised a hand and pointed into the downstream thickets, out toward the basin where the trio had fallen. "There are a dozen raiders coming up behind us. Can you stop them?"

Pendaran looked insulted. "Of course. But—"

"Then do it, or die with us," Cassius said.

Without waiting to see if the sorcerer obeyed, he returned to his position on the firing line. A hundred paces upstream, well beyond effective arrow range in the tangled thickets, thirty throgs were forming a ragged battle line across the canyon, using their bucklers to create a patchy wall of black steel between themselves and their enemy's arrows.

"We'll fire in volleys," Cassius called. "Take their legs, and start in the center of the line." He waited a few moments for their enemies to come into range, then said, "Now!"

The throb of bowstrings filled the wood, and three throgs near the middle of the line sprouted dark shafts in their legs. They howled in pain and went down grasping at their wounds.

Cassius nocked another arrow, then yelled, "And again!"

This time four tall marauders went down, one with an arrow in each leg. Without the shield-bearing throgs to protect them, the shargas following behind began to falter.

"Take the short ones!" Cassius commanded. "Now!"

The hunters loosed another volley, and five shargas fell with arrows in their breasts. The center of the line dissolved into a tangle of limbs and weapons, and the survivors dived for cover. Unable to ignore what was happening in the middle, the warriors on the end slowed to a crawl and glanced nervously toward their cowering comrades. The line was less than fifteen paces away now, within easy bow range.

"Well done!" Cassius called. "Fire as you will."

Bowstrings snapped one after the other. Each time, a throg cried out and went down, and the advance disintegrated entirely. Cassius breathed a sigh of relief and turned to check on the danger behind.

At first, the young lord could not quite grasp what he was seeing. A broad chasm had appeared across the canyon—but it was like no other chasm Cassius had seen. The ground appeared to have simply vanished beneath the bog spruce and willow thickets, but the plants themselves remained where they had been only moments before, their roots dangling over the dark abyss, bare and exposed.

As Cassius watched, the raiders from the basin began to emerge from the thickets and cross the chasm. If they noticed that they were walking on air, they gave no sign. The beasts simply continued their advance, keeping their eyes fixed on their enemies' backs and doing their best to maintain a line.

Cassius shook himself out of his astonishment and opened his mouth to shout a warning—then saw Pendaran lock gazes with one of the shargas and look toward the ground at the creature's feet. The little brute bared its fangs and aimed the tip of its halberd at Pendaran's chest, but the sorcerer only smirked and let his eyes drop again.

The sharga scowled and looked down.

When the beast saw the abyss below its feet, it let out a terrified scream and plunged out of sight. The creature's death scream jolted its fellows. One after the other, they glanced down to discover the chasm beneath their feet and plummet into the darkness. As they vanished, the spruces and willows began to fall after them, and an instant later all that remained was the black crevice itself.

"In the name of Thera!" Cassius gasped. "That's the strangest spell I've ever seen!"

Pendaran spun around scowling. "Thera had nothing to

do with it, you oaf! Is that the thanks I get for helping you?''

''No, of course not! I'm—uh—sorry if I offended you,'' Cassius stammered. ''When my father hears of your service, I'm certain he will reward you properly.''

''Your father is an ingrate, as your ignorance has already proven.'' Pendaran sneered. ''Nevertheless, I would like to return you to him in one piece.''

The sorcerer nodded up the canyon, and Cassius turned to see another line of raiders forty paces away. His companions were planting arrow after arrow in the dark rank, but every time one warrior fell, another stepped forward to take his place.

''You've been a very valiant boy, but the time has come to show some sense.''

Cassius swallowed and nearly gave the command to flee, then recalled the impressive magic he had just seen. He shook his head. ''A noble's first duty is to protect his people. If we leave now, the raiders will kill everything between here and Swafham.''

''And you intend to stop them how?'' Pendaran asked.

Cassius looked over at the sorcerer, still standing on his snowy log. ''Perhaps you have another spell?''

''I told you, I am not here to fight,'' Pendaran replied. ''It would not suit me to get you killed here.''

''I've no wish to die myself, but I will hold here.'' Cassius studied Pendaran, trying to guess from the reply whether or not the sorcerer had another spell ready. Using magic was a complicated business of drawing energy—called mana—from the earth's field of mystic power and storing it in a specially scribed rune, and that took time. If Pendaran did not have a spell ready now, the invaders would overrun Cassius and his companions long before any magic could save them.

When the little fellow did not look away, the young lord took a deep breath and shrugged. ''If you won't help us, then we have no choice but to try another way.''

Pendaran frowned. ''What way?''

Cassius tossed his bow aside and drew his sword. "Prepare to charge!"

Cassius's companions eyed him as though he were mad.

"A charge?" Pendaran gasped. "You're five against a hundred!"

"Five brave men against a hundred cowards," Cassius replied. He looked past the sorcerer and gave his companions a stern nod. "Do as I say! Their line will break the instant they see us coming."

A knowing twinkle came to Gareth's eye. "Aye!" He planted his last arrow in a throg's cheek, then tossed his bow aside and drew his sword. "They'll scatter like rabbits."

Pendaran's beady eyes grew as large as coins. "They'll swarm you like rats!"

"So be it." Cassius looked past Gareth to the rest of his companions, who had yet to draw their swords. "Go on! Toss those bows aside."

"Wait!" Pendaran jumped off the log. "I'll help you."

Cassius's companions breathed a sigh of relief, and those who had not yet dropped their bows continued to plant arrows in throgs and shargas.

Pendaran came to Cassius's side and held up his hand. "Give me your tinderbox."

"My tinderbox? Don't you have a spell ready?"

"So now you are a sorcerer as well as a great warrior?" Pendaran mocked. "Will you give me the box or not? You're the one who insists on holding here."

Cassius reluctantly reached inside his cloak and passed the box down. The raiders were only thirty paces away, and he was beginning to fear he had made a terrible mistake. The sorcerer could not possibly draw a rune and imbue it with mana in time to stop the marauders.

But Pendaran spoke no mystic words and drew no magic runes. He simply tore open the tinderbox and struck the steel, and a brilliant white spark went arcing through the trees to land a half step ahead of the invaders. A pair of throgs cried out in astonishment and leapt away, then the ember erupted into flames and instantly engulfed the six creatures nearest to it. Long tongues of alabaster fire shot out in every direction, hiding the marauders' entire line behind a blinding white inferno.

Cassius's jaw fell, for Pendaran had not done anything that resembled even slightly casting a spell. "How did you do that?"

"How does not matter," Pendaran snapped. "You wanted magic, I gave you magic—but I am warning you, I do not like extortion."

"I don't particularly care what you like," said Cassius. "Three of my friends are dead already, and the lives of many hundreds of good people are at risk. I'll take your help any way I can get it."

No sooner had Cassius said this than a small stretch of the sorcerer's fiery wall began to flicker and dim. Pendaran scowled, then raised his pallid brow as the weak spot darkened from brilliant white to deep crimson. In the reddening flames appeared a gaunt, spectral-faced figure that seemed part man, part beast, and part fire itself. It stood half again as tall as a man, with a grinning mouth full of red fangs, eyes ringed by whorls of crackling flame, and long fluttering hair that floated about its head like wisps of gray smoke.

"In the name of Red Azrael!" Cassius cried. "What have you summoned?"

"That's nothing I summoned," said Pendaran, sounding more interested than alarmed. "I do believe it's a galok."

Before Cassius could ask what a galok was, his companions fired three arrows into the chest of the fiery nightmare. The shafts sank barely deep enough to stick and crumbled to ash almost instantly. The galok merely stepped out of the fiery curtain, the flames clinging to its body like cloth and leaving a jagged hole in Pendaran's wall of white fire.

"Don't waste your arrows on him! Prepare to retreat." So dry with fear was Cassius's throat that he could barely choke out the words. He reached down to grasp Pendaran under the arm. "You can ride with me, sorcerer."

Pendaran jerked his arm away. "Where is your courage now, young lord? Gone with the smoke?"

"We won't save anyone by getting ourselves killed," Cassius croaked, still struggling with his dry throat. "That thing—that galok—is more than we can handle."

"More than *you* can handle, perhaps." Pendaran pointed toward the abyss he had created down the canyon. "Your horses should be able to leap the chasm, and we'll be safe enough on the other side."

Cassius frowned, confused. "I thought you wanted us to run."

Pendaran shrugged casually. "That was before they had a galok. Now things are more . . . interesting."

Cassius glanced back toward the galok, which was holding the fire curtain open for its beasts like some sort of hellish doorman. The doubts he had experienced after the deaths of his companions came flooding back, and he could not bring himself to give the order Pendaran suggested.

"What about Lord Alban's poor peasants, Cassius?" mocked Pendaran. "Are you not so brave, now that you think your enemies have a bigger sorcerer than you?"

Though that was exactly the case, Cassius did not want to further irritate Pendaran by admitting it. He glanced at his companions, who were continuing to loose arrows at the throgs and shargas as they came dodging through the fire curtain and dived for cover. The young lord was tempted to ask Gareth's opinion, but knew he should not. With so many lives at stake, the burden of this decision was not one to be shared.

Cassius looked back to Pendaran. "*Do* they have a better sorcerer?"

Pendaran's ears went flat against his head. "I will forgive that question because your ingrate of a father has not told you about me." The sorcerer cast an irritated glance at the gap in his fire curtain, then added, "The galok has not been hatched that is a match for my sorcery."

Cassius eyed the sorcerer warily. "I hope it is me you're trying to convince," he said. The young lord turned to his companions. "Gareth and Whitney, you'll stand rear guard and cross with me. Everyone else, over the chasm now!"

Three riders wheeled around at once, urging their mounts

into a gallop. Cassius pulled Pendaran up in front of his saddle, then saw the galok step away from fire curtain. The fiery brute whirled a burning staff overhead and whipped it forward, yelling something unintelligible. Cassius needed to see no more to know the creature was casting a rune stored on the staff; that was how spells normally worked—regardless of the strange magic of Pendaran Tremayne.

Cassius turned toward his friends. "War spell!"

Even as he shouted, a roiling ball of flame shot off the tip of the staff, arcing overhead to plunge into the chasm ahead of the charging riders. They hauled on their reins, but it was too late to stop their galloping mounts. The beasts leapt into the air just as a curtain of scarlet flame belched up from the chasm, and the three horsemen erupted into screaming scarecrows of flame.

Cassius cried out in grief and clutched Pendaran's shoulder hard enough to crush it. "You said you could stop that thing!"

"I said we would be safe on the other side of my magic abyss—which we will be, if you will get us out of here!" The little sorcerer glanced up the canyon.

Now that the rain of arrows had drizzled off to a trickle from Whitney's lone bow, the invaders were beginning to emerge from their hiding places. A big throg went down with one of Whitney's shafts through the chest, but that did not stop a dozen more from raising their swords to rush forward.

Whitney nocked another arrow, one of only two remaining in his quiver, and in of the corner of his eye Cassius glimpsed a red streak as the galok swung its burning staff toward the youth.

"No!" Cassius turned his horse in the boy's direction. "Cease fire!"

The galok's harsh voice crackled through the trees, then a tiny sphere of blue light began to shine through the flames at the tip of his rune staff.

Pendaran stood on the neck of Cassius's horse. "Whitney, my boy!" he called. "Over here!"

A blue streak of light sizzled off the end of the galok's

staff. In the same instant Whitney looked in Pendaran's direction, and the little sorcerer flicked his hand as though shooing the boy away. Whitney flew from his saddle, his horse flying apart beneath him as the galok's spell seared it in two.

Pendaran turned toward the galok and smirked. "How about that? You missed!"

"Quiet!" Cassius ordered. He spurred his horse toward his surviving companions. "Gareth, get Whitney and go!"

"Go?" Pendaran demanded. He fell into Cassius and dropped back to a seated position. "What do you mean, 'go'? That oversized pile of ash isn't half the sorcerer I am!"

"I've seen what you can do, sorcerer." The first of the marauders reached them. Cassius lashed out with his sword, cleaving a throg skull, then deflecting a sharga's halberd on the backstroke. "And three of my friends are dead because of it!"

"You cannot win a battle without casualties," Pendaran objected. "You will have to learn that, sooner or later."

"I have learned that already." Cassius used his knees to guide his mount over a pair of shargas attempting to lance Gareth from behind, then wheeled on two throgs rushing to attack from his flank. "And we are not winning anything here!"

"Got Whitney!" Gareth reported.

"Good! We'll meet in Swafham." Cassius reversed his grip and drove his sword down through the one throg's head, then smashed his boot heel into the other one's face. "Go!"

Gareth's hoofbeats were already pounding up the mountainside. Cassius raised his sword and worked his horse back and forth, momentarily holding the marauders at bay—at least until the galok roared and started forward, spurring the throgs and shargas into a frenzied charge.

Pendaran's long ears dropped flat against his head. "Then go, you coward—go!"

Cassius jerked his mount around and started up the shoulder of the mountain after his companions, who, despite the extra burden on Gareth's horse, were already nearing the crest of the ridge. He had lost six good friends today, and for what? To delay the marauders less than an hour? He could hardly bring himself to believe what had happened—much less understand it.

Cassius had nearly caught his friends when a deafening roar blasted his ears. The sky erupted into orange fury, and the ridge exploded ahead of him and engulfed his companions in crimson fire. Gareth and Whitney burst into columns of flame, then crumbled to ash without so much as a scream.

Cassius jerked his reins, guiding his mount around the conflagration, and disappeared over the crest of the ridge without looking back.

The invaders' assault line stretched across the entire width of Brookbury Basin, forming a distant black band that divided the white fields from the snow-blanketed mountains beyond. Thin tines of gray smoke streaked the afternoon sky, each marking the location of some peasanthold fallen to the torches. A great column of roiling fume in the heart of the plain betrayed the fate of Swafham and its granary. Ahead of the dark advance, splotches of dun-colored fur fanned out and grew steadily larger. The fast ones became squalling farm animals. The slow ones simply vanished.

Cassius stood holding his horse's reins, unable to take his eyes off the black line. After slaying his friends, the invaders had poured from the Dark Wood Canyon like rats from a burning barn. Instead of scattering to pillage peasantholds, as he had expected, the marauders had strewn themselves across the plain and started south, slaying anyone or anything not quick enough to flee before them. Looking at the dark horde now, spread across the entire width of Brookbury Basin, the young lord could not imagine how he had expected to hold them in the canyon. He had thrown away the lives of his friends, and part of him wished that he had not escaped the galok's last fireball. Anything would be easier than admitting to Sir Vinn and the other fathers that he had gotten their sons killed for nothing.

Pendaran Tremayne, standing on the other side of Cassius's horse, was studying the dark line as intently as the young lord. "What do you see out there?"

"You know what I see," Cassius answered bitterly. "You could have told me how many there were."

"And what would you have learned from that?" Pendaran demanded. "Next time you'll ask."

Cassius glared down at the little sorcerer. "I do not care for the price of your lessons, Pendaran. Those were my friends."

Pendaran shrugged. "Blame me for their deaths if you like," he said. "It's nothing to me if you want to deceive yourself."

The young lord ground his teeth together, biting back the urge to send the little sorcerer to join Gareth and his other dead companions. It was true that Pendaran had convinced him to stay when he knew he should run, but it was equally true that Cassius had ignored the sorcerer's earlier advice to flee.

"No, the blame is mine alone, as was the decision," said Cassius. "But the next time you want to test yourself against a galok, I will thank you not to involve me or my friends."

"It was hardly a test, as I would have proven, had you not been such a coward. Still, you did say 'next time,' so I may be able to make something of you yet." Pendaran's gaze returned to the marauders, then he asked again, "Cassius, what do you see out there?"

Cassius looked back into the basin. "Not much. A dark stripe and some panicked farm animals."

Pendaran rolled his eyes. "Is that what you intend to tell Lord Alban—that he is being invaded by a dark stripe?"

"Of course not." Cassius continued to study the line,

trying to guess what Pendaran expected of him. "I'll tell him that the raiders—"

"Raiders?" Pendaran scoffed. "Keep looking."

The winter air shimmered, and Cassius suddenly found himself staring at a jagged rank of ghastly throgs and scaly little shargas—seven hundred throgs and twice that many shargas. There was no need to count; somehow, he knew the numbers the moment he laid eyes on them. In the center of the line was a company of two hundred hulking, hairy beasts of a kind the young lord had never seen. Were it not for their long, pointed snouts, he might have thought them some type of giant mountain ape. Half again the height of a throg, their arms were bigger around than a sharga and their shoulders were as broad as those of an ox. In their hands they carried swords the size of men, and slung over their shoulders were bows longer than a deer lance.

"Ogares," said Pendaran, though Cassius had yet to ask the question—or even form it in his thoughts. "Those bows of theirs can send an arrow clear through a horse at a hundred paces."

Behind the ogares came the ugly galok who, just that morning, had breached Pendaran's wall of flames. With a spectral face and a scorched pate of singed hair stubble, the beast looked even more horrid now than he had burning. His leather armor hung from his body in charred tatters, exposing large expanses of blistered hide and blackened burn craters oozing with ichor. The fire had devoured his nose and mouth, leaving behind only four cavernous nostrils and a lipless meshwork of interlacing fangs. If there had ever been eyes in his sockets, they were gone now; there was nothing beneath his brow but a pair of cold black voids that opened into the murky hell of his soul.

The air shimmered again, and once again the assault line looked like nothing more than a black, distant stripe. "Tell me what you see, Cassius. What are the raiders doing?"

Cassius thought for a moment. "They're marching straight across the plain, and they're not stopping to plunder." He paused, then added, "They're invading."

"Very good, Cassius!" Pendaran's voice dripped with

unfelt enthusiasm. "And what should you do next?"

"There's nothing I can do, except warn my father," Cassius growled.

Pendaran slapped himself in the forehead. "Report to Lord Alban! Why didn't I think of that?"

Cassius shot his most withering scowl at the sorcerer. "If you knew they weren't raiders, you should have told me—or better yet, left me to my hunt and warned Lord Alban yourself."

"That ungrateful cur?" Pendaran looked away indignantly. "Your ignorance is proof enough of the help he deserves."

"Whatever your opinion of my father, he is not the one you would have been helping," Cassius said.

He turned and looked behind him, where a snarl of oxcarts and overburdened mules was cramming itself into the Giant's Gullet. Despite the panic, the tangle was shrinking rapidly as the last of the refugees poured into the twining gorge. The young lord waited until the last of the oxcarts had started down the winding road, then mounted his horse and forced himself to extend a hand to the arrogant sorcerer.

"It's time to go. Would you care to ride?"

"If you insist."

Pendaran raised a hand and allowed himself to be pulled up. Cassius swung his horse around and trotted after the refugees, taking a position at the rear of the column. The procession twined its way down the dusky gorge at a brisk pace, the eerie chime of jangling metalware and creaking axles echoing off the canyon's sheer granite walls. The road followed a narrow, twisting path along the side of a roaring creek, regularly crossing the water on wooden bridges, or occasionally climbing far above it on narrow ledges hewn from the living rock.

The column was about a third of the way down the canyon when Cassius glimpsed a dozen ogares loping around a bend behind them, some two hundred paces up the road. The hulking archers were moving quickly but carefully, scanning the canyon walls high and low for any sign of an ambush.

Cassius retreated around a bend, then spoke quietly to Pendaran. "If those brutes catch the column—"

"They will seize control of the canyon, of course—and that will thwart any hope of recovering Brookbury Basin before next summer," said Pendaran. "Do you think I'm blind, or stupid?"

"Neither," said Cassius, though he had been thinking less about the strategic implications than about what the ogares would do to the peasants. "But I was wondering if there is anything you can do."

Pendaran peered up and down the canyon, then twisted his head around to look at the young lord's hand. "That depends."

Cassius frowned and glanced down, then saw his bare signet finger. "I'm sure Lord Alban will—"

"Your father is not here," said Pendaran. "I am interested in what you have."

Cassius sighed. "A sapphire cloak clasp, in my room at Castle Kural."

"That would mean trusting you . . ." Pendaran flattened his ears, considering. Finally, he pointed down the gorge, to where a huge face of fissured rock ran from the bottom of the canyon wall up to its rim. "Stop down there."

Cassius did as instructed, and Pendaran dismounted long enough to stick a gnarly finger into the crack. Deep within the crevice, small stones began to gleam like rubies and sapphires. Recalling how he had been rebuffed in the Dark Wood Canyon, Cassius did not ask the sorcerer how he worked the magic without drawing any runes or summoning any mana from the earth's field of mystic energies. It was enough that the ogares would notice the sparkling stones and try to dig them out. The young lord helped Pendaran up in front of him, then slapped the reins and quickly caught up to the peasant column.

A quarter mile later, the Giant's Gullet was shaken by a tremendous rumble, and he looked back to see a great cloud of dust billowing down the gorge. The rock slide would block the invaders' advance—for now.

They continued down the gorge for another hour, until they neared the bottom and an excited murmur began to rise from the front of the column. The peasants began to crowd their carts against the canyon wall, warning those behind them to make way for Lord Alban. Cassius left his place at the rear of the procession and hurried forward, already working to compose his thoughts into a concise account of the situation.

Castle Kural's standard-bearer rounded the corner in a tempest of thundering hooves and choking dust, bringing with him a long double file of fiery-eyed warriors. Cassius's heart sank, for he saw at once that his father had not anticipated the enemy's rapid advance. The entire company was armored in full plate and mounted on barded warhorses, a cumbersome livery more suited to the open fields of the Brookbury Basin than the tight confines of the Giant's Gullet. Cassius's own warhorse, Crusher, was at the end of the line, loaded with battle armor and being led by Brenna the Swift—the only person aside from Cassius himself whose hand the big warhorse would abide.

Lord Alban himself was riding beside the standard-bearer, armed with a sturdy lance, horse bow, battle axe, and shield bearing the distinctive bear-and-hawk of Castle Kural. Though his legs and torso were protected by a full complement of gleaming plate, he had left his weapon arm bare so it would not be encumbered when the axework came. He wore his helmet visor raised, displaying a long lean face covered by a silky white beard. His eyes were narrow and fixed on the road ahead, and he did not seem to notice Cassius as he approached.

Cassius moved his horse into the middle of the road and stopped. "Father!"

Lord Alban reined his huge charger to a stop, bringing the entire column of horsemen to a slow, clamorous halt.

"Cassius, what are you doing down *here*?" As Lord Alban spoke, a crowd of peasants began to gather around. "Why are you not in the basin delaying the raiders?"

"He certainly tried!" answered Pendaran. The little sorcerer slipped down and stepped over to Lord Alban's stirrup. "But the intruders are hardly raiders."

Lord Alban glared at the sorcerer, and the look that came over his face was anything but pleased. "Pendaran Tremayne—I should have known you were part of this!" The duke glanced at his son's ring finger. "Cassius, where is your signet?"

Cassius flushed, surprised by his father's unexpected ire. "I—uh—gave it to Pendaran, as payment for his help."

If Pendaran noticed the anger creeping into Lord Alban's face, he did not acknowledge it. He simply craned his neck to look up at the duke.

"It was all I could do to save your boy, Alban." The sorcerer glanced at a grizzled knight directly behind Lord Alban, then added, "I'm sorry, Sir Vinn."

Sir Vinn's jaw fell. "What are you saying?"

"It was the duke's son, or . . ." Pendaran let the sentence trail off, then shrugged. "There was only so much I could do. I'm sure you understand."

Sir Vinn set his jaw and looked away.

"Pendaran!" Lord Alban commanded. "You will be silent!"

"Ingrate," whispered the sorcerer.

Lord Alban pretended not to hear the slur, then looked to his son. "What's this about raiders in the Brookbury Basin? Brenna came in with some wild tale about throgs and shargas."

"It's true, except they're not raiders. We thought that when I sent Brenna off, but . . ." Cassius took a deep breath, then continued, "I made a mistake. I tried to head them off and got everyone killed. Instead of a raiding party, we found ourselves facing an army."

The crowd murmured in sympathy for Sir Vinn, but the old warrior remained rigid in his saddle, saying nothing in return.

Cassius forced himself to address Gareth's father. "I apologize for my recklessness, Sir Vinn. I lack the words to tell you how sorry I am."

Vinn gathered himself up straight, then wiped his eyes and turned to face Cassius. "Those are the fortunes of war, milord. I'm sure Gareth thought as you did."

"Thank you." Despite the kind words, the young noble saw the doubt lingering in Vinn's grief-stricken eyes. "You are too kind by far."

"By far," agreed Pendaran. "If Cassius had listened to—"

"Yes, we all know how wise you are, Little One," said Lord Alban. "But I am interested in hearing what my son has to say."

"Matters are not good, milord," said Cassius. "The invaders have taken Brookbury Basin, and I saw their scouts coming down the canyon behind us. Pendaran blocked the road with a landslide, but by now they have climbed over and resumed their march."

Sir Vinn's expression changed from mournful to grim. "Then we are losing defensive terrain every minute." He spoke to Lord Alban. "We should rush up the canyon and mount a charge."

"No!" The urgency in Cassius's voice surprised even himself. "They'll slaughter you!"

Sir Vinn glared down from his big warhorse. "Cassius, get a hold on yourself." The grizzled knight's expression was not quite a sneer. "It's one thing to massacre an unsuspecting band of young hunters—quite another to kill two hundred veteran knights."

"Not if you outnumber those knights ten to one," replied Cassius. "And not if two hundred of your warriors carry bows as long as deer lances!"

Sir Vinn looked back to Lord Alban. "It must have been terrible for young Cassius to see his friends die. We shouldn't be surprised if the experience shook him."

"I am not shaken," Cassius said. "I know what I saw. Their line stretched clear across the basin."

Lord Alban flushed as though embarrassed, then glanced from Sir Vinn back to his son. "In the heat of battle, things often look more frightening than they are. Now, try to think clearly—and remember that there hasn't been a throg anywhere in Stonekeep for a hundred years."

"For two hundred years," said Pendaran. "But they're back, and the exact count is 737 throgs. There are also 1,377 shargas and 200 ogares—the ogares are the big ones with the bows. They'll put an arrow through those double-forged breastplates of yours at two hundred paces, so it really doesn't matter how badly you're outnumbered."

Lord Alban's face went blank. He stared at Pendaran for a long time without seeming to comprehend what the sorcerer was saying, and the crowd of peasants began to mutter about the possibility of never returning home.

After a time Sir Vinn moved forward and leaned close to Lord Alban. "I wouldn't trust the little bugger, milord. Remember how he bled you dry in the Cousins' War."

"You fought in the Cousins' War?" Cassius gasped, looking to the little sorcerer. The Cousins' War had taken place long before Cassius was born, when a disconsolate relative had attempted to seize Lord Alban's birthright.

"I did more than fight in it," said the sorcerer. "I won it."

"I've no doubt you also started it," growled Sir Vinn. "You certainly profited enough from the blood and death." He turned to Lord Alban. "I say we ride down these throgs and shargas and be done with this, or Pendaran will leave you as destitute as he did forty years ago!"

"Better broke than dead," Cassius interrupted. He turned to address his father directly. "I don't know what happened forty years ago, but I do know what happened this morning. Had I listened to Pendaran Tremayne in the first place, Gareth and the rest of my friends would still be alive—and probably many more of the people of Brookbury Basin, as well. This isn't a raid. They came with an army, and they mean to stay."

Lord Alban lifted his brow. "Are you saying they intend to seize Brookbury Basin?"

"They already have," said Cassius. "And they're going to hold it—at least for now."

"Ludicrous!" scoffed Sir Vinn. "A bunch of throgs and

shargas carving a province off the greatest realm in the world? No one is that stupid!"

"Perhaps they are not so stupid," said Pendaran. "If the High Lords fail to send help, who will stop them?"

"But Stonekeep will send help," said Lord Alban.

Pendaran rolled his eyes. "Just like they send money to keep the border forts in good repair—and troops to garrison them?" The sorcerer shook his head. "If I were you, I would count on no help from Keeplord Varden and his Council of Fools."

This drew a chorus of gasps from the peasants and villagers, all of whom viewed the leaders of their great realm as sages of almost godlike wisdom.

Lord Alban, who had met these leaders personally, appeared less astonished. "What are you saying, sorcerer?"

"I am saying that the High Lords did not send help when your cousin tried to seize your title," replied Pendaran. "And they will send no help now. They have better uses for their forces—such as quelling tax revolts and watching each other."

Lord Alban's posture stiffened. "I thank you for the advice, sorcerer." The duke's reply came quickly—too quickly—and he spoke loudly so the crowd would hear him. "Nevertheless, I am certain that Keeplord Varden and the Council of Eight will recognize the danger to Stonekeep and send help quickly."

Pendaran cocked an eyebrow, but said nothing.

Lord Alban turned toward Cassius. "My son, you will ride to Stonekeep at once to inform Keeplord Varden of our situation, then act as guide for the army the Council of Eight will surely send to our aid."

Cassius's heart sank. After what had happened that morning, the last thing he wanted was to be sent away. What he wanted was to stay and avenge the deaths of his friends.

"Lord Alban, my sword will serve Kural here better than my tongue will in Stonekeep," said Cassius. "Perhaps you could send Sir Vinn; he is much wiser and well regarded for his bravery in the Cousins' War."

"Sir Vinn is not my son," replied Lord Alban. "The Council of Eight is a prideful body, and they will place more weight in the words of someone with noble blood."

"The fact is, the High Lords won't listen to anyone but you or your father," said Sir Vinn, glaring at Cassius. "And Lord Alban's leadership will be needed here—if we are to hold until your return."

Cassius was not deaf to the message Sir Vinn left unspoken: after getting eight of their sons killed, the men would not trust his leadership. The young lord nodded reluctantly.

"Of course, I will do what is best for Kural," he said. "But my heart will be here with you—and with your sons, until I can return to make amends for their loss."

"They were the sons of Kural, milord, and they died defending her," said Vinn. "The best thing you can do for them is return with the Council's army."

"This will verify your identity," said Lord Alban. He made a great show of passing his signet to Cassius, then glanced down at Pendaran. "Try not to lose it to Pendaran Tremayne."

This drew a wry chuckle from the crowd, which did much to relieve the tension. Lord Alban pretended to join in the laughter, as did Cassius and Sir Vinn. Only Pendaran, whose gaze remained locked on the great ruby, seemed vexed by the joke.

Lord Alban took advantage of the crowd's good humor to address them. "My friends, the time has come for you to move along. The sorcerer's rock slide will not hold the invaders forever, and we must concentrate on our defenses. Go along to Castle Kural; my steward will see to your safety."

"Aye!" cried one of the villagers, a strapping fellow with the dark and blistered fingers of a blacksmith. "Aquila watch over you, milord!"

After the column had started to squeak and squeal its way down the gorge, Lord Alban turned to Pendaran Tremayne. "You will go with my son to Stonekeep."

The sorcerer shook his head. "You can waste your time

on that circle of fools if you like, but I'm going to take other measures. I'll need a horse and . . . oh, how about that emerald you bought last month?"

"I don't care about your 'other measures,' " said Lord Alban. "But you will have the emerald when Cassius returns safely from Stonekeep and not a moment before. He will be riding fast without escort, and I don't want him waylaid by highwaymen."

Pendaran sighed heavily. "I can see there is no use arguing the matter. I will take the emerald."

"Good." Lord Alban turned to Cassius and clasped his shoulder. "You are to leave at once. Take Brenna the Swift in case you need a messenger, and know that Pendaran's advice is as worthless as his magic is powerful. His words serve only himself."

The sorcerer's beady eyes grew black and angry. "Had you heeded my advice in the first place, there would never have been a Cousins' War!"

"Only a cousin's murder." As he spoke, Lord Alban continued to look at Cassius. "When you reach the Council, be patient—and don't let your tongue get your head cut off. Kural will be counting on you, as will we all." He removed his hand from Cassius's shoulder. "Go with Safrinni, my son."

"And may Aquila watch over you." Cassius waited for his father and the column to start up the road again, then gestured for the sorcerer to follow him down the road. "Meet me down there. We'll get my warhorse, and then you can borrow this one."

Leaving Pendaran to walk, Cassius rode down the narrow road to the end of the column, where Brenna was waiting with his warhorse. As he approached, her emerald eyes filled with unshed tears, and he knew that word of their friends' deaths had already rustled down the column to reach her.

"Cassius, I'm so sorry," she said. "I rode two horses to ground, but it took the knights so long to get ready. I kept telling Sir Vinn to hurry, but they had to call their squires and get their armor, and I just couldn't make anyone understand—''

''Brenna, stop it.'' Cassius rode up beside her and grasped her arm. ''You could have ridden as fast as the wind, and it would have made no difference. This was my fault.''

''Your fault?'' Brenna looked dazed. ''That can't be.''

''It can. We didn't last an hour,'' Cassius said. ''I got everyone killed.''

Brenna blinked twice, and the confusion in her eyes changed to anger. ''This wasn't your fault,'' she said. ''How could you think that?''

Pendaran arrived before Cassius could respond, and suddenly he did not feel like explaining. Instead, he dismounted and passed her his reins, saying, ''We'll talk about it later. But right now we've got to go back to Castle Kural.''

Brenna frowned, clearly as upset as Cassius at being sent away from the fighting. ''Back?''

''Don't look disappointed, child!'' Pendaran stepped up beside Cassius. ''You're going to see Stonekeep!''

Brenna looked to Cassius for confirmation.

The young lord nodded. ''I'm afraid so. Someone has to tell the Council what's happening here.''

He reached up and took Crusher's reins. The shire was enormous even for a warhorse, standing higher at the shoulder than most men were tall, and capable of carrying a fully armored knight at a full gallop for more than a mile. He snorted a welcome to Cassius, then glared down at Pendaran as though eyeing a snack.

''It's okay, Crusher. Pendaran's a friend.''

''More than you know,'' the sorcerer added. He eyed the horse thoughtfully, then suddenly smiled and caught Cassius by the arm. ''Young lord, surely you and Brenna can find your way to Stonekeep without me.''

Cassius narrowed his eyes. ''You told Lord Alban—''

''I told your father nothing, except that there was no use arguing the matter. I am not one of his lackeys, to be ordered here and there like some horse messenger.''

Cassius scowled. "You agreed to a price."

"My price was for saving Kural, which I cannot do if I must watch over you." Pendaran glared up the canyon. "Your father and Sir Vinn did not see how well you acquitted yourself against the invaders. They think you are some kind of child who cannot make a simple ride without a nursemaid to take care of him."

"That may be, but I don't see how it affects my father's command," Cassius insisted.

"It doesn't," agreed Pendaran. "And I fully intend to do as he wishes—after I see to it that his foolishness in trusting the Council of Eight does not cost you your legacy."

"My legacy is Lord Alban's to bestow," Cassius said.

"And it is also yours to protect," said Pendaran. "Did you not hear the doubt in your father's voice when he spoke of the army you were to fetch?"

"Doubt?" demanded Brenna, who had been too far away to hear the exchange in question. "What doubt? Of course Stonekeep will send an army!"

Pendaran ignored her and continued to look at Cassius. "And do you really think the celebrated Sir Vinn knows how to defeat those ogares—much less the galok? With your own ears, you heard what he suggested."

Cassius found himself nodding, despite his father's warning not to trust the sorcerer's advice. Sir Vinn's cavalry charge would have been disastrous—even more so than Cassius's own attempt to stop the invasion in the Dark Wood Canyon. The young lord glanced up the canyon and watched the last of his father's knights disappear around the corner, then looked back to the sorcerer.

"I'm not saying yes, but tell me what you're thinking—and it had better not violate Lord Alban's orders!"

"Of course! I'd never ignore the duke's command." Pendaran glanced again at Crusher, then said, "All I'm suggesting is a backup plan—one that will make up for your little mistake in the canyon, and almost certainly save Kural itself."

The cavern entrance was guarded by an ancient gatehouse, once proud but now decayed into a mass of mortarless stone and rusting chain. Even on the forest road, the air smelled of mildewing earth and musty stone, of moldering flesh and old powdery bones. Pendaran Tremayne shook his head at what became of a place when Vermatrix Goldenhide moved in, then urged Crusher forward across the turbid green moat. So rotten was the drawbridge that its beams trembled and sagged beneath the proud shire's hooves, and the big warhorse balked at trusting his weight to its soft planks.

"Go on!" Pendaran used the tail of the reins to slap the horse between the ears. "This is for the good of Kural, you gutless strewer of fly bait!"

Crusher raised his mane and started to back away, and Pendaran had no choice but to set his spurs to the beast. The shire whinnied in anger, then changed directions so abruptly that the sorcerer nearly fell from the saddle. Their whole trip had been much the same, from the moment Cassius had used a sweet apple to persuade Crusher to let Pendaran mount, until just that morning, when it had been necessary to summon a griffin to herd the stubborn creature back to him. The sooner they parted company, the happier Pendaran would be.

The sorcerer guided Crusher under the raised portcullis, then dismounted inside the archway and tethered the reins to the remnants of a drawbridge chain. The horse's large nostrils flared, and he turned to eye Pendaran suspiciously.

"I ought to," Pendaran said, guessing that Crusher feared being left to feed whatever caused the rank death smells wafting from the cave. "But you heard what I promised Cassius. I'm going to take good care of you."

The shire nickered doubtfully.

Pendaran ignored him and undid the ropes connecting the warhorse's saddle to a sturdy oaken log behind them—the unwelcome burden that had caused the warhorse's rebellion that morning. The sorcerer freed the log of its lines as well, then dragged it into the gateway and jammed one end up under the portcullis. The ease with which he did all this made Crusher raise his ears in curiosity.

The sorcerer bared his tusks in a haughty grin. "Full of surprises, am I not? Wait until I get you inside the cave."

Pendaran slipped into the gatehouse and climbed the moldering stairs to the winch room, where he knocked the sheave brake free of its stop. The portcullis gave a rusty groan, then dropped a few inches and settled onto its new support. Pendaran peered through the floor slot at his handiwork and, seeing the log lodged firmly in place, nodded in satisfaction. The precaution was probably not necessary, but it was always wise to have a backup plan when dealing with Vermatrix.

Pendaran returned to the archway and untethered Crusher, then clambered up into the saddle. The big shire turned around at once, starting across the drawbridge toward the mossy forest beyond.

Pendaran jerked on the reins, using the bit to force Crusher back toward the cave. "Not that way, you tick-bag coward!"

Crusher started forward, then a breath of brimstone came

wafting out of the murky depths. He stopped dead two steps into the cavern.

"And you call yourself a warhorse!"

Pendaran set his spurs—hard. The shire only nickered and started forward at a cautious trot. As they passed into the cavern, the smell of mildew and rot grew overpowering. Crusher snorted constantly, and Pendaran covered his nose to keep from retching. It was impossible to see anything in the darkness, though the distant echoes of clopping hooves hinted at the size of the cavern. Occasionally, the moist air would grow momentarily hot and dry, drawing an alarmed whinny from Crusher. Pendaran would stiffen in the saddle, then curse the beast for startling him and start forward again.

About a hundred paces into the cavern, the air on the right grew hot and dry and stayed that way. Pendaran guided Crusher around the corner into a dark vault filled with the throat-burning stench of brimstone. What sounded like brittle wooden sticks began to snap beneath Crusher's hooves, but the sorcerer knew them to be old bones by their mordant scent. A low, steady rumble filled the darkness, and every so often there came a long swishing clatter, like a wave tossing pebbles against the shore.

Pendaran sensed something moving in the black void ahead—something big and sinuous then a pair of huge red diamonds appeared in the air before him. It took even him a moment to recognize the shapes as the eyes of a huge reptile; each pupil was as large as his mount's head, and they were spaced a full lance length apart. Crusher began to tremble, and the sorcerer made no attempt to urge the warhorse on.

"Vermatrix Goldenhide, greetings!" said Pendaran. "I come with a brooding-gift from the mighty Wahooka."

"You are Wahooka—and less than mighty by any measure." The words rumbled from Vermatrix's throat on tiny tongues of crimson flame. "You cannot fool me, Trickster."

"I know that," replied the sorcerer. "I did not say I was

anyone else, only that I bear a brooding-gift from Wahooka."

The diamond eyes shot forward through the darkness, then Pendaran felt the cavity of an immense, scaly nostril snuffling Crusher's flank. The warhorse stood as still as a statue, hardly daring to breathe. Vermatrix inhaled, sniffing the horse's fear and drawing a hot draft across the sorcerer's leg.

"How long have you been sitting now?" asked Pendaran, or Wahooka—it made no difference to him what others called him. "A hundred and fifty years? And I smell no signs of a fresh meal. You must be hungry."

A thick, warm tongue brushed past the sorcerer's leg and snaked under Crusher's belly. The horse whinnied, then sprang away as lightly as a foal, his heart hammering so hard that Pendaran felt it pounding against his knees.

"So you have brought me a little snack?" When Vermatrix spoke this time, tiny wisps of flame shot from her mouth, illuminating the long, flattish snout of a gold-scaled dragon. "Well fed on narcissus blossoms, I am certain—to help me sleep while you rob me of my treasure!"

"To the Shadow with you," Pendaran scoffed. "Your treasure is nothing to me."

"Ha!" Vermatrix punctuated her exclamation by raising her head and spewing a plume of fire at the ceiling. Scintillating reflections of light danced across the great nest of gems in which she lay, and the cavern filled with the reek of sulfur. "I am as old as you are, Wahooka," said the dragon. "Do not take me for a fool."

"Never—in fact, I am here because of my great respect for you. There are dark stirrings in the north, and I need your help."

"Liar! You know I can't leave my lair."

"You don't need to," replied Pendaran. "All I want are a few scales—"

"From over my heart, no doubt—so you can shove a lance through it!"

"Vermatrix, you're practically my sister!" Pendaran was genuinely hurt. "Would I do that?"

"Of course, Pendaran—for the jewels." An unseen claw clattered out of the treasure pile and plucked at Pendaran's gem-lined cloak. "I know all about your Coat of Sparkles."

"What is there to know? I've got to wear something."

"Come, now!" A long clatter filled the cavern as a cascade of gems fell from Vermatrix's golden claw onto her nest. "We are both collectors. Don't we share a certain . . . love?"

"I don't know that I'd call it 'love.' "

"But you do value their beauty," observed Vermatrix. "Afri insists that your greed will bring you to a bad end—but what does she know? She is the goddess of wisdom, not beauty. She can never understand us."

"Never," agreed Pendaran, relieved at the dragon's sympathetic tone. He might persuade her to be reasonable after all. "And so what if I do ask my worshipers for jewels? Thera has her secret rites, Safrinni her songs, Red Azrael his bloody sacrifices—I've got to have something."

"You are entitled, I know."

The dragon's diamond-shaped pupils glowed above Pendaran, as mesmerizing as any moon. The sorcerer felt himself growing more relaxed and comfortable; no longer did he notice the brimstone stench of the cavern, or the creature's dry breath, or the moldering skulls crumbling to powder beneath Crusher's great hooves. He experienced a profound harmony, a peace as warm as any bliss he had ever known.

Vermatrix continued to speak in soothing tones. "We both know how the Young Gods slight you, Pendaran. Have they ever thanked you for helping Drake?"

"Helping Drake!" Pendaran said. "I practically shattered the Orbs myself!"

"But that is not what the Young Gods say." The dragon's eyes came closer. In the pale gleam, the viperous profile of her scaly head became barely visible. "They say you did nothing, that you only accompanied Drake to collect the gems."

"Liars!"

"I suppose so," said Vermatrix. "We both know how the Young Gods envy you."

Crusher nickered and stamped his hoof, and some deep-buried part of Pendaran's mind felt the air stirring beside him. For one instant the sorcerer shared the horse's instinctual fear of things that slither and bite—but then Vermatrix's soothing voice spoke again.

"We both know how they envy all the Elder Powers."

"They've always been jealous of me," Pendaran agreed. His fear had slipped away as quietly as it had come. "And with what cause? My tricks and traps hardly equal their power!"

"Because you were here before them," the dragon replied. "And you will be here when they are gone."

As Vermatrix spoke, flames licked up from her throat to fill the darkness with ripples of orange light. Pendaran glimpsed three huge talons rising up beside him as she reached out to comfort him—then his cowardly mount whinnied in alarm and leapt away, and the dragon's talons came whistling through the air above his head.

Crusher stretched out and darted under Vermatrix's upraised head, fleeing back toward the main chamber. Pendaran, as bewildered at the dragon's attack as he was at his mount's unexpected flight, simply grabbed the saddle horn and tried not to fall off. A second claw came hissing down from the darkness ahead. The shire cut away on his own, and a terrific clatter echoed off the stony floor beside them. They passed from the hot, dry air of the dragon's lair into the cooler breeze of the adjoining passage, and the big warhorse turned toward the exit's emerald light at a full charge.

Pendaran's head cleared in a heartbeat, and comprehension came crashing in on him in an angry rush. He hauled back on the reins, then wheeled Crusher around toward the foul-smelling lair. When the warhorse faltered and tried to back away, Pendaran did not curse or kick the beast. Instead, he patted the shire's neck and leaned down next to his big ear.

"I'm okay, you great bag of oats." In spite of his words, Pendaran was surprised to discover that the trembling he had noticed was his own. ''And thank you—Cassius would be proud.''

Crusher raised his head.

''Let's go, my boy.'' Pendaran urged the horse forward. ''It won't happen again, I promise.''

Crusher chomped down on the bit and clopped forward, his steel war shoes ringing off the cavern walls. When Pendaran felt the stifling breeze from the dragon's lair, he reined the shire to a stop.

''Cannibal!'' Pendaran's voice quavered with fury. ''You tried to eat me!''

Vermatrix's glowing eyes appeared high in the darkness. ''Cannibal? The last time I looked, you were not a dragon.''

''We were born of the same primordial seed!''

''Ha!'' A ball of flame filled the dragon's maw, illuminating her body coiled upon its nest of jewels. She was unbelievably large—but also terribly thin, with ribs as large as men showing along her torso. ''Born of the same seed, perhaps—but not the same. You are the joke of the heavens! The gods laugh at your Coat of Sparkles!''

Crusher snorted uneasily, and Pendaran realized that his knees were squeezing the breath out of the horse's chest. He forced himself to relax, then continued to address Vermatrix.

''I come here with this nice brooding-gift, and you greet me with attacks and insults?'' The sorcerer was genuinely pained. ''You're as much an ingrate as everyone else. I ought to leave and close the gates on you.''

''You wouldn't dare! I'd hunt you down and feed you to Khull-khuum myself!''

A faint spiral of light appeared beneath the dragon's body, and Pendaran realized that her belly was beginning to fill with fire. Crusher must have noticed the glow, too; the big warhorse began to clap his hooves against the floor, gathering himself for a charge. The sorcerer allowed himself a tusky smirk and kept a tight rein on his mount. There were better ways to vanquish a dragon than slaying it.

''Vermatrix,'' he asked, ''how long has it been since a

nice, juicy band of thieves came for your jewels? Three years? Five?"

"That is nothing to you."

The dragon's belly grew brighter, and the stripes of dappled shell began to show between the coils of her emaciated body. The egg was as large as an oxcart, with a ruby sheen deeper than any of the jewels in her lair.

"Five years, I think," said Pendaran. "Otherwise, you would never have tried to make a snack of me."

A long rumble sounded from deep within the dragon's coils, and Vermatrix's belly grew so bright that it lit the entire cavern. She filled the chamber completely, her sinuous body coiled up against the walls and twined about itself like a giant snarl of golden intestine.

"You must be very hungry." Pendaran reached down to pat Crusher's powerful shoulder. "Don't these big warhorses have a lot of meat on them? I'll bet this one goes a full ton."

The dragon's pupils broadened and took on a wild, faraway luster. Pendaran felt Crusher's mane bristle and reached down to give the horse a reassuring pat. Despite his words, the sorcerer had no intention of yielding his mount to Vermatrix—especially not after what the shire had done for him. But he did want her thinking of her belly instead of his tricks.

"You know," said Vermatrix, "it would not matter if I ate your narcissus-bloated horse—as long as I ate you first!"

Pendaran straightened in the saddle. "As if you could."

The dragon's tail crashed into a dark wall, then swished across the chamber to smash into the other one. Crusher whinnied and stamped his hooves. Pendaran remained silent, defiantly staring into the dragon's eyes. Her golden tail continued to twitch, shaking the entire cavern, unleashing a cascade of muddy moss and fetid water drops. With each crash, her stomach rumbled more loudly, her belly glowed more brilliantly, her eyes shone more wildly.

"Leave now, Wahooka—leave while you can, and take your stinking horse with you!" The dragon's breath puffed out of her lair as hot and dry as chimney smoke. "I will have none of your tricks!"

"As you wish, Vermatrix!" Pendaran wheeled Crusher around, calling over his shoulder, "I'll close the gates on my way out!"

The sorcerer tapped the shire's flanks lightly, and that was all the encouragement the horse needed. Crusher sprang forward, and the dragon's jaws cracked shut less than a tail length behind him. His hooves tore at the littered floor, catapulting him into a full sprint. Vermatrix launched herself after him, spraying sapphires and rubies everywhere as her serpentine body uncoiled.

A puff of hot breath filled the cavern, and Crusher dodged right, slamming Pendaran into the dark wall. The dragon's jaws banged shut beside them. The cavern's slick stone tore at the sorcerer's leg, threatening to drag him from the saddle. He howled in pain, but Crusher, expecting the same mettle from Pendaran as he would from any other rider, kept his eyes fixed straight ahead and galloped for the exit.

Vermatrix withdrew, and Pendaran sensed another strike coming. Before he could jerk the reins, Crusher cut left and slammed him into the opposite wall. The sorcerer screamed again, then the cavern mouth loomed ahead. A few steps beyond that lay the gatehouse, then the rotting drawbridge and the mossy green forest.

The dragon's jaws snapped again, and this time Crusher slowed abruptly, almost falling. Pendaran gave him a loose rein, and the shire caught himself in three short strides. The sorcerer glanced back to see a wisp of coarse tail caught between the dragon's fangs, then Crusher burst out of the cavern into the forest air, Vermatrix's hot breath billowing around them as they streaked toward the gatehouse.

Behind them, the dragon erupted from the cavern mouth in an explosion of rattling scales and snarling breath, her claws shooting out to flank the galloping warhorse on both sides. Pendaran pressed himself against the shire's neck, and Crusher lowered his head and lengthened his stride, flashing past the stout log the sorcerer had jammed under the portcullis before entering the cavern.

Vermatrix slammed into the log at a full sprint, shattering it with a single crack and peppering Pendaran's back with splinters. Crusher shot across the drawbridge at a full gallop, paying no heed to the soft spots beneath his hooves—nor to the shrill squeal of the falling portcullis. The shire simply ran. The instant his iron shoes touched the dry road, Pendaran jerked the reins hard, guiding the warhorse into the forest at a dead sprint.

A crashing roar erupted behind them, and a searing wall of heat caught them from behind. Pendaran huddled down inside his Coat of Sparkles, but even it could not keep his head from stinging and prickling all over. The acrid stench of singed mane and scorched saddle filled the air, then Crusher came to a fallen hickory tree and hurled himself into the air, screeching as though he would burst into flames before his hooves cleared the trunk.

They survived to come down on the other side, and Pendaran hauled back on the reins so hard that Crusher's snout rose straight into the air. Even then it took the warhorse a full ten paces to stop. The sorcerer wheeled the shire around and found the road ahead scorched and fuming, with ribbons of flame still smoldering in the mossy undergrowth along its edges. All that remained of the drawbridge were three charred beams and a few smoking cross supports.

The great Vermatrix lay trapped beneath the gatehouse's heavy portcullis, her golden-scaled forelegs and massive head filling the gateway completely, the coils of her gaunt body writhing in the cavern mouth beyond. Her eyes were burning red, and her nostrils were trailing wisps of smoke.

"Wahooka!" The dragon's speech was thick and clumsy, for the heavy portcullis prevented her from opening her mouth. "If you let my egg die—"

"If *I* let your egg die? I came bearing a gift—a gift which you received first with insults, then with a treacherous and unprovoked attack!"

"You have my apologies." Vermatrix's voice was sharp with hatred. "My deepest apologies!"

Pendaran considered her words, then said, "You do not sound very sorry."

The dragon's pupils narrowed to slits as tall as doors. "I warn you, Little One! Release me, or—"

Pendaran raised a restraining hand. "I am willing to forgive your ingratitude—and the price is small."

"Anything. My egg is cooling!" Vermatrix flapped one of her trapped claws toward the cavern behind her. "You can have my entire nest."

"I told you, I have no interest in your jewels." Pendaran dismounted and tethered Crusher to a tree.

The dragon's eyes narrowed. "No?"

"What good are jewels that don't come from worshipers?" Pendaran started toward the dragon, picking his way through the flames at the road's edge. "I told you what I need. There's trouble in the north, and all the gems in Stonekeep will not prevent it."

Vermatrix lifted her scaly brow. "And you mean me no harm?"

Pendaran rolled his eyes. "Just a few scales." He stepped onto a charred beam and crossed the moat, then stood before one of the dragon's immense eyes. "I promise."

"On your honor, then—though I know that is as worthless as your promise." Vermatrix extended a sword-length talon and bit it off at the base, then dropped it on the ground before Pendaran. "Use that to slice the scales off. It's one of the few things in this world that will cut them."

Pendaran picked up the talon, then crawled under the portcullis to begin work. "My thanks, Vermatrix. You won't regret this."

"I am sure I shall, Little One." The dragon twisted her head sideways, struggling to keep one eye on the sorcerer. "This better not take long. How many scales is 'a few'? "

"Not many," Pendaran replied. He cut off the first of the enormous scales and stuffed it into the magic pocket inside his cloak. "Only a thousand or so."

• • •

Like everything else in Stonekeep, the High Council hall struck Cassius as opulent to the point of absurdity. It was a cavernous chamber of hammered gold and ornate sculpture, of high-vaulted ceilings and tiers of marble benches vibrating with the half-whispered business of running a great realm like Stonekeep. The young lord stood on the floor of the small speaking arena, looking up at eight rosewood desks perched along the rim of a semicircular wall. Behind the desks sat the Lord High Councillors of Stonekeep, listening attentively to their wizened sorcerers or dictating orders to assistants crowded into the tiered seats above. In a place of honor between the two middle desks stood the squat figure of a single dwarf, stroking his beard and eyeing Cassius thoughtfully.

Of all the people in the room, only the dwarf showed any restraint in his attire, wearing a simple coat of white linen. The Lord High Councillors clothed themselves in billowing tunics with flamboyant capes, while their sorcerer advisers draped their frail frames in dazzling robes of golden silk. Even the pages wore doublets of shimmering sequins over brightly colored tunics.

The din faded as the chamber's occupants began to gawk at Cassius's plain attire. The young noble ignored the heat rising in his cheeks and raised his chin, keeping his eyes fixed on the face of the pensive dwarf. The stout little man could only be the Oath Envoy, the delegate of the dwarves who lived under the Stonekeep. According to the Ballads, Drake himself had granted this privilege to Clan Farli for their help in defeating Khull-khuum, guaranteeing the privilege with the Oath of Stonekeep. According to legend, the realm would endure only as long as the pact held and dwarves dwelled below.

After a time the voice of the last Lord High Councillor droned to a halt, plunging the hall into an unnerving silence. A stern-faced councillor with a long tail of graying hair leaned over his bench, fixing an angry stare on the nervous chamberlain at Cassius's side.

"Hortigern, explain this outrage!" The councillor

pointed at Cassius. "Are you in the habit of wasting the time of this august body on vagabonds?"

The chamberlain paled. "Certainly not, Keeplord Varden. But I had no—"

"My appearance is not Hortigern's fault," Cassius interrupted. "He warned me that my attire was an affront and suggested that I change."

"Then why didn't you?" demanded Varden. As a direct descendant of King Drake, he served as the Keeplord and council leader. "And who are you, anyway?"

"I am Cassius of Kural, son to Lord Alban." Cassius removed his father's signet ring and gave it to Hortigern, who carried it forward and passed it to one of the Keeplord's assistants. "I apologize for my attire, but I bear urgent news from Kural and did not wish the Council to wait on it while I visited a tailor."

This drew a chorus of incredulous laughter, and even Keeplord Varden's expression softened to a smirk.

"As much as the Council appreciates your consideration, you'll find us a very patient lot." Keeplord Varden examined Lord Alban's signet ring, then returned it to Hortigern with a bored expression. "Perhaps you would do us the kindness of showing the proper respect the next time you visit?"

"Certainly." Cassius inclined his head to the Keeplord. "My attire reflects no disrespect, only the great urgency of my mission. An army of throgs and shargas has—"

"Yes, yes," said the Keeplord. "You may tell us about it when you return."

"Return?" Cassius exclaimed. "But they've already taken Brookbury Basin! By now, they're in the Wilshire Bottoms!"

The young lord could not tell whether the startled gasp that followed was due to his outburst or to the news he brought. Keeplord Varden glared at him hotly, as though debating the best way to have him detongued, and the other seven councillors simply looked puzzled. Only the envoy from Clan Farli seemed to understand what he was saying.

"What of your father, son?" asked the dwarf. "Surely, he's trying to stop them?"

"Of course, but he can only support three hundred men under arms," Cassius replied. "By now, I imagine he's calling his retainers to service, but even with all two thousand, he's outnumbered."

The chamber burst into a tumult of disbelief. A burly, red-bearded councillor rose from his seat.

"Quiet!"

The din only seemed to grow louder, until Keeplord Varden finally recovered his wits and began banging his bench with the hilt of a bejeweled dagger.

"Silence!" He waited until the tumult quieted to a drone, then yelled, "One more word, and I will empty the chamber!"

The hall fell silent almost at once.

Varden looked back to Cassius, then said, "Do you expect us to believe your father allowed an entire army of throgs and shargas into Kural?"

Cassius raised his brow, stunned by the Keeplord's accusatory tone. "Lord Alban did not 'allow' anything."

Varden raised an eyebrow. "Really? Then how do you explain your presence here?"

"We were invaded!" Cassius felt his anger welling up and, not for the first time, wished that Brenna had been allowed into the chamber with him. She was a calming influence and a careful observer. He took a deep breath, then said, "When I left, there were more than seven hundred throgs and thirteen hundred shargas in Brookbury Basin, all under the command of a galok."

"A galok?" asked the dwarf. "What is that?"

"It's a sorcerer—a hideous, manlike thing," Cassius explained. "But much taller. I don't know how to describe it, except to say that it can walk through fire and cast runes."

Keeplord Varden rolled his eyes. "If you can't describe it, how do you know what it's called?"

"A sorcerer told me," Cassius explained. "Pendaran Tremayne."

The young noble watched carefully to see if the name drew a flicker of recognition from the High Lords, but all eight faces remained blank. Instead, the dwarf frowned at the galok's description and turned to Varden.

"Perhaps you would indulge me, Keeplord," he said. "I'd like to hear this tale from the beginning."

Varden raised his brow. "As you wish, Sir Asgrim."

Cassius recounted the invasion from the beginning, starting with the appearance of the sorcerer and his own efforts to stop the advance in the Dark Wood Canyon. He related how he caused his friends' deaths by trying to hold too long, and how Pendaran Tremayne had saved him from the galok. Varden and the High Lords listened ever more attentively, their expressions changing from disbelief to shock to indignant outrage. Their golden-robed advisers showed no emotion whatsoever; they simply watched the young noble with narrowed eyes, hardly blinking as he described the enemy's rapid advance across Brookbury Basin. Finally, he came to the peasants' escape down the Giant's Gullet and his meeting with his father.

"That is where I last saw Lord Alban and his knights," Cassius finished. "His intention was to hold the invaders in the canyon until reinforcements arrive from Stonekeep."

"And he shall not have to wait long!" vowed the red-bearded councillor who had tried to quiet the hall earlier. "The Council of Eight will teach that galok better than to bring his shargas into our lands!"

"Hear, hear!" cried another of the High Lords, this one a sharp-faced man with a hooked nose. "Belden is quite right. This incursion is an insult!"

"It is more than an insult—it is unthinkable." Keeplord Varden leaned over his bench and peered down at Cassius. "You are quite certain of what you are telling us? This is not some kind of hoax?"

Cassius's jaw dropped. "The invaders killed seven of my friends and drove the peasants out of Brookbury Basin! Who would joke about a thing like that?"

The Keeplord looked rather dazed. "I—I don't know."

"I think you'd better take Cassius at his word," said the

dwarf Sir Asgrim. "I've been telling you for years to garrison those border forts, and now you see why."

Varden flashed an annoyed glance at Sir Asgrim, then settled into his chair and looked toward the two lords who had already spoken.

"The Council applauds the enthusiasm of Lords Belden and Fiske. Are we to take it that you are pledging companies to this matter?"

"I will send the Crimson Hooves," said Belden.

"And I pledge both troops of the Grim Pikes," added Fiske. He ran his gaze around the circle, then stopped to stare at a bottle-nosed lord with florid cheeks and rheumy eyes. "That is five hundred men from my army alone. Who will match me? Lord Ramsay?"

The bottle-nosed lord started to rise, but stopped when his sorcerer leaned forward to whisper in his ear. The man listened for a moment, then tried to hide a smirk.

"Regrettably, my army is suffering from an outbreak of ague," said Lord Ramsay. "Perhaps I can send a company in a week or two."

This drew a frown from both Belden and Fiske, who quickly turned to consult with their own sorcerers. The dwarf looked as though he would have liked to spit on Lord Ramsay, and Varden eyed the man contemptuously.

"We are sorry to hear of your men's illness, Lord Ramsay," said the Keeplord. "Had you mentioned it before now, we would have made an offering to Aquila."

"I did not want to trouble the Council," replied Ramsay. "I'm certain they'll be better soon."

"No doubt." Varden turned to the next councillor in line. "How about you, Lord Tate? Is your army well?"

Lord Tate eyed Ramsay with ill-concealed loathing. "Well enough, Keeplord—but I fear all three of my companies will be occupied looking after Lord Ramsay's poor men."

This drew a wry chuckle from the tiers, and Cassius saw Kural's hope for reinforcements sinking into a quagmire of suspicion.

"Milords, without your help, Kural will fall!" Cassius

ran his gaze along the circle of councillors. "Surely, you value her furs and iron enough to send a company each to her defense?"

"I value Kural as much as the next man—and no more." As Lord Fiske spoke, he glared openly at Lord Ramsay. "Sadly, it appears I have need of all my troops here in Stonekeep."

"Aye," agreed Lord Belden. "But Stonekeep's loyal lords are hardly likely to revolt while she is threatened by invaders. Perhaps Keeplord Varden could spare a few Companies of the Realm?"

The Keeplord's retort came quickly. "At whose expense? Kural's safety is the responsibility of the entire Council, and I alone should not stand the cost of marching an army north—especially not in winter."

Varden had hardly finished speaking before the High Lords' sorcerers were leaning down to whisper in their ears. Sir Asgrim eyed the High Lords with an upturned lip, though he made no comment as they pleaded poverty one after the other, citing the unexpected claims that winter famines and delayed construction projects had placed on their wealth.

After the fourth such excuse, Cassius could tolerate the prevarications no longer. "Milords, even a boy from the provinces can see what is happening here." He did not bother to conceal his anger. "But you are faced with an enemy from the outside. If you cannot put aside your differences and meet him, you will lose all of Kural!"

A stunned silence fell over the council chamber, and the High Lords put aside their differences long enough to glare down at the fool who had dared to scold them. Lord Ramsay turned scarlet from the neck up, then rose and leaned forward to brace his arms on his desk.

"Are you lecturing us, young sir? Did you ride all the way from Kural to tell the High Lords how to conduct the business of this august body?"

Cassius felt himself flush, but refused to wither under the man's assault. "No, sir. I came to inform the Council of an invasion in my father's province."

"No, not in your father's province," said Varden. "Lord Alban is only a caretaker. The province belongs to Stonekeep, and *we* are Stonekeep." The Keeplord gestured at his fellow councillors. "The Council of Eight will study the finances and politics of the matter."

"Study?" Cassius could not prevent himself from shouting the question. "While you are 'studying,' my father and his men will be dying!"

"Which is their duty," said Sir Asgrim. "As yours is to await the Council's decision." The dwarf gave Cassius a level stare, then added, "Your hard ride is getting the best of your tongue, young man. You have done all you can here."

"Yes," agreed Keeplord Varden. "Hortigern will show you to an officer's chamber in the Council Guards' barracks. Perhaps you should rest until the Council reaches its decision."

Hortigern took Cassius's arm and started for the exit.

Cassius jerked free and whirled around to chastise the Council again, then remembered his father's admonishment to watch his tongue and simply bowed to Keeplord Varden. "I await your summons."

"Good. Rest assured that Kural will have its help." Much of the tension drained from Keeplord Varden's face. "In the meantime ask someone to recommend a good tailor."

Pendaran hurled himself through a jagged maw of emerald icicles and puffed down in a bank of powdery green snow, then rolled once and found himself staring at a mass of blossoming primrose. Behind him, two orbs of pink light came floating down the main passage of the catacombs, giggling merrily and calling, "Wahooka, Wahooka—come out, come out wherever you are!"

The sorcerer waited until they had passed, then tore the primrose plants out by the roots and flung them against the wall. The Faerie Realm was like that, a murky labyrinth of snow and flowers, filled with jade-colored darkness and sickly good cheer. Hoping the maudlin aura would not addle his brain as it had the faeries, Pendaran gathered himself up and turned away from the main passage—then quietly cursed when he found a tiny pearl of light hanging in the air before his eyes. The pearl quickly grew as large and long as a thumb, taking on the shape of a comely woman with cascades of flowing hair.

"I have been waiting, Wahooka," said the figure. "You are growing predictable in your old age."

"Quiet, sheafhead!" Pendaran held a finger to his lips

and glanced over his shoulder. "They'll find me!"

"Then leave, if you find them so disagreeable." Now almost as large as Pendaran, the glowing figure assumed Thera's doe-eyed aspect. "I am sure it would be best for all of us."

"What I am doing is best for all of us," said Pendaran.

The sorcerer stepped straight through Thera's glowing form and continued down the icy passage into which he had thrown himself. In contrast to the gridlike corridors of the Faerie Realm proper, this cavern meandered to and fro, angling ever downward into the murky depths of the earth.

Thera materialized in front of Pendaran again, this time in a form as solid as the passage's ice-caked walls. "Wahooka, I am warning you—"

"Warning me?" Pendaran stopped two paces from Thera and pulled open the Coat of Sparkles, ready to slip a hand inside. His magic pocket contained nothing capable of overpowering Thera in a fair fight—but then again, the Trickster never fought fair. "And how do you intend to stop me?"

"I am warning you that no good can come of this." Thera's gaze did not drop to Pendaran's coat, which he took as proof of her fear. "You cannot expect a mortal to wield the Sun Sword wisely."

"Who says I expect him to?" The sorcerer gestured toward the cavern wall. "Now stand aside. Stonekeep is in more danger than we thought."

"I know." Thera allowed Pendaran to pass, then shrank until she was small enough to walk at his side in the narrow cavern. "I have looked to the north, and there is a shadow there that even my eyes cannot pierce."

Pendaran kept his gaze on the tunnel ahead, taking care not to show his surprise. No galok on earth could cast a shadow capable of blocking Thera's eyes. If what she said was true, then Stonekeep needed him even more than he thought. He considered the good news for a moment, then peered down at the chest-high goddess and smirked.

"So, now that Stonekeep is in real danger, you have come crawling to me. Afraid they'll forget you after I return?'' Pendaran patted her on the head. ''No need, dear child. I'll have them keep a temple to you at some idyllic little lake in the Shadow Teeth Mountains—not too far up, at least if you ask nicely.''

Thera's eyes glowed green with fury. ''If Stonekeep ever chooses a new patron, it will not be the likes of you! You hardly know what a god is, much less have the compassion to be one.'' The goddess let out a long rumbling breath, then continued in a calmer voice. ''But yes, I did come to ask something of you—to beg it of you, in fact.''

''Beg?'' Pendaran stopped and turned to face her. ''Then by all means, go ahead and beg.''

Thera pursed her ripe lips, and she looked as though she had just swallowed a muddy toad. ''For the good of Stonekeep, I am begging you not to do this. Let the High Lords deal with the invaders by themselves—stand aside and let the realm grow strong by itself.''

''Stand aside and let you take my place, don't you mean?'' asked Pendaran. ''I know how you are—you forget that.''

Thera ignored the slight. ''If you love Stonekeep as much as you would have us believe, you will do as I ask.''

''Love?'' Pendaran scoffed. ''You are a fine one to talk! I have seen how you repay love.''

Thera rolled her eyes. ''You did not love the Young Gods.''

''Did I not offer you shelter when you had none?'' demanded the sorcerer. ''Did I not teach you how to be gods?''

''You taught us many things, but that was not among them.'' Thera spoke in a bitter tone. ''You called yourself our guide; what you wanted to be was our despot.''

''Despot?'' Pendaran stumbled back, genuinely hurt. ''How can you, of all the Young Gods, say that? You were my favorite!''

Thera sneered and shook her head. ''I was only the mirror in which you adored yourself.'' Her voice grew softer and she placed a warm hand on Pendaran's arm. ''But if you ever bore me any true love, you will not do this to

Stonekeep. You will leave the Sun Sword in its vault.''

Pendaran jerked his arm free. ''That time is long past, Thera.'' He shook his head angrily. ''You cannot call on my fatherly affections—not after what you did.''

''That was your own doing, Wahooka. True veneration must be earned. You cannot demand it—especially not from gods. Afri, Safrinni, and the others had turned from you long before I did . . . And your constant demand for gems will have the same effect on men that it had on us—no matter how many cheap gifts you give them in return.''

''I doubt that the people of Stonekeep regard their freedom as cheap,'' Pendaran countered. ''And if I demand gems in return, it is because gems are what men hold most dear. The favor of Wahooka is not to be bought with hollow words and empty gestures.''

The sorcerer turned away and started down the tunnel again, veering right where the cavern branched into a pair of look-alike passages. Thera sighed in exasperation.

''You are right not to sell your favor cheaply, and it is not my place to say how your followers show their respect,'' she said, scurrying after him. ''But in the end, what really matters is what you give them—or, in this instance, do not give them.'' The goddess stepped in front of him, then her voice grew more forceful. ''Wahooka, if you give the Sun Sword to a human, you know what will happen.''

Pendaran glared at the goddess. ''How dare you!'' He reached into his coat pocket, desperately trying to find something that might intimidate a deity as powerful as Thera. ''You have already seen what comes of threatening me!''

Thera looked confused. ''Threatening you?'' Her ripe lips curled into a smile. ''By the Orbs! I would never threaten you, Wahooka—I was talking about what would happen to the human—and to Stonekeep.''

Pendaran frowned doubtfully and did not take his hand from his pocket.

Thera eyed the hand for a moment, then broke into a fit of laughter. ''Wahooka, sometimes I forget how much fun you were!'' The goddess laid a hand on his arm, filling the sorcerer with such a feeling of warmth and tenderness that he nearly forgot how she had wronged him. "There are times I truly wish the Glass Palace had never been shattered."

"Not nearly so often as I do, I would wager." Pendaran cautiously withdrew the hand from his pocket, then allowed himself a tusky grin. "I would that I could build it again."

Thera's face grew serious. "I would visit."

"It wouldn't be the same, I fear. You're not a child anymore, and I . . . well, I'm not the same either."

Thera folded her hands around his. "I would come."

"Would you?" Pendaran squeezed her hand warmly, then began to rub his leathery fingers back and forth across Thera's feminine softness. "The others would talk, you know . . . but it wouldn't matter. I'd forget this nonsense with Stonekeep and let you have it. I'd let you have it forever."

Pendaran looked deeply into Thera's eyes and watched as the goddess struggled to grasp what he was saying. Her expression changed from compassion to confusion to concern, and her hands grew suddenly clammy in his.

"Wahooka, this is so . . . so unexpected." Thera blushed and looked away. "I do not know quite what to say."

"Say yes." Pendaran bared the tips of his tusks, giving her his most debonair grin. "You must say yes . . . if you love Stonekeep as much as you would have us believe."

Thera's gaze snapped back to Pendaran, her eyes bright with fury and disbelief. "Is that what you think of me?" She jerked her hands from his grasp. "That I would sell myself for a city?"

"Yes." Pendaran sneered. "That's what I think."

"You . . . you lying little . . ." So angry was Thera that she could not find strong enough words to curse him. "You swine-faced tick! How dare you treat me like a trollop!"

Pendaran shrugged. "If the name fits . . ." When Thera's eyes began to flicker, the sorcerer decided the time had come to be on his way. He slipped past the fuming goddess and started down the passage, saying, "But there's no need to trouble that pretty head about the Sun Sword falling into human hands. I'm trying to save Stonekeep, not raze it.''

Feeling more than a little foolish in his silk knee breeches and yellow stockings, Cassius followed the council chamberlain down a shaded arcade into the Keeplord's Privy Garden. Brenna walked to his right and a step behind, looking equally uncomfortable in the satin tunic and velvet doublet that passed for squire's garb in Stonekeep. The small courtyard into which Hortigern showed them was predictably flamboyant, enclosed on all sides by coffered walls of white marble and filled with beds of sweet-smelling flowers. Varden himself stood beside a bubbling fountain in the center of the lawn, conversing with Sir Asgrim and a wiry, rat-faced man in a ghastly suit of ceremonial armor.

The chamberlain stopped at the edge of the Privy Garden's soft lawn and cleared his throat. The Keeplord continued to converse with his companions for several moments, then finally turned toward the new arrivals. When he saw Cassius's new breeches and tunic, he smiled warmly.

''Welcome, young sir!'' Varden waved Cassius forward, in the same gesture dismissing the chamberlain and paying no attention at all to Brenna. ''I see you have made good use of your time in Stonekeep.''

''I visited Hortigern's tailor, yes.'' Cassius crossed the lawn and bowed to Varden, making a point not to introduce Brenna. Hortigern had already warned him that it was considered rude to force a high member of nobility to acknowledge a mere aide. ''I came as soon as I received your summons.''

''And a good thing you did.'' Varden gestured to the dwarf. ''You remember Sir Asgrim, of course.''

Cassius bowed. ''An honor.''

The dwarf returned the bow and eyed Brenna thoughtfully, but said nothing.

Varden gestured to the rat-faced man. ''And this is Sir Melwas, Lord Commander of the Home Guard.''

''Sir Melwas, an honor as well.'' Again, Cassius bowed.

Melwas smirked and nodded his acknowledgment.

Varden clasped Cassius's shoulder. "I wanted to give you the good news myself." The Keeplord glanced at Melwas and Asgrim. "I have persuaded all of the High Lords to aid in Kural's defense."

"That's wonderful!" Cassius cried.

"Isn't it?" Varden beamed. "Sir Melwas will lead the company."

Cassius frowned. "The company?"

"Yes." The Keeplord continued quickly, "Melwas is one of our most experienced officers. He crushed the Winter Rebellion two years ago, then single-handedly put down the Wheat Riots last fall."

"Really?" Cassius cocked an eyebrow, pretending to be impressed. Although he dimly recalled the names, no one could track the details of all the peasant revolts and lord wars that had been plaguing Stonekeep since before his birth. "But if Sir Melwas commands only one company, who will lead the others?"

"There will be no others." It was Melwas who said this. "I hardly need more to crush this little incursion."

"Little incursion! Haven't you been apprised of my father's dispatches?" Nearly every day, a new messenger had arrived from Kural bearing news of some new disaster and revising upward the number of invaders. Already, Lord Alban had lost five hundred retainers and been forced out of the Giant's Gullet. "In this war, a single company will hardly be noticed!"

"This company will," promised Varden. "It will consist of a hundred men from each of the High Lords. That's eight hundred soldiers, Cassius."

"Eight hundred!" Cassius cried. He felt Brenna's hand squeeze his elbow ever so quickly, then caught himself and realized he would accomplish nothing by shouting. He took a deep breath and forced himself to try another approach. "Forgive my outburst, Keeplord. Eight hundred men is indeed a good start. Such a company might even hold Kural until the rest of the army arrives."

"It will do more than hold." Melwas sneered. "These

are veteran soldiers. Under my command, they'll slaughter these intruders and send the survivors scuttling home with such tales of horror that the raiders will never trouble us again."

Cassius had to bite his lip to keep from naming Melwas for the fool he was. "With all due respect, Lord Commander, you have not fought these invaders. They are well disciplined and skilled in formations, and they are commanded by at least one rune caster."

Melwas glared through Cassius as though he were a window. "You will think less of these savages when you see a real army fight," he said. "And we shall have a wizard to match any barbarian witch doctor. The Keeplord has been kind enough to volunteer his own sorcerer for the duration of the campaign."

"Providing you have finished it by the spring planting," clarified Varden. He turned to Cassius. "You may place your trust in Melwas. He has never failed us. Besides, even if I could persuade the Council to send another company or two, Lord Alban can hardly afford more."

"Lord Alban?" Cassius could no longer contain himself, and this time Brenna did not bother to restrain him. "What are you saying?"

Varden scowled. "The Council can hardly be expected to pay the price for Lord Alban's improvidence."

"His improvidence?" Cassius roared. "It was the Council who abandoned the Border Forts, not Lord Alban! No duke could afford to garrison all those posts—even if he wasn't tithing half his income to Stonekeep!"

Varden's face darkened to the color of Cassius's crimson tunic. "See here, I've had just about enough of your insolence. You have no idea of the compromises I had to make just to assemble the Company of the Black Wyvern!"

The statement struck the young noble as so absurd that he could not reply. The Keeplord seemed genuinely disappointed in Cassius's ingratitude, as though the Council had more than fulfilled its obligations by sending a token force under the command of a boastful charlatan.

Finally, Cassius asked, "Why should you need to compromise?'' His anger had drained away and been replaced by a sense of weary foreboding. ''Isn't there something sick—and a little sad—about this? Stonekeep's being invaded, and it takes a week to convince the High Lords to defend her?''

The point seemed lost on Varden. ''These things take time. You can't rush the Council of Eight.''

''I'll tell that to the throgs and shargas in Kural.''

Not bothering to take his leave of Keeplord Varden or anyone else, Cassius whirled around and left. Brenna scurried after him, furtively trying to pluck at his sleeve and slow him down to think about what he was doing. He ignored her and continued toward the gate.

When it became clear that he intended to leave, Sir Asgrim called, ''Are we to take it, then, that you are turning down the Council's aid?''

Cassius paused long enough to face the dwarf. ''Not at all. We'll take any help we can get—but I'm through waiting for it.''

The dwarf's mouth opened into a broad smile. ''In that case, I'd like to offer you the services of the Brass Axe Company—four hundred crack troops, some of 'em old enough to remember what a throg looks like—and we never charge our friends.''

It was Cassius's turn to smile. ''How soon can you leave?''

''We'll be mustering outside the gate before you get there.'' The dwarf turned to Varden. ''You won't be seeing me at the Council until this is over—there's real work to be done.''

Asgrim bowed and started toward the exit.

The Keeplord's mouth fell open, then he scowled at Melwas. ''Are you going with them, Lord Commander?''

''Of course, Keeplord,'' said Melwas, recovering from his shock. ''Cassius, Sir Asgrim—one moment, please!''

The Lord Commander bowed to Varden, then came clanking toward the gate in his hideous ceremonial armor. The whole suit was etched in gilt floral patterns and edged in gold damascene, with the head of a fierce lion embossed in the center of every overpiece. The loins were guarded by a clumsy steel skirt, the kneecaps by winged poleyns, and the head by a curl-horned helm so ungainly Melwas could hardly carry it under his arm. All in all, it was the most ghastly suit of plate the young lord had ever seen, and any fool stupid enough to wear it into combat would deserve every arrow and bolt it drew.

Cassius sighed, then asked, "Can you change in twenty minutes?"

Melwas frowned. "Change? Into what?"

Cassius gestured at the Lord Commander's armor. "Into your field plate."

Melwas glanced down. "This is my field plate!"

After many hours of walking, of ducking down half-hidden offshoots and crawling through serpentine passages the size of snake holes, of scrambling over castle-sized monoliths and leaping abysses as wide as rivers, Pendaran came at last to the dead end he was seeking. The vault was an ancient chamber, far older than Stonekeep, perhaps even as old as the Trickster himself. At the far end, a wagon-sized boulder lay braced against the wall, having fallen from the ceiling in some ageless instant long before men invented time. The sorcerer stepped over beside this enormous boulder and shoved it lightly. The monolith rolled onto its side, exposing the small, hand-hewn archway that it had been concealing.

Pendaran passed through the doorway into a vast, low-ceilinged room filled with the smell of ash and brimstone. In the center of the chamber sat a large block of granite with a golden sword hilt protruding from its top. There was a little hollow in the pommel that had once held a magnificent topaz, which had long since been removed and put to far better use. The sorcerer climbed up on the granite block and grasped the hilt, then waited. A few moments later, after the gold had warmed in his hand, he slowly pulled the weapon from its rocky sheath.

As the blade came free, it shone with a yellow radiance so intense that Pendaran's vision filled with spots. His skin began to itch and sting as though he had been too long in the sun, and the room took on an eerie glow. The light seemed to soak into the walls and come beaming back from every direction, filling the chamber with all-encompassing radiance that washed out even the faintest hint of a shadow.

Pendaran turned the weapon upright, then stood on his toes and shoved the tip into the chamber ceiling. The spots began to fade from his vision, and the room no longer seemed quite so blindingly brilliant. He jiggled the sword to make certain it was securely lodged—he did not want the Sun Sword falling on him by accident—then climbed down to the floor and opened his Cloak of Sparkles. He reached through a silk pocket into the magic closet dimension where he stored his trove of treasures, then withdrew a handful of dry peat. It had been collected from the forest outside Vermatrix's lair and still reeked of the dragon's sulfurous breath, which—he hoped—would keep away beetles, rats, faeries, and any other such vermin. He tossed the moss onto the floor, then reached into his pocket for more.

When the floor was covered, Pendaran went to the back of the room and knelt down in the soft peat. He reached into his cloak and withdrew one of the platter-sized scales he had taken from Vermatrix, spreading it out carefully on the floor. Again he reached into his pocket, this time withdrawing a small, whip-tailed lizard he had snatched from a desert several days' ride outside the forest. The creature was covered in thornlike scales and had a mouthful of serrated teeth—ideal for devouring its favorite prey: venomous desert snakes.

Pendaran pricked his finger on one of the lizard's sharp incisors and squeezed a drop of blood into its mouth. After the reptile had swallowed this offering, he dangled it in the light until it grew sluggish, then folded its tail over its belly and tied it in place with a tress of human hair. Next, he put the lizard on the dragon scale and pointed its head toward the Sun Sword, holding it in place until the creature closed its eyes and fell into a deep, motionless slumber. By this time Vermatrix's scale had dried out and shriveled into a tight little cocoon, encasing the reptile in an impenetrable shell of yellow chitin.

Pendaran moved a few feet and began to repeat the process time after time, working slowly and carefully. Though the cocoons were no larger than a man's head, they would not always be so small, and he took great pains to leave at least an arm's length between them on every side.

Before long, the heat of the Sun Sword grew unbearable even for him. He had to remove his heavy cloak and lay it beside him, jewel side up, dragging it along whenever he moved. How long he labored there in the heat, even he could not guess; time in the Faerie Realm had a different meaning, and hours passed like minutes.

Finally, he placed the last lizard on its bed and watched Vermatrix's scale close over it, then picked up his cloak and stood. Nearly a thousand yellow cocoons lay baking beneath the glow of the Sun Sword, spread out across the mossy floor like eggs in the rookery of some strange seabird.

"Pheew!" mewled a high, chirpy voice. "What's that stink?"

"It ain't trolls!" twittered a second. "It smells like brimstone—brimstone and dragon breath!"

"Hey, how about turning down the light, Wahooka?" cried the first voice. "It hurts me eyes!"

Pendaran turned to find two globes of pinkish light floating through the door.

"Faeries!" Pendaran pointed at the door. "Leave!"

"Leave what?"

The faeries drifted apart, gliding past the sorcerer on either side. One globe settled into the moss along the far wall, and the other landed on the granite block under the Sun Sword.

"I'll leave a feather!" A single white feather fluttered out of the glowing orb at the wall.

"And I'll leave a leaf!" said the other. There was the sound of tearing, then the faerie atop the granite block tossed a single book page into the air. It turned brown in the Sun Sword's heat and burst into flames. "Hey!"

The faeries began to twinkle and glimmer, then erupted into bursts of sparkling light and changed into a pair of childlike figures. The one along the wall was a dainty female, with two diaphanous wings and a pair of perky ears rising from a cascade of golden hair. The faerie beneath the Sun Sword was a shabby male, lacking wings and dressed in a tattered robe of brown wool.

The male jumped up and grabbed the hilt of the Sun Sword, then braced his feet against the ceiling and tugged. Though the weapon did not come free, Pendaran knew the hilt would soon warm to the faerie's grasp.

"No!" Pendaran danced toward the middle of the room, raising his feet high to avoid stepping on the yellow cocoons. "The light must stay constant!"

"I know what you can leave, troll ears!" The female picked up the nearest cocoon and hurled it at Pendaran. "You can leave Bink alone!"

Pendaran flung up an arm and caught the cocoon, then skipped over another and stumbled into the granite block.

Bink looked down at him with a wild gleam in his eyes, then released the Sun Sword and dropped to the granite block. "Egg fight!"

Pendaran snatched at a thin leg and missed. Bink disappeared over the other side of the stone. Knowing what would happen if he went after the faerie, the sorcerer ducked down behind the square of granite.

"Come out, come out wherever you are!" cried the female.

"Listen to Wink!" added Bink. "Come out and play with your brother and sister!"

"I am no sibling to you!" Pendaran fumed. He was called many different things by many different people, and the names were all the same to him—save that of Faerie Brother. "I'd rather be a dwarf!"

"Hey, isn't that one of them old songs?" Wink began to sing. *"If you could be the king, wouldn't that be a dandy thing?"*

"I'd rather be a dwarf," Bink answered, singing chorus.

By the sound of their voices, the two faeries were sneaking up on either side of Pendaran. He laid aside the cocoon that Wink had thrown at him earlier, then withdrew a fresh dragon scale from his cloak and spread it out in his hands.

"A hero great and tall, vanquish foes one and all?"

"I'd rather be a dwarf!" Bink chorused.

"Enough of your inanity!" Pendaran was close enough to the Sun Sword that the dragon scale had already begun to curl. He plucked a small ruby from his cloak lining and wrapped it inside. "These 'eggs' are precious. I will not have you flinging them about like toys!"

"Too late!"

The faeries sprang around the granite block on either side, each holding an armful of golden cocoons. They caught Pendaran in a cross fire, pelting him with the missiles at point-blank range. He covered his head and curled into a ball, hiding the dragon scale in his hand.

"Stop, stop! You'll ruin them!"

Bink and Wink shrieked with glee and battered him with the last of their ammunition. The cocoons, sealed as they were with the Sun Sword's magic, would never burst open, but the faeries did not know that. Pendaran hurled himself flat on the floor, at the same time releasing the dragon scale he had been hiding in his hand.

The golden flake bounced in the moss, then opened like a flower, displaying the ruby Pendaran had wrapped inside.

Wink flitted over to the stone. "What's this?"

Bink danced to her side. "Is it glowing?"

"I think it is!" answered Wink.

Together, the two faeries chimed, "Magic jewels!"

Pendaran did not think it necessary to point out that the Sun Sword's brilliance made everything in the room glow.

"You two wouldn't know a magic ruby if you stepped on it." He lashed out and snatched up the gem. "That belongs to me!"

The faeries glanced around the room with gaping jaws. Wink began to count cocoons, and Bink tried to open one.

Pendaran snatched it from the faerie's hands. "Not yet!" He knelt on the floor and gently returned it to the moss. "It's not big enough."

The faeries' eyes grew as round as saucers. "They'll grow?"

"What concern is that of yours?" Pendaran frowned as though worried. "These are *my* eggs."

Bink shook his head. "This is the Faerie Realm, and what grows in the Faerie Realm belongs to the faeries."

"And you said yourself that you ain't no faerie!" Wink drew a tiny silver sword, then began to flutter about waving it at Pendaran's head. "So what are you doing here?"

"Get out, out, out, out!" Bink drew his sword and began to swing at the sorcerer's legs. "Wahooka's no faerie! Wahooka's a troll kisser!"

Pendaran dodged away from their assault. "You would not dare—"

Wink sank the tip of her blade into the sorcerer's rump, making clear that she *would* dare.

Pendaran let out a howl and dashed for the exit. "You will rue the day you cheated me!" He rushed out the archway, then spun on his heel. "I have given you fair warning!"

The faeries came at him, weaving a net of flashing silver with their blades. Pendaran stepped aside and pushed the boulder across the doorway, sealing Bink and Wink inside.

"And don't come back, sheep ears!" yelled Wink's muted voice.

"Yeah!" Bink added. "We'll be waiting right here!"

Stonekeep's reinforcements reached the border of Kural in a blizzard, with an icy wind howling in their faces and pellets of snow beating riffs on their armor. The craggy silhouettes of the Twin Spires loomed just ahead, all but lost in the white fury of the storm. Between the peaks, a band of scrawny little shadows was scuttling across the road, halberds balanced over their shoulders, apparently unaware of the approaching troops.

Cassius's heart fell. The scouting patrols had sent back word of free-roaming bands of marauders, but it pained him to see shargas at the very gateway to Kural. To penetrate this far, the galok's troops had to have the run of the entire province.

A gust of wind tore across the road, concealing the invaders behind a whirling curtain of snow. Sir Melwas raised his hand and called a halt. As the voices of the sergeants reverberated back along the column, the Lord Commander turned to Cassius.

"Did you see those shadows?"

Cassius nodded. "Shargas." He had to shout to make

himself heard above the wind. "They didn't seem to see us."

"All the same, we'll be careful," said Melwas. "The terrain ahead looks like dangerous country."

"It is," agreed Cassius. "At Shadow Gorge, the path narrows to thirty paces."

Melwas cocked a brow, and Cassius knew there was no need to point out that this would be an ideal place for an ambush. So far, the Lord Commander had proven as competent as he was vain, pushing hard to reach Kural quickly, but also being careful to scout ahead and keep his troops in good fighting condition.

"Is there a way around this Shadow Gorge?" asked Melwas.

"Not for an army," Cassius replied. "The gorge comes down through the Dark Step."

"What is this 'Dark Step'?" Melwas asked. "You can't expect someone of my station to know the minor geography of all Stonekeep's provinces."

Biting back a sharp retort, Cassius pointed into the blizzard-choked valley ahead. "About halfway up, the canyon is blocked by a hundred-foot cliff called the Dark Step. It separates the Low Valley from the High, and Shadow Gorge is the only way through."

"And is the rim of Shadow Gorge accessible from the High Valley?" Melwas asked.

Cassius nodded. "Unfortunately." Once again, he was impressed by the man's military acumen. "And only from the High Valley. If anyone's up there, we'll be easy targets."

Melwas turned to Boghos, the sorcerer whom Keeplord Varden had sent along. "What can you do for us?"

"I can scorch the earth or sunder it, but I cannot bring down a whole cliff," Boghos replied. A hollow-cheeked man with sagging jowls and a bladelike nose, the sorcerer dressed in a red-cowled, black sable robe almost as conspicuous as Sir Melwas's gilded armor. "I selected my runes to turn the course of a battle, not reshape the land."

Melwas turned and stared into the blizzard, thinking, and Brenna took the opportunity to speak.

"If I may, milord." She observed protocol by addressing Cassius, though her comments were loud enough for all to hear. "I'm sure I could scale the cliff and see if anyone's up there."

"And get a rock dropped on your head if there is?" Cassius retorted. "No."

"In this blizzard—"

"Brenna, I said no."

"But—"

"Cassius is quite right, young woman," interrupted Melwas. "If they are up there, you'll only get yourself killed, and this galok thing will still control the high ground. When your betters speak, you would do well to remember your place and listen."

Brenna's green eyes darkened to emerald, but she held her temper and nodded politely. "As you wish."

Melwas turned to Sir Asgrim without acknowledging her reply. "Our scouts have given us no reason to believe there is danger, but it won't do to risk both companies at once. You will take the Brass Axe Company through first."

"The whole company?" Cassius gasped, and then he saw what Melwas was doing. "You're using them as bait!"

"Not that it is your place to question my orders, but yes." Though Melwas's tone was calm, his eyes betrayed his ire. "If the enemy is at Shadow Gorge, we cannot allow him to remain. He could hold us in the Low Valley until spring."

"Aye—and with only a few hundred soldiers," added Asgrim. Though it was impossible to see the dwarf's expression beneath his ice-crusted beard, his eyes burned as fiercely as those of the Lord Commander. "Sir Melwas is right—and as much as I don't like playing his bait, it's a good plan."

"But you haven't seen the Shadow Gorge," Cassius said. "If the Brass Axe is ambushed there, you'll be helpless to defend yourselves. You won't even be able to retreat."

"Retreat won't be necessary," Melwas replied. "The Company of the Black Wyvern will be just far enough behind to stay out of sight. Once the fighting begins, the enemy will be too distracted to concern himself with the face of the Dark Step. Brenna will sneak Boghos and a troop of my best climbers up the cliff, and then it is the galok who will be surprised."

"Assuming all goes well," Cassius said. "And if it doesn't?"

It was Sir Asgrim who answered. "In war, you must sometimes take chances." The dwarf climbed down from his pony and asked a sergeant to have the Brass Axe come forward, then peered into the blowing snow ahead. "Besides, it'll most likely come to nothing. An archer couldn't see ten paces in this mess."

"It won't be like this in the Shadow Gorge." Brenna spoke directly to Sir Asgrim, for the dwarf had made clear that he preferred simple manners and plain talk. "The canyon is too deep and crooked for a wind like this."

Cassius nodded, then turned to Sir Melwas. "With your permission, I'll go along with the Brass Axe Company. If there is an ambush, the dwarves will need me to show them to what little shelter there is in the Shadow Gorge."

"How very brave of you," Melwas said. The smile that creased his lips was somewhat predatory. "Of course—as you wish."

Cassius dismounted and began to cinch down his field armor. "Stay twenty minutes behind us," he said. "There's a bridge around the corner from the Dark Step. If there's an ambush, you'll hear fighting by the time you reach it."

"And if we don't hear fighting?"

"Then we weren't ambushed," Cassius said.

The Brass Axe Company marched up, their hobnailed boots striking a distinct cadence even in the snow. Sir Asgrim ordered his soldiers to unsling their shields and prepare their weapons, and Cassius led the column forward. As they entered the valley, the gray silhouettes of the Twin Spires loomed ever higher, until they no longer seemed mountains at all, but only two soaring granite faces vanishing into the snow-white sky itself. Here, the company passed through the fallen gateway of the ancient border house that had once separated Kural from its neighboring kingdoms, back in the dark days before they had all become provinces of mighty Stonekeep. The wind grew stronger and more steady, hurling snow pellets at them face-on.

As the column traveled up the Low Valley, the sheer cliffs of the Twin Spires gave way to gentler slopes flecked with trees, boulders, and the occasional granite outcropping. The roar of the blizzard quieted enough that it became possible to hear the gurgling of a half-frozen river. The road passed back and forth over log bridges, and the valley itself began to twine and turn along the water's course.

Cassius watched carefully for signs of the enemy, looking for movement atop ice-draped outcroppings and beneath fluttering tree boughs. The task was impossible; even the tracks of the shargas they had glimpsed earlier were blown over, and the falling snow was thicker than fog.

After a time the road crossed a bridge and descended to only a few feet above the river, then rounded a corner to the Dark Step. In the storm, the cliff looked like an immense gray curtain strung across the valley, with the black gap of Shadow Gorge dividing it down the middle.

Sir Asgrim stopped outside the gorge and spent several minutes studying the shadowy cliff, then sent a handful of warriors to scout ahead. No matter what they found, the Company of the Brass Axe would proceed, of course—but it was important to put on a good show. If the dwarves made themselves look too careless, the galok would suspect the trap and take measures to counter it.

When the scouts returned with no word of trouble, Cassius took the point and led the company into Shadow Gorge. Almost instantly, the meandering depths robbed the winds of their vigor, and the blizzard quieted to a mere snowfall. Visibility improved, and the Brass Axe found itself marching up a cramped, serpentine canyon of cold shadows and roaring cataracts. The chasm sides stood no more than thirty paces apart, leaving room in the bottom for nothing but the half-frozen river and the narrow road that snaked along its bank.

The Company of the Brass Axe twined up the gorge at a quick-time march, simultaneously searching the icy rim above them for danger and the granite wall beside them for crannies of refuge. They rounded curving salients from which a few enemies could rain arrows down on them coming and going, and they wound through narrow bends where hundreds of foes could gather to deluge them from all sides. Twenty minutes seemed like twenty hours, and Cassius found himself jumping every time a dwarven boot sent a chunk of loose ice clattering across the river's frozen skin.

At last, the canyon began to reverberate with the muffled rumble of water falling under ice, and the Company of the Brass Axe rounded a corner to see a long horsetail of ice dangling down the gorge headwall. They followed the road up a steep side gulch that quickly climbed out of Shadow Gorge, then found themselves standing in another broad-bottomed valley, the wind howling in their faces and the river half-lost in the blizzard ahead.

Sir Asgrim brought the column to a halt, then peered into the blizzard. "It seems we worried for nothing."

"Better worried than surprised." Cassius turned to look back into the Shadow Gorge. Although the bottom was visible more than a hundred feet below, he could see less than thirty feet through the blowing snow along the top. "I think we'd be wise to scout back along the rims."

"There is no need for that," said a familiar voice.

Cassius turned to find a small figure with sheeplike ears peering down from atop Crusher. "Pendaran!"

With faces free of hoarfrost and the first pellets of snow accumulating on their shoulders, the sorcerer and horse both looked as though they had just ridden down from a dry barn.

"I thought you were going to meet me in Stonekeep!" Cassius said.

"I was there," replied Pendaran. "If you did not see me, that is your own fault."

Cassius scowled at the sorcerer's flippant reply. "And what of that company you borrowed my horse to fetch? I don't see them. Is that also my own fault?"

"Not at all!" Pendaran's beady eyes grew bright and proud. "You'll be very impressed. My enkavs will prove the match of ten thousand men when they arrive next month."

Cassius did not bother to ask what an enkav was. "Next month?"

He started to berate the sorcerer for neglecting to mention this detail earlier—then noticed the charred stump where the big shire should have had a beautiful tail broom.

"What did you do to my horse?" he screeched.

"Me? Nothing—but I fear Crusher is a little slower than he is brave." The sorcerer patted the warhorse's neck without offering any further explanation, then raised his arm and pointed into the blizzard. "But if I were you, I would be less concerned with my horse's tail than with those things on the other side of the gorge."

Cassius turned to find the blizzard's wind-driven snow pellets sparkling in his eyes like stars, shooting and whirling about, illuminating everything in the High Valley in a silvery faerie glow. Trees looked like shimmering cones of melted sugar, boulders shone with diamond halos, snowbanks beamed with the incandescence of pearls. The Shadow Gorge was a jagged black stripe that zigzagged back and forth through the twinkling landscape—a ribbon of black emptiness that divided the valley crookedly down the center.

The "things" Pendaran had mentioned stood near the entrance of the gorge on the opposite rim, only a few hundred yards from the Dark Step itself. From what he could tell—and he could tell a lot thanks to Pendaran's spell—the galok had assigned two hundred throgs and twice as many shargas to the ambush, with fifty hulking ogare archers to support them. The entire force was arrayed along the arc of a sweeping bend, with whole hills of melon-sized stones piled on the rim beside them.

Cassius turned to Asgrim. "We've got to warn Melwas off!"

"Warn him?" The dwarf squinted and peered into the storm. "About what?"

"The dwarf cannot see past the rime on his fat nose," explained Pendaran. "My magic is too valuable to waste on hairy little tunnel grubs."

Asgrim's eyes widened. "Who dares—"

"Pendaran Tremayne, that is who." Pendaran peered down his nose at the dwarf. "I should have thought Cassius would have told you all about me by now."

"There has been no time for singing your praises," Cassius said. "And we have no time to waste on insults now."

Cassius turned to Asgrim and explained what he saw. Even as he spoke, a distant rumble rolled up the valley as the throgs and shargas began to hurl head-sized stones down into the Shadow Gorge. The hairy ogare archers leaned out over the rim and started to fire their huge bows at anyone who looked important enough to merit an arrow as long as a lance. The young lord's first thought was of the young companion he had left behind to lead Sir Melwas's countertrap.

"Brenna!"

Asgrim glanced at the snowy ground, which was beginning to reverberate with distant fury of the ambush. "I take it they have attacked." The dwarf pulled the axe from his belt and started toward the Dark Step. "Let's hurry. With luck, we can make Melwas's plan work yet."

Cassius caught the dwarf by the arm. "They're on the other side of the gorge," he said, turning up the valley. "But there's another bridge just . . ."

Cassius let the sentence trail off, then cursed at what Pendaran's magic revealed ahead: a company of throgs crouching down behind a makeshift wall of stone and ice.

"They're guarding the bridge!"

"How many?"

Cassius saw at least a hundred heads sticking up behind the wall. "Not as many as us, but enough to hold for an hour."

Sir Asgrim tugged at his beard. "That's all they need, isn't it?" The dwarf did not need to spell out his thoughts; the Black Wyvern would be gone in an hour, and the marauders who had destroyed it would be free to turn on them. "That galok doesn't miss a trick."

Cassius cursed, then reluctantly glanced at Pendaran Tremayne. "I don't suppose you can get us across the gorge?"

"I thought you would never ask." The sorcerer smirked.

"Today?" Cassius clarified. "Right now?"

Pendaran scowled at the young lord's mistrust. "Of course—provided your dwarves are not too cowardly to trust me."

"Mistrusting the likes of you is never cowardly," growled Asgrim. "But if you lead the way, we will follow."

Pendaran smiled. "Good. Then there is only the matter of the toll—"

"Toll!" Asgrim growled.

"Every bridge has its toll," replied the sorcerer. "I deserve my due."

"You shall have your toll the moment we reach Castle Kural," snapped Cassius.

Pendaran cocked his brow. "I thought you wanted the bridge now."

"At once!" snarled Cassius. "Brenna is down there with them!"

"Then by all means, let us hurry." Pendaran cast his beady eyes upon Cassius's index finger, where he was wearing his father's oversized signet ring.

"But this is Lord Alban's!" Cassius objected.

"It would be yours soon enough." Pendaran rested both hands on the pommel of Crusher's saddle and looked away. "But if you are more worried about a piece of stone than about the life of your friend Brenna, perhaps the matter is not so urgent after all."

Cassius ripped the ring from his finger and slapped it into Pendaran's palm. "Now!"

The sorcerer smiled and closed his spindly fingers over the ring. "Follow me."

He guided Crusher around the Brass Axe Company and started down the valley, leaving Cassius and the dwarves to scurry after him on foot. As they struggled to keep pace with the warhorse's long stride, Cassius kept a watch on the invaders. The fury of their initial assault had slowed to a mere storm, with the throgs and shargas pouring a steady drizzle of stones into the canyon while the brutish archers moved back and forth along the rim searching for targets. Cassius imagined the scene below: men cowering behind rocks and dead comrades, bodies strewn up and down the road, death raining down from above—and a young woman not yet sixteen hiding somewhere in that maelstrom of death, sheltering herself beneath . . . what? A battered shield? The corpse of a dead comrade?

Though it could only have been a few minutes before Pendaran turned toward the gorge, it seemed like hours to Cassius. He could actually see the rock piles growing smaller as the throgs and shargas worked, and the care with which the ogares plucked their bows suggested they had run out of obvious targets. The young lord rushed to Pendaran's side and tried not to think of what must be happening below.

The sorcerer dismounted at the edge of the abyss and took up a handful of snow, then began packing it into an icy ball. The invaders were perhaps a quarter mile down the valley, still lined up along the bend in the gorge, flinging stones and arrows into the chasm. As far as the young noble could tell, they remained completely ignorant of the dwarves sneaking through the blizzard behind them.

"Our enemy could not have asked for better weather, had he created it himself," commented Asgrim.

"Are you so sure he didn't?"

Pendaran drew back his throwing arm and held it there, directing his energies into his new spell. Cassius's vision returned to normal. The far side of the chasm became only a dim gray outline, and the invaders disappeared back into the blizzard. Only the road below remained relatively visible, a gray snake lying alongside the half-frozen river.

Pendaran let out a long breath and hurled his snowball

into the air. The wind caught it and started to carry it down valley, and Cassius lost sight of it in the storm. He looked down into the canyon, expecting to see the white sphere drop out of the blizzard and plummet into the quiet depths below.

Instead, a long tongue of snow and ice began to gather at the canyon edge, pointing across the gorge in the same direction Pendaran's snowball had flown. Before Cassius's eyes, the projection stretched toward the far rim of the chasm, arcing up in the manner of the many graceful bridges on the road from Stonekeep.

"There you have it—a snowbridge." Pendaran stepped aside and waved Cassius across. "I suggest you move quickly; I cannot say how long it will last in this wind."

Cassius started across, his boots sinking deep into the snow. He felt as though he were walking on a cloud. The wind pushed against his body, threatening to sweep him down into the Low Valley, and he was surrounded by nothing but white, howling emptiness.

The young lord had advanced about ten paces when he realized no one was following. He looked back to see Sir Asgrim and the rest of the Brass Axe Company staring at the snowbridge with astonished, fearful expressions.

"What are you waiting for?" Cassius waved the dwarves forward. "Come on!"

Asgrim tore his gaze away from the bridge. "On what?" he demanded. "You're standing on empty air!"

"Dwarves do not have an eye for my magic." Pendaran rolled his eyes impatiently, then turned to Asgrim. "You see Cassius standing there, do you not?"

"Aye."

"And he must be standing on something, true?"

Asgrim regarded the sorcerer suspiciously. "That seems reasonable."

"Then follow!" Pendaran grabbed Crusher's reins and led the big shire onto the bridge. "Even a warhorse is smart enough not to question his common sense. If we are standing here, we must be standing on something!"

Sir Asgrim squinted at the unseen bridge, then reluctantly

tested its presence with one boot. When the boot struck the powdery surface and seemed to sink, he cried out in shock and leapt back to firmer land.

Pendaran scowled. "Sir Asgrim, did you not say that you would follow if I led the way across?"

Asgrim's cheeks reddened. "Aye, but—"

"Then I will thank you to keep your word!" Pendaran mounted Crusher and continued across the bridge, calling back over his shoulder, "Though, of course, I should know better than to trust a dwarf's promise!"

The taunt was too much for Asgrim. "Were you not Cassius's friend, I would make you another promise, wizard!"

Asgrim clenched his jaw and stepped onto the bridge, all the while glaring angrily at Pendaran's back. When his fellow dwarves saw him walking across the gorge, they gathered the courage to follow and also stepped into the empty air. Cassius fell into line at Sir Asgrim's side and led the column across, taking care to guide them squarely down the center of the bridge. It was impossible to see the expressions beneath the dwarves' frost-rimed beards, but their eyes kept darting between their own feet and those of the warrior in front of them.

By the time the column reached the other side of the gorge, the Brass Axe Company was more than ready for a fight. They strapped their shields on their arms and unsheathed their axes, and Pendaran led the way forward. With Crusher breaking trail, they moved quickly and quietly, and it was not long before the ground began to slope upward. The sorcerer stopped and turned back toward the center of the valley.

"They are fifty steps ahead," he said, speaking just loud enough to make himself heard above the wind. "You are outnumbered three to two—"

"But they don't know that," said Cassius. "In this storm, appearing from behind and taking them by surprise, we will appear ten times as many."

Asgrim nodded. "We'll give the Axe Cry as we hit—that'll be good for a hundred of them right there."

The dwarf turned and quietly gave his orders, arranging the dwarves in three ranks. Cassius drew his sword and took his place in the center of the line next to Asgrim, and the Brass Axe Company advanced at a walk. The dwarves moved as silently as an owl on the wing. They did not speak, their equipment did not clang, the snow did not crunch beneath their hobnailed boots. It was as if they had suddenly become a pack of hunting wolves, slipping through the snow in hushed pursuit of their prey.

The sound of throbbing bowstrings and chortling invaders began to drown out the howling wind, then a jagged line of brutish silhouettes appeared in the blizzard ahead. The throgs and shargas were standing around their rock piles in small groups, while the ogare archers continued to wander along the rim, firing arrows as thick as quarterstaffs down into the gorge.

Asgrim raised his gleaming axe. As one, the Brass Axe Company broke into a trot, and the silhouettes ahead began to take on the shapes and details of real figures. A few of the rock hurlers glimpsed movement and began to turn.

Asgrim lowered his axe, crying out, "For Stonekeep!"

The dwarves broke into a sprint, answering, "Clan Brassdeep!"

The cry cracked through the blizzard like a thunderclap, striking with such volume that Cassius felt as if someone had slapped him on the back. The invaders spun toward the sound, stones and arrows dropping from their hands like a heavy rain. A few throgs reached for their swords, but most turned and raced away along the rim of the Shadow Gorge, screeching like wounded animals and spreading panic among their fellows.

Then the Brass Axe Company was on them, hacking limbs and smashing skulls, flinging gore and spraying blood. Cassius split a sharga's head, then shouldered a fleeing throg into the gorge. He caught a hairy archer trying to draw its sword and opened its abdomen with a quick slash of his own blade, then saw a dwarf take the brute's leg off at the knee and send the creature cartwheeling to its death.

The battle roar grew deafening, and it seemed to Cassius

that every screaming voice echoed back to him a dozen times louder. The young lord found himself racing along a sickle-shaped bend in the gorge, leading half the Brass Axe Company down one side of the curve while Asgrim led the rest down the other side. In the confusion of the blizzard and the battle, the silhouettes following Asgrim looked closer to two thousand than two hundred. The whirling snow made every shadow look like ten, the wailing wind multiplied every yelling voice a dozenfold. The throgs and shargas reeled on each other in a panic, fleeing not only their attackers' silhouettes, but those of each other.

Cassius overran half a dozen throgs and shargas, cutting them down from behind or simply shoving them into the gorge, then found himself charging an ogare. The black-eyed brute had arms like trees and a pointed muzzle with two curved fangs hanging beneath his lip, and the sword in his hairy hands was as tall as Cassius. He was roaring madly in his chortling tongue, and throgs and shargas were beginning to rally around him and draw their melee weapons.

Cassius tapped the shoulder of the nearest dwarf and charged the beast, screaming, "For Stonekeep!"

The ogare's muzzle curled into a scornful snarl, then he raised his huge sword and stepped to meet the assault. Cassius feinted left, then right, but the ogare would not be lured into coming to meet him. The brute's gangling arms were easily three times the length of any man's, and he was cunning enough to know an advantage when he had it.

Cassius put on a burst of speed and was still three paces away when the ogare's sword came sweeping down. He hurled himself at the ground and rolled—then returned to his feet in time to glimpse a yellow-handled axe tumbling past his ear to bury itself in the creature's chest.

The ogare's muzzle gaped open, then the sword slipped from his big hand and went sailing into the gorge. The brute reached up to pull the axe out of his chest, but Cassius was already on him, driving his sword up through the huge stomach. The blade sank nearly to the hilt before finally finding the heart. The beast's knees went limp, then he let out a death rattle and pitched forward.

Cassius released his sword and braced himself, catching the ogare's horselike weight on his arms just long enough to slip aside and let the creature drop. The brute landed facedown in the snow, with the tip of Cassius's weapon protruding from his back. The young lord did not even try to retrieve his blade. He simply stepped back and jerked the sword from a dead throg's scabbard, then rejoined the charge.

The dwarves were already a dozen steps ahead, mere silhouettes in the blizzard. He raced to catch up, peering down into the chasm as he ran. The scene was pretty much what he had expected, with a few dead horses and hundreds of dead men lying crushed and broken beneath an avalanche of arrows and rubble. Still, the dwarven charge had not come entirely too late; several hundred stunned survivors were rushing along the road in both directions, carrying the wounded and keeping a watchful eye on the steady flow of invaders tumbling down upon their heads.

Near a curve at the upper end of the trap stood Melwas and Boghos, staring in horror at what had befallen the Company of the Black Wyvern. Brenna was between them, struggling to keep their skittish horses under control and—most probably—cursing the stunned pair for being too stupid to mount and ride.

All at once the wind died. The pellets of snow began to fall vertically instead of diagonally, then ceased to fall at all. Cassius found himself staring across the gorge at a salient of rock, where a shadow-caped figure stood slapping at the heavens with a pair of black-clawed hands. At first, the young lord took the thing for the galok sorcerer that had chased him out of the Dark Wood Canyon, but a second glance revealed that this could not be. Arrayed in ebony armor and an obsidian king's crown, the figure was no taller than a man and far too emaciated to be the galok. It had a hideous skeleton of a face, with a broad lipless grin and blue flames flickering in its empty eye sockets. Each time the dark king waved an arm, a gray snowcloud slipped out of the sky and freed another ray of weak afternoon light to illuminate the carnage of the battlefield.

The thing turned to sweep a snowcloud out of the sky over Cassius, momentarily touching him with its blue-burning gaze. A terrible chill passed through the young lord's body, turning his knees so cold and weak they buckled and nearly sent him plummeting into the gorge. He lay on the ground dizzy and trembling until the dark king finally looked away, then he rolled to his knees trembling and queasy—and more than a little ashamed of his weakness.

On the other side of the bend, Sir Asgrim and his men continued to press the attack. The throgs and shargas were fleeing en masse, only to find themselves trapped in a cluster along the edge of the chasm. The ogare archers, who had not been so quick to flee the dwarven charge, were barreling into the mob from behind and forcing their comrades in the front over the edge. Already, marauder bodies were beginning to dam the river below, and the young lord could see no sign that the cascade would end soon.

As Cassius returned to his feet, the man-thing swept another snowcloud from the sky, then turned its gaze in Asgrim's direction. At once, the dwarf and a dozen nearby warriors collapsed to the ground, their axes slipping from their hands and leaving them easy prey for their enemies—had there been a marauder within ten paces calm enough to notice.

The dark king raised its black claw and pointed in Asgrim's direction, sending a streak of blue light arcing from its talon into the chest of the dwarven lord. There was a brilliant flash and a sharp crack, then Sir Asgrim and the three warriors beside him vanished in a plume of greasy black smoke.

"No!" Cassius yelled, feeling somehow cheated that the brave Oath Envoy had died such an ignoble death. He began to run along the canyon rim, searching for a hand axe or other weapon to hurl at the man-thing across the chasm.

The warriors of the Brass Axe took Asgrim's death no better than Cassius. The angry dwarves charged the canyon rim in a fury, hewing the mob down like so many dead trees. The terrified ogares struggled to push forward, forcing shargas and throgs over the edge at an ever-increasing pace.

The dark king roared out in the strange tongue of the invaders, then stretched an arm out toward the place where Asgrim had fallen. It curled a single talon back toward itself as though dragging an object along a table, and a tremendous crack reverberated up from someplace deep beneath the High Valley. The ground started to quake, and a small section of canyon rim began to rumble toward the black-crowned sorcerer.

Cassius found himself looking across the canyon in utter awe, holding a huge arrow he did not remember grabbing, staring at the man-thing's back and knowing that even were he capable of drawing an ogare bow, the attack would do no good. The creature in front of him was more powerful than any sorcerer—certainly more powerful than Boghos or the galok, and probably even more powerful than Pendaran. It was ludicrous to think a simple shaft of wood could slay such a being.

"Thera help us!"

The young noble tossed the useless arrow aside, then heard four heavy hooves crunching over the throg bodies behind him.

"Thera?" demanded the voice of Pendaran Tremayne. "Why are you always calling on that heartless tramp?"

Cassius glanced up to see the sorcerer sitting above him in Crusher's saddle. "Watch your tongue." He pointed at the dark-crowned king across the gorge. "We have enough trouble without turning the gods against us."

No sooner had Cassius spoken than the dark king's skeletal face swung toward his side of the bend. The instant he glimpsed the flames burning in the creature's eyes, a terrible chill shot through him and his knees nearly buckled.

"Fool!" Pendaran came flying off Crusher's back and slammed into Cassius's shoulder, pushing him facedown into the cold snow. "Lie still!"

Cassius could not have disobeyed if he wanted to. Despite the sorcerer's small size, he suddenly seemed to weigh as much as an ogare. It was all the young lord could do to lift his chin and look across the gorge.

The dark king extended one arm and motioned with a talon as before, and again a tremendous crack reverberated up from deep beneath the High Valley. The ground began to tremble and rumble as Cassius's side of the gorge drew nearer the man-thing's, and the skeletal figure quickly began to grow larger.

As the hideous face grew more distinct, Cassius saw that there were several conspicuous hollows in its obsidian crown—hollows that had no doubt held a set of fabulously large jewels at one time.

"You know him!" Cassius whispered.

"Shhhh!" the sorcerer hissed. "You will not save Stonekeep by drawing his attention to us!"

"Save Stonekeep?" Cassius whispered.

But Pendaran only kept the young lord pressed tight to the ground and did not answer.

Finally, when the man-thing had drawn close enough to show the wisps of black breath slipping between its teeth, Cassius could bear to study it no longer. He began to quiver uncontrollably and, if not for Pendaran's weight, might well have leapt up and run.

With the canyon closed to a mere fissure, the surviving marauders began to leap across the gap to join their master on the salient. The dark king continually ran its gaze along the rim of the gorge, using its chill gaze to keep the Brass Axe at bay. Despite the man-thing's obvious power, the dwarves continued to press the attack as best they could, leaping forward to hack and chop at their enemies whenever the thing happened to be looking in another direction.

Cassius made no further attempt to move, sensing Pendaran's fear and deciding they had done well enough to spoil the king's trap and escape with as much of the Black Wyvern as they had. At length, the tide of refugees began to ebb, and the dwarves were content to back away. They stood shivering in the snow, glaring across the fissure at their fleeing foes until the last sharga jumped across.

The dark king raised its ebony talons, releasing its magic, and the Shadow Gorge rumbled open much quicker than it had closed, quaking and shaking so violently that Cassius could only lie under Pendaran and wait. Clearly, the sorcerer knew the identity of the dark king—but what else? And how long had he known it?

The moment the rumbling stopped, Cassius squirmed out from beneath the sorcerer and jumped to his feet.

"I want some answers!" He grabbed Pendaran by the lapels and lifted him out of the snow. "And don't tell me you have none! I saw the empty gem sets in that thing's crown!"

"Now that you mention it, perhaps I do know him." Pendaran turned to stare across the gorge, to where the dark king and his minions were already vanishing behind a curtain of blowing snow. "The last time I saw that crown, it was on the head of Ulger the Cruel."

Pendaran had last seen Ulger the Cruel more than 350 years before, when the dark king had been a handsome enough man of mere flesh and blood. They had been on a knoll overlooking Stonekeep's scorched and battered walls, standing next to a catapult filled with liquid fire and waiting for their battle-hardened legions to array themselves for the assault. Already, the weather was turning cold and wet, a harbinger of the cruel winter to follow. They both knew they would reclaim the city that day or not at all; their warriors had little stomach for killing their own brothers, and even less for the disease and starvation of a winter siege.

When the last legion had marched into place, Ulger stepped over to the catapult and personally jerked the slip hook free. The heavy arm shot up and slammed into the crossbar, flinging its fiery load high into the air. The thudding bang of a thousand more catapult launches reverberated up and down the line, turning the sky orange with comets of molten sulfur, and Ulger snatched the signal master's flag, determined that he himself would launch his legions into battle.

As the fireballs arced down toward Stonekeep's mighty walls, a shimmering curtain of magic fell from the sky to intercept them. The spheres slammed into the rippling shield one after the other, erupting into splashing starbursts of flame, then cascading down on the blood-sodden fields where so many of Ulger's thousands already lay dead and rotting. The unburied corpses began to catch fire and burn, bursting into flames almost eagerly, as though grateful for the cremation rites they had been so long denied by the circumstances of war.

Astonished shrieks and cries began rise from the battle lines. More than few warriors fell to their knees, making prayers and sacrifices to Red Azrael or Helion or whatever god they held responsible for the intervention. The nobles fidgeted in their saddles and twisted around to look at Ulger, their round eyes and pale faces making plain what their lips were reluctant to say: they had had their fill of civil war.

Still holding the signal flag high, Ulger turned to glare at Pendaran.

The sorcerer gnashed his tusks, then growled, "Thera again."

Ulger spewed a curse too foul for words, then turned with a wild look in his eye and waved the flag to signal the assault.

The nobles did not call their companies to the attack. They simply looked from the waving flag into the wall of greasy smoke that separated them from Stonekeep's walls, then sat up upon their horses and watched the bodies of their fallen comrades burn.

"Attack!" Ulger yelled. When even the nobles at the base of the knoll pretended not to hear, the dark king spun on Pendaran. "Strike one down! Make them obey."

"And then what?" Pendaran asked. "Watch the army burn? Who will keep your siege then?"

The madness in Ulger's eyes began to fade, abating to mere bitterness and anger. He turned to glare at the cheering masses atop Stonekeep's battered walls. "We won't take it, will we?"

"Not soon," the sorcerer admitted. "I fear Thera has embraced Terris for good . . . it would not be the first time that harlot has wronged me."

Ulger stared at the city in silence, then finally turned away and removed his crown. It was a beautiful circlet of obsidian set with thirteen huge jewels—one from each kingdom he had conquered.

"I take the blame for this, Wahooka," said Ulger. "You are strong enough to overcome the help rendered by any god—even that of Thera. I have been the one holding you back."

Pendaran furrowed his greenish brow, trying to recall when Ulger had ever discouraged him from any act necessary to defeat an army or topple a kingdom. "What do you mean? I've done all I can, short of razing Stonekeep itself."

"Yes . . . I know." The dark king turned to stare at Stonekeep's Grand Heights, where the king's palace complex loomed high above the rest of the city. "It is pity, is it not—that Prince Terris is the one who betrays his legacy, and I am the one who is cast out?"

"There are some who would say *you* are the traitor."

"Me? I did only what was best for Stonekeep." Without turning around, the king removed his dagger from its sheath and slipped the tip beneath one of his crown's magnificent gems. "It was Terris who divided the monarchy—who carved it up and passed it out to his lackeys like some hunter tossing scraps to his hounds."

Pendaran did not point out that Ulger had forced the concessions; had the dark king stepped down when Terris came of age, the young prince would not have been forced to recruit allies by agreeing to share the crown's power.

"Terris is too weak to rule," Ulger said. "In denying him, I have only done what was right for Stonekeep." The dark king came over and passed the gems to Pendaran as he pried them from the obsidian crown. "And now I want you to do what is right for Stonekeep."

"I've always done what is right for Stonekeep." Pendaran eyed the gems in his palm. There was an emerald the size of his thumb, and a pair of rubies larger than a man's eye, and a sapphire big enough to be a tooth—and many more, all just as striking. "I can't imagine what else you want me to do."

"One city does not make a realm." Ulger smiled and placed a brilliant blue diamond in Pendaran's hand. "Even without Stonekeep, I am strong enough to rule her lands."

Pendaran nearly dropped the gems—nearly, but not quite. "You cannot mean what you are saying!"

"Could you do it?" Ulger pried the last jewel from his crown, a brilliant fire opal with a blue starburst in its center, and placed it in the sorcerer's hands. "You were there when Khull-khuum drove Stonekeep into the earth. You must know how to do it yourself."

Pendaran was aghast. "There is a difference between knowing and doing."

"But you can, can't you?" Ulger displayed the empty settings in his crown, then returned it his head. "You have all my jewels, Wahooka. There is no use bargaining for more."

Pendaran eyed the gems in his hands. They were all as large as bird eggs and as brilliant as fire—each the prize of the land from which it had come, taken from its owner by sword and flame, coveted by the sorcerer from the moment he had laid eyes on them. He cupped his hands over the stones and looked into Ulger's mad blue eyes.

"Think of what you are asking!"

"I am," said Ulger. "I am thinking of Stonekeep and what is best for it. I am a generation closer to Drake than my nephew, and I have tripled the size of the realm in less than a decade."

"So you would have me sink the city?" Praying that he had somehow misunderstood the dark king's request, Pendaran searched for a look of surprise in Ulger's eyes. "You would have me destroy the very city that I have striven these hundreds of years to make great?"

The fire in Ulger's mad eyes did not waver. "Yes—for the good of the realm. When Terris is gone, who can doubt my right to rule?"

"I can."

Pendaran ground his palms together, using his primal strength to turn the jewels into so much sparkling dust, thus ending Wahooka's partnership with the dark king. When word had begun to circulate of the sorcerer's departure, all but the most loyal of Ulger's troops deserted, and it became an easy matter for Prince Terris and his newly formed Council of Eight to drive the Usurper into the cold northern wildernesses.

Now Ulger was back, and he was determined to stay.

After the battle in the High Valley, Ulger skulked north with his dark horde to rejoin the main part of his army. Cassius led the Brass Axe and the survivors of the Black Wyvern north to Castle Kural, where he was happy to discover that the assault at Shadow Gorge had been no more than a desperate attempt to keep Stonekeep's reinforcements at bay. The real fighting remained in the north, where Kural was putting its cavalry to good use in the open fields and meadows of the Wilshire Bottoms.

Sir Melwas assigned the surviving half of the Black Wyvern to guard Castle Kural, sending the normal garrison north with Cassius, Brenna, and the Brass Axe to join Lord Alban's forces in the Wilshire Bottoms. Kural's forces had been losing ground ever since—nine battles in eighteen days, always in the midst of one of Ulger's blizzards. The Usurper's horde never seemed to tire, and their numbers only swelled with every clash.

Finally, Lord Alban's forces were driven back to the rocky ridge above Castle Kural itself, and now another blizzard was starting to blow up the slope. Today, at least, Kural's defenders would have the shelter of the jagged plates of slate that ran like a spine along the crest of the mountain. They would need it; they were exhausted and battered, half-frozen and almost hungry enough to eat sharga.

A chorus of bowstrings sounded from the tree line below, and a flight of massive arrows came whistling up the slope. Cassius and his warriors cowered behind the ridgeline as the powerful missiles slammed home, cracking thick plates of slate and thumping into rocky ground. Not far from the young lord, a swordlady was unlucky enough to catch a shaft on her buckler; the steel head split the shield and pierced her breastplate, then passed all the way through her body and punched a thumb-shaped protrusion into her backplate.

A garbled roar rolled up the slope, and the throgs and shargas began their charge. The ogares stayed in the tree line to continue plucking their bows. Balls of fire and bolts of lightning started to slam the crest of the ridge, peppering Cassius's troops with slivers of stone and tongues of flame.

"Marksmen, up!"

Cassius's booming voice echoed from a hundred different places along the ridge, a precaution Pendaran had taken to prevent Ulger from finding the young lord "too soon." Cassius stood and peered over the jagged outcropping, as did Brenna and twelve other warriors scattered along the ridge. Advancing up the hill in front of them was a gray wall bristling with halberds and square-tipped swords. The marksmen raised their crossbows, then waited for a fireball or lightning bolt to draw their attention to the tall, gangly figure of a galok—after returning from Stonekeep, one of Cassius's greatest disappointments had been the discovery that Ulger's ranks included dozens of the huge rune casters.

One marksman fell screaming to a huge ogare arrow, but the others survived to find their targets. Brenna's bolt avenged the man's death by planting a quarrel deep in a galok's chest, but the iron bolt could not pierce the creature's leathery skin. She smiled at her aim nonetheless, then ducked down behind the ridge to reload. Cassius watched as each of the other crossbowmen planted a shaft in the tough hide of a galok. One of the lanky creatures fell to a lucky shot through the eye, but the others ignored the quarrels and continued to pummel the ridge with fireballs and lightning bolts. The young lord waited until he had heard the clack of all twelve crossbows, then ducked down behind the ridge and nodded to Pendaran.

"Now!"

The sorcerer poked his head up and grinned, then a series of dull thuds reverberated up the hillside as the crossbow quarrels exploded. The rain of enemy fireballs and lightning bolts diminished to a trickle, and Cassius peered down the slope again, hardly noticing the scintillating beauty with which Pendaran's magic allowed him to see through the blizzard. The fiery deaths of the galoks had left several gaping holes in the enemy lines, but the throgs and shargas hardly seemed to notice. With Ulger the Cruel somewhere behind them, they had more frightening things to worry about than the deaths of a few rune casters.

Ogare arrows continued to rain down along the ridge. Cassius waited until the invaders had charged to within twenty paces, then yelled, "Dwarves!"

Again, his voiced boomed across the ridge from hundreds of different places, and two hundred dwarves—all that remained of the Brass Axe Company—rose with crossbows in their hands. Almost instantly, six fell to the rain of ogare arrows.

"Volley!"

A deafening clatter rattled down the ridge, and a flurry of iron bolts shot out to thin the invaders' charge. The dwarves ducked down to reload, and four hundred Kuralian retainers—men and women alike—rose to take their place. The ogare arrows took a greater toll on the larger humans, and close to two dozen fell to the great shafts.

"Volley!" Cassius called.

The volley left gaping holes all along the invaders' line. The charge faltered, and four hundred Kuralian bowmen rose with arrows nocked.

"Volley!"

Throgs and shargas fell in bunches. The survivors glanced left and right and, finding their ranks too thin to carry the charge, lost the courage to continue. They began to turn and flee, their fear spreading down the line like a contagion.

Cassius's warriors began to fire at will, choosing their targets carefully and making every shot count. Ogare arrows continued to rain down on the ridge, pinning screaming warriors to the ground and sending corpses tumbling down the back side of the mountain. Pendaran stuck his head up and waved a finger across the slope below; a wall of thorns sprouted up before the fleeing invaders, entangling their hands and feet. Kural's archers felled throgs and shargas by the hundreds, and still they did not run short of targets.

After a few moments the wall of thorns burst into smoke, freeing the survivors to pour down the hill and vanish into the blizzard. Cassius's warriors ducked down behind the ridge and tended to their wounded, though there was seldom much that could be done for a man or woman rent open by a massive ogare arrow.

Cassius passed the order for his scouts to sneak into positions in advance of the battle line, then ducked behind the ridge. Ulger would regroup and send a throg company around to flank the ridgeline, or perhaps mount an advance behind the shields of his big ogares. Cassius and his men would hold as long as they could, then take their wounded and fall back, leaving behind a hundred brave volunteers to cover their retreat. There was no question of winning, even with Pendaran's magic; they had learned that sad truth in their second battle, when Ulger the Cruel kept hurling troops at them until they ran out of arrows and grew too tired to lift their swords. On that melancholy day, Lord Alban had lost a thousand retainers and suffered a grievous lung wound himself, and it was little consolation that his warriors had slain three invaders for every one of their own dead.

Cassius glanced down the back side of the ridge, where Castle Kural loomed over the village of Montabbey. The burg's streets were jammed with horses and oxen as the residents piled their possessions onto wagons and carts, trusting their lord's son to hold the line long enough for them to escape with their worldly goods.

On a stony hillock on the near side of the village stood the castle itself, a practical structure built in a pattern of concentric circles. The outer curtains were too high to look past, but the young noble did notice the men of the Black

Wyvern peering out from the wall turrets and standing guard atop the round keep. He was half-surprised to see them at their posts instead of packing to leave with the villagers. After losing half the company in the gorge ambush, Sir Melwas had not shown a great deal of bravery.

"Pendaran, how long before that company of yours arrives?" Cassius asked this without turning around.

"The longer we wait, the more powerful it will be," Pendaran replied. "But I can fetch it anytime next week."

Cassius's heart sank. "By next week Kural will be gone."

"Don't exaggerate. Kural may belong to Ulger, but it will still be here." Pendaran grinned, baring his tusklike teeth in what he probably imagined was a smile of reassurance. "Besides, you can hold for a month in the castle."

Cassius scowled doubtfully. "Against Ulger's magic?"

"You must," the sorcerer replied. "If Kural falls, his path will be clear all the way to Stonekeep."

Cassius stared at the sorcerer in disbelief. "You can't believe that would matter to me—not after the Council left Kural to fend for itself."

Pendaran scowled, though it was difficult to tell whether it was in confusion or annoyance. "Is that any way to talk? I have big plans for you."

"Unless those plans involve saving Kural, I'm not interested."

As Cassius spoke, he saw a single rider gallop out of the village and turn toward the ridge. The young noble thought at once of his ailing father and felt his heart rise into his throat, fearing that it was a messenger come to inform him of Lord Alban's death. Then, as the man raced past the castle, several of the Black Wyvern's soldiers rushed to the ramparts and began firing at him.

Cassius scowled and, forgetting where he was, rose. "Something's wrong!"

"That you have lost your mind?" Pendaran grabbed the young noble's arm and pulled him back down.

The dark streak of a crossbow bolt caught the rider in the side. The man pitched forward and nearly fell. The horse veered in the direction of his lean, then the fellow slipped completely out of the saddle and lay motionless on the ground. His mount slowed and circled back toward the castle gate.

Cassius turned to Pendaran. "Show me what is happening inside the castle."

The sorcerer frowned. "We have other concerns at the moment. If we can hold through the day—"

"What's happening?" Cassius started to grab Pendaran by the cloak, then thought better of laying hands on a sorcerer and turned down the hill in a half crouch. "I'll go see myself."

Pendaran grabbed his collar and pulled him back with surprising strength. "Sit."

The sorcerer glanced into the sky above the castle, then Cassius's stomach fluttered. He suddenly felt dizzy and found himself peering down on Castle Kural from a bird's-eye view. The scene on the walls looked normal enough, with the Black Wyvern marching along the ramparts and standing guard behind the crenellations.

But the inner ward was a shambles. Soldiers were running back and forth from the wallhouses, piling candlesticks, furniture, clothes, and anything else they could carry onto a great wagon parked in the center of the courtyard. Melwas and Boghos stood outside the keep tower, eye-catching as always in gilded armor and sable robe. In front of the pair, a detail of soldiers was assaulting the keep door with a battering ram.

"The thieves!" Cassius cried. "They're looting Castle Kural!"

A confused murmur began to spread down the line as warriors passed along what Cassius had seen.

"Are you trying to ruin their spirit?" Pendaran whispered. He scowled at Cassius, then, in a voice more hopeful than sincere, said loudly, "Maybe they are merely trying to protect your family's property."

Cassius's response was an angry glare.

"Perhaps you are right." The sorcerer sighed. "It seems more likely that they are safeguarding the Council's investment. After all, your father was to pay the Black Wyvern's expenses."

"My father has paid the Council's taxes for forty years—and that is a thousand times the worth of the Black Wyvern's help!"

"Be that as it may, it changes nothing up here." Pendaran allowed the bird's-eye view to fade. "We can hardly withdraw from the battle now."

"Why not?" Cassius glowered at the castle, his stomach churning with anger. "There is nothing left to defend."

Even as he said it, Cassius knew the sorcerer was right. If they abandoned the ridge, Ulger's monsters would pour down upon the fleeing refugees—and that he could not allow. Whatever he thought of Stonekeep, he owed the subjects of Kural a better defense than that.

The rain of ogare arrows began to thin out, and a few minutes later a female runner arrived from the far flank.

"Skagi Reist sends word that a company of two to three hundred ogares is working around his flank." As she spoke, the messenger could not help glancing down through the blizzard toward Castle Kural. Even on the run, she had heard rumors of what Cassius had seen. "The ogares are armed with swords and shields, and they have a galok with them."

"Ulger is trying a new tactic," observed Pendaran. "And now we can make him pay. If you slide a company of archers along behind the ridge, you can take the ogares from behind. That'll sting him."

"It is not Ulger I care about stinging," Cassius retorted. "That will change nothing, except that when we retreat into the castle, my father will be dead and Melwas will be gone."

"Milord?" The messenger looked confused.

Cassius summoned Brenna the Swift to his side. "Brenna, carry this message to Skagi—it is an unusual one, but coming from you, he will know it is what I want."

"Of course," Brenna said, looking weary and much older than her fifteen years. It pained Cassius to see her in the battle line, but with so little help from Stonekeep, Kural had already lost youths much younger than she. "What am I to tell him?"

"When Ulger attacks, he is to break his dwarves into skirmisher parties. They're to harass the ogares with flank assaults until nightfall."

"And after nightfall?" asked Brenna.

"You must help them find a way out of Kural," Cassius said. "Ulger will have Shadow Gorge by then, and I won't repay their loyalty by leaving them trapped in the mountains."

Brenna's eyes widened. "And what about you? I won't leave without—"

"Brenna, you must," said Cassius. "Everyone else will be gone or dead, and you're the only one who knows the mountains well enough to save them."

Pendaran grasped Cassius's arm, pulling him away from Brenna. "You mustn't do this!"

Cassius ignored him and motioned Brenna away. "Do this for me—I'm counting on you." Without waiting to see her obey, Cassius whirled on the sorcerer. "What else am I to do? Let Sir Melwas sack my family home and slay my father?"

"You would not be sorry." The sorcerer's beady eyes shifted away from Cassius, then he added, "I would give you as much power as the Keeplord."

"How?"

"My enkavs." A larcenous smile creased Pendaran's lips. "They will give you the strength you need to destroy Ulger."

"Enkavs?"

"The company I promised you. They are almost done incubating. When they are ready, so are we."

Cassius shook his head in disgust. "Pendaran, sometimes it worries me to think you're on my side. How can you even think that I would trade my father's life for a company of warriors?"

"You haven't seen these warriors," the sorcerer replied.

"Nor am I likely to, if those are your conditions."

Cassius waved a messenger to his side, then issued orders

for half his father's retainers to join the dwarven skirmishers and the other half to follow him. If there was any looting to be done in Castle Kural, the young noble was determined that it would be done by Ulger the Cruel and not Melwas the Betrayer.

Cassius and his men eased down the slope a short distance, then rose and started toward Castle Kural at a trot. With any luck, the invaders would not realize until they attacked that nearly half of Kural's defenders had slipped away from the battle line. It would take no luck at all to make certain the Black Wyvern remained blind to this tactic—until the company suddenly found itself surrounded.

Cassius led his company across the hillside into a thick copse, where Ulger's blizzard was no more than a gentle snowfall. They crept down the slope to a stream bank about two hundred paces from the castle's back wall, then crawled a short distance upcreek to a small footbridge. The young lord used his dagger to scrape away the dirt at the base of a foundation block, then reached underneath and began to pull.

The stone slipped out of its place, revealing a dark cavity beneath the bridge foundation—and drawing a muffled gasp from the surprised soldiers behind him. Cassius sheathed his dagger and squeezed through the narrow gap, then felt along the wall until he found a ledge with a small tinderbox. He quickly struck a fire and lit two tapers, giving one to the man behind him, along with a set of instructions to be passed along as the others entered the tunnel.

No one spoke as they proceeded down the passage, but the darkness was filled with the rasp of scuffing boots and the soft chime of clattering weapons. Cassius gritted his teeth and reminded himself that they were passing twenty feet beneath the walls. A criminal imprisoned in one of the castle's deep dungeons might hear them, or perhaps a scullery maid fetching potatoes from the root cellar—but no one from the Black Wyvern. Anything worth stealing was kept much higher, in the residence chambers and the great hall, in Lord Alban's private quarters and in the treasury vault atop the keep tower.

At last, they came to the spiraling stairs that ascended into the keep itself. Cassius led the way up, worrying now because he did not hear the thumping of the battering ram. As he climbed, he began to hear muffled shouts and the sound of running boots. He drew his sword and rushed up the stairwell, then ducked through a small crawlway and unlatched a slate panel leading into the archive vault beneath the keep's great hall.

The room had been ransacked, with every chest toppled on its side and dog-eared journal parchments strewn over the floor as deep as the snow outside. The chamber's oaken door hung splintered and cockeyed on its leather hinges, and a torch lay smoldering in the province's open book of taxes.

As Cassius studied the scene, an angry voice reverberated down through the wooden planks. "You will tell us, old man." It was Melwas.

"Lord Alban, be reasonable," added Boghos's silky voice. "The Council deserves its payment—or would you rather the invaders find your hoard?"

Lord Alban answered with a single word: "Thieves!"

There was the sound of an open hand striking a face, then Lord Alban groaned. Cassius was halfway out the vault's door when a firm hand caught him by the shoulder.

"Wait for your retainers, son. You'll need us at your back."

Cassius looked back to find Sir Vinn holding him by the arm. The young lord had not realized Vinn was among the warriors with him—indeed, he had lost track of the man two battles ago—but he was glad to see the old knight with him now.

"We'll try to do this without blood," said Cassius. "But if the Keeplord's sorcerer so much as raises a finger—"

"I will cut him down." Sir Vinn cocked his crossbow.

Cassius waited until the vault was packed with his retainers, then led the way past the kitchens and pantry, where a dozen of Melwas's men were looting the shelves of anything edible. When the thieves saw Lord Alban's son and retainers standing in the doorway, beards and armor still dripping with hoarfrost, they were too shocked to do anything but stammer.

Cassius merely pointed his sword at them. "Put it back."

Without waiting to see whether they obeyed, he led the way upstairs. In the corridors of the main floor, they met several more of Melwas's men, who immediately let their jaws fall and fled to inform their masters. By the time Cassius entered the hall itself, Lord Alban was seated in his chair behind the High Table, with Melwas to one side and Boghos to the other. At their backs stood fifty warriors with drawn weapons, but the number must have seemed pitifully small as Cassius's men filed into the great chamber.

"Cassius, what are you doing here?" Though Melwas's expression remained snide and confident, his white face betrayed emotions more fearful. "Did I not tell you to hold the ridge until the village was evacuated?"

"Don't you mean until you finished pillaging Castle Kural?"

As Cassius crossed the room, Sir Vinn stepped to his side and aimed his crossbow toward Boghos. The sorcerer smirked in response, but he was careful to keep his hands in plain sight. Cassius stopped across the table from Melwas and bowed to his father, who looked both tired and weak. There was a red mark on his cheek, and a fresh blossom of blood had stained his bed gown over his wound.

"Lord Alban, it appears you have been assaulted."

"Your father refuses to pay Lord Commander Melwas for the Black Wyvern's services," said Boghos. A lizard's smile crossed the sorcerer's face. "I am sure you recall the Keeplord's terms."

"I do," Cassius replied. He inclined his head to his father, then asked, "With your permission, Lord Alban?"

The duke met his son's eyes, then shot a querying glance over Cassius's shoulder at Sir Vinn. The look was so quick that the young noble doubted anyone else could have seen it, and before he had a chance to consider its implications, his father's gaze had returned.

"Cassius, you speak for me now." Lord Alban coughed

once, then allowed his eyes to betray his pain. "I fear my wound makes it difficult to think clearly."

A painful knot formed in Cassius's stomach, and the astonished murmur behind him made clear that his father's retainers understood what had just happened. Lord Alban had yielded complete authority to his son; for the moment, at least, Cassius was the Duke of Kural.

"Quiet now!" As he spoke, Sir Vinn kept his crossbow trained on Boghos. "Show Lord Cassius his due."

The retainers fell silent, and Melwas's sneer developed a nervous tick.

Cassius motioned two of his men around the High Table. "Return my father to his bed. A wounded man needs his rest."

"I am afraid Lord Alban will have to stay a little longer," said Boghos. "No lord may abdicate his responsibilities without the Council's blessing, and, as the Keeplord's representative, I cannot bestow that blessing until I have Cassius's assurances that he intends to honor his agreement with the Keeplord."

"I will not be held hostage!" Lord Alban's voice was raspy and gurgly, and when he tried to stand, he began to wheeze and cough.

Melwas pushed him back into the chair. "Stay here, old man."

Several retainers started forward.

Cassius motioned them to stop, then said, "Sir Melwas, if you touch my father again, I will take it to mean that you intend him harm." He glared at the Lord Commander, struggling to keep his sword under control, then turned to Boghos. "As for my agreement with the Keeplord, if Melwas will finally honor it, so will I."

"Finally!" Melwas's eyes grew narrow. "I hope you do not mean to impugn my honor."

"What I mean is to hold you to the Keeplord's word," Cassius said. "You may stay here and earn the Council's levy by defending Castle Kural, or you may flee without it. The choice is yours, but if you do not put an end to the Black Wyvern's looting, I will do it for you."

Melwas's eyes burned with anger, but it was Boghos who responded to the young lord's challenge.

"It is not your place to order the Black Wyvern—or any other company in the province—to do anything. Keeplord Varden named Sir Melwas Lord Commander of Kural's defense, and if he thinks it best to retreat with the wealth of Castle Kural in his possession, he will."

"He will try." Keeping his eyes fixed on Melwas, Cassius again waved two men toward his father. "You may return my father to his chambers."

The two men stepped around the High Table and, giving Melwas no chance to object, started toward the duke's seat. Lord Alban rose to meet them, holding his side and wheezing for breath. Kural's retainers and the warriors of the Black Wyvern eyed each other across the High Table, and for a moment Cassius thought the standoff would end as he had intended.

Then a wicked gleam came to Boghos's eye, and the sorcerer turned to face Sir Melwas. "Lord Commander, it would be better not to return to Stonekeep at all than to disgrace yourself by returning without the Council's levy."

Melwas glanced from Cassius to the sorcerer, then lunged to take Lord Alban hostage.

"No!" Cassius leapt forward, flinging his legs onto the High Table and sliding across on his seat. "Leave him alone!"

The young lord glimpsed a strange smirk of satisfaction on Boghos's face, then saw him reach for something inside his crimson robe. Sir Vinn's crossbow clacked, but the bolt ricocheted off the sorcerer's cloak and reversed its course, planting its tip in the old knight's throat. Sir Vinn's eyes widened, and he clutched at the wound, rasping hoarsely. Cassius came down in front of the Duke's Seat, a step behind Melwas.

Melwas caught Lord Alban around the shoulders and swung him around to face Cassius. "Call your men off."

Before Cassius could obey or disobey, Lord Alban reached back and grabbed his captor by the neck, then bent forward at the waist, hurling Melwas over his back into

Cassius. The pair went down in a clanging mass of weapons and steel, then the room erupted into a tumult of bellows and crashes as Lord Alban's retainers hurled themselves at the warriors of the Black Wyvern.

Cassius hardly had time to notice. Melwas spun onto his stomach, so that he lay on top of Cassius facing the opposite direction, and pulled his dagger from its sheath. The young lord rolled sideways, at the same time slamming the pommel of his sword hilt into Melwas's armored ribs. The Lord Commander cried out, then a dagger tip sliced into Cassius's thigh and started to cut upward.

Cassius whipped his sword around, then heard a wet slap as the blade cleaved the thin bone of an unarmored skull. Melwas went limp, leaving his dagger planted deep in Cassius's thigh. The young lord plucked it out and rolled to his feet—then was promptly knocked to his belly as a dead warrior crashed down on his back. Cassius dragged himself free and slashed his sword across the knees of one of Melwas's thieves, then struggled to his feet.

The battle was all but finished. The High Table lay toppled on its side, the floor behind it strewn with the bodies of Melwas's men and Cassius's warriors alike. The surviving retainers were streaming out the doors, screaming for blood and hurling curses upon the name of Keeplord Varden and his Lord Commander. Cassius began to realize the enormity of his treason and felt a hollow pit forming in his stomach—a feeling that quickly passed when he turned and discovered the corpse of his father.

Lord Alban lay beneath the two retainers Cassius had sent to take him to bed, half-buried and staring at the ceiling with lifeless eyes. A pink froth had bubbled from his mouth and spilled down his chin, and his white bed gown was crimson with blood. Cassius knelt and pulled the retainers off his father, discovering two fresh wounds in the duke's side. He righted the High Table and laid out his father, folding the lord's pale, withered hands across his bloodied chest and pulling the lids down over his eyes.

Cassius stood beside his father for a long time, eyes closed, too filled with grief and fury to move. He felt consumed by bitterness and anger; the lords of Stonekeep had done little enough to save Kural, and the one company they had sent had murdered Duke Alban. But the blame was not theirs alone. Had Cassius spoken less rashly in the Council Chamber, the High Lords might have given more weight to his words and sent a larger force. Or perhaps he should have let Melwas take Kural's treasure. With the province already lost, refusing Melwas his gold had accomplished nothing except to cause his father's death—though Lord Alban had made plain enough that he preferred death to surrendering his wealth to the thieving Lord Commander. How Cassius could have avoided the fight, he could not say—but he did know that he had done as his father wished, and at the moment that was all he could ask.

"May Thera keep you, Lord Alban." Cassius knelt and swept some dust off the floor, then rubbed it across his father's brow. "Great Mother, I restore to you the body of my body, the bone of my bone, the blood of my blood. I pray you, guard it well until I am returned to join it."

Only then did he notice the clamor outside and peer out an arrow loop to discover that his father's retainers had fallen on the thieves of the Black Wyvern. Though the battle was as fierce as any that Kural's warriors had fought against Ulger's minions, Cassius gave no thought to ending the fight. It would have been impossible to stop the slaughter—even if he had wanted to.

His father's personal servants began to drift into the room and tend to the wounded—at least to those from Kural. He allowed a scullery maid to stanch the bleeding on his thigh and push a cup of mulled wine into his hand, and then a terrible thought occurred to him.

"What happened to Boghos?" He rose and began to limp through the carnage, searching in vain for the sorcerer's red-cowled cloak. "Has anyone seen the sorcerer?"

"I doubt you will find Boghos among the dead." Pendaran spoke from the entrance of the great hall, where he stood watching Cassius with eyes like black embers. "High Sorcerers rarely make such mistakes."

Cassius started across the room toward Pendaran. "Where is he?"

"Stonekeep, by now," the sorcerer answered. "Reporting your treason."

Cassius cursed and hurled his wine against the wall.

Pendaran clucked his tongue, then glanced toward Lord Alban's body lying on the table. "What did I tell you, Cassius? They killed your father anyway, and now we have no choice but to flee Kural like lowborn cowards."

Stonekeep was a city of splashing fountains and white-bricked plazas, of marble colonnades and soaring monuments—a true splendor to behold, especially from the lofty height of Sentinel Pass. The impregnable walls loomed as high as the Dark Step on the way into Kural, and the mighty towers that guarded every corner were large enough to hold an entire company of archers. The great boulevards, always teeming with proud horsemen and elegant carriages, ran toward the city center like spokes in an immense wheel. In the heart of the metropolis soared the Grand Heights, a rocky knoll upon which stood the palaces of the High Lords, the Council Halls, and the Houses of the Young Gods—more than a hundred buildings in all, and every one a true wonder of the world.

Stonekeep was the last place Cassius wanted to go, especially when he saw the forces the Council had mustered to defend the city. In the week since Castle Kural's fall, the High Lords had assembled a column of warriors nearly three miles long, stretching from the city's North Gate halfway up to Sentinel Pass, where he and Pendaran sat watching from Crusher's back. So vast was the army that the mountain itself seemed to tremble beneath its weight. Had Keeplord Varden sent but a tenth of those troops to Kural, Cassius would have held the province and sent Ulger fleeing back into the wilderness.

A troop of outriders rounded the first switchback below and came prancing up the road on high-strung chargers. The men were young and eager looking, wearing crimson capes over burnished leather armor, carrying wooden lances posted alongside their legs and short bows holstered on their saddles.

Pendaran leaned forward, speaking softly to Cassius. "Slump down and hunch your shoulders. They may have heard about your treason at Castle Kural."

"It wasn't treason."

"Oh—how do you think Boghos described it to the Council?" The sorcerer dismounted and took Crusher's reins. "Don't look these men in the eye."

The young lord slouched down and hunched his shoulders, keeping his eyes fixed on the ground as instructed. As the sergeant urged his charger ahead of the others, an unexpected tremor shook the mountain. The sergeant's mount whinnied and began to dance sideways in alarm, and even Crusher gave an anxious snort.

Cassius looked to Pendaran and raised a questioning brow, but the sorcerer shook his head. "Not me."

The shuddering ceased as suddenly as it had started, subsiding into the almost imperceptible tremble Cassius had noticed before. The sergeant reined his nervous horse under control, then came over and stopped beside Crusher.

"You bumpkins, get that old plug off the road. Can't you see the High Lords and the Eight Armies coming?"

Crusher snorted and shot a glare at the man's charger, which did not seem to be fooled by Pendaran's spell and shied away from the larger warhorse. The sergeant scowled at his mount's skittishness and jerked its reins around, forcing it over to challenge the "plug."

"Go on, off with you!"

The sergeant raised his lance in a gesture more impatient than threatening, but it was enough to make Crusher whirl on the man's charger with bared teeth. Pendaran was taken by surprise and dragged along, and Cassius had to lean down to grab the big shire's bridle.

"That's enough, boy."

The sergeant's eyes grew wide. "That's an uppish scalawag you have, old man!" He pointed his lance up the hill. "Have your boy lead it off the road. We don't want it causing trouble when the High Lords come by."

Cassius nodded, and Pendaran tugged Crusher's reins. The warhorse cast one last glare at the nervous charger, then allowed himself to be led up the hill. The sergeant smirked in satisfaction, then turned to start down the other side of the pass—and stopped cold.

"Safrinni's rings!"

Coming up the other side of the pass were Brenna the Swift and what remained of the Company of the Brass Axe—a hundred and fifty battered, starved dwarves still marching in tight formation. Behind them followed a long line of oxcarts and pack mules from Stonekeep's northern provinces, all of which had fallen to Ulger's hordes since the collapse of Castle Kural. The column snaked clear down the back side of Lookout Mountain and stretched across the farmlands of the Magar Plain all the way to the Khera Vale. There was no sign of either the Company of the Black Wyvern or Cassius's retainers; the Black Wyvern had perished to a man at Castle Kural, and the new duke had disbanded his own followers as a precaution against retribution.

The sergeant's gaze traveled down the refugee column only as far as the third switchback. "We'll be all day clearing that mess!"

Another small tremor shook the ground, then the mountain quieted and resumed its gentle quivering.

"Yeah, and listen to that thunder," said one of the sergeant's outriders. He pointed across the valley to a tide of dark fog rolling out of the Khera Vale. "A storm—what a way to start a march!"

The sergeant cursed, then waved his outriders forward, commanding Brenna to assemble the Brass Axe on a hillside near "the old man on the plug" and await new orders. As she and the dwarves moved to obey, Cassius leaned down close to Pendaran.

"That wasn't thunder," he whispered.

Pendaran shrugged. "This part of the world is no stranger to earthquakes."

"Now?" Cassius glanced at the black fog coming out of Khera Vale. "I can think of more likely causes."

Pendaran shook his head. "Ulger is not that powerful. But whatever the cause, it is not our concern. Let Boghos worry about it."

Pendaran pointed far down the front of the pass, to where a company of fully armored bodyguards was escorting the Keeplord's magnificent coach around a distant switchback. Boghos's hollow-cheeked face could be seen peering out the uphill window, scanning the mountainside above. Cassius's hand dropped to the hilt of his sword—though he did not realize this until Pendaran pulled it away.

"Are you trying to ruin my illusion?" the sorcerer whispered. "There will be time for Boghos later. It's Ulger we must concern ourselves with."

"You concern yourself with him." Cassius spoke softly, for the Brass Axe was filing onto the hillside above him. They had yet to learn the full story of what had happened in Castle Kural and would probably frown on what he said next. "Ulger can have Stonekeep for all I care. It's Boghos I want."

"Can Ulger also have *her*?" Pendaran gestured at Brenna, who was walking over to join them. "And what of Kural? Do you wish leave your beloved home under his sway forever?"

Cassius looked away and did not reply.

"I thought not. Do as I say, and you will have your vengeance." The sorcerer's voice dropped low as Brenna came up. "We both will."

"Will what?" asked Brenna, stopping beside Cassius's stirrup. She and the dwarves were blind to Pendaran's spell, perceiving both Cassius and the sorcerer as usual. "Go back to fight?"

"Not right away." Cassius could not help smiling at the youthful enthusiasm in Brenna's voice. After standing beside her in so many battles—and watching her slay so many of Ulger's monsters—he found it impossible to regard her as a child any longer, but there were times when it seemed just as difficult to think of her as a young woman. "We'll let the Council of Eight do battle for a while."

Brenna's face fell.

"Don't be disappointed, child," said Pendaran. "We have a more important fight to prepare for."

"Watch who you call 'child,' sheep ears!" Brenna spat. "And who are you to decide what fight is important? Your advice did less to save Kural than your magic."

"Who am I?" Pendaran's beady eyes grew so narrow they disappeared. "I am the one who will destroy Ulger, that's who I am!"

"I'm sure you believe that." Brenna rolled her eyes, then turned to Cassius. "Really, what are we going to do?"

"Well . . ." Cassius eyed the sorcerer for a moment, then shrugged and shook his head. "I'm sorry, Brenna . . . I just don't know what to do."

Pendaran's jaw fell. "Cassius!" He turned to glower at Brenna. "If I can imprison Khull-khuum, I can handle an upstart like Ulger!"

Brenna returned the sorcerer's glare with a look of girlish skepticism. "So now you're King Drake? I thought he died about five centuries ago."

"I am not King Drake! I am not a king of any kind." Pendaran's face turned blue with rage. "I am a maker of kings! I am the one who saved Drake as a child, who saw to it that he grew up strong and proud—who armed him when he returned to Stonekeep and showed him how to defeat Khull-khuum!"

Brenna was unimpressed. "Old man, you'd better stop casting so many spells. They're beginning to—"

"That's enough, Brenna." Cassius eyed the sorcerer for a moment, then asked, "You really expect me to believe you knew King Drake?"

"Surely you've figured that out by now. I told you as much."

Cassius frowned. "You said you knew Ulger—and even that seemed a stretch."

"Believe what you will, but I'm speaking the truth." Pendaran led Crusher over to where the dwarves where sitting, then opened his cloak and began to run his fingers over some of the gems inside. "Drake gave me all these."

The sorcerer indicated rubies, sapphires, emeralds, and every sort of gem imaginable. Cassius could hardly tell if the jewels had actually been owned by Drake himself, but they certainly seemed large enough to have belonged to a king.

At last, the young lord nodded. "I doubt 'give' is the way Drake would have described it—at least if you had the same arrangement with him as you had with Lord Alban and me."

Pendaran ignored the slight, save that he closed his cloak rather quickly. "The king held my advice in great esteem, even after we defeated Khull-khuum. I am the one who persuaded him to drive the throgs and shargas out of the Khera Vale, to reopen the trading roads, to drive the wicked warlords from the neighboring lands, to hunt down those who sold their souls to learn the forbidden sorceries—even today, I am hunted for this last suggestion by the Fire Sorcerers of Ys."

"The Fire Sorcerers of Ys?" Cassius asked.

Pendaran dismissed the group with a wave. "A cabal of piddling little warlocks. Think nothing of it. On my worst day, the whole bunch is not a tenth the sorcerer I am."

But Cassius did not dismiss his thoughts of the cabal. Ys, he knew, had been one of two mighty island nations that had flourished centuries before. Like its rival, Atlantis, Ys had learned the art of rune casting early in its history, then used its magic to establish a vast merchant empire over much of the world. Eventually, the two realms began to fight over trading rights, and they fell to using their sorceries to make war. In their fury to destroy one another, they began to consume the earth's mystic energies—its magic-producing mana—ever faster, until one day their seers predicted the entire supply would soon be exhausted. Instead of doing the sensible thing and making peace, the dark warlocks of Ys spent years fashioning a spell that would destroy Atlantis completely.

It worked far better than even the dark warlocks had expected. Mountains burned and oceans boiled. Fires swept the forests from the land and filled the sky with impenetrable palls of smoke. The two island nations sank beneath the waves, and it took the scattered survivors centuries to rebuild—even with the generous help of the dwarves, who had escaped much of the Devastation by virtue of their subterranean homes.

Cassius frowned at the thought of any "Fire Sorcerers of Ys." If the secrets of Ys had survived the Devastation, then what was there to prevent it from happening again?

"Cassius, are you listening?" demanded Pendaran.

Though he had not been, the duke nodded. "You were saying that without you, Drake would never have made Stonekeep into a great kingdom."

The sorcerer frowned, but nodded. "More or less—but he didn't listen to me about the dwarves. I told him the true measure of a kingdom's wealth lies underground, but he made a pact with them anyway." Pendaran glared disdainfully at Skagi Reist, the dwarves' red-bearded, round-nosed leader. "Because of that damned Oath, Stonekeep can't even mine its own lands without opening one of their rat holes!"

Skagi and his warriors scowled.

"The dwarves have always proven valuable allies," said Cassius. "I have seen their worth for myself."

His careful praise was enough to prevent the dwarves from demanding that Pendaran retract his words, for the Brass Axe had grown tolerant of the sorcerer's constant slurs—perhaps because of the healthy respect they had developed for his magic.

But the little sorcerer would not let the matter drop. "Of course the dwarves are valuable allies! They know a good bargain when they see one."

"Our friendship has nothing to do with good bargains," retorted Skagi. "The Oath of Stonekeep is a sacred pact, reaffirmed by a long line of rulers both dwarven and human!"

"True enough. Drakeson reaffirmed it—but only because he needed the dwarves to win back his throne." Pendaran turned from the dwarf back to Cassius. "Had the fool listened to me and dealt with the malcontents before announcing his father's death, there would have been no need to reaffirm anything."

This drew a gasp of outrage from the entire Brass Axe.

Cassius was quick to defend them. "It seems to me that King Drakeson was wise to reaffirm the oath. Unlike his father's human vassals, the dwarves honored their oath." Cassius frowned at Pendaran, then continued, "Now, if you truly want my help in destroying Ulger, why don't you stop abusing my friends and tell me about him?"

Pendaran sighed. "Very well. When Drakeson died, I advised his son Calvar to start expanding Stonekeep's borders."

"And Calvar died in battle while still a young man," said Cassius. Although the history he had learned from the Ballads differed somewhat from the sorcerer's tales, the basic outlines were the same. "His brother Ulger was named regent, and Ulger wouldn't yield the crown when Terris came of age. That's why the trouble started."

Pendaran nodded. "That's right, but there were . . . circumstances. Ulger was a magnificent general who always listened to my advice. During his regency, he tripled the size of Stonekeep, and naturally he expected a fair reward when the time came to yield the throne."

"What kind of reward?" Brenna quipped. "The head of Prince Terris?"

Pendaran ignored her sarcasm. "Only what was his by rights. During the conquests, Ulger and his nobles had entrusted their own lands to the care of cousins and younger brothers. Naturally, Ulger expected these lands to be returned when he yielded the crown."

"But that didn't happen," Cassius said, guessing the rest of the story.

Pendaran nodded at Cassius's conclusion. "As Terris approached the age of majority, eight of the caretaker lords ingratiated themselves with the young fool and convinced him that Ulger and his followers posed a threat to the crown. Terris refused to reinstate the lands of his regent or followers, offering instead to make them each lord over one of the provinces they had conquered—Ulger, by the way, was to become Duke of Kural."

Cassius shuddered at the thought of the Usurper ruling his beloved Kural, but it was Brenna who objected. "You're making this up. The Ballads say nothing of such treachery."

Pendaran gave the girl a condescending look. "Come now, Brenna—it is the winners who pen history. Who do you think wrote the Ballads in the first place?"

A look of sick comprehension crept across the girl's face.

"That's right." Pendaran smirked. "The High Lords of Stonekeep—the very ancestors of today's Council of Eight."

"Surely, you aren't saying that Ulger was right to keep his nephew's crown?" gasped Skagi.

Pendaran gave the dwarf a level look. "I am saying he had a right to be angry," the sorcerer clarified. "Terris was a weak-willed puppet who let a pack of thieves tell him what to do. Had Ulger remained regent until the boy was old enough to think for himself, things would have worked out better."

"The kingship belonged to Terris by rights!" Skagi declared.

"Just the nonsense I'd expect from a dwarf," Pendaran said. "If your ancestors hadn't been spouting that drivel three hundred years ago, Terris would have been too weak to deny Ulger, and there would never have been a war. Instead, the Oath Envoy started rattling on about divine rights and obedience to the crown, and the next morning Terris and Ulger were at war—without any troops from the thieves who started the whole thing, I might add. Unlike your idiot dwarven ancestors, the caretaker lords were smart enough to withhold their support until Terris agreed to divide the crown with them."

Skagi folded his arms. "An oath is an oath."

"And it seems to me that Prince Terris would have done well to remember that," said Cassius. Pendaran's story sounded all too similar to his own experiences in the courts of high nobility. "Every oath has two parts."

Skagi's eyes widened, and he turned to stare at Cassius. "From the likes of Pendaran Tremayne, I expect that kind of talk. But from you? You are a duke of the realm!"

Being unsure of whether that was true any longer, Cassius made no reply. At least he knew how the Brass Axe would react if they ever learned the whole truth about what had happened in Castle Kural. So far, the dwarves had heard only the story he had instructed his retainers to tell: that Cassius had caught some cowards from the Black Wyvern looting the castle and preparing to desert, and that he had ordered his men to put a stop to it when he could not find Melwas or Boghos to do it themselves—which was a half-truth, at least.

When no one attempted to fill the tense silence, Brenna turned away from the others. "Speaking of the realm, maybe it's a good thing we've talked ourselves out."

"True enough," said Pendaran. "Whatever Ulger's justifications, we're all against him now."

"That's not really what I was thinking," said Brenna. She pointed at the road, where Keeplord Varden's coach procession was rounding the last switchback before the pass summit. "I was thinking we should call the Brass Axe to attention."

"Right you are." Skagi turned to his dwarves and barked, "Stand for inspection!"

The Brass Axe sprang to its feet and formed a neat rectangle of tiered rows around Cassius and Pendaran. Although the battered dwarves numbered less than half their original strength and looked like refugees themselves, the entire company stood straight and proud, with their bucklers across their chests and their free hands resting on their belted axes. As the first of Varden's bodyguards began to clang past on their steel-barded warhorses, the stout little warriors struck their fists to their breasts in salute.

Cassius started to ease Crusher toward a nearby stand of cedar trees, but Pendaran caught him by the stirrup. "Don't trust my powers, Cassius?" he whispered. "We are better hidden in the open."

An especially noticeable tremor shook the mountain as Varden's coach crested the pass, but the quake did not seem to disturb the Keeplord's bodyguards or his High Sorcerer. Boghos's face appeared in the window, scanning the grim faces of the Brass Axe, but lingering only briefly on Cassius and Pendaran. The sorcerer did not speak to the dwarves, nor betray any sign that he recognized their companions, and Cassius began to hope that Varden's coach would not stop.

That was when Skagi Reist stepped forward. "By your leave, Keeplord! The Company of the Brass Axe begs to report!"

Pendaran cursed under his breath, consigning all dwarves to the deepest pits of Shadow, and Varden's face appeared in the window next to Boghos. The Keeplord was wearing a silken battle doublet and holding a handkerchief across his nose to keep out the dust. When he saw the Brass Axe standing beside the road, he raised his brow and dropped the cloth from his face.

"Halt!" he yelled.

His driver hauled back on the reins, bringing the coach to a quick stop. The captain of the rear guard threw up his hand and ordered a halt, and the command began to echo down the hillside from one company to another, until Cassius could imagine the order passing from one mouth to another all the way to Stonekeep.

The Keeplord scowled at Boghos. "Why didn't you tell me we were passing the Brass Axe?"

"My apologies, Keeplord Varden." Boghos motioned Skagi over to the coach, saying, "I wasn't aware you wished to speak with them."

Cassius thought it more likely that the sorcerer did not

want to draw attention to the fact that he had spent the entire Kural campaign holed up in the castle with Melwas.

Varden settled back into his seat, looking out upon the dwarf from the shadowy recesses of his coach. "The Council was most distressed to hear of Sir Asgrim's death. We understand he died valiantly."

Skagi bowed. "Most valiantly, Keeplord."

"Tell me, are our enemies as fiendish as my sorcerer claims?" asked Varden. "I must admit to being surprised at how quickly he allowed Kural to fall."

Boghos's eyes flashed, and he spoke before Skagi could answer. "As I have said, Kural was secure until the castle fell."

This caused Skagi's brow to rise, and Brenna stormed down to stand at his side. If Varden recognized her from their earlier meeting in his garden, he showed no sign and kept his gaze fixed on the dwarf.

"I take it you do not agree, Sir . . . dwarf?" asked Varden.

"My name is Skagi, Keeplord," said Skagi. "And no, I cannot agree with the High Sorcerer. We might have held the castle for a week or two, but Kural was doomed without reinforcements."

"Which we would have sent for, had we had a chance," said Boghos. "It was the mutiny that cost us the castle, and losing the castle that cost us the province."

Skagi lifted his bushy brow. "Mutiny?"

Brenna looked as though someone had struck her, and closer to Cassius, several dwarves broke discipline to look in his direction. The young lord glanced at Pendaran, wondering if the time had come to flee, but the sorcerer's beady eyes looked more angry than worried.

Boghos peered down his nose at Skagi. "You wouldn't know," he said. "Young Cassius and his sorcerer turned traitor."

"Liar!" Brenna yelled.

Boghos's jaw dropped, while Varden recoiled from the hatred in her voice and glanced toward his rear guard. The captain quietly urged his horse forward to take her into custody.

Skagi grabbed Brenna's wrist and pulled her to his side, squeezing until she winced. "I beg you to forgive the girl, Keeplord. She has fought in many battles, and I fear all the galoks and throgs she has killed have addled her mind."

"Truly?" Varden studied her carefully. "A little thing like her has actually killed some of these creatures?"

Brenna fumed, but did not try to escape Skagi's grasp.

The dwarf nodded. "More than any warrior in the Brass Axe." He gestured at the dwarves behind him, who all gave a single curt nod. "Fifty at least, and many of those were galoks."

The Keeplord's gaze slid from Brenna to his sorcerer, and a smile tugged at the corners of his mouth. "Very well, I forgive her outburst." His gaze swung back to the young woman's face. "This time."

"Thank you, Keeplord." It was Skagi who spoke, though Brenna did have enough sense to lower her eyes. "Now, about this mutiny, I find it difficult to believe that Cassius would turn traitor. I did hear about some trouble with the Black Wyvern looting—"

"We were not looting!" Boghos shot back. "We were preparing to send Castle Kural's wealth to the south for safekeeping."

Skagi looked doubtful. "You could hardly have expected to get it past Ulger's forces without the entire Company of the Black Wyvern—which, of course, would have meant abandoning Castle Kural."

This drew a scowl from Keeplord Varden, who was looking less pleased with his High Sorcerer by the moment. Cassius smiled; he could not have hired a better speaker in any of the law houses that ringed Stonekeep's Grand Heights.

Unfortunately, Boghos's confidence took only a moment to return. "Milord Varden, Sir Melwas had every right to recover the expenses you incurred mustering the Company of the Black Wyvern. By refusing to pay, Cassius was guilty of treason—even before he incited your subjects to murder the very men you had sent to help him.''

At the mere mention of money, the Keeplord's face turned crimson with rage. ''The High Sorcerer is quite right.'' He leaned out of the carriage to glare down at Skagi. ''Cassius and his wizard are traitors no matter how one looks at it. The Council of Eight would be in Clan Brassdeep's debt if you could tell us what happened to them.''

Skagi's bushy eyebrows came together in puzzlement. The dwarf half turned to look in Cassius's direction, and the young lord's pulse began to ring in his ears.

''Witless, backstabbing dwarves!'' Pendaran cursed, stepping to Crusher's side. ''Let's go.''

The sorcerer raised one hand for Cassius to pull him up, but Boghos was already pointing in their direction.

''Seize them!''

Cassius grabbed Pendaran's arm and set his heels to Crusher's flanks, but the little sorcerer had insulted the warriors of the Brass Axe once too often. As the warhorse sprang away, six dwarves leapt forward and seized Pendaran's legs, jerking the young lord half out of the saddle. He felt both the sorcerer's hand and Crusher's reins slip free of his grasp, and then he was bouncing up the hill, his wounded thigh burning with the strain of holding his foot in the stirrup.

Cassius caught hold of his saddle horn and pulled himself up. Behind him, the dwarves were cursing, Boghos was shouting for them to hold Pendaran still, and a terrific clamor was ringing up the hill as the Keeplord's bodyguards urged their steel-barded mounts into pursuit. The young lord stretched forward and, after several attempts, finally caught hold of Crusher's reins. He pulled up short and wheeled around to see the dwarves wrestling what appeared to be a giant octopus. Boghos was struggling along with them, trying to fasten a pair of smoky black manacles around the creature's writhing tentacles, while Skagi was finding it equally difficult to keep Brenna from drawing her blade and rushing to Cassius's aid. A dozen of the Keeplord's bodyguards steered their horses past the edge of the melee, starting up the hill in what was certain to prove a futile pursuit of the young duke. Weighed down as they were with armor and barding, their mounts had no chance whatsoever of catching Crusher.

Cassius turned toward Khera Vale and urged the shire into a gallop, as though trying to escape in that direction. Brenna gave up struggling and started to urge him on—until Skagi clamped a hand over her mouth. Varden's bodyguards spurred their clanging mounts after the young lord, losing ground with every step, and a dozen more started across the hillside to cut him off. Cassius continued uphill for the space of thirty or forty hoofbeats—then stopped and wheeled around, angling back toward the chaos below.

The octopus—Pendaran—lay buried beneath a pile of stout little warriors, a smoky manacle clasped around one writhing tentacle and Boghos struggling to cuff another. The rest of the appendages were wrapped around dwarven necks, apparently bent on choking them to death.

Cassius plowed into the Brass Axe from behind and sent astonished dwarves tumbling in every direction. "Pendaran, no!" he yelled. "Don't kill them—it isn't their fault!"

Boghos snapped the second cuff around a tentacle, and the writhing appendage suddenly became an ankle. The other tendrils vanished at once, leaving half a dozen dwarves coughing and choking and grasping at their throats. Boghos rose from the center of the pile, holding Pendaran Tremayne manacled one wrist to one ankle. Cassius drew his sword, and dwarves and bodyguards began to fumble for their crossbows.

Finally, Boghos noticed the heavy hoofbeats bearing down from behind and turned to see the young lord closing. The astonished sorcerer dropped Pendaran and hurled himself to the ground. Cassius flung his sword aside and stretched down to catch the back of Pendaran's cloak, then jerked him up across Crusher's neck. Varden's bodyguards turned their horses to pursue, but the clamor of their barded horses was not enough to drown out the sound of Brenna's desperate voice.

"Cassius!"

The young lord glanced back to see the girl struggling to free herself from Skagi's grasp. When the dwarf did not release her, she stomped on his instep and twisted around to slam an elbow into his head. Skagi's knees buckled, but he managed to catch hold of her ankle as he went down. She hit the ground kicking, trying in vain to free herself of his clutch.

"Cassius, wait!"

"No, Brenna!" Cassius looked away. "This battle isn't yours."

He and Pendaran thundered over the hilltop down toward Stonekeep, the clamor of their pursuers' overburdened mounts growing more distant with every step. Cassius angled across the slope away from the road, determined to open the distance between them and the Keeplord's army as quickly as possible.

"By the burning skies!" Pendaran's curse, referring as it did to the Devastation wrought by the warlocks of Ys, was the foulest oath in Stonekeep. "They won't come off!"

Cassius glanced down to see Pendaran grabbing at the wispy manacles on his wrist and ankle. Every time the sorcerer tried to pull them off, his fingers slipped through as though he were trying to grasp smoke. At the same time a thin line of darkness was reeling off the cord between the cuffs, pulling them closer together with every hoofbeat.

Cassius pointed at the thin cord. "What's that?"

Pendaran's eyes widened. "A leash!"

The sorcerer stopped struggling and concentrated on the string for a long moment, then shook his head in despair. "I can't believe it—my magic doesn't work."

"What do you mean, 'doesn't work'?" Cassius hazarded a glance behind them and saw a virtual wall of armor coming across the hill behind them. Crossbows began to clack, but the bolts thudded into distant trees or whizzed past harmlessly, not even close. "Do something!"

Pendaran looked up, his pasty brow raised in astonishment. "I can't." He sounded more amazed than frightened.

Cassius drew his dagger and sliced at the manacle cord. The shadowy line passed through the knife as if the blade were made of smoke instead of steel. The tip dropped away beside Crusher.

"Fire in the sky!" he cursed, tossing the useless hilt aside.

"Why should steel work when magic won't?" The cord between Pendaran's manacles had grown so short that his wrist and ankle were almost touching. He grasped Cassius's wrist, then said, "Stop. You have to leave me, and there's something—"

"I'm not leaving you—"

"Do it!"

Pendaran shoved himself off Crusher and bounced down the hill—then drew up short as his manacles came together and his black leash finally reached its end. Cassius wheeled around and rode back to Pendaran, where he found the sorcerer withdrawing a huge, curved talon from inside his Cloak of Sparkles.

"What's that?" he gasped.

"This is no time to ask questions," Pendaran replied. He glanced back at the Keeplord's bodyguards, who were less than a hundred paces away and closing fast, then thrust the butt of the claw toward Cassius. "Take this to the Tower of Rathe in Stonekeep and go into the cellars. Step into a ring of mushrooms and spin around three times—three times—saying, 'Spin when you win, win when you spin, when you spin you win!"

Cassius scowled and did not touch the wicked-looking talon. " 'Spin when you win'?" he repeated. "What the—"

"It's faerie drivel!" Pendaran hissed.

A crossbow quarrel zinged past, and Cassius looked up to find the Keeplord's bodyguards only fifty paces away. Behind them, Boghos stood at the crest of the hill, holding the other end of Pendaran's leash. The High Sorcerer began to pull the dark line hand over hand, reeling in his captive like a fish.

Pendaran started to slide across the hill on his back. "Just do it!" Again, he thrust the talon at Cassius. "I'm depending on you!"

This time the young lord accepted the claw. It was as

long as a sword, with a tip as sharp as any needle. He glanced down at Pendaran's manacles, then rode after the sorcerer and leaned down to slash the black cord.

"No!" Pendaran rolled away. "You'll need that to free the enkavs!"

"Free them?" Cassius continued to follow. "From what?"

"Just go to the bottom of the realm, and follow my tracks through the green snow." Pendaran rolled onto his belly and scratched at the ground, trying in vain to hold himself in place. "Once you have the enkavs, I expect you to free me—and don't touch the Sun Sword!"

"Green snow?" Cassius asked. He reined Crusher around, preparing to flee again. "Sun Sword?"

His only answer came in the form of clattering crossbows and zinging quarrels.

A low, grating shudder rumbled up through the tower foundations, as if Stonekeep herself quivered at the mighty battle about to unfold just beyond the mountain. Curtains of dust cascaded off the ancient timbers above Cassius's head, slicing the dank cellar into thin aisles of candlelit gloom. He tried not think about the smell of rotten wood, or about the staggering weight resting on all those floors above. The tremors were stronger in Stonekeep than they had been on Sentinel Pass. The whole city shivered with foot-tickling vibrations, punctuated at odd intervals by jolts and quakes violent enough to send roof tiles sliding to the street. The nervous citizens, far wealthier than the refugees from the northern provinces, were packing whole wagons with their belongings and making uneasy jokes about long holidays in country villas. They did not seem to grasp that when they came back, they might well find their homes inhabited by Ulger's monsters. Even now, with the Usurper on the doorstep and their own armies marching to battle, it seemed unthinkable that Stonekeep would fall.

Cassius only hoped that the city did not succumb before he returned from the Faerie Realm—assuming he could find the realm at all. Pendaran's instructions had been imprecise, if not downright silly. Could he really reach the Faerie Realm through a circle of mushrooms beneath the Tower of Rathe? And if he did, then what? He still had to find the enkavs and free them, and even if he managed that, he had no real idea what to do next. Return to Stonekeep and lead the enkavs against . . . who? Ulger, in defense of Stonekeep? Or Boghos, in defense of Pendaran?

A great deal would depend on what became of Brenna the Swift. Certainly, she was better off sharing the companionship of the Brass Axe than that of a renegade lord. Skagi Reist would attest to the fact that she had taken no part in the mutiny, and the dwarf's word would certainly be enough to prevent Varden from imprisoning her with Pendaran—especially considering how he seemed to feel about Boghos at the moment. Still, the High Sorcerer might try to find some way to use the girl as a tool against Cassius; if that happened, nothing in the realm would prevent the young duke from using the enkavs to hunt down and destroy the sorcerer.

But first Cassius had to find the enkavs and ascertain exactly what they were. Holding his candle in one hand and the talon Pendaran had given him in the other, the young lord stepped into the ring of mushrooms and began to turn in a circle, reciting the sorcerer's words once for each revolution. "Spin when you win, win when you spin, when you spin you win!"

"Fire!" cried a shrill, chirrupy voice.

Cassius glimpsed a ball of rosy light overhead, then a cascade of icy water crashed down on him from behind. He cried out in shock and spun around to find two tiny women hovering above him, each supported by a pair of colorful butterfly wings. They were dressed in gauzy gowns and held an empty bucket between them.

The candle in Cassius's hand remained aflame.

Something jabbed his sore leg. He turned to see that the glowing sphere in front of him had become a small, child-like figure in a shabby brown robe. With long pointed ears and a round mischievous face, the little man bore a certain resemblance to Pendaran Tremayne. He pointed at the candle in Cassius's hand.

"Fire!"

At once, another bucket of icy water doused the young lord, and the women behind him fell into a fit of giggling.

Cassius blew out his candle. "Very funny."

He found himself standing in a strange colonnade of granite columns and gloomy corridors, awash in emerald faerie glow and buried knee-deep in a blanket of lime-colored snow. Between the pillars hung icy curtains of jade stalactites, and growing up through the snow were thousands of summer flowers—marigolds and primrose, gladiola and foxglove, iris and half a dozen others. The blossoms were swaying back and forth on their stems, though Cassius did not feel any wind, and it took him a moment to realize that the ground was still shuddering beneath his feet.

Fearing he had not left Stonekeep after all, Cassius stooped down to address the little man in the brown robe. "Is this the Faerie Realm?"

"That depends on you." The little man chortled. "Are you a faerie fellow?"

"Faerie isn't a place," chirped one of the females. She fluttered around in front of Cassius. "It's a state of being."

"If you being with us, you being faerie!" added the second.

"Thank Thera!" Cassius exclaimed.

"If you say so," said the male. "Thanks, Thera!"

"Thera, we are most grateful," added the first female.

"Not so fast, Lina!" The second furrowed her brow, then asked, "What are we thanking Thera for?"

"Nothing," Cassius said. "It's just an—"

"Thanks for nothing, Thera!" the second female burst out. "And we mean it!"

Cassius groaned, then said, "I'm looking—"

"Looking! That's right—I forgot!" said the male. A rosy aura appeared around his body, then quickly brightened into a brilliant, opaque glow. As the radiance grew more luminous, it rounded into a sphere and began to float down the corridor. "We're supposed to be looking for a big, strong man!"

The two females allowed him to drift another dozen paces down the corridor, then called, "Oh, Flip?"

Flip stopped, though it was impossible for Cassius to tell whether the glowing sphere turned around. "Yeah?"

The two females pointed at Cassius.

"You found one!" he exclaimed.

The females shook their heads sadly. "Poor Flip," said Lina.

"More shine than mind," agreed the other female.

Flip's rosy orb turned crimson, then started down the corridor. "Come quick!"

The two females fluttered after him. As they flew, they also vanished into their own rosy auras. Cassius found himself limping down the corridor after three spheres of pinkish light, with no real idea where they were going or why.

"Wait!" he called. "Where are you taking me?"

"You'll see!" came Flip's answer, and the three orbs disappeared around the corner.

Cassius stopped running and took a moment to study his surroundings. This corridor looked the same as the one he had first entered, with flowers growing out of green snow and emerald icicles hanging along the sides. Pendaran had said to go to the bottom of the Faerie Realm and follow his tracks—but as far as Cassius could tell, this corridor was as level as a lake. He turned around and retraced his own trail, hoping to return to the place where he had entered and find some indication of how to reach the bottom.

They had come farther than Cassius realized. He followed his tracks around three corners, passing two intersections that he had not even noticed as he chased after Flip and the females. He peered down each of the side corridors, searching for a slope or set of stairs. He found none. All of the passages looked exactly the same, save that the flowers grew in different places.

A loud fluttering sound began to reverberate down the corridor, swelling in volume as Cassius moved forward. He stopped at a corner to listen. The pulsing continued to grow louder, and he realized it was coming in his direction. He tried to imagine what kind of creature the thing could be. The sound reminded him of a hummingbird's throbbing wings, save that it was a hundred times too loud. He began to edge away, then looked down in the green snow and realized the thing was following his tracks.

Cassius pressed himself against the wall, clutching the giant talon Pendaran had given him and wishing it was a sword. The fluttering became almost deafening, and powdery swirls of snow began to billow down the corridor. He glimpsed a flash of movement ahead and jumped into the intersection, thrusting his claw forward to defend himself.

He found himself pressing the talon to the nose of an astonished faerie woman. She was hovering just off the ground, beating her wings madly and stirring up clouds of powdery green snow. Her eyes crossed as she considered the sharp point in front of her face.

"Nice dragon claw you got there, fella!"

Cassius pulled the talon away. "I beg your pardon. I didn't mean to startle you, but the noise—"

"Cleaning up is noisy business."

Cassius looked past the faerie and saw that she had swept away his tracks. "What are you doing?" he shrieked.

"Just sweeping up." The faerie retreated up the corridor, eyeing Cassius's talon as though he were about to throw it at her. "Say, shouldn't you be helping Bink and Wink?"

"Not I." Cassius shook his head. "I'm supposed to be in the bottom of the Faerie Realm, following my friend's tracks to the enkavs—if you haven't swept away his footprints."

The faerie looked doubtful. "What are enkavs?"

"Uh—I don't know, exactly."

"Do you know approximately?"

Cassius thought for a moment, then shrugged. "All I can say is they're supposed to be great warriors."

"Sorry, nothing like that down here." The faerie turned to leave.

"Wait!" Cassius cried. "Please!"

The faerie stopped a cautious distance away and slowly turned. "Well—since you said 'please.' "

"Can you at least tell me how to find the bottom?"

"Sure." She smiled, then looked at the floor. "There it is." A rosy aura appeared around her body, and she pointed at the ceiling. "There's the top."

"What?" Cassius cried.

"Sorry!"

The faerie vanished into her glowing ball and zipped around the corner, leaving Cassius to his own thoughts. He did not know whom to be angrier with, Pendaran for sending him down here to find the bottom of something that had no bottom, or the faerie for erasing any hope he had of finding the enkavs. He began to trudge up the corridor, using the dragon claw to knock the blossoms off every flower he passed. He had no idea how large the realm was, or even if he would be able to recognize the entrance when he found it, but at least he would know if he began to walk in circles.

A few minutes later a tremendous shudder shook the colonnade, filling the gloomy corridors with ominous creaks and crackles.

"Say, that was a doozy!" chirped a voice ahead.

"This can't be good," added another. "Khull-khuum's way too excited."

"Way too," agreed a third.

"Khull-khuum?" Cassius rushed around the corner to find three glow balls hovering in the air ahead of him. "What do you mean, Khull-khuum?"

"You know—the Shadow King!"

"The Dark One!"

"He who sleeps in a bed of Drake's making!"

The orbs erupted into dazzling sprays of light. When Cassius could see again, Flip and the two females were standing in the corridor before him.

"Khull-khuum!" they chimed together.

"He's causing the tremors?" Cassius gasped.

"It ain't Aquila," said Lina.

"It ain't Thera," said Flip.

"You figure it out," said the second female.

"If you were about to get out of the dungeon after five hundred years, wouldn't you be excited?" asked Lina.

"What do you mean, get out?" Cassius asked. "How's he going to get out?"

"How do we know, silly?" retorted Lina. "We're only faeries."

The three faeries started down the corridor, Flip in the middle and the two females flanking him on either side.

"Now come along quiet," said Flip. "It won't hurt at all, and we'll fix that sore leg when you're done."

"Done doing what?" Cassius demanded.

"Moving a little rock for us," said the second female. "That shouldn't be hard for a big strong man like you."

Cassius began to back away. "I'll make you a deal. First you help me find the enkavs, then I'll move the rock."

Flip shook his head. "No time. Bink and Wink are starving!"

"Do you know what that means?" asked Lina.

"Of course!" answered the second female. "When faeries want something real bad and don't get it, they turn into trolls! And Bink and Wink want food!"

"You move the rock first," said Flip. "Then we'll take you to the enkavs."

Cassius would have been happy to accept the deal, save that he did not trust the faeries to keep their word.

"It's a good deal—the rock's on your way to the enkavs," urged Lina.

Cassius narrowed his eyes, recalling that the faerie sweeper had seemed completely ignorant of the term "enkav." "If you know where to find the enkavs, then tell me what they are."

"The same as outkavs!" Lina darted in to kiss him on the cheek. "Only smaller!"

As she spoke, Flip leapt forward to kick him in the shins. The second female swooped down and wrapped both arms around the dragon claw, tearing it from Cassius's arms. She had flitted three paces down the corridor before he quite realized what was happening. He lunged after her, but stumbled over Flip and nearly fell.

"Stop!" Cassius caught Flip in his arms and clutched the faerie tightly to his chest. "Bring that back here!"

"You want it—you come and get it!" answered Lina.

The two females started down the passage, using the claw to wave good-bye.

"What about Flip?" Cassius cried. "You don't know what I'll do to him!"

"And we don't care!" retorted the second female.

"Hey, take that back!" Flip yelled. A rosy aura rose around the faerie's body, and Cassius's fingers began to sink through his flesh. "That's no way to talk about your husband!"

With that, Flip became a ball of light and slipped through Cassius's fingers, then drifted down the corridor after the two females.

Cassius hobbled after them, stumbling through the snow and yelling for them to stop. His demands were met with giggles and taunts. Every now and then, the faeries would vanish around a corner and disappear, leaving him to stand in the intersection panting for breath. They would return a few moments later, swishing past his head like swallows on the hunt, or scratching the tip of the talon along the icy wall.

Finally, a chorus of distant, gaggling voices began to echo down the halls. Cassius followed the faeries around the next corner and saw a flickering pink glow ahead, spilling out into the corridor from the jagged, ice-draped mouth of a side passage. Flip and the two females paused only long enough to make certain their pursuer knew where they were going, then ducked through the opening.

"Where is he?" asked a female. Her voice sounded deeper and less chirrupy than any faerie Cassius had heard so far. "Tell me you didn't lose him again!"

"Okay—we didn't lose him again!" said Flip. A glowing sphere floated back into the corridor. "Really, we didn't!"

Cassius reached the opening and peered into a small,

rough-hewn tunnel. Although it was filled with the same green snow and long-stalked flowers as the corridors he had been traveling, it had no faerie glow; the passage was lit only by the dozens of glowing spheres that hovered along its course, illuminating the way into the jade depths of the earth. Lina was flitting down the passage, flying backward and waving his dragon claw at him.

At the tunnel mouth, one of the orbs began to sparkle brightly, then erupted into a burst of dazzling white and assumed the shape of a lovely faerie woman of no certain age. She had beautiful emerald eyes and a pearl-white smile. In her dark hair she wore a small tiara of flashing diamonds, while a pair of gossamer wings shimmered behind her white-gowned shoulders.

She scowled at Flip. "This man is limping! Why didn't you help him?"

"I—um—er—said I'd fix him up, if he helped us."

"That is not the faerie way, Flip." The woman—Cassius guessed she was some sort of queen—reached into a fold of her gown and produced a small white cake. "Take this. It will ease your pain."

"Thank you, milady." Cassius accepted the cake, but made no move to eat it. "If you would be kind enough to have—"

"You need not fear treachery here, good sir." The queen's eyes sparkled with good-humored mockery. "Our faerie cake is not poison."

"I beg your pardon." Cassius took a small bite, and at once the pain began to fade from his throbbing leg. "I meant no offense—but one of your subjects has taken something important to me."

"You must forgive Flip and his wives. Property means nothing to a faerie, so it is difficult for us to understand the concept of stealing." The queen held out a hand, inviting Cassius into the tunnel. "I would like to ask a small favor. Your agreement has no bearing on the return of your filthy dragon claw, of course, but it seems an enemy of our race has trapped two of my people behind a small boulder and ensorcelled the stone to prevent us from moving it."

Cassius scowled. "This enemy—is he a small, round-faced sorcerer with beady eyes and pointy ears?"

The queen raised her brow. "You know him?"

"He has been involved in some trouble I'm having." Cassius said no more, reluctant to anger the queen by admitting that he was in the Faerie Realm on Pendaran's behalf. He started down the tunnel. "I'll be happy to move this boulder, if I can."

Cassius followed the queen and her subjects through an icy maze of cramped tunnels, meandering back and forth past a hundred intersections, ducking down half-hidden offshoots that he would surely have missed if not for the guiding lights of the glowing faerie orbs. At last, they came to a bottleneck, a long meandering wormhole so narrow and cramped that the faeries squeezed through single file. Cassius had to stretch out on his belly and shimmy forward, using his toes to push and his hands to pull.

He emerged in a dead-end chamber filled with hundreds of the queen's people. They were packed shoulder to shoulder, the males standing jammed into nooks and crannies and the females hovering among the icy stalactites. Nearly a dozen were pressing themselves against a large boulder, trying in vain to roll it away from a half-concealed hollow in the wall.

"Stand aside," the queen called. "The human is here."

The faeries spun toward the entrance and cut loose with a shrill, chirrupy cheer that nearly split Cassius's eardrums. He pushed through the crowd, keeping one hand on his purse as tiny hand after tiny hand reached out to slap him on the back. As he drew closer to the boulder, he saw that it appeared to be sitting in something of a hole. Though he doubted it would budge, he went around to the side and laid his shoulder to it.

The stone gave way at once, rolling aside as easily as an empty handcart. Cassius stumbled past a brilliantly lit archway, then something like a wall struck his shoulder and slammed him to the floor. The next instant he was face-down in the powdery green snow, pinned beneath an avalanche of round, stonelike objects as large as ponies. From somewhere above came another shrill cheer.

"Faerie cake!" cried a weak, chirrupy voice. "Let us eat cake!"

The chamber exploded into a series of happy trills and gleeful twitters.

"Wait!" cried the queen. "Where is the human?"

"The hero!"

"The strong man!"

A confused murmur rustled through the chamber. When Cassius tried to call out, green snow filled his mouth, and he started to cough.

"There!"

"Down under the eggs!"

A dull rumble echoed through the room, and the weight quickly vanished from atop Cassius's body. Several small hands caught him beneath the arms and pulled him to a seated position. A fan of brilliant yellow light was shining on the snow around him, bleaching its green hue and causing it to melt.

The queen came over and offered him a faerie cake. "We thank you." She gestured behind him. "Bink and Wink thank you, too."

Cassius accepted the cake, then turned around to see a pair of haggard-looking faeries standing in the archway. Both were so white that he could practically see through their gaunt bodies. The female's wings were withered and cracked, and they both had deep, sunken eyes that made them look more like shargas than faeries.

In front of the archway lay six or seven huge golden eggs with leathery shells, each nearly as high as Cassius's waist. They were rocking back and forth and emitting sharp scraping sounds, as though something inside were attempting to break free.

"The enkavs!" Cassius gasped.

"In what?" Wink narrowed her eyes at him.

"Enkavs," said Flip. "What he's looking for."

Cassius barely heard the exchange. In the vast chamber beyond the archway lay more eggs than he could fathom, all rocking back and forth and emitting the same sounds as those outside. They were stacked two high in much of the room, and so deep that he could see nothing but eggs and the source of the golden light in which they were bathed. In the middle of the chamber, with its blade stuck firmly in the ceiling, hung the most magnificent sword Cassius had ever seen.

It had to be the Sun Sword Pendaran had warned him about, and Cassius wanted it the moment he laid eyes on it. He rose to his feet and stepped toward the archway without thinking, drawn toward the glowing weapon by some inborn power lust he had never before felt.

"Not so fast, fella!" Bink dashed in front of Cassius, his sunken eyes burning with menace. The faerie raised a tiny sword and pointed the tip at the duke's chest. "Where do you think you're going?"

"Bink!" scolded the queen. "That's no way to treat your savior. He didn't have to come down here and rescue you."

The interruption brought Cassius back to his senses. He backed away, then turned to the queen. "No, Bink is right. I didn't come for the Sun Sword."

"You didn't?" Wink appeared at Bink's side, her eyes even darker and more menacing than those of her companion. "Then what do you want?"

Cassius pointed at the eggs.

"No!" Bink and Wink shouted the word at once, their voices suddenly low and gravelly. "Them's our eggs! We been sitting 'em for two months!"

Both faeries became a shade paler, growing so translucent that Cassius could see through their bodies to the eggs behind. A collective gasp rose from the rest of the faeries, and the queen began to ease forward, her hands raised in a calming fashion.

"Bink, Wink—calm down," she said. "This nice man came to help you. He's not going to take anything he shouldn't."

"Oh no?"

Wink darted forward, pulling her sword and slicing Cassius's purse off his belt before he could leap away.

"That's mine!" Cassius cried. The purse contained what little of his family's wealth he had salvaged from Castle Kural—and not yet paid to Pendaran Tremayne. He lashed out, trying to snatch it back. "Give that to me!"

"Why?" Wink demanded, dodging aside. She jerked the pouch open, then reached inside and withdrew a handful of gems. "Trying to hide something?"

"Jewel thief!" Bink cried.

"Egg poacher!" said Wink.

Their voices were as raspy and deep as a bear's growl, and their noses were growing lumpy and long before Cassius's eyes. Wink folded the stolen purse closed and stuffed it into her gown, then both she and Bink turned so translucent they became mere blurs in the air.

"Trolls!" screamed a faerie.

The cavern exploded into flashes and streaks as hundreds of panicked faeries assumed glow form and fled, streaming into the narrow worm tunnel one after the other. The queen grabbed Cassius by the arm and tried to pull him toward the exit.

"Bink and Wink are lost to us," she said sadly. "If we stay, they'll kill us."

"I'm not leaving without my purse."

Cassius jerked free of the queen's grasp and reached out to grab the blur that was Wink then cursed as the troll's tiny blade slashed across his palm.

"Mine!" The voice sounded so low and guttural that Cassius could not tell whether it was Wink's or Bink's.

A red gash opened across the queen's abdomen. "Manlover! Kill you, too!"

The queen cried out in pain, then assumed glow form and floated toward the exit. "Come along, human!"

Ignoring her, Cassius lashed out at what he thought was a blur, but his hand met empty air.

"Can't see us!" cried a gravelly voice.

The tip of an invisible blade jabbed Cassius in the hip, then a stinging gash opened down his back.

"Can't hit us!"

Cassius leapt forward, hurling himself onto the heap of

enkav eggs. He landed belly down on a leathery shell and scrambled through the archway toward the Sun Sword. Pendaran's warning against touching it was fresh in his mind, but he needed a weapon to survive—or so he told himself. As he drew nearer to it, he felt a stirring of secret delight deep within himself; the Sun Sword's magic was plain to see. With such a weapon in his grasp, he might be able to turn Ulger back and reclaim Kural—or slay Boghos and avenge his father's death.

Something brushed the side of Cassius's leg, and he realized the trolls had caught him. He spun around, lashed out with his forearm, and caught one across the chest. The invisible creature gave an ''oomph'' and tumbled away across the eggs, leaving a trail of bouncing shells in its wake.

As Cassius's first attacker rolled to a rest, a throbbing ache shot through his calf. He looked down to see a stream of blood spurting from a thumb-sized hole, then thrust his foot out and launched the second attacker into the air. He could not see where the troll landed; the eggs seemed to be pitching and rocking even more frantically than before. Beyond the arch, he noticed a streak of pulsing pink streaming into the worm tunnel as the last of the faeries fled the anteroom.

Cassius scrambled to his feet and managed to run several steps across the shifting egg bed, then lost his footing and went down just a few paces from the sword's golden hilt. A fiery ache lanced through his shoulder as one of the trolls stuck again. He rolled toward the blow, smashing into the creature's legs, and a second blade thudded down where he had been, bouncing off the leathery shell of an enkav egg without so much as scratching it.

Cassius caught hold of his first attacker and punched blindly, hitting and missing, then felt the troll's sharp teeth sink into his neck. At least he knew where its head was. He rolled again, then caught the creature by its nose and gave a savage twist. There was a sharp crackle, and the creature opened its mouth. Cassius whipped his arm out, hurling his attacker across the room.

"Nosebreaker!" cried the second troll.

The young duke heard a blade whistling toward his head and whirled away. The blow bounced harmlessly off the eggshell beside him, and he rolled back toward it, swinging both arms like clubs. He caught his foe high and low, catapulting it away and knocking the little sword from its hand.

The weapon became visible as soon as the troll dropped it. Cassius could have picked it up; it was about the size of a long dagger, and certainly more dangerous than his bare hands, but he wanted the Sun Sword—he wanted it as badly as he wanted to avenge his father's death and drive Ulger from the land. He wanted it as badly as he wanted to kill Boghos and ensure that no harm ever came to young Brenna.

The duke scrambled to his feet and bounced across the enkay eggs, stepping onto a granite platform directly beneath the weapon. Its golden hilt was a true wonder to behold, cast in the form of two twining serpents rising to strike at a flaming globe that could only represent the sun. Embedded in the top of this pommel was an empty gem setting—a sign, no doubt, of having once fallen into the hands of Pendaran Tremayne.

The heat of the glowing blade nettled Cassius's skin, and its brilliance made his eyes ache. He recalled the sorcerer's warning and began to wonder what would happen when he grabbed it. Perhaps he would burst into flames or go blind, but the thought of not touching it never crossed his mind. Now that he was this close, he would have it or die.

Cassius grasped the golden hilt and pulled.

The glowing blade remained lodged in the stone.

"In the name of Red Azrael!"

Cassius jerked down with all his might, to no avail. The blade's heat coursed through his body, filling him with a warm confidence he had not known since the days before Ulger's invasion. He began to feel stronger and quicker, though he could not tell whether this was due to the sword's magic or the pleasure he experienced simply touching such a weapon. If he could only dislodge it, there was no limit to what he might accomplish—drive Ulger from the land and avenge himself on the entire Council of Eight.

Cassius glimpsed movement out of the corner of his eye, then turned to find the trolls sneaking toward him. With leathery round faces and beady black eyes set deep in the sockets, they resembled an ugly cross between Pendaran and the faeries. One of their long noses was bent and draining blood; otherwise they looked identical.

Cassius dropped into a fighting crouch and, before realizing the significance of what he had just seen, released the Sun Sword. The trolls vanished at once. The young lord rose to grasp the blade again and saw his attackers again.

When the pair noticed Cassius's eyes following their movement, they split to approach from different sides.

"These are our jewels!" said Crooked Nose.

"Jewels? What jewels?" Cassius switched grips, turning to keep them on either flank, rather than one in front and one behind. "Jewels don't grow in eggs."

"Magic jewels do," said Crooked Nose.

"Get him!" said the other.

The trolls raised their swords and hurled themselves forward.

Now that Cassius could see his attackers, they were no longer quite so dangerous. He smashed a hammerfist into Crooked Nose's temple, then lashed out with his uninjured leg and drove his heel through the other one's sternum. Both trolls went limp, dropping their weapons and tumbling onto the granite platform to lie in lifeless heaps.

Cassius turned to tell the faeries the danger was past, but found the chamber outside empty and dark. The dragon claw was nowhere in sight. In the panic, Lina had no doubt dropped it in some dark corner—or simply carried it out of the room with her.

"Cowards."

Still grasping the Sun Sword's golden hilt overhead, Cassius stretched a toe out to lift Crooked Nose's shabby cloak and search for his purse.

The Sun Sword's tip suddenly hissed free of the ceiling and came arcing downward. Cassius stumbled out of its path, swinging the heavy blade away from his body and into one of the eggs that filled the room.

A smoking seam opened where he touched the shell. A black, almond-shaped pupil peered out, blinking and staring at the glowing blade in Cassius's hand. The eye watched the Sun Sword for several moments, then a scaly hand pushed through the gash and began to scratch at the leathery shell. With a broad palm and opposable thumb, the shimmering appendage looked vaguely human, save that the fingers ended in small sharp talons.

As sharp as those claws were, they could not tear the egg open. Cassius drew the Sun Sword along the length of the shell, splitting it open. A huge, strange-looking lizard slipped out in a slime-covered ball, panting and stinking of sulfur. Its body shape was more or less humanoid, with a lanky neck, two long arms, and a pair of sturdy legs, but the semblance ended there. It had a scaly head with smoky emotionless eyes, a beaklike snout, and a grinning reptilian mouth that looked as though it could swallow a dwarf whole. It was covered head to toe in small, brightly colored scales, and its body had a sinuous, vaguely cylindrical look that seemed more serpentine than manlike.

Cassius squatted down to look into its black eyes. "So you're an enkav?"

The enkav's only response was to stare at the Sun Sword. Slowly and tentatively, it began to stretch out its slick limbs, which unfurled with a strange smacking sound, then started to lick the egg slime off its armor. To Cassius's amazement, the creature was nearly a head taller than he was.

Cassius took a moment to bandage his throbbing wounds, then sliced open another shell. The second huge lizard-man came sliding out and stared blinking at the Sun Sword for a moment, then started to lick its armor clean. The young duke began to open the eggs one after the other, working his way outward in a great circle. Soon, the entire chamber was filled with enkavs, all licking themselves clean and blinking in the brilliant light of the Sun Sword. Their eyes followed the glowing blade wherever it went. If their view was blocked, they raised their heads or dragged themselves over their fellows until they could see it again. Cassius kept expecting the formidable-looking creatures to do something else—speak, perhaps, or show some sign that they were intelligent enough to make war, but all they did was blink and watch.

At last, Cassius had opened all the eggs on top of the pile, and the room was so filled with empty shells and squirming enkavs that he could not work. Indeed, the duke could barely move, and reaching the eggs below had become a matter of haphazard slashing.

"All right, we've got to clean this mess up." He pointed at the empty shells scattered around him, then waved his hand toward the other room. "Take those into the other room."

The enkavs merely stared, their dark eyes showing no sign of comprehension.

Cassius dragged a shell over to the archway and tossed it into the other room, then pointed at the empty shells, the enkavs, and the empty room. The lizard beasts lifted their heads and slithered all over each other in an attempt to keep the Sun Sword in view.

"Fine warriors you'll make," he grumbled. "Can't even follow a simple order. What can Pendaran be thinking?"

Cassius stepped through the archway and opened the eggs that had spilled out, then ducked into a hidden corner. The enkavs flooded into the chamber after him, clambering across the floor on all fours. After the last one had crawled through the archway, he squeezed over to the door and began to work his way back into the hatchery, rolling each egg around behind him before slicing it open. In this way, he kept the enkavs at his back as he worked, and many hours later he finally reached the back wall.

After opening the last shell, the duke looked up to find himself surrounded by a chin-high tangle of scaly limbs and spike-covered bodies. Their faces were all turned toward him, so that their eyes, gleaming golden with reflections of the Sun Sword's brilliance, shone back at him like a sky full of stars. He had grown accustomed to their sulfurous egg stench and barely noticed it anymore, but the constant rattle of their rustling scales was beginning to set his teeth on edge.

"We've got to get out of here."

Cassius stepped forward, holding the Sun Sword before him. Much to his relief, the enkavs retreated when its brilliance came too near, and he slowly made his way to the archway. His wounds continued to throb and seep blood through the bandages, but they did not hinder him—save for a slight limp caused by the hole in his calf. When he reached the other room, he was able to make his way to the wormhole exit quickly, as the enkavs had all crawled back into the hatchery while he worked to free their nest mates. The duke could not imagine how he was going to make the docile creatures into warriors; they looked ferocious, but they hardly seemed intelligent enough to make good soldiers.

As Cassius started through the worm tunnel, he realized it would prove difficult for the enkavs to follow. They were huge creatures, at least a head taller than he was and a good deal heavier. If he had to crawl on his belly, he could not imagine how they would make it through the cramped tunnel.

The answer came when a series of loud crackles sounded behind him. He looked back to see an enkav pulling itself up the passage, both of its shoulders popped out of the sockets. The sight made Cassius wince, but if the enkav felt any pain, its reptilian face showed no sign. The duke scrambled up the tunnel all the faster.

At the other end, the enkav emerged from the worm tunnel right behind Cassius, all four of its limbs pushed out of the joints. It squirmed through the powdery green snow for the space of half a dozen paces, then its arms and legs popped back where they belonged. It raised itself up on all fours and scurried over to the duke no worse for the experience.

When the next enkav emerged from the worm tunnel and did the same thing, Cassius started up the meandering passage, following his own tracks back toward the realm's pillared catacombs. He did not know whether the faerie sweepers had been too frightened of trolls to enter the side passage or simply did not tidy up in such places, but he was grateful for their neglect. Without his own tracks to follow, he would have quickly lost his way.

Soon, the enkavs began to swarm around Cassius on all sides, threatening to spill ahead and wipe out his tracks. He had not bothered to count the eggs as he opened them, but it would not have surprised him to learn there were a thousand of the creatures. They filled the tunnel as far back as he could see, welling over into offshoots and by-passages. To stay ahead of them, he had to break into a limping trot, and the exertion caused his wounds to start bleeding again. The pain grew worse, and before long, he was beginning to feel tired and weak.

Cassius was just about ready to give up when he rounded a corner and saw a dozen orbs of pink light hovering in the darkness ahead. Behind them was the jagged mouth of the tunnel, opening into the emerald glow of the main catacombs. One of the glow balls separated from the others and drifted toward him.

"Human!" It was the queen's voice. "You survived!"

"Apparently," he gasped.

Cassius stopped running and stooped over to catch his breath. The enkavs began to swarm around him. For the first time their dark eyes began to glance away from the Sun Sword, flickering toward the glowing faerie balls ahead.

The queen stopped in front of Cassius, hovering five feet above an enkav's head. "And you brought your pets," she said. "How nice."

"They're not exactly pets." Cassius scowled at the way the enkav was eyeing the queen's glowing form. "Maybe you shouldn't get so close."

The queen's pink orb grew a shade paler and drifted another foot into the air. "You need a faerie cake." One of the little biscuits dropped into his free hand, then she began to retreat toward the mouth of the tunnel. "And Lina still has your—"

An enkav sprang up as quick as lightning and snapped its gaping jaws around the pink sphere, then dropped back to the floor and swallowed. For an instant no one said anything. Cassius stared at the beast in dumbfounded shock, half expecting it to let out a great belch and send the queen fluttering back across the cavern.

But that did not happen. The enkav's fellows turned their heads toward the other orbs at the mouth of the cave, and the tips of their forked tongues began to flicker between their scaly lips. Cassius grabbed the beast that had swallowed the queen and thumped it squarely in the back, hoping to dislodge the thing's snack—then a horrified screech echoed through the passage.

"The queen!" One of the glowing orbs erupted into the figure of a female faerie, her finger extended toward the offending enkav. "It ate the queen!"

The faeries turned to flee, filling the corridor with panicked chirps and sparkling colors. The enkavs sprang after the streaking spheres of light, bowling Cassius over. He rose as far as his hands and knees before a passing talon snagged his armpit and dragged him up the tunnel. A searing pain shot down his arm, then his hand came open and released the Sun Sword. He pushed off the creature's side and dropped into the snow, then covered his head and waited.

Cassius suffered a few more bruises and scratches as the stampede passed, then rolled onto his hands and knees and watched the last of the enkavs charge out into the pillared catacombs. He thought of the havoc the beasts would wreak on the faeries and began to have a sick, hollow feeling. These had to be the creatures Pendaran had sent him to fetch, but he still could not see how the sorcerer expected him to control them—or what good they would be in a battle if he could not.

Cassius stood, then raised his injured arm and made a fist. Gingerly he swung his hand around in a circle, testing his shoulder. He could still wield a weapon. He turned toward the back of the tunnel, where the Sun Sword lay in a basin of melting snow. A huge, brightly scaled figure was standing over the weapon, staring down at the glowing blade as though in a trance.

The guilty feeling in Cassius's stomach changed to panic. "Get away!" Without stopping to think, he dashed over and snatched the weapon up, then spun around to face the looming figure. "The sword is mine!"

Only then did he recognize the creature as an enkav, now standing on its legs like a man. It raised its scaly brow, then pointed at Cassius with two spindly fingers.

"Sword?" The word was at once shrill and rasping, as though the creature were speaking with a faerie's voice and a serpent's. "Sword!"

Cassius saw the pink sparkle in its eyes, then his jaw dropped in horror as he suddenly saw how Pendaran meant to control the creatures. He backed away, trembling in revulsion at the abomination the sorcerer had made him a part of.

The enkav followed.

Cassius stopped and looked back toward the tunnel mouth, where several more enkavs were walking into the passage on two legs. Like the huge warrior before him, their eyes gleamed with a pink faerie twinkle. The first enkav turned to its fellows and, still pointing at Cassius, touched a fist to its chest.

"Sword!" it declared.

The others stopped and repeated the gesture. "Sword!"

In their voices, Cassius could have sworn he heard Flip and Lina.

9

Lookout Mountain trembled beneath Pendaran's feet, as though the earth itself craved the blood that would soon drench the farmlands below. Ulger's hordes had advanced halfway across the Magar Plain, an unseen multitude hidden behind the swirling wall of fog slowly rolling across the fields.

At the base of the mountain, Stonekeep's Eight Armies stood ready to meet them. A solid line of armored cavalry extended across the entire width of the plain, with the Keeplord's own Royal Sabers anchoring the center. Behind the horsemen stood rank after rank of grim-jawed pikers and broad-shouldered swordsmen, the best warriors the High Lords had to offer. A short distance up the hillside, Brenna and the Brass Axe waited in reserve with several companies of volunteer militia. With any luck, she and her companions would see the disaster coming and have time to flee; Cassius was overfond of the girl and would be no use to anyone if something happened to her.

The Eight Armies were protected on each end by troops of archers. They were hidden on a gentle slope just inside the tree line, where they could surprise the invaders at the last moment by stepping forward to shower their flanks with arrows. To prevent Ulger's marauders from flanking them, both troops of archers were screened by a full company of dwarven axemen. The Council's strategy was simple: stop the advance with an enormous arrow assault, break up the enemy lines with a cavalry charge, then send the footmen in to finish the job.

"It won't work," said Pendaran.

Still shackled in Boghos's shadowy manacles, the wizard was standing with the High Sorcerer and Keeplord Varden about halfway down the mountain from Sentinel Pass, gazing down on the battlefield from atop a granite outcropping. They were surrounded by adjutants, messengers, signalmen, and assorted aides—all the men needed to run an effective command post, plus more to make an impression. The other High Lords were scattered across the mountainside in similar gatherings. By previous agreement, each of the councillors had a hundred plate-armored bodyguards standing on the hillside above him—a heated battle, after all, was a perfect place for an assassination.

When Varden paid him no attention, Pendaran repeated his warning more loudly. "Your plan won't work."

"Silence, traitor!" Boghos jerked the shadowy leash attached to Pendaran's manacles. "One more word, and I'll gag you."

"That won't be necessary, Boghos." Keeplord Varden peered down his nose at Pendaran, then asked, "Is there something you wish to tell us?"

Pendaran nodded. "Your battle plan is ludicrous. Ulger is five times the general as the fool who dreamed this up."

Varden's face turned crimson. "The Council has agreed to this plan," he said, as though that alone were enough to refute the sorcerer. "I am sure that eight heads are better than one."

Pendaran shrugged. "Believe what you will." He cast an angry glance at Boghos, then added, "It makes no difference to me whether you fall to Ulger or abdicate to Cassius. Stonekeep will be the better for it either way."

Varden's eyes flashed in anger. "I shall enjoy watching your execution, traitor. Perhaps I will make it the main event at the victory celebration."

The Keeplord turned away, nodding to the signal master standing just up the mountain. The man raised a twelve-foot pole high into the air, then began waving the red pennant on top. On the third dip, clouds of arrows sailed up from the flanking hills, aimed toward the swirling fog that masked Ulger's advance. As the deadly shafts arced down into Ulger's fog, the horses along the cavalry line grew agitated at the sound of so much dying, but all that reached Pendaran's ears at the command post were a few distant shrieks. A satisfied smile spread among the adjutants and aides, and even Keeplord Varden shot Pendaran a smug glance.

The sorcerer smirked back. "Your twig-flingers are nothing to Ulger's archers. If the ogares are not returning fire, it can only mean trouble for you."

Varden's smile remained confident. "His archers cannot fire at what they cannot see." The Keeplord looked to his High Sorcerer. "Is that not so, Boghos?"

"Undoubtedly," Boghos replied.

Stonekeep's archers continued to pour arrows into the dark fog as it moved closer. The shrill cries of dying throgs and shargas grew louder and more common, and still Ulger's archers did not answer. Pendaran peered helplessly at the swirling clouds below and, not for the first time that day, cursed Thera for a meddling harlot. It had to have been the All Mother who forged the fetters for Boghos; certainly, no human sorcerer could have created them. He had tried a dozen times to snap the wispy chain or slip the dark cuffs, and each time the bonds only seemed to grow tighter. And when he tried to use his magic, the results were even worse; his head seemed to implode, collapsing on itself in blinding black pain. What could the trollop be thinking? That Ulger would be a better king for Stonekeep than Cassius?

Varden turned toward the signal master, and Pendaran saw that the fool was about to fall into Ulger's trap. The sorcerer shook his head, then turned to address the Keeplord.

"Keeplord Varden, one moment—I beseech you." The situation was desperate enough that Pendaran would try anything—even begging. "Perhaps you would enjoy watching your armies crush the enemy. If you would only—"

"Silence!" Boghos ordered. "One more word from you—"

The Keeplord raised his hand, silencing the High Sorcerer. "Let's hear him out, Boghos."

Pendaran sneered at Boghos, then addressed himself to the Keeplord. "If you would have your sorcerer remove these manacles, I would be happy to clear away that fog so you can see."

Varden glanced down at the advancing clouds, which were only two hundred paces from the cavalry line. "I'm sure you would be happy to clear the fog away so someone can see." When the Keeplord turned back to Pendaran, there was an angry scowl on his face. "You want Ulger to see what awaits him on the other side of Boghos's cloud."

"Boghos's cloud?" Pendaran gasped.

"Of course." Boghos glared at Pendaran with narrowed eyes. "I created it to render the enemy blind."

Pendaran's jaw dropped at the magnitude of the deceit. It was one of those big lies, so enormous and brazen that it stunned even him. The Trickster's mind whirled, thoughts flying in a thousand directions as he struggled to work out the implications.

"You should hardly look so stunned, spy," said Varden. "It is one thing to corrupt a young noble from the provinces, and quite another to deceive the Keeplord of Stonekeep itself. Really, you should have expected this."

Pendaran glared up at the Keeplord. "Lord Varden, as much as I despise the idea of guarding your life, I'll give you one more chance to save yourself—and Stonekeep. The fogbank is Ulger's, whatever Boghos claims. It is the Usurper who is luring you into an ambush, not the other way around. Take these manacles off and let me show you what's under the fog—it will prove what I say.''

Varden glared back at him. ''You must take me for a fool. Boghos has told me all about your 'runeless' magic, and I know what will happen if I remove his manacles.'' The Keeplord looked back toward the signal master. ''And now I have heard enough from you. One more word, and I shall forget what I have planned for our victory celebration.''

Varden lifted two fingers, and the signal master waved a black pennant. The Eight Armies started forward, the cavalry quickly urging their mounts into a trot. The first rank of footsoldiers, Lord Fiske's Grim Pikes and Lord Tate's Long Forks, gave a rousing cheer and rushed after the horsemen. They were answered by a guttural roar from deep within the fog.

The cavalry broke into a gallop and disappeared into the dark mists, the line just beginning to break ranks as the faster horses sprinted out ahead. Stonekeep's archers stopped firing for fear of hitting their own cavalry. The thunderous rumble of twenty thousand pounding hooves reverberated up the slope, and the fog came alive with bolts of flashing magic and blossoms of roiling flame. The entire mountain began to tremble, though it was impossible to say whether this was caused by the battle or by an earthquake.

The cavalry smashed into the enemy ranks with a tremendous crash, then the sound of clanging steel and pained howls began to underscore the rumble of the hooves. Pendaran imagined the scene inside the cloud: an uneven line of horsemen bowling over invaders, silver sabers flashing, throg heads flying this way and that, long halberd blades glancing off barding and shields, steel-shod hooves trampling shargas into red pulp. The sorcerer had seen it all a hundred times before, all those centuries ago when Ulger the Cruel had launched his hordes against the enemies of Stonekeep and won the lands that Varden and his Council of Fools now claimed for their own. The High Lords were attempting to defeat the Usurper with his own tactic, and the only possible result was a disaster of the worst proportions.

The footsoldiers began to run, disappearing into the fog one rank after the other. Knowing the battle to be lost already, Pendaran turned his thoughts from saving the Eight Armies to saving himself. Ulger was about as likely to forgive his desertion as to have forgotten it, and the last thing the sorcerer wanted was to let the Usurper catch him helpless.

The rumble below faded abruptly as the cavalry charge rode itself out. Horses began to whinny in pain and anger as they whirled about, their riders slashing and hacking at the enemies closing in from every direction. Pendaran turned away. Trusting the battle to keep all eyes riveted on the fog-cloaked plain below, he leaned down and addressed the granite outcropping in a soft whisper.

"Thera, listen—do you hear the cries of those dying thousands? Do you feel the blood soaking in, turning your fertile soil to warm mud?"

The goddess's face appeared between Pendaran's feet. "Why do you ask when you know the answer, Little One?" She looked sick and sorrowful, and perhaps a little angry. "I hear all things, and not a drop of blood falls that I do not feel."

"Then why allow that?" Pendaran gestured at the raging battle below. "This has gone far beyond what we believed at the start—now that Ulger has returned, you can no longer believe this is good for Stonekeep."

Thera half-closed her stone eyes. "No, of course not. But the Keeplord will have to stand or fall on his own. Khull-khuum is rattling his prison, and it is all I can do to keep him from shaking Stonekeep to stones."

"Khull-khuum is part of this?" Pendaran frowned at the trembling ground, and another piece of the puzzle fell into place. "Can Ulger have found his way to the Shadow King?"

"So it would seem." Thera winced as the mountain gave an especially powerful tremor, then said, "I do not see why that should surprise you."

"It surprises me that he succeeded—but it explains much." Pendaran squatted close to her face and stretched the manacle cord between its cuffs. "How about removing these? Surely even you can see that the time has come for us to work together."

"Conspire with you?" The goddess shook her head. "I would sooner treat with one of Ulger's galoks."

Pendaran frowned, genuinely hurt. "That was uncalled for."

"Really?" Thera demanded. "Did you not promise me that you would not let any mortal touch the Sun Sword?"

Pendaran's eyes grew round. "He didn't!"

"Do not act the innocent with me," said Thera. "You sent him there. What did you expect?"

The sorcerer raised his brow. "You can hardly blame me if humans can't be trusted," he hissed. "Did he at least free the enkavs?"

"What do you think?" Thera's stormy face told him the answer—and what had happened to the faeries. "I can hardly tell who is worse for the world—you or Khullkhuum."

Pendaran breathed a quiet sigh of relief. "At least there's still hope. We don't have to work together, but there's no need for you to interfere." He nodded toward Boghos's back. "At least call off your pet."

"Gladly—if he were my pet." A sadistic smile crossed Thera's lips, then she added, "But he is not."

"What?" Pendaran shot to a standing position. "Liar!"

"Deception is *your* talent, Wahooka—not mine."

"As I recall, you're pretty good at it," Pendaran snapped. "Or was it some other traitor who opened the Glass Palace to her ingrate siblings?"

Thera's smile remained. "No, that was me—and I would do it again. You were wrong to play us against each other." Thera's stony eyes glanced briefly past Pendaran's shoulder, then her face faded back into the rock. "And I am glad I saw through your flattery in time to be the one who rallied the Young Gods against you."

"Wait!" Pendaran shook his fetters. "What about these?"

"I told you. They are not mine." Thera's voice came to

Pendaran inside his head. "Look to your enemy."

A bony hand clasped his shoulder. "What about them?" Boghos jerked the little sorcerer back, then scowled at the rocky ground. "Who are you talking to?"

"I thought it was you," said Pendaran. "Or maybe that was just a horse tick crawling by."

Boghos's eyes narrowed. "I trust you will prove as amusing on the executioner's stage." The High Sorcerer jerked him around to face the battle. "Why don't you watch with us? I'm sure you'll be very interested in the way things play out."

Boghos's words pushed the last piece of the puzzle into place, and suddenly Pendaran saw how carefully and how long the Usurper had been planning for this day. It was the High Sorcerer himself who was Ulger's spy; Boghos had spent decades manipulating Stonekeep into a position of weakness, convincing the Keeplord that there was no need to garrison the borders, or even concern himself about threats from the wilderness. After all, what could a mere band of savages do against the might of Stonekeep? No doubt, Boghos had also persuaded Varden that he could not afford to send more than a small force north to defend Kural, then volunteered to go along with the company to make sure even that token force was ineffective.

But most telling were the manacles on Pendaran's wrists. If they had not come from Thera, then Boghos had gotten them from someone just as powerful. Pendaran's thoughts flashed backward along the twisted course the shadowy fetters had taken onto his limbs; to Boghos from Ulger, the one enemy who might know both the Trickster's true identity and how to disarm him; to Ulger from Khull-khuum, the only being aside from Thera with the power to make such a pair of bonds.

And how had Ulger found his way to Khull-khuum in the first place? There was only one way. The Usurper had joined the Fire Sorcerers of Ys and used their dark ways to contact Khull-khuum inside his prison. He had called upon the Shadow Lord's magic to keep him whole through the ages, and asked him for the power to seize what Terris and the Council of Eight had wrongly denied him so long ago.

And Khull-khuum had answered, placing the Usurper beyond the reach of death and giving him dominion over the weather. Ulger had made an army of the throgs and shargas and all the other creatures the High Lords had dispossessed over the centuries, then led them back to reclaim what had been taken so long ago.

Whether the changes in the throgs and shargas were part of the Cruel One's plan or merely a side effect of the Shadow Lord's corrupting magic, Pendaran did not know. But he was certain of this much: if Khull-khuum was aiding Ulger, it had to be because Ulger intended to free Khull-khuum; and if Ulger freed Khull-khuum, then Pendaran was doomed—as were Stonekeep and Thera, and all the other Young Gods.

Pendaran barely noticed when the first rank of footsoldiers reached the battle line and plunged their long war forks into Ulger's monsters, filling the air with a cacophony of roaring voices and pained cries. The sorcerer had things more important than the battle to think about—such as his own survival.

Though he had tried it a dozen times before, he folded his thumb into his palm and began to work his wrist back and forth, trying to squeeze his hand tight enough to slip through the manacle. It was a useless endeavor. No matter how small he made his hand, the cuff always seemed smaller. He tried to grab it with his free hand and stretch it larger, but he could clutch the shadowy circle no more than he could grasp a passing ray of light. His fingers simply passed through the darkness, shooting needles of bone-stinging cold up his hand.

The prattle of sharp steel cleaving soft flesh began to drift up the hill as Stonekeep's horsemen wheeled their mounts around. Pendaran knew that down in the fog, the riders would be taking up positions in the bristling wall of polearms and starting to advance at a slow walk, hacking down any foe not quick enough to flee. He had seen Ulger's men do it a hundred times, and it had never failed to drive the enemy from the field.

Varden turned to smirk at Pendaran. "What say you now, sorcerer? Do you still think Ulger is luring us into a trap?"

"It matters less to me than to you." Pendaran spread his hands, at the same time glancing at his wrist and imagining that he was no longer manacled. "I will be long gone when he is pulling your ribs through your navel."

Varden's gaze shifted briefly to the sorcerer's wrist, where the shadowy manacle cuff remained in place, then furrowed his brow. "I doubt that, but the rib maneuver sounds entertaining. I shall remember your suggestion when I plan your role in our victory celebration."

The Keeplord turned back to the battle.

Pendaran cursed under his breath. Though he had experienced the same result when he tried his magic before, he could not understand how the manacles crippled his spell. His sorcery was driven by the most potent kind of magic, the mystic energies of the mind. To cast an enchantment, the Trickster had but to visualize the result he wanted, then impart the slightest hint of that image to any onlooker. The power of suggestion did the rest, utilizing the force of the victim's mind to make the spell real and tangible. This magic was as simple as it was mighty, available only to immortals like himself—and thwartable only by a powerful deity like Khull-khuum. If he had had any doubts about the identity of his ultimate enemy, they were gone now.

A sudden jolt shook the ground, nearly buckling Pendaran's knees and flinging tiny puffclouds of dust into the air. The crowd let out a collective gasp, and an abrupt clamor of steel echoed down the slope from the bodyguards. A second jolt shook the hill, then a third. The adjutants began to murmur to the aides, and the messengers and signalmen began to cast wary gazes at the granite beneath their feet.

"In the name of Thera!" The Keeplord turned to Boghos, demanding, "Did you do that?"

"Not without consulting you, Keeplord Varden."

Boghos looked slowly in his prisoner's direction, implying by expression alone that Pendaran might have something to do with the tremors. Before the sorcerer could make any denial, the battlefield itself began to quiet; the clang of clashing steel faded away, and the roar of angry voices gave way to the muted groans of the dying. The aides and messengers began to murmur in confusion.

The Keeplord turned to Boghos. "What's happening?"

Before the High Sorcerer could reply, a distant human voice cried, "After them!"

The roar of a Stonekeep victory cheer rose out of the fog, then the low rumble of running feet began to shake the plain.

"We've broken their lines!" Varden concluded. He turned to Boghos and pointed at the fogbank below. "I want to see this. You may lift your fog."

Boghos's face went white. "Are you sure that is wise, Keeplord? If the enemy sees our men—"

"Your sorcerer cannot lift the fog because he did not create it," said Pendaran. "Ulger will spring his trap any moment now."

Varden backhanded Pendaran across the face. The blow would have split any mortal's lip, but it simply snapped the Trickster's head back and knocked him to the ground.

"I have warned you about fouling my ears with your nonsense," said the Keeplord. "One more word, and I'll execute you myself."

Pendaran glared at the Keeplord. "I am going to enjoy what Ulger does to you."

Varden's face grew crimson. "Guards!"

A dozen armored bodyguards rushed to the Keeplord's side. He drew one of their heavy swords and pointed it at Pendaran.

"Hold him on his knees!"

A pair of guards grabbed the sorcerer by the elbows and forced him to kneel. Boghos quickly stepped forward to place himself between Pendaran and the Keeplord's blade.

"Milord, wouldn't it be wiser to hold the prisoner until we return to Stonekeep?" Boghos's request surprised no one more than Pendaran. "He may well prove our best source of information about Ulger."

"I think we know all we need to about Ulger." The Keeplord glanced toward the fog-shrouded plain below, where the sounds of the rout continued to build. "After today, he'll trouble us no more."

Boghos did not move. "True, but if Ulger himself escapes—"

"Why are you trying to spare my life?" Pendaran demanded. "Does Ulger want me alive?"

Boghos's boot rose and caught Pendaran square in the nose. As before, the blow drew no blood.

"You see?" Varden shook his head. "We'll get nothing but back talk from him. Now step aside and let me finish this."

When Boghos did not obey, Pendaran knew he had guessed right. "Which master will you obey, Boghos—the Keeplord or the Usurper?"

Varden braced a hand on his hip. "Yes, Boghos—I am beginning to wonder the same thing."

The High Sorcerer backed away, paling. "I was only trying to prepare for all contingencies, Keeplord."

"I will tell you what to prepare for—but right now I want you to lift your fogbank. When I am finished here, I want to see what is happening on my battlefield." Varden nodded to the guards. "Let's get this done."

The guards bent Pendaran over at the waist, exposing his neck to the Keeplord's blade. Varden raised his sword to strike, and the sorcerer twisted his manacled hand free of its captor's grasp.

"Wait!" the guard cried.

He was too late. The Keeplord's blade was already on its way down, and Pendaran was laying his manacled wrist over the back of his neck. Even if the blow took only part of his hand, he would be able to slip the cuff and use his sorcery to escape.

But when the sword fell, it did not touch his neck.

Instead, the blade dropped without force, the tip swinging down in front of him to strike a single spark off the granite outcropping. When no one reached up to remove his hand from the back of his neck, Pendaran grew aware of a strange chugging sound down on the plain and looked up to see blossoms of green fume spreading over the battlefield, billowing up from someplace beneath the fog. The roar of victory cries had ceased, as had the rumble of charging feet. Now there was only the chugging whoosh of the green vapor, the hacking rasps of thousands upon thousands of burning throats, the anguished whinnies of a horde of choking horses.

"Boghos?" The Keeplord seemed unable to tear his eyes from the field. "What's happening?"

The High Sorcerer simply continued to stare out over the plain, standing with his hands at his sides and his jaw gaping open, doing his best to look as shocked as everyone else. Boghos's gaze suddenly shifted toward the edges of the battlefield, where Stonekeep's shocked archers stood staring out over the poisoned plain. A full second after he looked, the crack and boom of galok war spells began to erupt from the woods behind the bowmen.

"Boghos!" Varden was more insistent now, shaking the sorcerer by the arm. "Snap out of it! We must decide what to do!"

"There is only one thing you can do," Pendaran said, speaking from his knees. "Had you listened to me, Stonekeep would still have its army. But now your only choice is to run—run like the coward you are!"

Varden whirled on the sorcerer. "You!" he hissed. "This is your fault!"

"My fault? I told you this was going to happen."

"How could you have known about the trap—unless *you* are Ulger's spy?" asked Boghos. "You knew the Keeplord would discern your guilt when the trap was sprung, and so you tried to lay the blame on me."

"Just so!" said Varden. He looked to the guards. "Did I not tell you to hold him?"

Again, the guards pinned Pendaran's arms to his sides and bent him forward. The sorcerer tried to jerk his manacled wrist free, but this time the guards were ready and held the arm firmly in place. The Keeplord raised his sword.

Pendaran felt a dull shock at the base of his skull. There was a terrible pop as the blade cleaved his spine, then he lost all control of his neck muscles. His chin swung down to touch his chest, leaving his head to dangle by the skin and gristle of the front of his throat, and only then did he realize that the Keeplord's blow had not been powerful enough to cut completely through his neck.

Pendaran glared at Varden from the corner of his eye. "This hurts!" With all of his neck muscles severed, he could not lift his head, nor even turn it to look at the Keeplord. "I suppose it was too much to ask that you do it in one blow?"

Varden's jaw began to work without speaking. The color drained from his face. The sword slipped from his grasp, and he turned to flee—then, before he had taken a step, his eyes rolled back and he fainted.

Boghos was not nearly so shocked. He stooped down and pulled Pendaran's head up by the hair. "My, my—a tricky little wizard who can't be killed," he said. "I wonder who you can be?"

In the end, leaving the Faerie Realm proved too easy.

Cassius had been wandering the emerald catacombs for hours, searching in vain for the Tower of Rathe—or any other route out of the Faerie Realm. Then the last enkav walked down the corridor on two legs, its scaly brow arched in awe and its eyes twinkling with pink faerie light. The army of enkavs following Cassius thumped their fists to their chests and pointed at him, chorusing, "Sword!" The newcomer repeated the gesture and stood blinking in the Sun Sword's light, and in the next instant the Faerie Realm vanished. Cassius had no way of knowing whether they had simply been moved or the realm had suddenly ceased to exist—and he was not sure he wanted to find out. If Faerie was a state of being, did its disappearance mean the last faerie had ceased to be?

Now he was beginning to sound like a faerie himself.

Cassius shook the thought off as too morbid, then found himself standing in a place as desolate and forlorn as his soul. The ground was trembling as before, a faint shuddering so constant it was forgotten almost before it was noticed, but the duke needed a moment to recognize the city as Stonekeep. The houses around him were narrow and tall, with ornate stonework and raised thresholds guarded by flamboyant statues, built so closely together that only their steeply pitched gables separated one from another. Every building had been closed up tight, windows shuttered and doors shut fast. All manner of refuse—broken furniture, discarded foodstuffs, odd tatters of clothing—lay strewn over the cobblestone pavement. Aside from Cassius and his reptilian warriors, the only living things appeared to be the crows and rats rustling through the trash. The enkavs gazed at these scavengers with bright hungry eyes and occasionally licked their lips, but—much to the duke's relief—the reptiles made no attempt to eat the filthy vermin.

The desolation made Cassius think for a moment that he had returned too late to save the city, but he quickly realized this could not be. Had Ulger sacked Stonekeep, there would be fires and smashed doors, the awful reek of death, the wails of the grieving. This place simply looked empty.

Having never before visited this quarter of the city, Cassius had no idea where he was. He started down the street, looking for some plaza or parkway where he could see past the tall houses and find the Grand Heights to orient himself. The army of enkavs followed close behind, their scaly feet whispering across the pavement so softly that he heard their toe talons ticking on the cobblestones. When he stopped, they stopped; when he peered into an alley, they peered into the same alley. After devouring the faeries, the reptiles seemed to be developing a strange sort of intelligence, at once incredibly alert and completely obedient to his will. Whenever he spoke, even to himself, they chorused the words back to him, and when he turned to listen to some distant rumble, they turned in the same direction and cocked their heads. They even favored one leg as they walked, mimicking the limp he had acquired in the fight against Bink and Wink.

The imitation did not flatter Cassius. He could hardly look at the enkavs without recalling the source of their intelligence. It sickened him to think of his part in so many deaths—much less the extinction of an entire race—and he could not escape the suspicion that his sorcerer had planned things that way. Before he freed the little man from Boghos or anyone else, Pendaran Tremayne would have some explaining to do.

After a short walk, Cassius came to a small square with a clear view to the Grand Heights. In the low battlements that ringed the great hill, tiny figures were running along the ramparts and leaning out through the embrasures to peer northward. From his position relative to the Keeplord's Palace and the Hall of Eight, the duke guessed that he had emerged on the west side of the city, about a third of the way around from the North Gate—almost directly opposite the Tower of Rathe, where he had left Crusher in a nearby boarding stable. Given the condition of his leg, it would have been nice to have his mount with him, but he was not worried about anyone stealing his warhorse. The big shire would be quick to chase any such thoughts from a thief's mind.

Cassius looked toward the North Gate, trying to determine what had become of Stonekeep's armies. Though the high buildings of the city blocked any view of either the gate itself or Lookout Mountain beyond, the dust cloud billowing into the sky told him all he needed to know. The Eight Armies were in a rout.

As Cassius started to turn northward, he glimpsed the shutter of a corner tavern being pulled shut. With his slithering army at his back, he marched over and banged on the shutter with the hilt of his glowing sword.

"You inside, will you open up?" he asked. "I need to know the fastest way—"

The shutter flew open, and Cassius saw the tips of half a dozen iron bolts pointed in his direction.

"Duck!" he yelled, flinging himself to the ground.

The crossbows clacked.

In the same instant a thousand enkavs followed his lead, hurling themselves down and yelling, "Duck!"

Their bodies thundered to the ground with a single rumbling crash, then Cassius looked up to see a red-bearded tavern keeper and several wide-eyed customers frantically cranking their bowstrings back toward the locking nut. Behind the duke, several enkavs were staring curiously at the strange iron spikes that had suddenly sprouted from their scaly chests. They seemed neither hurt nor angry, although one was scratching at a bolt that had split a shoulder scale and sunk deep into the one beneath.

Cassius looked back to the tavern keeper. "Put those crossbows away before you kill someone!"

When the enkavs repeated the command in their shrill, raspy voices, the tavern keeper and his fellows turned the color of milk. The weapons slipped from their hands, and two of the men fainted.

Cassius rose. "There's no need to be frightened." When the enkavs repeated this, he turned to them and held his finger to his lips. "That's enough. Be quiet."

The enkavs in front passed his command back, and a hush slowly settled over the packed square. When Cassius turned back to the window, only the tavern keeper remained, standing at the casement with his hands hidden beneath the sill.

Cassius gestured at the three streets that led out of the square's east side. "Can you tell me which of these leads to Karzak's Belt?" Karzak's Belt was a broad boulevard that circled the Grand Heights, providing the fastest means of moving from one quarter of the city to another. "I seem to be lost."

"I'll tell you nothing." The keeper spat on the ground, then looked from the enkavs behind Cassius to the glowing sword in his hand. "I'm no traitor."

"Traitor?" Cassius glanced at the enkavs and suddenly realized how their brightly scaled bodies must have looked to the keeper. "Safrinni's rings! Forgive me for alarming you—we're not Ulger's monsters. We're here to defend the city."

The keeper looked doubtful. "I've never heard tell of any lizard companies in the service of the realm. Where'd you come from?"

"Where they came from is a story too long to tell." Cassius gestured at the enkavs. "But I am from Kural."

"Lord Alban's son?" The keeper raised his hands to display a suddenly loaded crossbow. "The traitor duke?"

Cassius felt the angry heat rise to his face, but did not deny the charge. "A traitor to the Keeplord's lackeys, perhaps, but not to Stonekeep."

"And how would that be?" The keeper kept the crossbow trained on Cassius's chest.

"While I was fighting Ulger and his monsters, the High Sorcerer Boghos and Sir Melwas were busy looting Castle Kural. When I demanded that they stop, matters got out of hand, and Lord Alban was killed. I am responsible for what followed, but that does not mean I have sided with Ulger. Now I believe the Usurper's troops are knocking at the North Gate, and even if you refuse to tell me how to get there, I advise you not to shoot me in the back—I have no idea how my companions might take it."

Cassius motioned at the enkavs, then turned to leave.

"Not so fast."

When Cassius looked back, the keeper had lowered his crossbow.

"You'll need a Stonekeep standard, or you're liable to start a panic as you approach the gate." He turned and spoke to someone outside Cassius's view, then stepped back and swung a wooden leg up onto the sill. "I'd carry it myself, except for what Sir Melwas cost me the last time I picked up a sword."

Cassius raised his brow. "You served with Melwas?"

"Long enough to believe what you say—and to be happy he's dead." The keeper accepted a flag from someone inside the tavern, then passed it out the window. "Melwas was always a shrewd commander—shrewd enough to stay out of the fight while we won his glory. We called him the Coward Cat."

"A fitting description." Cassius unfurled the pennant, revealing the emblem of a male lion rearing up to defend the walls of Stonekeep. "I'll try to do your standard more honor than he did."

"You have already—though I don't see why you bother.

From the sound of it, the High Lords have done you no favors."

"It is not the High Lords I am fighting for. Before this is over, they will get what is coming to them."

The words spilled from Cassius's mouth before he realized he had spoken them—indeed, even before he realized he had thought them. He found himself squeezing the Sun Sword's golden hilt, as surprised by the harsh words as the innkeeper—but meaning them no less. Cassius passed the standard to an enkav, then struggled to regain his composure.

"But I seem to be getting ahead of myself," he said. "First there is Ulger to deal with, and that alone will be enough to kill me."

"I doubt that." The keeper eyed Cassius and his sword thoughtfully, then pointed toward the opposite end of the block. "That's the street you want."

Cassius led the enkavs down the indicated street and was surprised to notice a few scattered shutters swinging open as he passed. The occupants would peer out at Stonekeep's pennant, then stare at the enkavs and let their jaws drop. Some managed to voice an astonished cheer or ask if they were really looking at the Company of the Standing Lion, but most were too dazed to do more than watch in stunned silence as the reptiles clattered past. Cassius carried himself proudly, with the Sun Sword held upright before him, and whenever anyone asked his identity, he always identified himself as Duke Cassius of Kural.

By the time the Company of the Standing Lion reached Karzak's Belt, people were beginning to line the streets to cheer the "Traitor Duke." Bearing heirloom swords, wood axes, smithy's hammers, and any tool that could be used as a weapon, men and women of all ages began to fall into line behind the enkavs. From these volunteers, Cassius learned that despite Keeplord Varden's promise to turn the invaders back, the largest part of Stonekeep's population had departed for the south; the people cheering him now were refugees from the north and a few residents who could not or would not leave.

Like most of the city's largest boulevards, Karzak's Belt was lined by the grand manors of the wealthy—all occupied by small troops of guards hired especially to defend the mansions from refugee squatters. As the procession passed, the volunteers at Cassius's back scolded these sell-swords mercilessly, calling them cowards and traitors and bootlickers of the rich. Occasionally the harangues had an effect, compelling a small group of mercenaries to forsake their contracts to join the makeshift army. More often, the sentries watched the column pass in silence, their thoughts veiled behind callous masks of indifference.

At last, Karzak's Belt passed beneath a massive obelisk and spilled into the broad, monument-strewn ribbon of Drake's Way. As the procession turned toward the gate, the carnival-like atmosphere gave way to a more nervous mood. Ahead lay a mile-long boulevard cluttered with victory arches and granite statues, all quivering in time to the shuddering ground. The low rumble of an army on the move filled the air, and a dark curtain of dust was billowing into the sky from someplace just beyond the city walls.

Cassius led the way up road at his best limp. Before long, a haggard-looking rider in battered armor came galloping down the road, slumped over in his saddle and staring vacantly at the Grand Heights. When Cassius stepped out to stop him, the man did not seem to see him and would have ridden him down, had the duke not been quick enough to leap aside.

More riders began to appear in groups of two and three, then four and five, and soon in a steady stream. Like the first, they were mangled and stunned, many with huge ogare arrows lodged through their breastplates, some with limbs that ended in scorched stumps. The horses seemed as battle-shocked as the men, galloping past with hardly a glance at the Traitor Duke or his fierce-looking enkavs. Cassius's thoughts turned to Brenna the Swift and the Brass Axe, but none of the vacant-eyed riders would pause to answer his questions.

The great North Gate came into view down the street, a blocky two-legged tower that straddled the road like a giant.

The walls were festooned with narrow arrow loops, through which tiny defenders could be glimpsed scurrying about their duties. As Cassius and his followers rushed forward, the High Lords themselves began to stream from the gate's dark vault in a thundering torrent of carriages and riders. The entire cavalcade looked as though it had endured a firestorm. The bodyguards were scorched and blistered, some so badly they held their hands up before their faces and guided their mounts with their knees. The horses had lost most of their barding; their manes were singed, their hides seared and hairless, their legs covered with draining sores. The splendid carriages had been reduced to mere tinder, with melted curtain wisps flying from the windows, gilded body panels scorched to charcoal, and vacant-eyed, soot-smudged faces rocking to and fro inside.

"Stand aside!" The leading rider waved at Cassius from fifty paces up the street. "Out of the way!"

Cassius started to obey, then heard the chime of steel on steel coming from the other side of the distant gatehouse. A huge ogare arrow came sailing out of the dark archway, and the men on the ramparts began to fire crossbows down toward the ground. The volley was answered by a flight of lightning bolts that blasted half a dozen men out of their embrasures and launched starbursts of stone out over the city.

"Make way for the High Lords!" the bodyguard demanded again, still leading the ravaged cavalcade toward Cassius and his followers.

Cassius raised the Sun Sword. "You make way!" He pointed down an alley perhaps twenty paces ahead. "I'm going to reinforce the gate!"

The bodyguard scowled, then looked past Cassius's shoulder and finally seemed to comprehend what he was seeing. His jaw dropped, then he reined his horse and wheeled down the alley, motioning for the procession to follow. Another volley of lightning bolts blasted the battlements, all but silencing the crossbowmen on the ramparts. Cassius continued to hobble forward, and he was only a few paces from the alley when the first carriage turned down it. So battered and blackened was the coach that he did not even recognize it as Keeplord Varden's until he saw the sorcerer Boghos glaring out the window.

What Cassius spied next made him stop in his tracks. Tied to the carriage's rear boot, with his wrist and ankle still shackled by Boghos's shadowy manacles, was Pendaran Tremayne. The sorcerer's captors had hung him upside down, facing inward so that the gaping wound on the back of his neck was exposed to view. Cassius's anger over the fate of the faeries vanished at once; suddenly he could think of nothing but how much Pendaran had done to save Stonekeep, and of how the sorcerer's efforts had been frustrated at every turn by the incompetence of Keeplord Varden and his Council of Fools.

"Pendaran!" Cassius screamed, unable to believe the sorcerer was dead. "No!"

The carriage banged over a piece of stony rubble, bouncing Pendaran's head off the boot so that it flopped over to face the grief-stricken duke. Much to Cassius's surprise, the sorcerer's beady eyes blinked once, then swung toward the Sun Sword and fixed on the glowing blade. The disembodied head frowned and began to speak. Though it was impossible to hear the corpse's words over the din of battle, the lips seemed to be saying, "Ungrateful cur!"

The coach banged off a wall and vanished down the alley, leaving Cassius to wonder if he was seeing things. Certainly, Pendaran was a great sorcerer—but that great?

An outburst of savage bellowing drew the duke's attention back toward the gate, where two more carriages were barreling out of the archway. In the dark recesses behind them, the silhouettes of weary horsemen and squat bearded warriors struggled in vain to hold back a churning tide of hulking, gangly-armed shapes. Though it was impossible to tell if the dwarves were of the Brass Axe, Cassius's heart leapt at the mere possibility that Brenna was with them. He raised the Sun Sword and charged.

"For Kural!"

The enkavs mimicked the gesture with their taloned hands and roared, "For Kural!"

Astonished faces peered out through the gatehouse's narrow arrow loops and the windows of passing coaches. Cassius rushed forward, squeezing along the side of the street so the High Lords' cavalcade could pass and not block the road. The enkavs squeezed together and followed close behind, casting half-starved looks at the passing parade of horseflesh. Only once was there a collision, when a bodyguard's jittery mount noticed their hungry leers and shied away, crashing into a carriage at its side. Man and beast fell together, perishing beneath the hooves of their own fellows.

Cassius had nearly reached the gate when the ogares broke through, spilling out of the dark vault alongside a burned out coach. The hulking brutes were battling the High Lord's bodyguards as they ran, shouldering aside horses and yanking riders out of the saddle with their bare hands. The savage attacks did nothing to slow the torrent of riders and coaches behind them; invaders and defenders poured through the gate in a single roiling flood of steel and claw and hoof.

As Cassius raised his sword to join the battle, the nearest ogare caught hold of a High Lord's carriage window. It swung onto the doorstep, then reached inside to throttle the passenger. Had the coach not been passing by at the moment, Cassius might not have troubled himself to save the councillor's life; as matters were, he flicked the tip of his weapon toward the brute's thick neck and felt the blade bite. There was a brief sizzle and the smell of charred flesh, then the ogare dropped from the coach and tumbled down the road. The duke caught a brief glimpse of a round face with wide eyes peering out the window, and then the carriage was gone.

Cassius turned to find a huge iron blade arcing down toward his head, the ogare behind it stepping into the attack. By reflex, the duke snapped his own weapon into a high guard, bracing his legs in what he was sure would be a vain effort to weather the blow.

The Sun Sword sliced through the ogare's blade as though it were lard, leaving the hairy brute off balance and pitching forward. Cassius barely had time to pivot out of the way as the beast crashed to the ground; he finished it with a quick chop to the back of the neck, then heard another of the monsters crashing up beside him. He turned his head to find the thing already upon him, its huge sword arcing in from his blind side.

A passing bodyguard laid a blade across the back of the ogare's shoulders. Even with the momentum of a racing horse behind the blow, the assault did not fell the hulking brute—but it did cause the ogare to roar and spin toward its attacker, who by that time had galloped half a dozen paces down the street. Cassius seized the advantage, whirling his Sun Sword around to open a deep gash in the ogare's midsection. The creature's pointed muzzle fell open in shock, then it dropped to the ground and began to bellow its pain.

Cassius looked up to see a dozen ogares swarming up the side of the gatehouse, clinging to the sheer stone and reaching around to thrust their long arms into the arrow loops. One of the beasts jerked a screaming defender out through an opening, then slammed the poor man against the wall until he fell silent.

When Cassius looked away, he saw another dozen ogares rushing toward him through the gate. He quickly retreated to the safety of his enkavs—and found the reptiles staring around in wide eyed wonder. As far as he could tell, not a one of them had blood on its claws.

"Fight!" Cassius screamed, hefting his sword.

"Fight!" screamed the enkavs.

They hefted their arms, but made no move to attack, even when the ogares came crashing into their ranks. Cassius blocked a vicious overhead slash, in the same gesture snapping his foe's sword and beheading the beast. He continued the swing and opened another brute from scapula to sternum, dropping it at the feet of the enkav beside him. The reptile lowered its chin and stared at the dying creature in dumbfounded amazement—until the sword of another ogare crashed down on its collarbone, cleaving it down to the heart.

The enkav collapsed in heap of shattered bone and spurting blood, then looked up and asked, "Fight?"

"Fight!" yelled Cassius.

But the enkav was already dead. Cassius stepped over to cut down its slayer, and after that he could be sure of only one thing: the enkavs were learning fast. The lizard-beasts came lurching past him with a deafening roar, driving the ogares back toward the gatehouse. Every time an iron sword rose to attack, it was answered by a flurry of talons. The hulking invaders fell one after the other, their hairy bodies shredded to pink ribbons. The blood and mayhem only fed the fury of the reptiles. They pushed past Cassius, swarming up the gatehouse walls after their climbing enemies, either dragging the brutes down by their ankles or clambering up their backs to claw at their throats and eyes. Usually, the reptilian warrior rode its victim to the ground, then bounced up and scrambled back up the wall. By the time the duke reached the gatehouse, the enkavs were swarming across the archway to assail their foes on the other side of the road.

The largest part the enkav horde rushed straight into the gateway, carrying Cassius along in the middle. Though he no longer had room to wield the Sun Sword, its light illuminated the archway in brilliant arcs of white gold and silver yellow. He became a mere spectator, peering between his warriors' scaly shoulders and trying not to let their thrashing arms knock him off his feet.

The ogares, crammed into the narrow space between the thundering horsemen and the gateway wall, could stand only one abreast—and even then, it was difficult to swing their massive swords. When one of the brutes did manage to land a blow, more often than not it glanced off the enkav's thick armor, doing no damage more serious than cutting off a few scales and opening a nasty gash. The reptiles, smaller and quicker, attacked in pairs. While one moved in behind a flurry of slashing claws, the second dropped to all fours and launched itself at the foe's knees, or came up under the brute's guard to attack the soft belly. The result was always the same; the invader fell screaming, and the enkavs scrambled over the body to find a new mark.

Determined not to lose their foothold in the gatehouse, the ogares at the back of the archway broadened their line across the road, chopping the legs from beneath a dozen screaming mounts. Rider and beast alike hit the ground tumbling. The horses behind them sprang into the air, trying to leap over their somersaulting fellows, then came down in a jumbled heap. In the space of two breaths, the gateway became an impassable tangle of horses and men—and it was into this mess that the last coach came racing.

The driver had no time to stop or turn or cry out. He simply let his jaw drop and watched as his thundering team smashed into the ogares from behind. There was a great cracking and booming, and the horses screamed and went down. The coach swung toward Cassius's side of the road, then toppled onto its side and tumbled, flinging splintered footboards and charred body panels in all directions.

The duke soon saw why the ogares had not interfered with the High Lords' cavalcade before now. As the hairy brutes flooded in to fill the gap, a company of charging bodyguards crashed in from behind. With a great rasp of delight, the enkavs rushed forward to join the battle, and the archway was instantly blocked by a maelstrom of whirling blades and swift death.

Cassius stormed into the fray with his reptiles, not quite sure whether he was leading the charge or being carried along by it. He leapt over a screaming horse and found himself standing on a pile of writhing limbs, then ducked past two whistling blades as long as he was tall. He leapt again, chopping at one hulking chest and three huge hairy arms as he charged forward, struggling all the while to keep his balance on a pile of blood-slickened bodies.

A short distance ahead, the gilt-armored figure of a High Lord began to crawl from the wrecked coach, his back turned to Cassius. Though the man was surrounded on all sides by hulking ogares with arms as big as his waist, he did not hesitate to jab his flimsy rapier into the nearest hairy thigh. The victim roared in surprise, then whirled around so angry that it missed its target and drove its sword clear through the coach undercarriage.

The High Lord shoved his rapier into the ogare's stomach, then left it there and ducked back into the wrecked carriage. "Guards!"

The wounded ogare plucked the rapier from its abdomen, then knelt down and began to feel around inside the passenger compartment.

Cassius ducked a wild swing and darted between two ogares toward the wreckage, not quite sure why he was taking such a risk. The coach was surrounded by ogares, and the High Lord might well be dead by the time he arrived anyway, but there was something about the man's courage—or perhaps arrogance—that touched a nerve. He unlimbed an ogare at the knee, then dodged past the bellowing creature and found himself standing behind the carriage.

The ogare was stooped over the side of the coach, growling angrily and pulling something from inside. Cassius brought the Sun Sword down, severing the brute's thick arm at the elbow. The beast screeched and spun around, smashing the bloody stump into the duke's face. His vision blackened, and he felt himself falling, and that was when he heard the enkavs roaring.

Cassius concentrated on his sword, gripping it tightly in both hands and bringing it around in front of him. For a moment he could neither see nor feel, and when his senses finally came flooding back, he had already landed in a pile of battle offal. The combat swirled around him, enkavs and bodyguards swarming the huge ogares and dragging them down. Directly ahead lay the toppled coach, and beside it lay the claw-savaged corpse of a one-armed ogare.

Cassius rose and stepped over the creature's body. When he peered down through the smashed sidewall, he found a High Lord cowering against a blood soaked seat, the ogare's huge hand still clutching him by the head. Cassius reached inside and pulled the severed hand away, revealing a hook-nosed man with sharp features.

The High Lord's expression changed from one of terror to confusion. "You?"

"Lord Fiske," said Cassius crisply. He took the councillor by the arm and gently extracted him from the carriage. "Perhaps you should leave."

He pushed the High Lord toward the far end of the archway, then turned back to the battle without waiting to see what became of him. A steady stream of ogares and bodyguards continued to pour in from the other end of the gate, slashing and hacking as they came. Cassius clambered up on a pile of bodies and began to swing the Sun Sword again. In the close quarters, the clamor grew as deafening as the stench did foul—clanging steel and reeking entrails, rattling scales, anguished cries—it all became one sensation, unbearably acute and dizzying in its madness. Any semblance to an organized battle vanished; enemies attacked from everywhere, and allies came to the rescue from every side. The bodies continued to fall, until it became as much work to stay atop the heap as it was to keep from becoming a part of it. As the corpse pile grew deeper, Cassius sensed the vaulted ceiling creeping closer, and he began to see squat, bearded figures wielding their axes around him.

The duke's entire body began to ache and throb with fatigue. He was covered in blood, though it was impossible to tell how much was his own. He had no sensation of being wounded, but he could have been cut a dozen times in the mad melee and not have known it. He had no perception of anything, save a growing awareness of being forced toward the exterior end of the gateway.

Gradually, Cassius realized that he was ducking fewer and fewer attacks, and that he was having trouble finding enemies upon which to wield his blade. A strange numbness settled over his mind and body, something akin to the emptiness he had felt when Castle Kural fell, save that now he experienced neither despair nor anger. Beneath his feet lay a red tangle of limbs and torsos, many still moving and some crying for help. The duke was too dazed to give it. Of all the combats he had fought in Kural, none had been as savage as this—and what was this battle, really? A minor skirmish for a gate. The thought left him drained.

Cassius let the press from behind carry him completely out of the archway, where he stumbled down a grisly delta of bodies onto the dirt road outside the city. The field around him was littered with hundreds of bodies—ogare and human alike—and there were perhaps another two thousand warriors—mostly dwarves—limping toward the safety of the gate. In the distance, the mountains around Sentinel Pass stood dark and tall, looking somehow more heavily forested than he remembered.

"By the jewel, Cassius!" said a familiar dwarven voice. "It was good to see you and those lizards coming through that gate!"

Cassius looked down to see Skagi Reist standing beside him, smeared with blood up to his eyebrows.

"Skagi!" Cassius gasped. He extended a gore-covered hand to clasp the one offered by the dwarf. "What happened to Brenna?"

"I'm well enough—not that you care."

Brenna's voice came from behind Cassius, and he turned to see her stuffing a handful of bloody shafts into her empty quiver. Like everyone else, she was smeared in gore—though in her case, she seemed to have acquired much of it while retrieving arrows from fallen targets.

"What kind of coward are you, leaving me with the likes of Varden and Boghos?"

Cassius felt the heat rise to his cheeks, but he could see just by looking at the girl that they had done nothing to harm her. "It was for your own good. You had nothing to do with my trouble, and I—"

"That knife doesn't skin!" Brenna snapped. She stepped over to stand toe-to-toe, truly angry with him for abandoning her. "Now that you're not a duke, you don't get to decide what's good for me or any one else!"

"Brenna, that is not for you to decide!" Skagi scolded. The dwarf cast an apologetic glance at Cassius. "The duke will have to answer to the Council for what happened in

Castle Kural—and he may be sure I will speak on his behalf—but until Keeplord Varden says otherwise, he is still your duke."

Brenna's anger instantly withered to embarrassment, and her gaze dropped to the ground. "He should have told me what happened. I had a right to know."

"Perhaps," said Cassius. "But it was better that you didn't."

Brenna kicked a rock, then nodded at the Sun Sword. "Nice sword," she said.

Cassius laughed, then hugged her to his side. "You keep your hands off my sword, young woman. You wouldn't believe what I had to do to get this."

"Whatever it was, I am glad you did it," said Skagi. "Without you and your lizards, Brenna and I would have been throg meat."

"Really?" Cassius looked around, frowning, and it was only then that he realized what he did not see. Save for the dead ogares, who had apparently been sent forward to seize the gatehouse, there was no sign of the enemy. "I don't see any throgs—and what happened to the Eight Armies?"

"You have already seen what remains of the Eight Armies." Skagi gestured at the bloody battlefield. "The Council will be lucky if it can still muster an eighth of an army. As for the throgs, they're right behind us."

The dwarf pointed toward Lookout Mountain.

Cassius turned to study the horizon above the mountains, searching for the familiar storm clouds that always heralded the approach of Ulger's army. "I don't see anything. The sky is clear."

"Not the sky," Skagi prompted. "The mountain."

Cassius squinted at the forested slopes again. It took a moment for him to see it, but eventually he noticed the faint undulations and realized he was not looking at trees at all. He was looking at an army.

"I don't suppose you have more of these lizard troops?" Brenna jerked her head at the enkavs, who were beginning to gather around the trio. "Like maybe another ten thousand?"

"I'm afraid not," said Cassius. He turned toward Stonekeep, wondering how difficult it was going to be to free Pendaran. "But maybe we can ask for more."

The Keeplord's carriage was already nearing the summit of Stonekeep's Grand Heights when the battle ended at the North Gate. Pendaran could see his enkavs swarming the archway, mad with hunger and desperate to pull the ogares out into the open. That would mean another long delay before he was rescued. What could Cassius have been thinking, going off to defend the gate instead of freeing his loyal sorcerer? The Sun Sword had to be boiling the boy's brain.

Cassius's mob of volunteers was streaming into the gatehouse like a long line of ants, rushing up the interior stairs to emerge on the ramparts above. They were spreading along the wall in both directions, taking positions in the battlements and giving the appearance, at least, of being ready to put up a fight. That Ulger's hordes would slaughter them like insects made Pendaran a little sad; over the centuries, he had developed a certain affinity for humans, and it pained him to see them throw their short lives away so foolishly.

In the distance beyond the walls, the Usurper's hosts were creeping down the mountainside around Sentinel Pass, obscured only by the dust of their own passing. With the shadow manacles still depriving him of his powers, Pendaran could see no details—only a dark, amorphous mass sliding toward Stonekeep. Now that the Eight Armies had been smashed, Ulger no longer bothered to conceal his hordes behind clouds and storms; he wanted the city to see its death coming.

The coach rounded the last bend in the Cliff Road and entered the Lords' Gate. Pendaran's half-severed head, still dangling by the skin and muscles of his throat, twisted around to stare in the opposite direction. He saw the dark slit of an arrow loop slip past, then heard the Keeplord's voice call out to the coachman.

"Stop here."

The coach squealed to a halt in the gateway, forcing the rear guard to rein their mounts so sharply that they nearly crashed into the back of the coach. Pendaran's head rolled back to center, leaving him to stare at the carriage's leather boot while a bodyguard's horse snorted into the wound on the back of his neck.

"Sergeant!" called the Keeplord. "I want you to close this gate behind me."

"Of course, Keeplord, when the time comes—"

"No, Sergeant." Now it was Boghos who spoke. "Right behind us."

In the silence that followed, Pendaran found his own mind racing as fast as the sergeant's must have been. After Varden had recovered from his fainting spell at the battlefield, the High Lords had fallen into such a bickering match that Pendaran had thought they might save Ulger the trouble of killing them. The Council had united in blaming the disaster on Varden, and he had countered by pointing out the contributions each of them had made to the disastrous plan. There had been talk of selecting a new Keeplord, but this had come to a swift end when a company of galoks and ogares emerged from the trees flinging fire and arrows. The High Lords had quickly joined forces to organize their escape, and Pendaran had expected the truce to hold after they returned to Stonekeep. Apparently, Boghos and Varden did not intend to take that chance.

At last, the sergeant said, "Keeplord, you know I can't close the gate until the other councillors are inside. The Guard is sworn to protect all the High Lords."

"And Keeplord Varden is the Highest of the High," retorted Boghos. "There are happenings afoot of which you know nothing—"

"I can see what is happening, Lord Sorcerer." The sergeant's voice grew hard, and Pendaran heard the leathery scrape of a sword clearing its scabbard. "Keeplord, may I suggest that you move along to your palace? A lot of people are going to be coming through this gate, and you're holding things up."

"Don't take that tone with me!" Varden's command sounded less like a rebuke than a plea. "You weren't there. You don't know what happened."

"But I can tell you," called Pendaran. "Sergeant, if you will just cut me loose—"

"That's enough," said one of Varden's bodyguards. The man touched the tip of a lance to Pendaran's back, then said, "The sergeant has his duties to attend to."

But the little wizard had already piqued the sergeant's curiosity, and heavy footsteps echoed around to the back of the carriage. Pendaran jerked his torso up, flopping his head around to see his savior's weathered face.

"In the name of Aquila!" the sergeant gasped. He backed away, instinctively bringing his sword around. "What have you here?"

"A spy," said Boghos. By the sound of the High Sorcerer's voice, Pendaran guessed he was craning his scrawny neck out the window. "The reason the Eight Armies were lost."

"I am not the spy," Pendaran growled. "Boghos is the traitor here. Sergeant, if you love Stonekeep, you will cut me free."

The sergeant cast an inquiring glance at the bodyguard.

The bodyguard shrugged. "All I know is he's not human. Neither are the things we're fighting."

"Don't listen to him!" hissed Pendaran. "He's a fool. They all are!"

"Not all of us," said Boghos. "I will have the truth from you soon enough . . . And you, Sergeant, will rue the day you defied the Keeplord."

"Not when the rest of the Council hears what the Keeplord ordered," the sergeant countered. "Now clear my gate!"

There was a loud ringing slap, then a horse screamed and the carriage bolted forward. They passed from the dim vault of the gate into the marble-paved haven of the Grand Heights, with its vast market halls flanking Council Boulevard and its two-story colonnade running down the center. The ground was shaking more violently here than in any other part of the city, so that the trembling statues along the street looked almost alive with fright. Aside from the quivering statuary and the High Lords' bodyguards, the district appeared far more deserted than the rest of Stonekeep; the wealthy residents had long ago fled to their villas in the south, entrusting the care of their homes to the Young Gods and the Council Guard.

As the coach raced down the boulevard, Boghos called to the driver, ordering him to take them into the temple ward instead of the palace quarter. Keeplord Varden said something that Pendaran could not quite understand over the rumbling wheels. The sorcerer jerked his chest up several times, until at last his head flopped around so that his ear was pressed tightly against the carriage boot. Even then, the conversation was so muffled he could barely understand it.

". . . the palace?" asked Varden.

"They'll expect that," replied Boghos. "We'll be safer in the temples."

"Safer? You think they'll attack me?" gasped Varden. "They wouldn't dare!"

"Who can say what they will dare?" countered Boghos. "You did try to lock them out . . . the Grand Heights."

"Your idea, not mine!"

"To reaffirm your control," said Boghos. "As much as

it galled the Council to ask your leave, it would also have humbled them. They would not have dared call for a new Keeplord."

There was a moment of silence, then Varden complained, "They shouldn't blame me. The entire Council approved the plan."

"It's easier to blame you than themselves," said Boghos. "But I have something in mind that will change their thinking—if you will trust me."

"Of course. You're my one true friend." A moment later Varden added, "You know this wasn't my fault."

Pendaran's chest tightened. Cassius would come looking for him in the Keeplord's Palace, not the temples; by the time the boy found him, Ulger would be marching down Drake's Way. The sorcerer began to tug against the rope binding his wrist to the coach. With some grunting and cursing, he managed to pull his hand close enough to his chest to reach inside his cloak. He slipped his fingers into his magic pocket.

And felt nothing but cloth. The shadow manacles prevented even his robe's magic from working.

"Fireclouds!"

Thinking to leave a trail of gems instead, Pendaran clutched at his cloak lining—then looked down to find himself grasping the ruby Cassius had given him north of Brookbury Basin. He reached farther inside, but this time caught hold of the diamonds Drakeson had presented him for his services against the Traitor Lords. Then he grasped a magnificent opal that Calvar's wife, Lady Diamanta, had presented him for holding his silence about a certain encounter in the Privy Garden . . .

The carriage swung down a side street and suddenly they were careening along the Sacred Way, with Thera's Pavilion looming up on one side and the Singing Fountains of Aquila arcing up on the other. The bodyguards, surprised by the unexpected change of direction, reacted slowly and rounded the corner in a cacophony of neighing horses and clattering hooves. The next coach in line trundled past the intersection without slowing, and Pendaran saw Lord Belden's red-bearded face scowling out the window.

The sorcerer pulled his hand from his cloak empty. He would not waste any of his precious jewels making Cassius's job easier. Had the oaf done his duty in the first place, Pendaran would be free by now.

The Keeplord's carriage raced under the Eternal Flame of Helion, then bounced down a narrow lane between Azrael's Altar of Blood and the House of Marif. The city here was shaking so hard that marble cobblestones were popping out of the road. Pendaran's head smashed into the coach boot time after time, twisting back and forth so wildly that he barely glimpsed the trailing bodyguards. Whole sections of friezework were crashing down from the entablature atop of the great temples, shattering on the street and spraying the sorcerer with stinging shards of stone. They passed the sweeping curve of the rear wall of Safrinni's Amphitheater, and Pendaran began to have a bad feeling about where they were going.

The coach came to a stop beside a small circular structure with a domed roof. Made entirely of black obsidian, the building had no means of entrance—no doorways, no windows, no chimney, no portals of any kind. Even the seams between the glassy blocks had been polished and smoothed so carefully that an insect could not have crawled between them.

The coach door opened and Boghos stepped out, followed closely by Keeplord Varden.

"The Temple of Shadow!" Varden exclaimed. "What are we doing here?"

Boghos's tone was dismissing. "It's the last place the Council will think to search for us."

"With good reason!" Varden said. "I don't see—"

"You said you would trust me," said Boghos. He stepped to the rear of the coach. "Do so, and you may come through this yet."

"May?" Varden studied the temple doubtfully.

As the Keeplord spoke, Boghos cut Pendaran's feet free. The little sorcerer's legs came down over the back of his head, leaving his body to hang by his outstretched arms.

His head lolled forward, chin to chest, and he strained his eye sockets trying to look in Varden's direction.

"Don't be a fool, Keeplord," said Pendaran. "Khull-khuum's temple is sealed for good reason. There is a better way to save your title."

"You have said enough, faerie ears." Boghos pointed the tip of his dagger at Pendaran's mouth. "One more word, and I'll see if you can talk without a tongue."

"No, I want to hear this." Varden turned to Pendaran. "Please continue."

Pendaran pulled one arm up, so that his head rolled toward the Keeplord, and gave a tusky grin. "The High Lords are not fools. They know a spy has been working against you." The sorcerer shifted his eyes toward Boghos. "Give them their scapegoat, and you have nothing to fear."

Varden nodded sagely, then stood and turned to Boghos. "There's something to what he says."

Boghos clenched his dagger until his knuckles whitened, and he glanced nervously in the bodyguards' direction. "You mean to turn me over?"

Varden frowned at the sorcerer's stupidity. "Of course not—they'd never believe you to be the spy." The Keeplord pulled Pendaran's head up by the hair and looked him in the eyes. "I'm talking about our friend here. Everyone knows he was in the middle of that mess in Kural. It will take nothing to prove that he passed our battle plan to the enemy."

"Passed your plan to Ulger?" Pendaran fumed. "I tried to warn you off!"

Varden let the sorcerer's head drop, then stepped back with a satisfied smirk. "There—he already admits he knew what Ulger was going to do."

Boghos shook his head, then knelt to tie Pendaran's feet together. "I have better uses for Pendaran."

Varden frowned. "Who is the Keeplord here?"

"You are, Lord Varden—and I am only thinking of your well-being." Boghos stood and cut one of Pendaran's hands free of the coach, then tied the little sorcerer's wrists together. "The High Lords understand only one thing:

power. And I am going to give you more power than you ever dreamed of—power not only to control the Council, but to save Stonekeep from Ulger."

"Defeat Ulger?" Varden seemed more frightened than eager. "How?"

Boghos gestured to the Shadow Temple. "The answer lies inside—but you must be brave enough to go after it."

"Or you have to be the biggest Drake idiot since Terris himself," scoffed Pendaran. "It's madness to toy with Shadow."

"The choice is yours, Keeplord." Boghos tied Pendaran's hands to his ankles. Only then did he cut the little sorcerer free of the coach, dropping him on the bucking street and leaving him to lie there on his side. "Will you trust the Council with your life, or seize the power to save Stonekeep—and yourself?"

Varden looked from Boghos to the Temple of Shadow. "What would I have to do?"

Boghos gave the Keeplord a crooked smile. "Just follow me."

The High Sorcerer sheathed his dagger, then took his rune staff from the carriage and pressed its length to the obsidian wall. He pressed his thumb to one of the mystical patterns near the top and spoke a single word, "Shadowpass."

A curtain of dull gloom spread across the glassy wall, surrounding the staff with an oval of wispy drabness. Boghos held his hand in place until the last of the spell's mana—the raw mystic energy that powered the magic of all rune casters—passed from the staff into the glassy obsidian, then stepped aside. He waved one hand into the dark circle, motioning the Keeplord into the temple ahead of himself.

Varden hesitated, licking his lips.

"There is nothing to worry about, milord," said Boghos. "But if you do not wish to enter—"

"I'll do it—for Stonekeep." Varden turned to his bodyguards. "You men, form a perimeter. Let no one disturb us."

"And pay no attention when you hear the Keeplord's death screams ringing inside the temple," added Pendaran. "It will only be Khull-khuum devouring his soul."

Boghos's foot snapped out, catching the little sorcerer in the forehead and snapping his head around to face the bodyguards. They were all dismounting, looking as uneasy as their horses.

Boghos leaned down and grabbed Pendaran by the shadow manacles, whispering, "It is your soul he will devour, Little One."

The High Sorcerer followed Varden into the shadowy portal, dragging Pendaran along behind him. They passed through a curtain of inky fumes into a vault of curving black glass where shadows seemed to drag across the flesh like cobwebs. In the wall sconces burned ebon-flamed torches, casting just enough flickering blue light to reveal the myriad runes etched into the walls and ceiling.

In the center of the chamber stood a long altar of black marble, and behind this table rose four broken pillars, each with a piece of silver jewelry pressed into the top—an ankh, a crescent, a cross, and a circle. Floating in the center of the columns was a pulsing sphere of darkness, careening madly from one pillar to another. Each time the sphere struck a post, a powerful shock shot through chamber, reverberating inside Pendaran's chest before he felt it through the floor. The sorcerer experienced a strange sensation he had never before known—a certain lightness in his stomach, a pulsing in his ears, a profuse sweating, an uncontrollable trembling. Fear.

Boghos stopped three paces from the broken pillars. He laid his rune staff aside, then bowed to the ricocheting sphere of darkness and hefted Pendaran onto the altar. The sorcerer's head landed so that he was looking away from the black sphere toward Varden and Boghos.

"I have brought you a gift, Dark One," said Boghos. "The gift of freedom."

The crashing and shaking suddenly ceased, and Varden demanded, "What is that sphere, Boghos? Who are you talking to?"

"That should be apparent, Lord Varden—even to you," said Pendaran. "Some fool has brought Khull-khuum up from the depths."

Varden took an involuntary step back, then looked to the High Sorcerer. "Is that true?"

"You have nothing to fear from me, Varden," boomed a deep, all-too-familiar voice. The last time Pendaran had heard it was five centuries earlier, when he was leading Drake into the Tower of the Shadowking. "I have been watching you, and I will have use for you when I am free."

Varden's jaw fell, and he stared at Boghos in indignation. "You betrayed me!"

"I saved you." Boghos stooped down to reach into a shadowy recess beneath the altar. "Ulger has been studying the secrets of Ys for three and a half centuries. Did you really think you could stop him with mere men and weapons?"

"Not by listening to your advice," said Pendaran.

"The Council needed no advice from me to lose that war," said Boghos. He rose with a rune brush and inkwell in his hands, then stepped around to the top of the altar. "Hold his head for me, Keeplord."

Varden simply stared at Boghos, showing no sign that he had heard the sorcerer's command. "How long have you been—"

"Obey!" thundered Khull-khuum. The Orb of the Shadowking slammed against the pillars, sending another shock wave through all of Stonekeep. "Five hundred years I have waited, and I will wait no more!"

Varden leapt forward to do as instructed. Boghos uncapped the inkwell and dipped his brush, then began to paint on Pendaran's forehead. It did not take the little sorcerer long to identify the rune—a burning crescent moon, the sacred symbol of the Fire Sorcerers of Ys. Pendaran had no doubt that he would find an identical mark tattooed over Boghos's heart; in return for the dark sorceries Khull-khuum had taught them, the Fire Sorcerers had long been servants of the Shadowking.

"Lord Varden, you will find the same tattoo over Ulger's

heart you find over your own High Sorcerer's," said Pendaran. Though Boghos's torso was covered by a silk robe, Varden could not help glancing at the High Sorcerer's chest. "When Ulger takes the city, who do you think Khull-khuum will present it to—you, or the one who has served him for three and half centuries?"

"Silence!" Khull-khuum crashed into another pillar.

The impact jarred the altar so badly that Boghos dragged a crooked line across Pendaran's brow, spoiling the rune. The High Sorcerer cursed—but so softly that even Pendaran barely heard it—then wiped the symbol off to begin again.

Pendaran smirked at the outburst, then continued to speak to Varden. "You have nothing to fear from Khull-khuum, Keeplord." He glanced toward the shadowy portal that Boghos's spell had opened in the temple wall. "You can walk outside and call your guards. The Shadowking can't stop you—but if you free him, your city will belong to Ulger."

Varden glanced toward the door.

"Do not even think of defying me!" This time Khull-khuum managed to restrain himself from slamming into the pillars and ruining another of Boghos's runes.

"Go ahead," said Pendaran. "If the Shadowsop could stop you, would I still be talking?"

"Khull-khuum will be free sooner or later," said Boghos. The High Sorcerer did not even look up, so confident was he of his control over the weak-willed Keeplord. "Even if your bodyguards kill me, there is still Ulger to contend with—and he will free Khull-khuum after he conquers the city."

"I have a long memory," said Khull-khuum. "I reward those who aid me—and punish those who do not."

Varden looked away from the shadow portal and continued to hold the sorcerer's head. Boghos lifted his brush and, with a smug grin, began to paint the Lost Circle of Atlantis on Pendaran's cheek.

"Look at how Boghos is smirking, Varden," said Pendaran. "He's played you like a puppet all your life, and he's doing it still. Are you so stupid you don't see that everything depends on you?"

"What can I do?" Varden asked. "I've already proven I can't stop Ulger."

"But there is one who can," Pendaran retorted. "You saw him at the gate—"

"Silence him!" Khull-khuum ordered.

Boghos slapped his hand over Pendaran's mouth—then cried out in pain as the little sorcerer caught two fingers between his jaws and clamped down, grinding his tusks back and forth. His mouth filled with blood, then he felt the satisfying crunch of bone. The High Sorcerer jerked his arm free and stumbled away, holding his hand and pale with pain.

Pendaran spit out two fingers, then winked at Varden. "You see? What are they frightened of?"

Boghos rushed back to the altar clutching his dagger in his good hand. Pendaran barely had time to pull his arms up before the knife arced down at his chest; it sliced across the rope binding his wrists together, then crossed the cord between the shadow manacles and snapped in two.

Something jagged and cold scraped past a rib low on Pendaran's chest, but he paid it no attention and rolled off the altar. He landed in a heap, driving the broken dagger deeper into his torso, and found himself facing Varden instead of his attacker. He cursed, then began to work his wrists back and forth. Boghos's dagger had done nothing to Khull-khuum's shadow manacles, of course, but it had slashed into the hemp rope that bound his wrists together.

"Varden! What are you waiting for?" Pendaran's breath whistled from his chest wound, making it hard to speak. "Go!"

The Keeplord, as pliant as ever, turned toward the dull oval on the opposite wall. Khull-khuum slammed into his imprisoning pillars, and the floor bucked like a horse, sweeping Varden's legs out from beneath him. The Keeplord landed hard and rolled once, then scrambled to his feet.

"Guards!" Varden started toward the exit. "Guards!"

Pendaran gave a last, savage twist and finally broke the frayed rope between his wrists. Boghos came rushing around the altar and raced after Varden.

"Boghos, forget that one!" commanded Khull-khuum. "Close the portal. We will finish with Wahooka first."

Varden stopped short at the mention of Pendaran's other name. "Wahooka?" The Keeplord spun around to stare at the little sorcerer, then gasped, "The Trickster?"

"What's in a name?" Pendaran cried. "Go!"

"And be your fool?" The Keeplord stayed where he was, shaking his head. "I know your tricks, Wahooka. Do not think you can dupe me!"

Pendaran's voice grew angry and mocking. "I wouldn't dream of it—I prefer a challenge."

Boghos stopped beside the Keeplord. "You have made a wise decision, Lord Varden." The High Sorcerer used his good hand to take Varden's arm and start back toward the altar. "The Shadowking would have been most displeased."

Pendaran plucked the dagger blade from his chest. His breath wheezed in and out through the hole, but the wound did not bleed, and he felt no discomfort. He began to saw at his ankle ropes with the broken blade, determined to be as mobile as possible when the Keeplord's bodyguards came rushing in—and then the first battle cries drifted in from the street outside.

Cassius's timing was as miserable as ever.

Boghos's eyes flashed toward the altar, where his rune staff lay on the floor behind Pendaran. Khull-khuum slammed himself against his pillars again and roared for his servant to seal the portal, but the command came an instant too late. Even as Boghos rushed to obey, Pendaran scrambled to his feet and snatched the High Sorcerer's staff away from the altar.

"No!" Boghos sprang forward, his mangled hand flinging blood in every direction. "Put that down!"

Pendaran ducked around behind the altar. Behind him, Khull-khuum went wild, hurtling his shadowy sphere against the pillars so ferociously that both sorcerers and the

Keeplord were thrown from their feet. A deafening rumble filled the temple, and from outside came the sound of crashing stone and howling men and splintering streets.

As Pendaran bounced across the floor, he turned the rune staff over in his hands, studying the symbols etched into its faces—no easy task, what with his head flopping about like the ball at the end of a morningstar. Although the shadow manacles denied him the use of his own sorcery, the runes' power came from the magical energy—the mana—stored within the staff itself. If the sorcerer could find the appropriate symbol and speak its name aloud, he would dissolve the manacles.

He had just discovered one possibility when Boghos crawled around one side of the altar and Varden came around the other. The Shadowking's earthquake was pummeling both men as mercilessly as it was Pendaran, flinging them a foot into the air and slamming them back to the floor on their faces and flanks.

Pendaran pointed the rune staff at his shadow manacles. "Shadow open!"

The altar's side panel fell open, opening a bloody gash along the back of Varden's head and revealing a sacrificial dagger with a blade of wavering shadow. The manacles remained cuffed to Pendaran's ankle and wrist.

Boghos lunged forward, reaching for his staff. "Give me that!"

Pendaran jerked the rune staff out of reach. Seeing that he would have no more chances to try its magic, he cocked his arms back to swing.

"No!" Boghos raised his injured hand to block the stroke.

Pendaran stopped and met the High Sorcerer's gaze. "What will you give me?" he asked. "Do you have any nice jewels?"

Boghos frowned, confused. "What?"

"No?" Pendaran shrugged, then kicked the High Sorcerer's arm out of the way. "Too bad."

He slammed the staff into the corner of the altar. The rod snapped with a thunderous crack, and the temple burst into silver brilliance. Raw, sizzling mana flooded the room, hurling Boghos in one direction and Varden in the other and Pendaran in yet a third. Pendaran's vision went white and his entire body began to prickle, then he slammed into a barrier at once unyielding and cushioning—the mystic enclosure that kept Khull-khuum's sphere in place. The sorcerer's wounds filled with acid anguish, and he slumped to the floor, too dazed and pained to move.

Slowly, Pendaran's vision cleared, and the ringing in his ears began to clear. He felt something cold and wispy around his brow, throat, and chest, holding him in place as firmly as any set of chains. When he lowered his eyes, the sorcerer found himself lodged inside a shimmering wall of force, held in place by black tentacles of shadow.

"Boghos!" Khull-khuum commanded. "Stop lying about. There is still time to finish!"

It took Pendaran a moment to understand what was happening. So great was Khull-khuum's power that he had to be imprisoned inside two prisons: the wispy orb of shadow bouncing around inside the pillars, and the pillars themselves, which were the corner posts of a mystic fence through which only a being wearing the appropriate symbols could pass. With two of the four sigils painted on his face, Pendaran had been blasted halfway into the barrier holding Khull-khuum's sphere. When all four runes were finished, the sorcerer would pass completely through. Hampered as he was by Boghos's shadow manacles, he would be unable to prevent the Shadowking from changing places with him; he would be absorbed into the prison orb, and Khull-khuum would escape.

Boghos staggered into view, rune brush in his good hand. The High Sorcerer's hair was completely gone—eyebrows, lashes, beard, everything—and his skin had turned white and papery. Though he looked three decades younger, he moved with the creaky awkwardness of an old man, and his cloak had been seared away, revealing the tattoo that Pendaran had expected to find over his heart all along: the Burning Moon of the Fire Sorcerers of Ys.

Now that Khull-khuum had stopped bouncing around off

the pillars, the battle sounds outside had grown more audible. The sorcerer could hear scuffling feet and grunting men just beyond the portal—and also the clanging of dwarven axes and the rasping growls of his enkavs.

Boghos dipped his brush in a pool of spilled ink, then knelt in front of Pendaran. The sorcerer bit back the urge to kick at the rune brush or call for help, knowing that Khull-khuum would be prepared to counter either tactic.

"My compliments, Shadowking," said Pendaran, trying to think of a way to distract his captor. "You have made the best of an unexpected boon."

"Hardly unexpected, Wahooka," rumbled the Shadowking. "You have been the prize from the start. For five centuries have I waited to trade places with you."

"Truly? I am flattered." Pendaran did not resist as Boghos painted the third rune, the Cross of Life and Death, on his cheek. "So much trouble for a small gem."

"Small, but predictable—and therein lies your value," said Khull-khuum. "Ever have you meddled in Stonekeep's affairs. To draw you out, I had only to threaten the city."

The truth of this was more than Pendaran cared to admit. "Predictable?" He brought a knee up, slamming it into Boghos's chin. "Predict this!"

Taken off guard, Khull-khuum could not react fast enough to stop the blow. Boghos's head snapped back, and Pendaran twisted his hips around, swinging one leg behind the High Sorcerer's neck and locking him in a scissors hold.

"Cassius! Get in—"

Pendaran's cry was drowned out by Khull-khuum's booming voice. "Varden!"

The Keeplord staggered into view, looking as pale and hairless as Boghos. He reluctantly grabbed a leg and began to pull, and that is when the first bodyguard came tumbling through portal. The man hit the floor with clamorous crash and lay there groaning, holding his hands to a bloody split in his armor.

Boghos slipped free of Pendaran's legs, then pinned the little sorcerer's knees to the floor and shoved Varden down to hold them in place. He dipped his rune brush in the ink spilled on the altar, saying, "We still have time!"

The stout figure of Skagi Reist stepped through the portal and stood squinting into the gloomy chamber, his axe blade dripping blood. Boghos knelt and touched his rune brush to Pendaran's chin. The little sorcerer started to call out, then felt one of Khull-khuum's shadowy tentacles snaking toward his mouth. He clamped his jaw shut and kicked his heels against the floor, desperately trying to draw the dwarf's attention.

Skagi cocked his head, then finally squinted in Pendaran's direction. "Pendaran?"

Pendaran slapped the flat of his foot against the floor, silently cursing the entire dwarven race for the idiots they were. He felt himself sinking deeper into Khull-khuum's grasp as Boghos traced the ankh's stem down his chin, but he did not dare cry out. He could still feel the tentacle lurking at the corner of his mouth, ready to silence him the instant he tried to speak, and there was something he would need to warn Cassius about.

At last, Skagi's eyes grew accustomed to the gloom. "In here!" he called, rushing across the room.

Boghos made the mistake of glancing back before he had completed the fourth symbol, and that was all the time Skagi's axe needed to come tumbling through the air and bury itself in his back. The High Sorcerer let the rune brush slip from his hand, then gasped once and lurched forward into Pendaran's chest.

"Finish!" Khull-khuum boomed. He began to tug at Pendaran, trying in vain to pull the sorcerer through the mystic barrier. "Rise, Boghos, I command you!"

Varden reached for rune brush—then cried out in pain when Skagi Reist's hobnailed boot came down on his wrist. "Perhaps you'd best leave it lay, Keeplord. We need to figure out what's happening here."

Cassius rushed into the chamber, burning the shadow out of the portal as he carried the Sun Sword through. At once, the gloom vanished from the room, and Keeplord Varden looked toward the source of the light. When he saw the Traitor Duke coming toward him, he cried out in fear, then tore his hand from beneath Skagi's boot and scrambled into a dim corner. With Khull-khuum still trying to pull him through the mystic barrier, Pendaran could do little more than kick his feet against the floor.

Cassius rushed over at once, raising the Sun Sword to strike.

"No!" Pendaran screeched. "You'll free—"

The warning was cut short as Khull-khuum's tentacle shot down the sorcerer's throat. Cassius continued forward with the glowing blade raised, and it looked as though he would strike despite the warning. Pendaran looked away, unable to bear the thought of what would happen when the Sun Sword's brilliance sundered Khull-khuum's shadowy prison.

The blow never came. Khull-khuum simply continued to pull, though he certainly knew as well as Pendaran that it was impossible to break the mystic barrier without the proper runes. When the sorcerer finally looked back, Cassius was standing above him, scowling in confusion and staring at the black tentacles wrapped around Pendaran's chest.

The sorcerer raised his manacled leg.

Cassius's eyes lit in understanding. He touched the tip of the glowing blade to the shadowy cuff on Pendaran's ankle, and the manacles fell open. For a moment nothing else happened. The duke frowned—then Pendaran caught his eye and glanced down at the wheezing hole in his side.

Cassius's gaze followed, and then the sorcerer used his magic.

"That's the last time I count on you for a rescue!" cried Pendaran's wound. "Do you know how long I've been waiting?"

Cassius stood beside the black altar in the Temple of Shadow, holding the Sun Sword aloft while Skagi used a wet thumb to wipe the runes off Pendaran's face. Khull-khuum's dark orb continued to hover behind the little sorcerer, his wispy tentacles still struggling to pull his quarry through the mystic barrier. In his fury, the Shadowking did not seem to care that he was attempting the impossible—and that even if he somehow succeeded, Pendaran now had full use of his sorcery and might well defeat him in the ensuing battle.

Skagi touched his wet thumb to the last rune and began to rub. The mystic barrier instantly discharged Pendaran, severing the Shadowking's tenuous hold. Khull-khuum went mad, crashing from one corner to another, rocking the temple so violently that black, glassy shards began to rain down from the ceiling. Through the portal came panicked screams of those outside and the roar of walls tumbling into the streets.

Skagi pulled Pendaran to his feet and turned toward the exit. "Let's get out of here!" He blanched as he saw Pendaran's half-severed head loll forward.

"Just like a dwarf to leave the job half-finished!"

Pendaran jerked free and lurched across the bucking floor to brace himself against the altar, then reached up and began to wipe the dirt and gravel from his wound. The sight sent a shiver down Cassius's spine. He had seen plenty of gruesome injuries during the last few weeks, but there was something lurid about seeing the victim of a decapitation rub the stump of his own neck.

"Are you just going to stand there and gawk?" Pendaran demanded, eyeing Cassius from his capsized head. "Come here and hold my head in place."

The duke staggered around behind Pendaran and pulled the sorcerer's head up by the hair.

"Is it straight?" Pendaran demanded.

"More or—" The floor jumped beneath his feet. "Less."

At once, the two edges of the wound fused, leaving only a smooth red line to indicate Pendaran's neck had ever been severed. Unfortunately, a slight kink in the spine betrayed the difficulty of trying to align both halves in the middle of an earthquake.

Pendaran rolled his head in a circle, then grimaced painfully. "Liar."

Cassius started to say something in his own defense, but was interrupted when Brenna rushed into the quaking temple.

"Cassius, you'll never believe who's here!"

Before the duke could ask, the High Lords Fiske and Belden stumbled through the portal behind her, still wearing their scorched battle armor. He sank into a fighting stance, raising the Sun Sword to a middle guard, and only then did he realize they had brought no guards.

The Lords braced themselves just inside the door, as astonished at the scene before them as Cassius was at seeing them. They kept glancing from the Keeplord, cowering wild-eyed in the corner, to Boghos's body to Khullkhuum's black orb, careening madly between the magic pillars.

To everyone's surprise, it was Keeplord Varden who

spoke first. "Fiske, Belden—call your men!" He gathered himself up and staggered across the floor toward the High Lords, waving a hand at Cassius and Pendaran. "Those traitors are trying to free Khull-khuum!"

This was too much for Cassius. Without saying a word, he stepped away from the altar and started after the Keeplord.

Skagi leapt after him, grabbing the duke's arm and jerking him to a stop. "Can't let you do that, Cassius. Varden may be a coward and a liar, but he has sworn the Oath of Stonekeep. I'm obliged to defend him—to the death if need be."

"No matter," said Lord Belden. He cast a distasteful glance over his shoulder at the Keeplord. "Varden will not be Keeplord much longer."

Varden's eyes widened at this.

"The Council has agreed to vote Varden out." Lord Belden started across the floor toward Cassius, almost shouting to make himself heard above Khull-khuum's earthshaking fury. "And we are prepared to pardon the charges against you and your sorcerer, good Duke."

"What?" gasped Pendaran. "Wait—I want to hear this clearly."

The Trickster turned toward Khull-khuum, then traced a square in the air, moving his finger from one broken pillar to the next. When that was done, he spread his arms wide, hands turned inward as though holding a large box. He slowly brought his palms together, stopping when they were a few inches apart. The mystic barrier enclosing the Shadowking's sphere narrowed to the same width. The dark orb shrank accordingly, though it seemed to gather in speed what it lost in size, and the earthquakes continued unabated.

Keeplord Varden took advantage of the distraction to quietly slip out of the temple. Cassius made no effort to go after him. During the past weeks he had learned enough about dwarves to take Skagi at his word, and his thirst for vengeance was not so great that he would take it over a friend's body.

Pendaran spread his arms and repeated his earlier gesture

in two more directions, front to back, then top to bottom. When he finished, Khull-khuum's prison had shrunk to the size of a lark cage, and the dark orb itself had become a web of inky black streaks flashing about inside. The temple—and the city outside—continued to shake. If anything, the crash and rumble of the Dark One's fury had intensified, bucking the floor so violently that the sorcerer fell twice as he staggered over to the bouncing box.

After two tries, Pendaran managed to catch the container between his palms and lift it off the floor. The temple stopped shaking at once, and the roar outside gradually faded to astonished silence.

"Much better." Grasping the box securely in both hands, Pendaran returned to the middle of the chamber and passed the container to Skagi. "You dwarves are big on duty. Hold this."

The dwarf stared wide-eyed at the box in his hands. "But—"

"And whatever you do, don't drop him," Pendaran added. "At that size, Khull-khuum would split the Grand Heights clear down to your wormholes."

Skagi paled from the crown of his bald head to the nub of his round nose, and he squeezed the box so hard his knuckles turned white.

Pendaran turned back to the High Lords. "Now, what's this about a pardon?"

"If Cassius will lead the defense of Stonekeep," explained Lord Belden—he and Fiske could not take their eyes off the box in Skagi's hands—"your crimes against the Council would be forgiven."

"You seem to have reached this decision rather quickly," observed Pendaran. "There must be some urgency."

Fiske cast a questioning glance at his fellow lord, who answered with a short nod.

"Ulger's hordes are at the North Gate," said Fiske. "As we speak, they are rolling their siege towers forward to storm the walls."

Pendaran turned to Cassius with a smug grin, but the

duke did not share the sorcerer's delight at how things had worked out. He glared at Fiske and Belden in equal measure, then shook his head in disgust.

"You come to me to save your mansions on the hill?" He felt all the hopelessness and desperation of the last six weeks raging up inside him, transforming itself into a bitter fury, the likes of which he had experienced only when Melwas's looters had slain his father. "Why should I? The Council did nothing to save Kural. It did nothing to aid my father, except send the butcher who murdered him!"

The High Lords blanched at his anger, but Lord Fiske managed to collect himself enough to say, "Should you prove successful, your family lands would be completely restored—"

"No."

The High Lords reddened and glanced at each other anxiously, but it was Brenna who appeared most surprised.

"No?" She caught Cassius by the arm. "What do you mean, 'no'?"

"The duke knows what he is doing, child," said Pendaran. He looked to the councillors. "For saving a realm, surely he deserves a realm."

The High Lords' jaws dropped, and Lord Fiske said, "I have seen for myself what a valiant fighter Cassius is, but he hardly has the experience to sit on the Council."

"It is not a seat on the Council that he wants," said Pendaran. "You must think bigger."

A distant roar began to echo through the portal. It was not the sound of an earthquake or a battle, but of thousands of yelling voices. Not bothering to excuse himself, Cassius started toward the exit to investigate.

"Wait." Lord Fiske caught Cassius by the arm, then turned to Belden, then said, "I suppose we could make him the next Keeplord."

"What?" Skagi was so astonished that he nearly dropped Khull-khuum's box. "But the Keeplord must be descended from the Line of Drake!"

"Ulger is Drake's grandson." Pendaran smirked. "Perhaps the Council would prefer him?"

The narrow-eyed looks the High Lords shot at the sorcerer made clear what they thought of his humor.

"If we go back far enough," said Lord Belden, "I am sure we can find Drake blood somewhere in Cassius's ancestry."

"What say you, Cassius?" Fiske continued to hold his arm. "When you came before the Council, I know you were . . . frustrated with our deliberations. As Keeplord, you would have the power to change our ways."

Cassius studied the High Lord, tempted. If he could defeat Ulger—and that was a big if—he might be able to correct the abuses that had plagued his father. He could reduce taxes, stop the outflow of wealth from the provinces, relieve the border lords of the burden of defending the realm's frontiers, arrange matters so that Stonekeep's blessings flowed down to the peasants instead of being squandered by a few noble families in unbelievable displays of bad taste.

As Cassius contemplated these matters, the roar outside grew loud enough that he became aware of a two-syllable rhythm. Footsteps began to clatter past the exit toward the outer edges of the Grand Heights.

"Cassius, we are running out of time," said Lord Belden. "If it is Varden you are worried about, there is no need. The Council will take care of him."

Cassius saw with sudden clarity what life would be like as Keeplord: an endless cycle of convenient alliances and cold betrayals, of halfhearted agreements and compromises of necessity. In the company of such jackals, he would be lucky to survive a year. He pulled his arm free of Fiske's grasp.

"You can save your own mansions. The last thing I want is to be your Keeplord."

He turned to leave, but Pendaran was instantly in front of him. "You're mad! Do you know how hard I've worked to make this happen?"

Cassius shrugged, then glanced at the High Lords. "I wouldn't lower myself to sit on their Council."

"Lower yourself?" Belden fumed. "What would you be, our king?"

Cassius ignored the man's sarcasm and shook his head. "If you want my help, you'll have to do better than that."

The Traitor Duke stepped around Pendaran and into the portal. As he passed through, he heard Lord Belden complaining, "What's he want? I don't understand."

"Councillor, I think you do understand," said Pendaran. "And I suggest you think about it."

Outside, the strange two-syllable roar that Cassius had noticed earlier grew louder and more distinct, though it was still too muffled to understand. The duke found his enkavs packed along one side of the narrow street, standing amidst piles of rubble that had once been the curving frieze atop Safrinni's Amphitheater. Their heads were pirouetting back and forth, watching curiously as armored dwarves and poorly armed humans streamed down the street. The procession did not seem panicked so much as excited, though no one showed Varden's dead bodyguards the respect of not walking on their corpses.

As soon Cassius's enkav standard-bearer saw him, it raised the Standing Lion banner and cried, "Sword!"

"Sword!" answered the other enkavs.

Cassius raised the Sun Sword and waved it in response, and that was when a passerby stopped and caught him by the shoulder.

"You'd better come, milord!" said the man. Though he carried nothing more than a forester's axe, the blood on the blade suggested he was hardly shy of battle. "They're calling for you!"

"What?"

A dwarf stopped beside the first man, smiling broadly. "Come along. You'll see."

As Cassius stepped into the procession, men and dwarves alike seemed to want to be near. They closed in around him, clasping his free hand or clapping him on the shoulder, uttering words of encouragement and vowing to stand with him to the death. The enkavs, as confused as the duke, merged into the torrent of flesh, and soon they were all streaming down the narrow lane together. The procession curved around the base of Safrinni's Amphitheater and turned down a short alley, where it entered a slender stone tower barely large enough to enclose the spiral staircase inside. Cassius followed the line up the winding stairs, then emerged onto the narrow ramparts of a small fortified wall.

The duke found himself on the rim of the Grand Heights, looking westward over Stonekeep. In that direction, the city appeared peaceful and virtually abandoned, with narrow streets zigging past shuttered buildings and through empty plazas. The only beings he could see were a handful of distant sentries, pacing along the ramparts of the city's great wall.

The press of the crowd forced Cassius onward. The roaring below grew clear enough to understand: *Ca-shus-Ca-shus-Ca-shus* . . . They were shouting his name. He began to see men and women running through the streets fifty feet below, carrying makeshift weapons and moving in the general direction of Drake's Way. The dwarves had also sent several more companies up from the depths beneath Stonekeep, though these were marching northward in orderly columns.

As the ramparts curved around to the north side of the Grand Heights, Cassius saw the first siege tower in the distance. It was a mammoth structure of tree-length logs, draped with hides and rocking from side to side as it rolled forward over uneven ground. The uppermost level was packed with ogare archers, so huge that he could identify their gangly-armed figures from a over a mile away. The middle level had a long bridge sticking out like a tongue; the dark recess behind it bristled with tiny points that could only be sharga halberds. The lower level was hidden from view behind a screen of rough-hewn planks, but Cassius could see a dark fan of eager invaders marching along behind it, ready to clamber up the ladders inside and cross into Stonekeep.

Cassius counted ten more siege towers rolling toward the city's outer wall, most so close that Stonekeep's defenders were already trading arrows with the ogares. To his surprise, it looked as though the humans on the ramparts might repel the assaults. A hundred armored soldiers stood clustered in front of each siege tower, hiding behind the merlons and ready to fight the instant the bridges touched the wall.

The sight made Cassius uneasy. He had learned in Kural that Ulger's first blow was seldom the lethal one, and he soon saw that the Usurper had not changed tactics. As the duke approached the Cliff Road Gatehouse, which faced due north along Drake's Way, he noticed Ulger's siege towers avoiding the North Gate. Stonekeep's defenders, anxious to prevent their foes from gaining the top of the outer wall, were streaming along the ramparts toward the siege towers, leaving the gate itself vulnerable to a wedge of invaders advancing straight down North Road.

Cassius pushed his way through a mass of human and dwarven warriors to look down from the wall. The road below angled down the face of the Grand Heights to an unruly mob armed with tools and heirloom weapons. While most of the volunteers had the tattered look of refugees, there were also many residents from the city, better fed and dressed in something other than rags.

The crowd quickly noticed the Sun Sword's glowing blade and realized Cassius was above them. Their chant slowly became a cheer, which only grew louder and more clamorous as the bewildered enkavs also began to gather along the wall. The duke raised his arms and spread them wide, and the cheer became a roar. He could feel the mob's excitement coursing through him, filling him with faith and strength.

Still, as much as he enjoyed their adulation, he did not quite fathom it. "I don't understand," he said, to nobody in particular. "Why are they calling to me?"

"Word has been spreading of your victory at the North Gate," said a dwarf next to Cassius. The warrior's battered shield bore the insignia of the Brass Axe. "They think you can save the city."

Cassius eyed the gathering crowd, wondering why they had all chosen to trust their lives to him—yet feeling, somehow, that their faith was well placed. Had he not driven Ulger back once already? His enkavs would prove even more formidable now that they understood fighting, and no one knew the Usurper's tactics better than he did. But most importantly, Cassius had the Sun Sword.

"Maybe I can save Stonekeep at that," said the duke. He looked back toward the North Road, where the gate guards continued to stream from their post as Ulger's wedge of troops advanced toward them. "But not if we give up the gate. What are those fools doing?"

The dwarf squinted toward the gate. "Going to where they are most needed, I imagine."

"They are needed at their posts." Cassius pointed at the invaders on North Road. "Do they think a barred gate alone will stop that?"

The dwarf scowled and continued to squint at the gate. "What?"

"That." Cassius used his finger to outline the wedge-shaped throng. "There must be thousands."

"He can't see them," said Pendaran, pushing his way to Cassius's side. "He's not holding the Sun Sword."

"Can't see what?" asked Brenna.

She and Skagi followed close behind Pendaran, the dwarf clutching Khull-khuum's prison to his chest like a jewel box.

Cassius turned to Pendaran. "You're telling me that you and I are the only ones who see what's coming down the road?"

"I am afraid so." Being too short to see comfortably, Pendaran pulled himself up into the crenature gap and stood staring out at the North Road. After a moment he let out a low whistle and said, "Oh, my."

The air shimmered briefly, and Cassius found himself studying his enemies on the North Road as though from a distance of a hundred paces. The wedge contained close to ten thousand invaders, mostly throgs and shargas arrayed in alternating ranks—but that was not what dismayed the duke. Leading the formation was a lanky, shadow-caped man-thing in ebony armor and an obsidian crown.

"Ulger!" Cassius exclaimed softly.

"Yes—better than I thought." Pendaran cackled.

"Better? I don't see anything better about that!" Cassius gestured toward the disaster looming at the North Gate.

The wizard gave a sly smile. "I do—your little scheme just might work after all." He glanced in the direction of the Temple of Shadow, then lowered his voice so that Cassius could barely hear him. "When Ulger enters the city, the Council will come begging to make you emperor."

"Emperor?" Brenna hissed. "What are you talking about?"

"You were there," Pendaran said. "You heard him."

Brenna frowned and looked to the duke. "What's he talking about, Cassius?"

"It's the only way, Brenna," said Cassius. "I have seen how the Council works—how the High Lords keep the Keeplord weak and connive against each other and never think of the good of the realm. If I am going to change Stonekeep, I will have to be as far above them as a master above his dog."

"Change Stonekeep?" Brenna gasped. "Cassius, what has gotten into you?"

"It has to been done, Brenna." As Cassius spoke, he raised the Sun Sword into the air and drew a thunderous cheer from the crowd below. "For them."

Brenna cast a doubtful glance over the wall. "If Ulger gets into the city, there won't be any *them*," she whispered. "He'll trap them against the cliffs and slaughter them all."

Pendaran shrugged. "Every crown has its cost."

"A crown bought at that price is worthless." Cassius stepped away from the wall and started for the stairs. "I'm going to stop Ulger—outside the city."

Pendaran jumped down and caught Cassius by the arm. "Don't be a country moron! The High Lords haven't conceded to anything. You must have their agreement before you act. They won't show any gratitude after you save Stonekeep . . . I know!"

Cassius whirled on Pendaran and glared at him a long time. When the sorcerer finally released his arm, Cassius said, ''You've already made me party to one atrocity in the Faerie Realm. Don't try such a thing again.''

Pendaran returned the glare with a sneer as cold as Khullkhuum's heart. ''Do you think you can threaten me, boy?'' The sorcerer shook his head in mock pity. ''Already, the Sun Sword is making you foolish.''

The attack started with a booming crack that did not stop, then a long arrow of dust billowed up from plains outside Stonekeep, slowly advancing down North Road toward the great gatehouse. The few defenders within the tower poured out the rampart doors and fled along the wall in both directions, gawking out over the empty plain and shaking their heads.

Cassius and Pendaran could see nothing more from their post, a cramped lamp chamber high inside Calvar's Arch. They were crouching on opposite sides of a huge glass lantern, peering north along Drake's Way through a small star-shaped portal. Everything in the room was covered with soot, including Cassius and the sorcerer. The grime seemed not to bother Pendaran, but the acrid stench of the place burned the duke's nostrils and made his throat close up. Skagi and Brenna were not with them. The dwarf had been ordered to stay at the Cliff Road Gate and safeguard Khull-khuum's prison. If worse came to worse, he was to flee to the farthest corner of the world and hide the box in the deepest, loneliest cavern on earth. Brenna had been sent to fetch Crusher; the duke did not really expect the errand to keep her out of the battle, but he hoped it might delay her long enough to avoid the initial shock.

The enkavs stood a quarter mile ahead, spread across the avenue just inside the North Gate. The human volunteers were not so easy to find, concealed as they were behind buildings along both sides of Drake's Way. When the enemy hordes broke through, the enkavs were to give ground slowly, retreating down the boulevard toward the great arch. Once Ulger was trapped inside the city, Cassius would unsheathe the Sun Sword and show its blade through the star portal atop Calvar's Arch. The volunteers, along with a few seasoned dwarf companies, would rush in from both flanks and destroy the Usurper's horde. Cassius and Pendaran would take care of the dark king himself.

The dust cloud continued to advance down the North Road, filling the air with a sharp crackling as loud as it was interminable. Cassius tried to guess what kind of spell was causing the sound, and failed. Opening a chasm beneath the gatehouse would only make it more difficult for Ulger's hordes to enter the city, while a boulder huge enough to smash the fortifications would get stuck in the rubble and bar the entrance itself.

Cassius grasped the hilt of the sheathed Sun Sword and peered northward. A few ranks of dark, nebulous shapes appeared inside the dust cloud, but most of Ulger's strike force was already hidden behind the bulk of the high gatehouse. He could see nothing at all of the magic that caused the loud cracking. The duke's brow began to sweat, washing soot into his eyes. He wiped his filthy sleeve across his forehead and succeeded only in making the situation worse.

Finally, he released the hilt of the Sun Sword and asked, "Pendaran, what's going on out there?"

"You are asking me—the abominator?" The sorcerer's tone was as bitter as his eyes were dark. "If you are so worried, you should have listened to me and held your attack."

"And buy my crown with the blood of innocents? I will be an emperor of the people or nothing at all."

Pendaran shook his head disparagingly. "This is why you should return the Sun Sword to me." The sorcerer laid his palm out, as though actually expecting Cassius to place the weapon in his hand. "With a weapon of power, you think you don't have to be ruthless. You think you can rule without the burden of guilt."

"Give you the sword? So *you* can be emperor?" Cassius eyed the golden serpents twined about the weapon's hilt. "I think it will be better for Stonekeep if I keep it."

"No." Pendaran continued to extend his hand. "The sword will overpower you. I see it happening already."

"I don't." Cassius pulled the weapon around to his side, where he would have more time to react if the sorcerer tried to snatch it from him. "The Sun Sword has some magic to it, I'll grant you—but it isn't going to overpower me."

"Isn't it?" Pendaran reluctantly lowered his hand, then glanced toward the volunteers outside. "So you are accustomed to swarms of people flocking to your side? This happened to you often in Kural?"

"Those people are fighting for their lives, not flocking to my side."

Pendaran shrugged dismissively. "Men are always fighting for their lives. When someone unites them, that is power." The sorcerer gave him a tusky sneer. "And if you do not know how to use power, it will use you."

"Then you have nothing to worry about." Cassius looked out the window. "The High Lords have already shown me how not to use power, and knowing what should not be done is the hardest part of learning anything."

Pendaran looked doubtful, but said nothing, and the crackling outside built to a banging crescendo. A roiling plume of dust shot up from the other side of the gatehouse, obscuring everything behind it and robbing the attack of all sense of motion. Something brown, huge, and ribbonlike rose up inside the billowing dust cloud, and Cassius recognized it a moment later as the North Road, arching up like the tail of a cracking whip.

An instant later the gatehouse blossomed into rubble and billowed briefly up above the walls. Another dust column shot skyward, drawing a gray curtain across the gateway, and Calvar's Arch shook with the fury of shattered stones crashing back to earth. The enkavs stood awestruck before the devastation, and there was a moment of peace as the haze began to dissipate and the growl of settling stones faded to a whisper.

Then the rubble started to clatter. The enkavs tensed and peered into the dust, their scales bristling and their claws flexed. The occasional chime of steel on stone echoed down the street, and the eerie chortling of the invaders' voices began to fill the air.

Cassius grasped the Sun Sword's hilt and suddenly saw the invaders, clambering over the rubble pile in a ragged wedge, a pair of gaunt galok overseers cursing and whipping them in an attempt to maintain their formation. They were advancing in alternating ranks, with the sword-wielding throgs in front and sharga halberders in the line behind. Being too smart to risk himself in the first wave, Ulger had withdrawn to someplace deeper in the formation.

The enkavs cocked their heads and stood waiting, for they could hear their foes but could not see them. When the first rank closed to within sword's reach, the galok commanders gave a strange, chuckling war cry. The wedge lunged ahead in a solid mass, sharga halberds pointed up to spear the enkavs' bellies, while throggish swords sliced down to cleave their collarbones.

Unable to see the attack coming, the enkavs made no attempt to defend themselves, filling the air with an angry chorus of lisps and hisses as the blows rained down. The entire first rank flinched and recoiled from the unexpected assault, but only a handful fell. Even their thin belly scales were sturdy enough to turn aside the weak halberd thrusts of shargas, while their tough shoulder armor nicked and chipped the brittle throg swords more often than the reverse.

Roused at last, the enkavs lashed out in blind fury, rending whatever their sharp talons touched—be it throat, skull, or breastplate. A hundred invaders fell in as many seconds, and in the next hundred seconds their casualties doubled.

The enkavs surged forward, slashing and kicking, felling throgs and shargas by the score.

"You said they understood," growled Pendaran. "If this goes on much longer, Ulger will never make it into the city."

"I told them to make it look good," Cassius replied, hoping the reptiles had not misunderstood how good.

A cramp formed in Cassius's forearm, and he realized he was clenching the Sun Sword tight enough to crack a walnut shell. He opened his hand, and the invaders vanished at once. Where before he had seen heaps of dead throgs and shargas, now he saw only jumbled stones, glistening and wet. Some of his enkavs appeared to be walking on air as they clambered forward over the corpses of their fallen enemies, claws slashing and ripping at no visible target. Often, they would recoil or stumble back for no apparent reason, then leap forward even more furiously, arms flailing madly until they found their unseen attacker and rent him into small pieces.

The enkavs were halfway through the demolished gateway when lightning bolts and fireballs began to rain down from atop a rubble pile, blasting the scaly warriors in the chest and hurtling them back into their own ranks. To Cassius's surprise, the reptiles simply picked themselves up and started wobbling up the pile toward their unseen attackers.

"Stupid lizards!" Pendaran growled. "Don't they know when to quit?"

Cassius grasped his sword hilt again and saw two galoks standing back-to-back, frantically waving their rune staffs at the approaching reptiles. Sometimes, on the second or third strike, a scaly warrior would burst into flames or go down with a smoking hole in its chest, but another enkav always clambered up to take its place.

The enkavs had almost reached the top of the rubble pile when one of the rune staffs ran out of mana and nothing happened after the galok gestured with it. The rune caster's ugly maw fell open, then it grasped the staff like a club and smashed it across a reptile's head.

The shaft snapped. The enkav caught its attacker in a sharp-taloned bear hug and squeezed until blood began to ooze from the victim's mouth. The galok threw its head back, screeching, then bared its fangs and ripped through the enkav's thick neck scales. The reptile mirrored the attack, and they fell together, locked in an embrace of gore and death.

The second galok fell an instant later, taken from behind by a flurry of flashing claws.

The enkavs surged past the rubble pile, pressing the throgs and shargas back toward the plain—and then a sheet of dancing shadow fanned out from the center of the invaders' line, striking the first rank of enkavs square in the midsection. Their voices rose in a single cry of fear and anguish, then abruptly fell silent as their bodies folded over backward, blood and gore spilling out from where the dark scythe had cut them open.

Before the remaining enkavs could react, another fan of darkness danced out, slaughtering the second rank. The throgs and shargas roared a chortling cheer and rushed forward to attack, driving their bewildered foes back onto Drake's Way. Only then did Cassius spy the spell's caster, a tall gaunt figure adorned in an obsidian crown and a cape of shadow, advancing at a walk while his army streamed past on both sides.

"There's Ulger." Cassius pointed toward the crowned figure.

"So I see," Pendaran replied. "He is not invisible, you know."

Cassius released the hilt of his Sun Sword and discovered that he could still see the Usurper and his hordes.

"He cannot cast one spell while he is focused on another. Even Ulger has his limits." Pendaran cast a sideways look at Cassius. "Remember that, young Duke—it is the difference between him and me."

"Your power has its limits as well—or I doubt we would be here."

Cassius looked outside to find the enkavs falling back toward Calvar's Arch. The reptiles were giving ground slowly, suffering few casualties and dealing many, just as the duke had instructed. Twice, when in the heat of battle they forgot their orders and began to drive the invaders back, Ulger spread his fingers and used his magic to cut them down by the rank. Each time the duke cringed and felt a queasy shame in his stomach; as fierce and fearless as the reptiles were, they were still his followers, and it made him feel guilty to use them in this way.

As the enkavs drew near the arch, Cassius caught glimpses of the volunteers along the side streets beginning to stir, checking their weapons and tightening whatever stray pieces of armor they had managed to find. The duke opened his purse and removed two big emeralds, then held them out to Pendaran.

"Here is your payment, sorcerer."

Pendaran snatched the stones from Cassius's hand, then asked, "You are sure you can do this?"

Cassius raised the Sun Sword. "I have this, don't I?"

Pendaran eyed the sword warily. "Place too much faith in that, and it will do more harm than good." He opened his cloak and pressed the emeralds into its lining, then looked back to Cassius. "The blows of Ulger's minions will not hurt you, but I can do nothing to protect you from the Usurper himself—and remember, do not look into his eyes. If you do, you are lost."

"With luck, I won't even see his face."

Cassius peered down at Drake's Way, which was packed with throgs and shargas from the base of Calvar's Arch back to the demolished gate. Ulger was standing just inside the city, at the foot of the rubble pile that had once been the gatehouse. Even if the trap worked as planned, some of the invaders behind him might escape back into the plain—but that would hardly matter if Cassius succeeded. He grasped his scabbard in one hand and the sword's hilt in the other, preparing to unsheathe the blade.

"And there is no need to ask about me, Cassius," said Pendaran, obviously disappointed Cassius had not. "I'll be fine. The likes of Ulger will never destroy me."

Cassius started to apologize for his thoughtlessness, then

thought better of it and simply smiled. "I knew that—you've certainly told me so often enough."

Pendaran almost scowled, then broke into a sheepish grin. "So you *do* listen."

Cassius answered with a half-serious nod, then squatted in front of the star-shaped portal and pulled the Sun Sword from his scabbard. A brilliant golden light filled the lamp chamber, and even before he thrust the glowing blade out into the sky, a tremendous roar arose from both sides of Drake's Way. The volunteers began to pour onto the boulevard from the side streets and alleys, pinning Ulger's horde in the jaws of a howling vise.

The throgs and shargas stopped in their tracks and spun around to meet the attacks, in their confusion tangling their weapons and disordering their neat formations. The enkavs renewed their assault, tearing into their foes with all the fury they had been stifling as they retreated toward Calvar's Arch.

Ulger raised his head, turning his dark gaze upon the arch. Cassius waited just long enough to glimpse the blue flames burning in the Usurper's hollow eye sockets, then looked away.

"He sees us."

Pendaran peered out one of the star portal's arms. "Go!" he called. "And don't go calling on Thera. She won't help you anyway."

Cassius stepped out into the air, seventy feet off the ground, and his stomach rose into his chest. He had a brief sensation of falling, then came down in the demolished gateway, standing amidst a throng of bewildered enemies. Though the landing was soft, his foot turned on the loose rubble, and jagged pain shot through his ankle. He stumbled forward and nearly cried out, but caught himself when he saw a gaunt, shadow-caped figure just two paces ahead, facing the opposite direction and pointing at Calvar's Arch.

The duke shouldered aside two stunned throgs and lunged forward, bringing the Sun Sword around in an overhead swing. A half-dozen throgs recovered their wits, sputtering in alarm and lashing out to stop him. In the same instant a blue bolt streaked from Ulger's finger toward Calvar's Arch, where Pendaran Tremayne was still peering out through the star portal.

Cassius continued his swing, watching the blade drop toward Ulger's obsidian crown as if time had slowed. Half a dozen throg swords struck his back. The blows drove the breath from his lungs and filled his head with an eerie thumping, but they opened no wounds and broke no bones. The Sun Sword came down across Ulger's shoulder, opening him to the breast and filling the air with the stench of rotten, scorched flesh.

Such a blow would have killed an ordinary man, but the Usurper only threw back his head and let out an earsplitting howl. The throgs rained more blows on Cassius and nearly drove him to his knees. Ulger took one plodding step toward the smoking ruin that had been Calvar's Arch and pulled himself off the searing blade the duke had buried in his torso.

Determined to strike again before his foe could turn on him, Cassius raised the Sun Sword and hobbled forward. He did not even realize Ulger's foot had moved until he felt it slam into his chest, lifting him off his feet and launching him into the throgs who had been attacking him from behind. They all went down together, and in the next instant his world became a tangle of flailing limbs and dark blades.

Still protected by Pendaran's magic, Cassius ignored the assaults and concentrated on one thing: keeping hold of the Sun Sword. He slashed back and forth, jabbed the tip forward, whipped the blade around blindly above his head. His attackers screeched and bled and crawled away or died, leaving the rocks slick with gore and the air bitter with the reek of charred flesh. The duke gathered up his aching body and scrambled to his feet.

Cassius found himself surrounded by a ragged circle of shargas and throgs, all standing just beyond his sword's reach. The rubble pile was high enough to afford a view of his refugee volunteers, each group hacking their way toward the center of Drake's Way. The enkavs were slashing their way up the street at a near sprint, cutting foes down as though they were weeds. To the duke's dismay, Brenna the Swift was leading the charge, a tiny figure riding a big horse, her arm whirling madly as she whipped her small saber back and forth, felling throgs as rapidly as any enkav.

The circle of throgs opened in front of Cassius, and Ulger came forward. "Assassin!"

The Usurper's ebony breastplate was as finely wrought as the best dwarven plate, save that it was shaped more like a skeleton than a suit of armor, with sternum, ribs, and a sunken abdominal cavity. His injured shoulder was dangling uselessly at his side, separated from his torso by a chasm of scorched decay. Cassius did not raise his eyes any higher, heeding Pendaran's warning not to meet Ulger's gaze—and recalling from the battle at Shadow Gorge the chilling weakness he would suffer if he did.

"Assassin, who is helping you?" Ulger continued to come closer, his good hand clenching a long sword with a blade of wavering darkness. "Speak, and you will suffer less."

A terrific clatter arose at the base of the rubble pile as throgs and shargas began to stream past, chortling in fear as they fled Brenna and the enkavs. Cassius cursed the girl and blessed her in the same breath—she had no business trying to save him from Ulger, but she was proving a far more reliable ally than Pendaran, who was so late arriving from Calvar's Arch that Cassius was beginning to fear the little sorcerer had not escaped.

"Who gave you the Sun Sword?" Ulger demanded. "Thera? Azrael?"

Cassius fixed his gaze on Ulger's dangling shoulder and refused to answer. With Brenna and the enkavs chasing his hordes from the field, the Usurper would have to turn and use his sorcery against the reptiles soon—and the duke knew better than to think the dark king would leave him alive when he did.

"Assassin, look at me!" Ulger commanded.

"My name is Cassius!" The duke raised his eyes only as high as the Usurper's chin. "Duke of Kural!"

Launching himself off his good foot, Cassius sprang forward and feigned a blow at Ulger's dangling arm. The Usurper snorted his contempt, twisting around to protect his injured side as the duke had expected. Cassius flipped the Sun Sword around, striking at Ulger's neck from behind.

Almost casually, the Usurper leaned away, at the same time flipping his shadowy sword up behind his head to catch the blow. The blades met in sizzling spray of light and dark, then Ulger swung his foot out, kicking Cassius's front leg from beneath him. At once the injured ankle collapsed, and the duke slammed down on his back.

Ulger stepped forward, pinning Cassius's wrist to the ground. The duke's arm went numb with cold, and his hand slowly opened to release the Sun Sword. The Usurper waited until the golden hilt had slipped completely free, then laid the tip of his shadowy sword beneath the duke's chin.

"Now, *Duke* Cassius, look at me."

Ulger used his sword to raise the duke's chin, and Cassius found himself gazing into the blue flames in the man-thing's hollow eye sockets. He began to tremble as before, and not even the sound of Crusher's heavy hooves clamoring up the rubble pile could give him the strength to look away.

Ulger paid the big horse no heed and kept his gaze locked on Cassius. "Who sent you?"

"P-Pen—" Cassius bit his tongue, knowing he would die the moment he answered, but his foe's icy eyes robbed his spirit of defiance, just as they sapped his body of strength. His mouth fell open almost of its own accord, and then he heard his voice saying, "Pendaran Tremayne."

Cassius closed his eyes, expecting the Usurper's cold blade to slide into his throat.

But Ulger seemed baffled. "Who?"

Cassius was so shocked to be alive that he almost made the mistake of opening his eyes again—but then he heard Brenna crying out and Crusher snorting in fury, and he rocked up on his hips and twisted around to slam a shin into the back of Ulger's knees.

The blow did not topple the Usurper, but it did stagger him and make him step off Cassius's wrist. In a single motion, the duke snatched up his sword and brought it around, severing Ulger's foot at the ankle. The Usurper bellowed in pain and began to tilt, swinging his own weapon as he fell.

Cassius rolled away from the descending blade, but he could not avoid the blow. Ulger's sword caught his side, sending waves of searing numbness through his abdomen. He cried out and tried to roll away—then saw a silvery saber come down across the back of the Usurper's head.

It was the steel that shattered, of course, and not the dark king's neck—but then Crusher was between Cassius and his attacker, snorting and gnashing as Brenna screeched and flailed at Ulger with her broken blade.

"Brenna, no!"

Cassius scrambled to his feet and pulled the girl from the saddle, bringing her down on his side of the horse. A shower of blood and grave rot came with her, and still Brenna fought, screaming in terror and blindly swiping the stump of her blade across Crusher's flank. The horse whinnied in surprise and sidestepped, trying to shoulder Ulger over.

Cassius dropped Brenna to the ground as gently as possible, then stumbled back as Ulger met the warhorse's shove with one of his own. The big shire danced sideways to keep from going down, straddling Brenna and sending Cassius reeling back into a pair of scaly arms.

"Sword hurt?"

Cassius glanced up long enough to glimpse the twinkling eyes of an enkav, then launched himself back toward Crusher. As he reached for the reins, the big shire whinnied in alarm and danced forward. Ulger's obsidian crown appeared on the other side of the saddle, and Cassius looked away just in time to see a black, footless leg swinging over the warhorse's rump as the Usurper mounted.

The stump caught the duke square in the head.

Cassius fell spinning, then heard an earsplitting whack. He looked up to see the flat of a shadowy sword slapping at the shire's flank, raising welts the size of a man's arm, and the big warhorse shrieked in pain, springing forward to race down the rubble pile and into Ulger's dark, fleeing horde.

Cassius scrambled to his feet in time to see the dark horde close in behind Crusher's docked tail and spill across the plain toward Lookout Mountain. He raised the Sun Sword high and started forward, oblivious to his wound and everything else—everything except catching the routed horde and cutting it down from behind.

"After them!" He waved the Sun Sword forward. "Cut them—"

"No." A small, spindly-fingered hand caught his arm from behind, then pulled it down. "Don't be a fool."

Cassius turned to find Pendaran Tremayne standing behind him, covered in soot and blood and surrounded by startled enkavs. The sorcerer yanked the duke into the sheltering midst of reptiles and started back into the city.

"Have you forgotten what happened to Asgrim?" Pendaran hissed.

"Let me go!" Cassius tried to jerk free, but found the sorcerer's grip unbreakable. "We can finish this!"

"Not in the way you think," Pendaran countered. "We have already lost this fight, which you would realize if you were not blinded by the Sun Sword's power."

"I am not blinded, by the Sun Sword or anything else," Cassius retorted. "I know the risk."

"Do you?" Pendaran stepped over a pair of dead shargas, then nodded at his feet, where Brenna lay half-buried beneath the savaged remains of a throg corpse. "Or have you forgotten something?"

"Brenna!"

Cassius knelt down and scooped her blood-smeared figure into his arms. A gash as long as his hand ran along one side of her head and her breath came in erratic rasps, but he saw no other apparent wounds.

Cassius glared up at Pendaran. "Where were you? This is your fault! If you hadn't held back, we would have had Ulger—"

"Even I cannot be in ten places at once," the sorcerer interrupted. "The siege towers were breaking through, and it was all I could do to keep Ulger's galoks from catching us in their vise—which they still might do, by the way."

Pendaran pointed toward the Grand Heights, where hundreds of men and dwarves were fleeing down Drake's Way toward the relative safety of the Cliff Road. Although Cassius did not see any galoks or ogares chasing them, a sporadic rain of arrows and lightning bolts suggested the creatures were not far behind.

"They've breached the wall?"

"In half a dozen places. You should have listened to me and stayed in the Grand Heights. It all worked out the same anyway." Pendaran pointed to Brenna. "But now you'd better look to your friend. Pull her eyelids up and see if her wound has made her eyes crazy."

Cassius did as instructed and saw to his dismay that Brenna's pupils had opened to nearly the size of the irises. They were deeper than wells and as black and glassy as Ulger's crown, with tiny disks of crimson fire burning at the bottom of their measureless depths.

Cassius gasped, and Pendaran said, "Keep looking."

The crimson fires began to grow brighter and larger. Cassius lost sight of Brenna's face and had a feeling of plummeting, as though he had fallen into her eyes. The smell of brimstone and acrid oil smoke filled his nose, and he heard low voices speaking gently over the crackle of flames.

"It speaks well of Ulger's strength that he found us."

"And better of his cunning that he knew to look at all."

A ring of scarlet-robed figures appeared around the fire pit, arrayed along a black stony rim with their hands folded in their sleeves and their faces hidden beneath large pointed cowls. On one side of the circle stood a bitter-eyed man in Ulger's jewelless obsidian crown, while directly opposite him loomed an especially tall figure in a black hood and robe.

"Perhaps Ulger's presence is a warning as well, my brothers," said the tall figure. "A warning that others may follow—others who will not come alone to beg our help, but in hundreds and thousands to destroy us."

"You need have no fear of that," said Ulger. The Usurper's voice sounded remarkably similar to the one that had spoken to Cassius during their battle, save that now it was human and did not fill him with terror. "The Drake Kings have long known of the Fire Sorcerers of Ys. Indeed, they have been watching you since you first thought to draw upon the caged might of Khull-khuum."

The black hood rose ever so slightly. "That cannot be so, or we would be dead."

The circle rustled its agreement, and Cassius caught the reflection of more than a few hidden daggers glinting out from their wielders' sleeves. Ulger eyed the sorcerers contemptuously and looked across the fire pit to the leader.

"It is no service to flatter your followers with empty admonitions, Morholt." Ulger's use of the leader's name drew a gasp of uneasy surprise from the other sorcerers. "Every good king knows it is easier to watch the enemy he knows than one he doesn't. Had we ever felt threatened, rest assured that you would be long dead—as would Algaral, Bersules, Evrawg, Fanewulf, Escanor, Melecaun, Rion . . ."

The circle burst into a startled cacophony as Ulger named each of the sorcerers present, making plain that he, at least, could have assassinated the entire ring as easily as he claimed. The hooded figures seemed to wither in their robes, and they began to glance about self-consciously, avoiding Morholt's gaze but studying each other, as though trying to guess who had been betraying their secrets to the hated Drakes.

Morholt allowed the anarchy to continue a moment longer, then recovered from his own shock. "If we were so little to you as a king, then why come to us now?" The black hood pivoted as the sorcerer looked around the circle. "Can you think we have the power to win your crown back?"

The mockery won a chuckle from Morholt's fellows, but Ulger paid them no attention. "At the moment your power could not win me a quiet minute in one of Stonekeep's garderobes." The Usurper allowed a moment for the gasps of outrage to pass, then continued, "But that can be changed, which is why I'm here: to make real what you only dream."

The circle was silent for a moment, then one of the sorcerers closest to Ulger burst, "Absurd! No Drake would join—"

"I am no longer a Drake—or haven't you heard?" Ulger removed his signet ring. "The name has no honor. Drake is the name of thieves and betrayers, and I will not be called by it."

Ulger tossed his ring into the fire pit, and the crimson flames shot up to chin height. The sorcerers flinched at the heat but did not dare back away, and little crescent eyes of reflected light began to shine beneath their cowls.

"So you are no longer a Drake," said Morholt, his tone spiteful and haughty. "But neither are you a king. You come to us defeated and alone and ignorant of even the simplest spells, and it is you who would make us great?"

Ulger nodded. "I may not know the Path of Fire, but I do know who has been betraying you to the Drakes." To avoid giving his secret away for free, the Usurper avoided looking in the direction of any of the sorcerers. "And I know how to free Khull-khuum."

The flames roared at this, flashing so brilliantly that for

a moment it was impossible to see anything except crimson tongues and orange fangs. The sorcerers' robes began to steam and smoke, and their faces shone beneath their hoods like blurry yellow moons. Morholt stepped forward to the very edge of the pit and held his arms over the pit, paying no attention as his dangling sleeves burst into flames. He lowered his arms, and the fire subsided enough for the sorcerers to see each other across the pit.

"Your words are brave, Usurper—but so far, they are only words." Morholt shook the fire off his sleeves with a single quick flutter, then reached up and grasped the sides of his cowl. "Do you have the courage to make them real, I wonder?"

The sorcerer pulled his hood back, revealing a flat, scarred face that had lost its nose to a searing fire. When Ulger gasped at the gruesome sight, Morholt grinned, then turned to the figure beside him.

"Show him," he said. "Show Ulger what it takes to become a Fire Sorcerer of Ys."

The next sorcerer pulled back only one side of her hood, revealing the hairless wreckage around a melted hole that had once been her ear. The sorcerer after her thrust a withered length of melted arm from his sleeve, then, one after the other, the remaining sorcerers revealed what they, too, had sacrificed to the fires of Khull-khuum. Some mutilations were obvious, while others were more subtle or private. There were women with no lips and men with fingers fused together. One sorceress had allowed the flames to consume the entirety of her womanly shape, and another had contented herself with a mere swath of melted flesh along her inner thigh. One man had burned off all his toes, while another had immolated something more personal.

Ulger looked increasingly ill with each revelation, yet not once did he glance away. He calmly observed each mutilation as it was presented, gazed briefly into the eyes of the presenter, then turned to the next one. Nor did his expression betray the sight of any affliction he had seen before on his spy. His eyes remained as cold and stony as sapphires, and when he had at last completed the circuit, Morholt's bitter expression made clear that he was no closer to learning the identity of the group's betrayer than before.

"What say you, Ulger?" asked the sorcerer. "Do you still wish to join us?"

Ulger thrust one arm into the fire and met Morholt's gaze levelly. "I did not come here to join you." He watched as the arm erupted into flames, then thrust his second out to join it. "I came here to make something of you."

The Usurper's expression remained as impassive as when he had observed the mutilations of the others, and the jaw beneath Morholt's noseless face dropped in surprise. Ulger waited until the flesh had melted from both arms, then thrust a leg out over the fire pit.

"And make something of you I will!"

The dark king lowered his burning leg into the pit, then rocked forward and stepped off into the flames.

A terrible scream filled the air, and the sensation of falling returned to Cassius. The fire disk grew smaller and vanished before his eyes, and then he found himself staring into a pair of frightened emerald eyes, with Brenna's voice ringing in his ears.

"No! No, Cassius! Stop!"

It took the duke a moment to locate himself again and realize that he was kneeling in the rubble of the North Gate, clutching the Sun Sword in one hand and Brenna in the other, squeezing the back of the poor girl's neck so hard that he was surprised it had not snapped.

"By the burning sky!" Cassius released Brenna's neck and fell backward. "I am sorry, Brenna!"

The girl's frightened eyes remained as round as coins, and she pushed herself out from under him.

"It was Ulger!" Cassius gasped. When he reached out for her, she flinched and rolled away, scrambling into the arms of a nearby dwarf. "I was with him . . . We were at the Fire Pit of Ys, with a ring of sorcerers . . . !"

"You weren't with him," said Pendaran. "What you saw happened long ago. You had to see what he did to win his power."

Cassius lowered the Sun Sword and calmed himself, then

looked from Brenna's trembling form to the sorcerer. "And you showed that to her?"

Pendaran shook his head. "Not at all—she saw what you would do to win *your* power."

The High Lords came at dusk, when Cassius stood alone in the watchtower of the Cliff Road Gate, looking out over the smoke that hovered like fog above the rooftops of the lower city. Scattered blossoms of orange shone up through the gray pall, uncontrolled fires set by stubborn citizens who would rather burn their property than yield it to Ulger's hordes. Hulking silhouettes materialized suddenly in the haze and vanished like ghosts. Occasionally, there were screams, long and anguished, and the crash of an incinerated building falling in on itself. The air was so mordant with ash that it hurt to breathe.

Wheezing and gasping, the High Lords gathered beside Cassius and looked out over their city in silence. They had exchanged their gilded armor for less ridiculous attire, simple tunics or doublets covered by plain breastplates bearing the eight-pointed star of the Council Guard. Their swords were heavy double-edged weapons more suited to the bloody work ahead than the elegant rapiers they usually carried.

With a nod, Lord Belden directed the watch sentries toward the stair turret. He did not speak until the astonished men had closed the door and descended into the gatehouse proper.

"Can you win?" He pointed his red beard toward the pall of smoke below.

Cassius had lost half his enkavs. He could only guess at Ulger's strength, though he knew the Usurper to have plenty of ogares and galoks left. The wound in his side was suppurating, filling him with poison and fever, but he answered without hesitation.

"Of course. What other choice does Stonekeep have?"

Lord Ramsay's rheumy eyes grew glassier than ever. "We could ask for terms."

Cassius glanced down at the ramparts below, where the

refugees from the northern provinces were laboring alongside the city's wealthy to stock the walls with oil and boulders.

"If Stonekeep wanted terms from Ulger the Cruel, it should have asked three and a half centuries ago. If you want to live now, you must fight."

"Just so." Lord Fiske glared at Ramsay, his sharp features set with ill-concealed contempt. "If we have not served our ancestors well in looking after their city, at least let us make them proud in how we lose it."

"It is decided, then." Lord Belden turned to Cassius. "We yield to your terms."

"My terms?" Cassius asked, determined to make them say it.

"You will be emperor, if you save us," said Fiske.

"And if I don't?"

"It will not matter," said Lord Ramsay. He had to fold his bloated hands to stop them from trembling. "May Thera have mercy on us."

"I'll do what I am able," said Cassius. "But I will be emperor now—win or lose."

The High Lords frowned and looked to one another in confusion. "You will have complete control of the armies, of course," said Belden. "But until you actually win—"

"Now," Cassius said. "I will not have the Council questioning my decisions—or trying to escape with the city's treasure."

Lord Fiske turned to his fellows and shrugged. "Why not? If we lose, at least history will blame him."

Before the other lords could voice their agreement, the door from the stair turret swung open. Together, Cassius and the High Lords turned to find Brenna the Swift stepping onto the watchtower deck, her head bandaged and her arms held out before her as though she would rather not get too close to what she was carrying.

"Young woman!" barked Lord Belden. "You're interrupting us."

"I beg your pardon." Despite her apology, Brenna continued across the deck, walking rather unsteadily and staring at the item in her hands. As she drew closer, it grew apparent she was carrying a small box with tiny corner posts and a web of flashing Shadow inside. "Skagi Reist told me to deliver this to Cassius at once."

Lord Ramsay stepped forward. "And you put the command of a dwarf above ours?"

Cassius pulled the councillor back—an unthinkable affront just a few days before—then smiled at Brenna. "It's okay, Lord Ramsay. Brenna is my personal adjutant."

Brenna passed the box over without returning his smile. As he accepted it, Cassius was astonished to discover that the thing weighed exactly nothing, especially considering that Pendaran had said dropping it would level the entire city. He displayed the box to those who had not seen it before.

"This is Khull-khuum's prison." He looked back to Brenna. "What are you doing with it?"

"Skagi told me to deliver it to you." Her face reddened, and she glanced uncomfortably at the High Lords. "His words were 'Return this to the Oathbreaker. Tell him I hope he lives to have his empire, but the dwarves can have no part in his treachery.' "

Cassius had a sinking feeling. "Treachery?"

"You must know, milord." Brenna's expression grew incredulous. She glanced nervously at the High Lords, then leaned close and whispered, "The enkavs."

"What about my enkavs?"

The heat of the question made Brenna draw back. "Keeplord Varden," she said. "They killed him."

The High Lords instantly fell to whispering amongst themselves, but Cassius was too stunned to say anything—so stunned that he almost dropped Khull-khuum's prison. He would be the last one to claim he understood the reptiles, but so far he had encountered no trouble controlling them. Even in the heat of battle, they had never made the mistake of killing anyone he did not instruct them to, and he saw only one reason they would start now: Pendaran Tremayne.

When Cassius said nothing for several moments, Brenna

ventured, "That's why the dwarves left, Cassius. Because you had the Keeplord assassinated."

"And what of his family?" asked Fiske.

"They're missing," Brenna answered. She cast an uneasy glance in Cassius's direction. "Nobody knows if the dwarves took them, or . . ." She let the sentence trail off.

The High Lords were silent for a moment, then Belden said, "Well, it seems our new wyrm has fangs."

"Aye. Perhaps the High Lords had less choice in this than we thought," agreed Ramsay. "Still, I am glad that we made the right choice . . . on our own."

Lord Fiske nodded, then turned to Cassius. "It would have been better to leave no doubts, but the family can hardly make a claim on the Keeplord's throne if they're not here." He clamped a fist to his breast. "Hail to the emperor!"

"Emperor?" gasped Brenna. She began to back toward the stairs. "Then it's true?"

Cassius shook his head. "No—not what you think. I had nothing to do with the Keeplord's death." He started after her, still holding the box in his hands. "Is this what Pendaran showed you at the North Gate?"

Instead of answering, Brenna turned to descend the stairs. "It's that sword, Cassius—just like Pendaran said!"

"Wait, Brenna!"

She was already gone, bounding down the stairs somewhat dizzily, but still as lightly as the deer she had so loved to hunt back in Kural. Realizing he would not catch her until she wanted to be caught—and especially not with Khull-khuum's prison in his hands—Cassius stopped and simply stared after her.

"Have no fear, milord." Lord Fiske clasped Cassius's shoulder. "She's just a young thing. She'll be back soon enough."

"And if she is not, there will be no shortage of pretty girls to take her place," added Lord Ramsay. "You're emperor now."

Cassius scowled at the man. "A hundred of Stonekeep's courtesans would not be the equal of that young woman—

and the one who cost me her respect will soon have reason to regret it.'' He thrust Khull-khuum's prison into Lord Fiske's hands and started across the floor, calling over his shoulder, ''Don't drop that!''

Cassius raced down six stories of spiraling stairs to the gatehouse's street-level exit and stepped out onto Council Boulevard. The surviving enkavs were standing gape-mouthed in the street, peering up into the twilight sky and gasping at the twinkling stars. With the Sun Sword sheathed in his scabbard, they paid no more attention to him than to any of the humans bustling past with defense supplies for the wall. The duke did not bother to check their claws for blood—the reptiles were meticulously careful about licking them clean after each battle—nor to question them about what had happened. Even if he could make them understand what he was asking, he doubted they would have the answers he sought.

Cassius rushed up the street to the Sacred Way, then ducked into the public fountain house that Pendaran had claimed as his temporary home. With a high domed ceiling and a gurgling fountain, the building was meant to serve as a sort of meditation chamber where people would pause to cleanse their hands and souls before entering the temple district. The fountain should have been surrounded by four curved benches, but these had been pulled to the north end of the room and arranged in a circle around Pendaran. Seated on the benches were the seven sorcerer-advisers of the High Lords, all listening to the little wizard with rapt attention.

''You have no need of these sticks!''

Pendaran took a rune staff from Cajetan, Lord Fiske's black-bearded sorcerer, and tossed it aside. Instead of coming down, the stick rose into the air and hovered near the ceiling, drawing an appreciative murmur from the little wizard's audience.

''But without staffs, how will we cast our runes?'' asked Cajetan, his head craned back to stare at his staff. ''And where will we store our mana?''

''You don't need mana—''

''Pendaran!'' Cassius yelled, not caring that he had interrupted the wizard in mid-sentence. He stepped around the fountain and continued forward, one hand on the hilt of the Sun Sword. ''Murderer! What have you done?''

Pendaran scowled in Cassius's direction. ''Can you not see that I'm busy?'' He raised his hand, motioning Cassius to wait, and the duke suddenly found himself looking at the little wizard from across a very great distance. Pendaran turned back to his fellow sorcerers. ''Emperors! Have they no manners?''

The High Sorcerers glanced in Cassius's direction and chuckled nervously.

''Manners! I will teach you manners!''

Cassius's exclamation faded almost as soon as it left his lips, so that even he barely heard his words. He broke into a sprint, but the faster he ran, the farther away Pendaran seemed to be.

The little wizard smirked and turned back to his audience. ''Now, as I was saying, the world is almost out of mana.'' The words sounded hollow and tinny, as though they were coming to Cassius through the bottom of a jar. ''There is so little left that you can cast only small spells, and even then you must haul around unwieldy sticks like that.''

Pendaran glanced up, and the rune staff hovering up near the ceiling suddenly plunged back down. Cajetan cried out and leapt up to catch it, then tripped over a bench and fell flat on his face.

''You see?'' Pendaran said. ''They're more trouble than they're worth.''

This drew another nervous laugh from his audience. Lord Belden's sorcerer, a red-haired woman named Melvina, said, ''You still have not answered Cajetan's question. Without mana, how do we power our runes—''

''Your spells,'' Pendaran corrected. ''A rune is nothing but a spell traced out in letter form; a spell is the figure that shapes your magic, whether you trace it in your mind, dance it on the ground, sing it with your voice, paint it as a ward, write it in a scroll, or inscribe it on an item of magic."

Melvina knitted her brow. "Very well, spells. I still do not see how we will power them."

"That is the simplest thing of all." Pendaran gave her a broad smile, revealing the four snaggled tusks that rose from behind his lower lip. "Venerate Wahooka. Build shrines to him and offer him gems and jewels. Call on him when you cast your spells, and he will give you magic."

When Cassius heard these words, his heart leapt so high into his throat that he thought he would choke. The demand for gems was familiar—all too familiar, except that Pendaran had never before demanded his payment in Wahooka's name.

After a moment of silence, a chubby sorcerer with bejeweled fingers joked, "Give away my gems and jewels? I'd rather take my chances with mana!"

"Then you will die on the morrow." Pendaran's reply was sharp. "I am teaching you what you must know to win in battle. Ulger's magic is mighty, and if you try to stop him with mana, he will boil your brains in your skulls."

A solemn silence fell over the gathering. Pendaran turned slowly around the circle, staring in turn into each sorcerer's eyes. When he returned to the chubby man, he pointed at one of the fellow's fingers.

"Give me that citrine, Kolinkar. I will show you."

Kolinkar frowned, glancing about at his companions.

"Go ahead," urged Melvina. "There's no use being cheap, for tomorrow we die."

"Ha, ha—very funny."

Despite his complaint, Kolinkar twisted the ring off his finger and passed it over. With a practiced pinch, Pendaran plucked the gem from its setting and returned the empty ring to its owner. He withdrew a piece of charcoal from inside his cloak, then drew a simple rune on the floor.

"Trace this pattern in your head over and over," he said. "Do it until you can see it in your mind's eye without concentrating."

Kolinkar leaned forward and stared at the rune. The charcoal began to fade away. A moment later the chubby sorcerer closed his eyes in concentration, and the pattern vanished completely.

"It's there!" he said, excited.

"Good." Pendaran tossed the man's yellow gem into the fountain's catch basin. The stone vanished at once, and nobody except Cassius seemed to notice when it reappeared in the little wizard's palm. "Now look at someone and wipe the pattern from your mind."

Kolinkar turned to Cajetan, and in the next instant the man's clothes were gone. Melvina smiled appreciatively, while the others burst out laughing.

Cajetan glanced down and turned red. "Very funny," he said, crossing his legs. "But if we must sacrifice a jewel just to take off our clothes, we will not be casting many spells."

"You do not have to offer a gem with every spell." Pendaran gestured at Cajetan's feet, and his neatly folded robe appeared on the floor. "Wahooka is not greedy. If you make an offering once or twice a week, I am sure he will hear when you call."

"And this will work with any of our runes?" asked Melvina.

Pendaran shook his head. "I have made lists of some of his favorite spells." He reached into his cloak and withdrew seven small rolls of parchment, which he passed out to the circle of sorcerers. "These spells will serve you well tomorrow."

As Cajetan accepted his scroll, he said, "This all seems so very simple—too simple. Will Wahooka let anyone with a symbol and a jewel cast one of his spells?"

Pendaran shook his head. "Oh no, you are all experienced in the ways of sorcery, much practiced in the tracing and making of runes," he said. "If a novice were to try these symbols, the results could be bad, very bad indeed. And do not try to use any other spells—Wahooka will answer your calls only for his spells."

This caused several of the sorcerers to exchange knowing

glances, but they said nothing and simply accepted Pendaran's scrolls with thanks.

"Now go." Pendaran waved them toward the exit. "Trace your spells in your minds tonight and make your offerings. Tomorrow, you will be happy you did."

Pendaran waited until the last sorcerer was safely out the door, then turned to Cassius. "What is so important that you interrupted my lessons?"

Cassius stumbled forward and suddenly found himself standing at the sorcerer's side. "You—you liar!" he exclaimed. "Now I know why the name Pendaran is not in the Ballads!"

"But I am mentioned," Pendaran replied. "Or do you still fail to recognize me? I'm beginning to wonder if you really are clever enough to be emperor."

The word "emperor" reminded Cassius why he had come after Pendaran in the first place. Still, the wizard's taunt gave him pause. If Pendaran and Wahooka were one and the same—and it had grown impossible to doubt it—then he was facing the legendary Trickster, an entity more ancient than the gods themselves.

"What happened to Varden's family?" Cassius demanded.

"How should I know?" Wahooka asked. "It was not my enkavs who killed the Keeplord."

"And it was not by my order," Cassius replied.

Wahooka shook his head in disgust. "Have you not learned by now? You cannot rule without blood on your hands." He glanced down at the golden hilt rising out of Cassius's scabbard. "Do not let the Sun Sword's power deceive you."

"I am less worried about ruling than surviving," Cassius said. "The dwarves have left, and our only chance of getting them back is to produce Varden's family—safe and alive."

"Then the dwarves will not be back," said Wahooka. "It is a small loss, and you are better off for it. Any one of Varden's family could challenge your right to be emperor."

"I will not buy my crown at the price of innocent children!"

Wahooka stepped toward Cassius, and suddenly the duke found himself staring up into the Little One's eyes—though he could not say whether it was because he had shrunk or Wahooka had grown larger.

"Varden's children were born as corrupt as their father." Wahooka's eyes burned with an angry, obsidian darkness. "And your honor means nothing to me. If you wish to save Stonekeep, you will be emperor—and I will have my due."

Cassius backed away—he could not help himself. "I'll—I'll tell them who you are," he threatened. "Melvina, Cajetan, and the others."

"Tell them, and if the sorcerers turn away from me, how many more of your innocents will Ulger slay?" Suddenly Wahooka was as small as before, standing on a bench in front of Cassius. "You need me, Emperor. You need me more than you need the Sun Sword."

"If that is true, it is only because you have made it so."

"And what does that change?" Wahooka smiled and glanced down at Cassius's festering wound, then patted him on the cheek. "Now get some sleep. You are ill, and you will need your rest come morning."

The pounding at the door came almost as a relief, rousing Cassius from a fevered dream filled with shadowy skeletons and smirking sheep-eared midgets. His wound felt as heavy and swollen as a fist and reeked of sour purulence.

"Lord Emperor, it's time!" cried a young voice. "They're coming!"

"Brenna?" Cassius threw back his blanket and, ignoring the fiery ache in his side, swung his feet to the floor. "Brenna, come in. I've been worried—"

"Lord Emperor!" the voice cried again, and now Cassius recognized it as that of a young boy. "Wake up! They're on the march!"

"Yes, yes." Still struggling to recall who "they" might be, he called, "I'm awake."

Intending to illuminate the still-dark room, Cassius located his scabbard leaning against the wall and grabbed for Sun Sword's golden hilt. When his hand closed on empty air, he came completely awake.

"Wahooka!"

"Milord?" The door opened, and a page rushed in, cupping his hand around a candle flame. "Are you all right?"

"No!" Cassius shoved his feet into his boots. "Have you seen Wah—Pendaran, my sorcerer?"

"He is on the roof, with the High Lords."

Only then did Cassius recall fully that he was in the Cliff Road Gatehouse awaiting Ulger's attack. He raced out into the corridor, where his enkavs lay sleeping in a scaly tangle, packed in the hall so tightly that it was impossible to move without stepping on them. The emperor hurried toward the stairwell, using the tip of his scabbard to wake them as he passed.

"Come along. Fight!"

The enkavs opened their eyes long enough to slap the scabbard away or roll over, but none rose. Cassius spent a few puzzled moments trying to rouse the reptiles and make them obey, only to receive a few hisses and beakish snaps. He finally gave up and climbed the stairs to the roof, where the night was just giving way to gray dawn.

The cold morning air bustled with Council Guards wheeling forward barrels of iron crossbow bolts, stoking firepots to boil the oil, winding the cords of two small mangonel catapults. Cassius shouldered his way through the crowd and found Wahooka at the front of the roof, standing between two merlons so he could see over the crenellations down into the lower city. The Trickster had the High Sorcerers arrayed along the wall beside him, and a short distance from them stood the seven remaining High Lords. Brenna was nowhere to be seen, and Cassius had the uneasy feeling she had elected to fight with the other refugee volunteers, down on the cliff walls.

When no one noticed his approach, the emperor peered over the gatehouse battlements to see what was consuming their attention. Spread along the base of the Grand Heights he saw two thousand ogares, just starting to scale the cliffs with their great swords slung over their backs. On the Cliff Road, several dozen ghoul-faced galoks had already scrambled over the Low Gate's smoking ruins and started up the hill, their yellow eyes burning with hatred and their needlelike fangs gnashing with bloodlust. Behind them came a column of throgs at least two thousand strong, with half again as many shargas waiting along Drake's Way. Ulger himself, still dangling one arm and missing one foot, sat at the rear of the horde astride Crusher's massive back. The warhorse was so caked with ash and filth that the emperor barely recognized him.

After taking in the sight, Cassius grabbed Wahooka's arm and jerked him out of the crenature, then pulled him to the back of the roof.

"Where is my sword?" He waved his empty scabbard under the Trickster's nose.

Wahooka regarded the scabbard. "How unfortunate," he said. "At least it won't give you away to Ulger. You remember what happened to Asgrim."

"Don't play games with me," Cassius said. "I want it back."

"And what makes you think that lies in my power?"

"Don't pretend innocence," Cassius said. "You're the only one who could have taken it."

"Really?" Wahooka's eyes darted toward the lower city. "Could you be underestimating our enemy?"

The spoon of a mangonel banged against its crosspiece, hurling a boulder toward the galoks advancing up the Cliff Road. Instantly the sound was answered by the crack of a magic bolt, then the distant rattle of a hundred stone shards clattering to the ground. The throgs roared in delight.

Cassius glanced briefly toward the battle, then looked back to Wahooka. "We have no time for games. The enkavs won't follow me without the Sun Sword, and without them, we lack the strength to hold."

"And whose fault is that?" Wahooka's tone grew defensive. "The Sun Sword has been your undoing all along. Had you opened their eggs with the dragon claw as I instructed, it would have been your face they saw instead of the sword's brilliance. If they have abandoned you now, that is hardly my fault."

The second mangonel banged its crossbar; again, the attack was answered by the crack of a lightning bolt.

"I don't care whose fault it is." Cassius pulled his purse from his belt and placed it in the Trickster's hand. "Those are all the jewels I own. Just return the Sun Sword."

"That I cannot do—but I can give you something almost as good, if you promise to give it back." As Wahooka spoke, he slipped Cassius's purse into his cloak pocket and withdrew a plain-hilted sword with a blade of gleaming silver. "It will not call the enkavs back to your side, but it will stop Ulger if you use it well."

"No." Cassius refused to touch the hilt.

"Take it," Wahooka urged. "Sooner or later you'll have to deal with Ulger, and you'll need the best blade available."

"I want the Sun Sword."

Wahooka did not lower the weapon. "What are you afraid of?" he asked. "That you need the Sun Sword to defeat Ulger—or that you cannot lead without it?"

A tremendous crash shook the gatehouse, and a merlon burst apart, spraying shards across the roof and downing a dozen men. From the front of the tower, Lord Belden called, "Cassius—we are awaiting your orders!"

Cassius glanced in the lord's direction, then extended his hand to take the sword. "You win, but if you are deceiving me—"

"If I am deceiving you, it will not matter." Wahooka eyed Cassius's hand, but withheld the sword. "First you must promise to return it after the battle. This is no Sun Sword, but it is still a weapon of considerable magic, and I won't have you losing it like you did the Sun Sword."

Cassius eyed the Trickster angrily. "I promise," he said. "On one condition."

Wahooka's eyes grew beadier than usual. "Which is?"

"You must look after Brenna. If she comes to harm, I won't return the sword."

"You place too much faith in my abilities," Wahooka said. "The fortunes of war—"

"That is my condition." Cassius eyed the sword contemptuously. "Otherwise, I would sooner fight Ulger himself bare-handed."

Wahooka gave him a tusky sneer. "Be careful what you wish for." The Trickster laid the sword in Cassius's hand.

"I will keep an eye on her—but it will tax my concentration, and there may come a time when you wish my full attention had been on the battle at hand."

"I'll take that chance."

Cassius put the sword in his scabbard, then joined the councillors at the front of the tower. To his surprise, Lord Fiske still had Khull-khuum in his hands. The little box was a weblike blur of black streaks as the mad Shadowking continued to bounce around inside his prison, but if the councillor felt the impact, his relaxed grasp did not show it. Cassius started to suggest taking the prison to a safer place, then changed his mind. Khull-khuum was the one thing that frightened Wahooka; if circumstances grew desperate enough, the box might prove useful.

As the volunteers on the ramparts noticed the emperor's presence atop the gatehouse, they raised a great cheer. Cassius was dismayed to see that the refugees, interspersed with small companies of High Lord bodyguards, were already hefting their oil kettles into the crenatures. The ogares were only halfway up the cliff; if his men dumped the oil now, most of it would splash harmlessly off the rocks.

Cassius turned to the signal master. "Have the ramparts hold their oil. They are to drop boulders first."

As the signal man raised the appropriate flags, Cassius turned to inspect matters on the Cliff Road—and glimpsed Ulger's arm rising in his direction.

"Everybody down!"

Cassius hurled himself to the floor, groaning in pain as he landed on his wounded side. A chugging roar rumbled up from below, then a roiling cloud of fire crashed into the wall and shook the entire gatehouse. Tongues of crimson flame came shooting through the crenellations, licking his back with searing heat and turning his world the color of blood. Men screamed, and wood began to crackle and burn, and the air filled with a sick, acrid stench.

Cassius rose to his knees, waving his hand at the flames. "Put out that fire!"

A dozen guardsmen were already slapping at the blazes with their cloaks, while several more rushed forward with large buckets of water. Cassius turned and peered down through the charred crenature to find Ulger's flickering blue eyes searching for him along the rooftop. At once, the emperor began to feel sickly and chill, and he found himself wondering if it had been the Usurper who had stolen the Sun Sword after all.

In the next instant a fork of red lightning shot out of a crenature beside him, arcing down toward Ulger. The bolt struck its target full in the chest, engulfing rider and horse in a crackling flash of scarlet energy. Crusher reared, lifting his dazed and smoking rider high into the air.

Cassius looked over, expecting to find Wahooka's short figure standing in the next crenature. Instead, it was Melvina pointing at the target, with Cajetan standing beside her. Cajetan rolled his hand in the direction of the lower city, and a tiny ball of flame tumbled off his fingertips to hiss down toward the Usurper, throbbing and growing larger as it flew.

By the time the sphere struck, it was as large as an ogare. It blossomed across the street like a huge carnation, engulfing Ulger and two dozen shargas along with him. Crusher screamed and vanished inside the flames. Cassius thought he had seen the last of his poor horse until the shire galloped out the other side, his hide smoking and Ulger's skeletal figure jerking at the reins. The warhorse cut sharply and vanished down a side street.

The ramparts erupted in a frenzy of hurrahs and catcalls. Cassius turned to congratulate the sorcerers and found Wahooka standing in their midst, glaring angrily at all seven.

"Those are not Wahooka's spells!" snarled the Trickster. "I certainly did not give them to you!"

"Your lesson was most enlightening, Pendaran." Melvina's smile was not quite a smirk. "We took what you taught us and applied it to other gods besides Wahooka. I converted one of my runes into Helion's Bolt of Justice."

"I call my spell Red Azrael's Cleansing Fire," said Cajetan. He stooped down and assumed a conspiratorial tone. "Pendaran, you might consider calling upon someone besides Wahooka for your own magic. The other gods do not demand jewels as offerings."

Wahooka's face screwed into a mask of rage. "Ingrates!"

Cassius stifled the impulse to laugh—though only because he feared making the Trickster angry enough to turn against them. On the Cliff Road below, the galoks crossed the halfway point at a dead run, waving their rune staffs at the gatehouse and showering the walls with all manner of magic bolts. Close behind came the throgs, roaring in fury and ready to pour through the first breach in the Grand Heights' defenses.

Cassius gestured at the head of the column. "If you have any more spells . . ."

No sooner had he spoken than the High Sorcerers unleashed a barrage of flame and fury. The sky rained burning hail, and the earth belched steaming clouds of poison. The wind tore the enemy from the road and hurled them down in the broken streets of the lower city. The galoks countered with fire and bolt, shattering merlons, blasting whole lengths of crenellation into rubble, setting the roof aflame in a dozen places, and splintering the crossbar of a mangonel. Lord Belden fell with a cracked skull. The sorcerer Kolinkar erupted into flames and plummeted, screaming, down along the gatehouse wall. Even Pendaran took a lightning bolt in the chest and went tumbling across the planks, cursing and howling. Upon reaching the far wall, he bounced up and started back toward the front, pausing along the way to snatch up the sparkling line of gems strewn along his path.

In the end, the galoks' runes were no match for the sorcerers' new magic. The galoks fell by the handful. With each loss, the fury of their attack abated. Their charge slowed, then stopped, then became a retreat and finally a rout, and still the attacks of the High Sorcerers did not diminish. They reduced the galoks' numbers to ten, five, and finally Melvina struck the last one down with a shooting star. Left with no protection from the onslaught, the throgs fled and in their frenzy to escape trampled every sharga in the way.

The gatehouse shook with the cheers of the Council Guard, but Cassius had not forgotten yesterday's lesson, when a few ogares succeeded where a horde of throgs had failed. He looked down along the cliffs and saw that fifteen hundred of the hairy beasts had climbed to within a few feet of the top. The refugees and bodyguards were pelting them with boulder after boulder, and sometimes a stone would cause the target to loose its grip and bounce down into the low city, roaring and growling all the way. More often, the ogare merely hunkered down and shook its head, then glared at its attacker and resumed the climb.

Cassius studied the scene somewhat longer than necessary, hoping to spy Brenna's lithe form among the thousands laboring along the ramparts. She was probably safer down on the wall than with him in the gatehouse, where Ulger had so far focused the greatest fury of his attack—but it was disconcerting not to have her at his side, if only because she had chosen to be somewhere else. He spent a few moments longer searching for her bandaged head, then noticed that the ogares had stopped climbing.

The brutes were taking shelter just below the rim of the cliff, clinging beneath craggy outcroppings and little overhangs, wedging themselves into the few crevices and crannies large enough to hold them—in short, hiding anywhere they would be protected from the constant bombardment above. Cassius had a sinking feeling and looked down the Cliff Road again. He found the throgs and shargas charging back up the hill, sprinting along as though the death awaiting above was as nothing compared with their dark master's anger. The ogares had stopped climbing because Ulger wanted them to; the Usurper was coordinating attacks.

Cassius turned to his signal master. "Have the ramparts dump their oil kettles. They've got to dislodge the ogares before the throgs reach us."

The signal master raised a flag, and the refugees began to dump their kettles over the wall. Much of the oil splashed harmlessly off rocky overhangs, but many vats found their targets. Often the scalding oil did nothing more than singe the ogares' thick fur and elicit an angry bellow. Occasionally, however, one of the hairy brutes would catch a faceful of the black bubbling stuff and go tumbling down into the lower city.

The situation at the gatehouse was little better. Even with half the Council Guard battling flames, several fires continued to burn out of control. The roof had already collapsed in half a dozen places, and it was beginning to sag under the weight of the mangonels. The initial assault had left the entire front wall cratered and crumbling, blasting hollows around the arrow loops and opening cracks in the foundation large enough for a sharga to scramble through.

The remaining mangonel hurled a boulder down into the lower city. When the spoon banged into the crossbar, the entire roof shook, and a burning support beam gave way. One corner of the little catapult sagged toward a fiery hole, and Cassius ordered everyone who was not fighting fires or invaders to depart the rooftop. Lord Ramsay and the other High Lords were only too happy to go, but the emperor ordered Fiske to stay. The councillor was still holding Khull-khuum's shadow-webbed prison, and with matters deteriorating as rapidly as they were, Cassius did not want to lose his only leverage over Wahooka the Trickster.

As the throgs charged past the halfway point on the Cliff Road, the High Sorcerers unleashed a torrent of fire and lightning. Many of their assaults landed on target, blasting dozens of invaders off the road or dropping them where they stood—but many more spells arced away at the last minute, ricocheting into the cliffside or arcing out over the lower city.

"What's happening?" gasped Fiske. "What's wrong with the new magic?"

The councillor's question was nearly lost in the roar of cheering throg voices. The invaders rushed up the slope with renewed vigor, screaming madly and waving their swords. Crossbow quarrels began to streak down at them from gatehouse arrow loops, but the toll taken by the iron bolts was too small to slow the charge. To Cassius's surprise, he saw no ladder or battering ram anywhere in the crowd. He studied the mob more carefully, then noticed a small emptiness in the otherwise close-packed horde.

"Ulger's with them!" he hissed.

"Oh, bravo," said Wahooka. "You noticed. Didn't I say you would have to deal with him?"

Lord Fiske scowled. "I don't see him."

"It's the same trick he used at the North Road Gate." Cassius pointed to the small emptiness he had noticed. "He's invisible."

Fiske's face went pale, and he turned to Wahooka. "Can't you do something?"

The Trickster shrugged. "What can I do?" He motioned at the High Sorcerers, who were continuing to rain spells down on the column with little effect. "They are the ones who turned their backs on Wahooka!"

Cassius gave Wahooka a sidelong glance. "I doubt the Trickster could do any better," he said. With the horde almost at the gatehouse, the ogares began to peer out from beneath the cliff rim, eyeing the short fifteen feet between them and the top of the wall. "Wahooka could never break Ulger's magic. How could he? Wahooka's magic is mere illusion; the Usurper's is real."

Wahooka would not take the bait. He merely flattened his ears and glared at Cassius with ill-concealed spite, then said, "Wahooka's magic is real enough for those who please him."

The clacking of a massive crossbow volley throbbed up from below, followed at once by the staccato patter of iron bolts ripping into leathery hide. The road broke into a cacophony of hoarse wails and endless screeches, and Cassius looked down to see a hundred bloodied throgs collapsing between the gatehouse's salient towers.

In the next instant a tremendous boom shook the gatehouse, and the sturdy outer gate erupted into a flaming spray of shredded tin and splintered oak. Suddenly Cassius could see Ulger, sitting on Crusher's singed back amidst the gaggling throg horde, looking left and right along the cliff as his hulking ogares crawled out from their hiding places to clamber up the low battlement walls. The volunteers fought back as best they could with axes and spears, but as ogare after ogare gained a foothold on the ramparts, it quickly grew apparent that ill-equipped refugees and outnumbered bodyguards were no match for the overwhelming strength of their huge foes.

"We'll never hold," whispered Cassius.

The certainty of that statement settled over him with an unbearable weight, and he could not imagine why he had ever thought they might win. The Usurper had devoted more than three centuries to his plans and preparations, and now what did Cassius have to resist him with? A battered empire thrown together overnight from the dregs of a defeated kingdom. He stumbled back from the battlements, struggling to accept what he knew to be true.

"Stonekeep is lost!"

"Not yet!" Lord Fiske sounded less certain of himself than desperate. "We still have the Council Guard. We can send half of them out to drive the ogares back."

"And once they leave, Ulger's shargas will pour through the breaches like rats," said Cassius. "As it is, we barely hold the gatehouse."

As if to confirm the emperor's conclusion, Ulger twisted his hand into a gnarled claw and began to make a fist. A great screeching rang out from the hidden archway, and the entire structure began to vibrate, gently but steadily. A long series of pops and pings echoed up from the portcullis as its iron rivets began to give way.

Cassius turned to the signal master. "Call the retreat."

"Retreat?" Wahooka gasped. The screeching of the portcullis continued to shake the gatehouse, but the Trickster ignored it and asked in a mocking voice, "To where—the Temple of Shadow?"

"Where is for you to decide." Cassius turned toward the broken mangonel behind him. "I want you to go to Council Boulevard and open an escape route to Lookout Mountain, or the Magar Plain—or the Faerie Realm, for all I care."

Wahooka scowled. "Even if I wanted to help you abandon Stonekeep, what makes you think I could do such a thing?''

''Shadow Gorge,'' Cassius replied. ''You and Crusher appeared from nowhere, dry and warm in the middle of a blizzard.''

He drew the sword Wahooka had given him and used it to cut free one end of the mangonel's windlass line. As promised, the weapon was a fine one, well balanced and sharp. It bit through the sturdy winch rope in a single blow.

''Just get everybody as far away from the city as you can.''

The Trickster's eyes narrowed. ''Why?''

Cassius glanced at the box in Lord Fiske's hands, then asked, ''Is what you told Skagi about Khull-khuum true?'' He wrapped the line around his chest and tied it under his arms. ''That if he dropped the box, it would sink the city?''

Fiske's jaw fell, and his knuckles whitened on the box.

Wahooka glared at Cassius in astonishment, then began to shake his head. ''Oh no! I won't allow you to sink Stonekeep—not after I have done so much to save it!'' He turned and reached for Khull-khuum's prison. ''Give that here!''

Cassius shook his head, and Lord Fiske backed away, deftly lifting the box out of Wahooka's grasp. In the gatehouse below, the screech of the twisting portcullis grew louder and sharper, and the sound of popping rivets came too rapidly to count.

Everyone's eyes dropped to the floor, then Cassius said, ''A city can be rebuilt—but not a realm. If Ulger wins, Stonekeep is lost forever.''

A chorus of bloodcurdling battle cries rang out on the ramparts to the east, and Wahooka looked toward the sound. Through the curtains of smoke billowing off the gatehouse roof, a trio of ogares could be seen cutting its way toward the gatehouse. The Trickster cursed, then reluctantly nodded and turned to Lord Fiske.

''You mustn't throw the box until Cassius attacks Ulger. If the Usurper is not occupied when the city begins to sink, he may be quick enough to retrieve the box—and then we are lost.''

Khull-khuum began to bounce around inside his prison so furiously that the box turned solid black. Fiske eyed his burden nervously, then nodded to the Trickster.

"As you instruct."

Wahooka turned to join the bloody swarm rushing for the stairs, then stopped to look back at Cassius. "Brenna was safe the last time I looked," he said. "But I cannot do this and watch over her, too."

Cassius nodded. "I understand. It's on my head now."

The Trickster vanished into the mob descending the stairs, and then a final series of pings echoed up through the gatehouse. The screech of twisting metal gave way to the terrific clamor of iron bars collapsing into a twisted heap, and Cassius knew there was no time to measure the rope off the mangonel. He simply pulled the ratchet lever from its socket and tossed it aside, then started toward the front of the gatehouse, dragging the rope behind him and fighting against the resistance of the windlass. Fiske ran along at his side, looking both frightened and uncertain of himself.

"I am sorry to ask this of you, Lord Fiske," Cassius said.

"Think nothing of it." Though Fiske's pale face and trembling lip showed that he knew he was about as likely to survive his assignment as Cassius, the lord's gaze remained steady. "If the Council had listened to you earlier, perhaps I would not be here now."

Cassius reached the wall and crouched behind a crenature, then looked down upon the sea of sharp blades pressing forward into the archway. The mob's progress was slow and bloody, for a few brave guardsmen had stayed behind in the gatehouse to man the murder holes along the narrow passage, turning the corridor into a cramped killing zone of zinging crossbow bolts, thrusting halberds, and flaming oil. Ulger himself sat just a few paces outside the threshold, hurling thunderbolts and fireballs into the gateway with no regard for his own troops.

As soon as Cassius laid eyes on the Usurper, a cold terror seeped over him. His arms began to quiver at the mere thought of meeting his foe's flickering blue gaze, but he could think of no way except attacking to keep the dark king occupied long enough for Khull-khuum's prison to sink Stonekeep. How long would that take? Three seconds for the box to sail from Fiske's hand to the lower city, and perhaps another minute to drag the city into the abyss after it? That was a long time to stand against a foe such as Ulger—only a few moments less than Cassius had lasted at the North Gate, when the dark king had taken time to stop and talk.

The Usurper's firebolts soon silenced the last of the gatehouse defenders, and the shargas began to clamber inside through spell-craters and stress fissures. Ulger raised his hand and waved the rest of his throng into the archway, calling to them in their strange chortling language. The dark horde swirled past with ever increasing speed, and the momentum began to carry even the dark king's big mount toward the demolished gateway.

Only then, when his army could not have stopped if it wanted to, did Ulger take Crusher's reins and join the flood. Without so much as a good-bye to Lord Fiske, Cassius scrambled into the crenature and launched himself over the disintegrating battlements. Even with the rope and the drag of the windlass slowing his descent, the plummet was dizzying. He flashed past the gatehouse's third story, the second story, then raised his sword to strike—and reached the end of the rope, snapping to a halt mere feet above Ulger's obsidian crown.

Crusher continued forward, carrying the Usurper forward. Cassius whistled, as he often did when calling his horse to the fence for an apple.

The shire's ears perked, and he stopped at the gateway threshold, knocking two throgs to the ground as he turned to investigate the sound. Ulger twisted around to see what had distracted his mount, and Cassius cut the windlass line.

He plummeted the last few feet, then struck heels first, snapping Ulger's head to the side. The Usurper slipped from the saddle and crashed down amidst his charging minions, taking a handful to the ground with him. Cassius bounced off Crusher and knocked another half-dozen invaders off their feet, then found himself lying upon a cushion of flailing limbs and facing the stump of the dark king's truncated leg.

He brought his sword around and slammed it into the Usurper's thigh. There was the muffled snap of breaking bone, then Ulger howled—and that was when Cassius saw that his sword had turned into a staff. The hilt was the same one Wahooka had given him as the battle started, but the blade had become a weathered gray length of crooked branch.

As Cassius cursed, Crusher reared up beside him and came down upon the invaders in a flurry of flailing hooves and gnashing teeth. A chorus of startled throg voices cried out, and the big warhorse did as he had been trained, whirling to defend his fallen master in a tornado of kicks, stomps, and neck-crushing chomps.

Far above, a tiny square of darkness came sailing off the gatehouse roof and arced out over the lower city. Recovering from the shock of finding himself fighting Ulger with a stick, Cassius rolled to his feet and swung again. The Usurper thrust an arm up to block, then wailed in astonishment when the blow shattered the bone and left his forearm dangling at a crooked angle. The emperor began to think his wooden staff might not be such a bad weapon after all.

Then Ulger sat up, driving his good fist into Cassius's solar plexus and slamming him back into Crusher's hip. The warhorse spun at the contact, hurling the emperor back toward his foe. Ulger met him with a fist to the chest, then brought his broken arm around in a wild flailing arc and smashed his elbow into Cassius's ear.

There was a deafening crack, then everything fell silent and the emperor's head exploded into white agony. His knees buckled and his feet went out from beneath him. He slammed down on the hard street, and then Ulger was on him, kicking and striking and clawing. Cassius felt ribs crack, flesh tear, joints pop. His whole body erupted into anguish, and still he counted himself lucky. Had Ulger been holding his shadowy sword at the moment of attack, Stonekeep would have already lost its first emperor.

Cassius thought only of holding on to his weapon, of swinging it back and forth before him. There was no need to avert his eyes, or even remind himself to avoid his foe's fiery gaze. Cassius could not have looked into Ulger's eyes if he wanted to; his own eyes could no longer focus, and all his perceptions had come together in one endless experience of pain. He heard tendons popping and saw bones snapping and smelled blood gushing and did not know whether any of it belonged to him. His lungs were empty of breath and full of the fetor of death, and he felt the earth shaking the cobblestones loose beneath his legs.

Cassius circled his staff around in front of him in a figure-eight clearing pattern and raised it over his head for a final, overhand blow that would either beat through his enemy's guard or open himself up for Ulger's final blow—then Crusher screamed, and the beating stopped.

Cassius brought his weapon down and felt it cleave dead limbs, then heard a torrent of booted feet stumbling past. He noticed the pit of his stomach vibrating with a rumble almost too deep to hear, and his legs reverberating to the resonance of shaking ground. He tried to rise and found himself trapped by the weight of a dozen moaning bodies. His vision changed from white agony to blurry red, and he realized that he was buried to his chest in a sea of twisted limbs, some truncated and smoking, some broken and writhing, some ominously still. He beat them away with his wooden club and saw a horde of leathery legs clambering past—downhill, he thought, as impossible as that seemed.

As the legs scurried by, Cassius began to catch glimpses of a battered, shadow-cloaked form standing at the edge of the road, one footless leg held off the ground and a mangled arm dangling uselessly from one shoulder. He was looking out over the lower city, extending his good arm into the empty air, his palm turned skyward as if to hold something up.

"No!"

Though Cassius had yelled the word at the top of his lungs, it came out as an unrecognizable gurgle. He clawed at the sea of limbs until he could hoist himself to his feet, then lurched forward toward Ulger.

A leathery hand snatched at him from behind. Cassius whirled on his attacker, bringing the staff around to defend himself, and caught a throg in the neck. The blow separated the squarish head from the shoulders beneath as cleanly as any executioner's axe. Cassius had no time to consider this. He spun around and stumbled forward, slipped around to Ulger's side.

At the last moment the Usurper heard Cassius coming and pivoted to face him, but even had Ulger been quick enough, he made no move to lower his outstretched hand. Cassius brought his staff down across the arm.

The limb came off at the elbow and bounced down the cliff face, disappearing into a cloud of dust roiling up from below. For the merest instant Ulger and Cassius stood beside each other in stunned silence, the Usurper staring aghast at his severed arm and Cassius gaping at the wreckage below. A whole block of the lower city seemed to be flowing inward on itself, spiraling down a small well-like shaft perhaps fifty paces from the base of the cliff.

Then Ulger fixed his gaze on Cassius, his empty eye sockets blazing with angry tongues of blue flame. "Shadow take you!"

Cassius's legs buckled as he had known they would. He collapsed to his knees and began to tremble as he had before, though this time he felt more weary than frightened. The Usurper raised his mutilated arms and lurched forward on his good leg, trying to bowl the emperor over and carry him into the swirling abyss below. Cassius brought his stick around and struck his attacker in the shin, then ducked out of the way.

When the leg came off at the knees, the emperor knew he had guessed correctly about the staff; whatever its appearance, the weapon in his hands could only be the Sun Sword. He glanced down in time to see Ulger's mangled body crash through the roof of a house. A sharp crack—merely one of a hundred echoing up from the lower city—sounded inside the building, then it collapsed inward and disappeared down the hole after Khull-khuum's prison. There was a column of smoke, then a muffled rumble, and the hole began to fall in on itself, spreading outward to become a huge gaping pit that would soon be as large as Stonekeep itself.

"Milord, come away from there!"

The rough hand of a Council Guardsman caught Cassius by the arm and jerked him back from the road's edge. The emperor turned to find a whole company of Council Guards rushing past, chasing the last of the throgs and shargas away from the shattered gatehouse.

Without asking permission, the guard lifted Cassius and rushed up the road toward Crusher. Though the big shire had a long gash along the neck and was blood-smeared to the shoulder, he seemed little the worse for battle.

"Milord, are you hurt badly?" the guardsman asked, hoisting Cassius into Crusher's saddle. "You certainly should be. Imagine, attacking Ulger with nothing more than a stick! How could you expect us to retreat after that?"

Cassius's reply was drowned by a thunderous roar from the lower city, and he looked down to see it collapsing at an ever-increasing pace. When the Low Gate crumbled and disappeared into the hole, the throgs and shargas fleeing down the Cliff Road abruptly reversed course and started to fight their way back up the hill.

Cassius's guardsman quickly took Crusher's reins and led the big shire back through the gatehouse archway onto Council Boulevard. The avenue was packed with refugees and soldiers, many wounded and all hastening up the street toward a shimmering curtain of air, where Wahooka stood on a pedestal ushering the multitude to safety—and collecting whatever trinkets people had to offer.

When he saw Cassius coming, Wahooka called, "Make way!" He waved his hand, and the column of refugees spun sideways to create a narrow aisle. "Make way for Cassius the Vanquisher!"

Cassius took the reins from the guard and pulled Crusher to a halt beside the Wahooka's pedestal, then glared down at the Trickster. "Cassius the Vanquisher?"

Wahooka shrugged. ''An emperor must have an emperor's name.'' He glanced at the staff in Cassius's hand. ''Isn't there something you should give me?''

Cassius moved the weapon out of the Trickster's reach. ''I know what this is—and where you got it.''

''All that is true, but we still made an agreement.'' Wahooka looked toward the corner of the shimmering escape curtain, where Brenna the Swift, soot-covered and blood-smeared, stood watching Cassius with an expression of great uncertainty. ''I kept my word. The question is, will you keep yours?''

Cassius studied the rod for a long time, until Brenna finally turned to step through the shimmering portal, then thrust it into the Trickster's hands. ''You could have told me.''

''What would have been the fun in that?'' Wahooka raised the piece of wood above his head and waved it at the crowd, which erupted into a great cheer. ''My way, you are a legend already.''

Epilogue

It was the deepest, darkest place Wahooka knew, a jagged grotto of sharp corners and jumbled walls, where the air stank of smoke and stone, still trembling with the memory of the cataclysm above. The Trickster crept along the perimeter of the cave, peering into every cranny, cocking his ears in all directions, testing the still wind for the slightest whiff of something untoward. When he found nothing, he walked to the center of the chamber, where a vast pit lay filled with the moldering bones of a thousand thieves and warriors—relics of one of Vermatrix's ancient broodings, in the days before she had grown quite so slovenly.

This would do, Wahooka thought to himself. Chuckling, he stepped to the edge of the pit, then opened his cloak. He reached inside and withdrew the staff that Cassius had given him just a few minutes earlier—the staff that had slain Ulger the Cruel, the staff that had made an emperor of a naive boy fresh from the provinces. This would do very nicely indeed.

As Wahooka cocked the stick back to throw, a dulcet voice spoke to him from above. "Are you happy now?

Now that Stonekeep is lost and the line of Drake has been broken?''

Wahooka looked up to find Thera's doe-eyed face peering down on him from the stub of a broken stalactite.

''There is more gained than lost.'' He tossed the staff into the center of the pit, where it clattered down among the bones and vanished from sight. ''The Young Gods should thank me. Stonekeep will rise again, stronger than before.''

''Stronger, perhaps.'' Thera granted. ''But better?''

''Stronger *is* better.'' Wahooka stepped back to admire his handiwork. The staff was practically invisible down among the bones, imperceptible to all but the most careful observers. ''Isn't that what you've been trying to tell me?''